Do You Promise Not to Tell?

"Clark, who in real life is a writer and producer f̶ CBS News, understands how to hang on to her audience. H̶ ̶ ̶s̶ ̶s̶ are the sorts with whom many readers identify. H̶ ̶ ̶ ̶ *Want to Know a Secret?*, had pluses. It was ̶ ̶ ̶ ̶ ̶s̶ and plot were compelling. But *Promise* is̶ ̶ ̶ ̶ a fun read with some nifty twists."

—USA Today

"The suspense never flags, and the kill̶ ̶ remains a secret long into the tale . . . for those who can't g̶ ̶ ̶ough of the competitively backbiting world of network news, this novel offers entertaining verisimilitude."

—*Publishers Weekly*

"In news, as in life, luck often counts as much as hard work. Clark captures the spirit of an enterprising reporter who relies on both to 'get' the story of her life."

—Deborah Norville, anchor, *Inside Edition*

"Nail-biting suspense, two budding romances, and the heartwarming tale of an elderly Russian émigré make *Do You Promise Not to Tell?* a top-notch read. The story grabbed me from page one and kept me mesmerized until the surprising finale. Clark, a producer and writer for *CBS News,* knows the industry well and her expertise adds realism to her tale."

—*Romantic Times*

"Fast, fun, and informative, *Do You Promise Not to Tell?* is a winner from the start. I couldn't put it down!"

—Christopher Reich, author of *The Patriot's Club*

Do You Want to Know a Secret?

"A polished page-turner with a smart, appealing TV anchorwoman as the main character. Twists, turns, and a terrific plot. I loved it."

—Mary Higgins Clark

"Clark . . . spins a tightly knit whodunit with engaging characters and a suspenseful plot."

—*Publishers Weekly*

"The secret is out: Mary Jane Clark is one of the most exciting novelists in America today. Her debut thriller takes us on a suspense-filled insider's tour of the corridors of power in politics and journalism where everybody's got a secret, everybody wants a scoop—and now somebody has murder in mind. *Do You Want to Know a Secret?* is an unabashed edge-of-the-seat, they-don't-write-'em-like-that-anymore, unplug-the-phone-and-disconnect-the-TV, page-turning stunner!"

—Dan Rather

Do You Want to Know a Secret? is a brilliantly structured thriller. The secrets and surprises just keep coming and make perfect sense in the TV media world that Mary Jane Clark has absolutely nailed."

—Janet Evanovich, author of *Eleven on Top*

"Secrets . . . ambition . . . intrigue . . . Mary Jane Clark knowingly seduces you in this intensely suspenseful behind-the-media-scenes thriller."

—Joan Rivers

DO YOU PROMISE NOT TO TELL?

∞

DO YOU WANT TO KNOW A SECRET?

Don't Miss These Other Novels by Mary Jane Clark

Hide Yourself Away
Nowhere to Run
Nobody Knows
Close to You
Let Me Whisper in Your Ear

AND DON'T MISS

Dancing in the Dark

A HARDCOVER FROM ST. MARTIN'S PRESS

DO YOU PROMISE NOT TO TELL?

∞

DO YOU WANT TO KNOW A SECRET?

MARY JANE CLARK

St. Martin's Griffin ⚓ New York

www.stmartins.com

ISBN 0-312-35565-3
EAN 978-0-312-35565-4

Do You Promise Not to Tell? was originally published
by St. Martin's Press in August 1999

Do You Want to Know a Secret? was originally published
by St. Martin's Press in November 1998

First St. Martin's Griffin Edition: October 2005

10 9 8 7 6 5 4 3 2 1

Do you promise not to tell?

JUST FOR ELIZABETH . . .

My sparkling, intricate, miraculous treasure

✣ Acknowledgments

It takes a village to write and publish a book. I'd like to express my appreciation to the support population of *Do You Promise Not to Tell?*

Roberta Golubock took me to lunch at the Metropolitan Museum of Art while the Fabergé exhibit glittered. An idea was born and Roberta encouraged me to see it through to fruition.

Margaret Trombly, Director of the Forbes Museum, Associate Curator Robin Troemer-Brenner and George Tempro, Director of Administration, helped me with my early research on "Fauxbergé". Geza Von Hapsburg, Thomas Hoving, and the late Robert Woolley assisted too, with their respective tomes on Fabergé, art forgery, and auctions.

Norma Nutman and the late Deena Teitlebaum guided me through Brighton Beach as I tried to absorb the local color of "Little Odessa."

Margot Dennedy, Director of Security at Sotheby's, helped me find the one spot to get away with murder in a world class auction house without security cameras watching.

An FBI agent, who wishes to remain nameless, generously

volunteered inside information on how today's Federal Bureau of Investigation works. I promise not to tell.

Louise and Joel Albert, Cathy and David Holmes and Barbara and Reginald Brack opened their "writer's retreats" to me.

Father Paul Holmes was my sounding board, hole-finder, and cheerleader, "egging" me on as I labored to make deadline. His editorial help made the book better.

Laura Dail, my agent and friend, seems to be thinking constantly of my career, which frees me up to think about my writing. I always feel I am in good hands with Laura and her enthusiastic assistant, Francheska Farinacci.

The St. Martin's Press team is led by Sally Richardson, who has made me feel quite special. My editor Jennifer Weis, her assistant, Joanna Jacobs, publicist Walter Halee and paperback quarterback Matthew Shear tackle their work hard, determined to score. My thanks to them and everyone at St. Martin's who worked on this project.

Frances Twoomey, what would I do without you?

Louise Albert, Joy Blake, Liz Flock, Cathy White Haffler, Katharine Hayden, Elizabeth Kaledin and Steve Simring: the ones I called when I was ready to shave my head. That happened alot.

Doris and Fred Behrends, my parents, constantly tried to help me.

Finally and always, Elizabeth and David, my children. They bear with their mother. I love you both, very, very much.

❧ Prologue

Fat Tuesday

Why hassle with buying a gun when you can just cruise the aisles of Home Depot? It's all there.

A box of heavy-duty black plastic garbage bags was thrown into the wire shopping cart. Industrial Strength, the package boasted.

No one would miss Misha—at least no one that the police would bother trying to satisfy.

Slowly up and down the busy aisles. Pruning shears. Big ones. Into the basket they went.

Either you're on the team, or you're not, Misha.

So many axes, so little time. A salesman in an orange, bib-fronted apron appeared amid the axes.

"Can I help you?"

"Yes. I'm doing some yard work. I have to clear some trees and brush."

"How thick are the tree trunks?"

The salesman was assessed. "A little thicker than your waist."

The salesman selected a large, wooden-handled ax from the bin. "This one's a beauty. Double-edged. When one side gets dull, you just flip to the other."

"Okay."

"You said you have to clear some brush, too? It's a waste of your energy to use an ax as heavy as this one if you don't have to. You'd better have a smaller hatchet in your toolbox."

The hatchet found a home on top of the garbage bags.

"You'll want one of these files, too. That way, you can keep your tools keen. You'd be surprised at how much easier your job is when they're razor sharp."

In went a shiny new hammer for good luck.

It was essential to get out while the going was good. Many people would get away with their crimes if they just knew when to stop. Instead, their egos got in the way. You gotta know when to quit.

The pimply-faced high-school kid at the register scanned the tools that would make Misha . . . well, "go all to pieces."

The kid looked up and felt a chill creep up his spine. He ignored it.

"Spring cleanup, huh?"

❧ Chapter 1

Farrell Slater knew her days were numbered. Her contract was up and Range Bullock, executive producer of *KEY Evening Headlines*, didn't like her. A lethal combination. Unless she could redeem herself, Farrell knew her contract would not be renewed and her days as one of the producers of the network's highly-rated evening-news broadcast would be over unless she could pull a journalistic rabbit out of a hat.

She'd even started going to church again. Funny how worry led one back to the kneeler. On the way to the office this morning, Farrell had stopped for ashes at St. Gabriel's. It was the first time in years she'd bothered. Might as well start the Lenten season off right. Having God on her side right now wouldn't hurt.

How the mighty had fallen. Eight years ago, as just a thirty-year-old, Farrell had been the talk of KEY News, having won three Emmy Awards in one season—industry recognition for her outstanding achievements in television news production. Everyone had loved her then, everyone had wanted to be her friend. She was a hot property, admired and sought after by her colleagues.

What had happened?

Part of it, she had to admit to herself, was that she hadn't been able to sustain the momentum and enthusiasm for her job. She had started to coast—just slightly at first, then a little bit more. So, to some degree it was her own fault she was where she was. But not entirely.

There was no doubt in Farrell's mind. Her boss detested her. Was there any way she could redeem herself? Did she want to? Bullock had written her off. The stories he was assigning to Farrell now were always "below the line," iffy stories listed way down on the morning's rundown, beneath the pieces sure to make air.

Occasionally one of Farrell's stories developed into something more than Bullock had anticipated. The executive producer was then forced, grudgingly, to give it a slot in the *Evening Headlines* lineup. If the piece came out well, Bullock credited its depth, creativity, and impact to the correspondent. If the piece came up short, Producer Farrell, ever the goat, got the blame.

Hanging her violet wool coat on the back of the door, Farrell, dressed in a simple turtleneck and black wool slacks, headed for her desk in the office she shared with Bullock's pet producer, Dean Cohen. Farrell lifted a cup of coffee from the Strokos Delicatessen's brown paper bag and studying her office mate, tried to remember what it was like to be the favored one.

Dean certainly wasn't any smarter or more aggressive than Farrell. His pieces were solid, never outstanding. But Dean was a skilled player in the KEY political game. He knew when to keep his mouth shut. Farrell did not. His sucking up to Range Bullock made Farrell want to gag.

"Happy Ash Wednesday," Dean nodded, acknowledging the black smudge on Farrell's forehead.

"That's a contradiction in terms," Farrell corrected.

"Oh yeah, right. Ashes to ashes, dust to dust, and all that." Dean turned his attention back to his *New York Times*.

Now, why had she done that? She could have just smiled and said a simple thank-you. That's what most people would have done. But no. She had to put Dean in his place. It was a constant game of one-upmanship between them and she knew it. It didn't play well.

Perhaps if she were prettier, she could get away with it. But Farrell wasn't a conventionally pretty woman. Quirky, maybe—exotic, on a good day. She'd known since she was a little girl that she would make her way in life with her strongest asset, her brain. A coarse cloud of black curly hair crowned her high forehead. Large (almost too large) brown eyes gave her a look of wide-eyed wonder—not very reassuring in the television news business. The appearance of control could be more important than actual control.

Booting up her computer, Farrell groaned inwardly as she viewed her lot for the day. How could she change Bullock's mind when he kept assigning her the dreck? The Fabergé auction over at Churchill's?

Below the line.

✥ Chapter 2

Pat struggled to stay seated. Please, God, just let the bidding go up.

The gavel snapped crisply. "Sold! To number four-ten. Fifteen thousand dollars for the Fabergé brooch."

Patricia Devereaux craned her auburn head, eager to see who had captured Olga's treasured crescent pin. Searching the crowd, she saw movement two rows ahead. Sitting on one of the folding chairs in the venerable Churchill's auction gallery, a wraithlike old woman dressed entirely in black smoothly replaced her green auction paddle in her lap. As the woman rose to leave, Pat got a better look.

Luminous dark eyes peered out from her magnolia-skinned face. The woman's raven hair could not be untinted, but Pat suspected that years ago the shiny black had been its natural color. In her time, she must have been a real beauty, Pat decided.

But now the former beauty would be wearing Olga's brooch. Pat felt a tug of sadness. Dear Olga. How many times had the tiny Russian woman lovingly attached that pin to the collar of her carefully starched linen blouses? Olga had cher-

ished the white enamel crescent studded with tiny sapphires—
a gift from her father who had once worked in the studios of
the famed jeweler Carl Fabergé. If an old woman was to wear
this unique pin, Pat preferred that it be Olga.

Fabergé. The Imperial jeweler to the last Romanov czars.

Pat and her nineteen-year-old son Peter watched the
distinguished-looking auctioneer standing at the raised walnut
platform stationed in front of the large room. Well-dressed
men and women spoke softly into the telephones at desks
banking either side of the auctioneer's podium. Their job was
to efficiently express bids made by potential buyers not on
the floor of the salesroom.

The auctioneer expertly moved through the numbered
items in the Churchill's catalogue. A small copper ashtray
embossed with the Russian Imperial Eagles went for fourteen
hundred dollars. A pair of silver Fabergé asparagus tongs
earned over its estimate of two thousand. A silver table lighter
in the form of a crouching monkey went for twenty-five thousand. The monkey's expressive face and lined forehead had
clearly charmed its new owner.

"What do we have for the gold cigarette case?"

Pat studied the picture of the cigarette case featured in her
program. The fourteen-karat golden cover was monogrammed and featured a diamond-set Imperial Eagle. When
pressed, the sapphire thumbpiece opened the elegant container. Beautiful.

"Four thousand once.

"Four thousand twice.

"Sold! Four thousand dollars to number one-ninety-six."

Pat recognized the buyer. It was the same man who had
purchased Olga's silver cigarette case at last year's auction.

The tall, pleasant-looking man was wearing a tweed sports jacket. She guessed him to be about forty-five, maybe older. As she studied him, he looked in her direction and smiled.

Did he remember her from last year?

"That's Professor Kavanagh! My Russian Studies prof." Peter was out of his seat and headed for the cigarette-case buyer. The men shook hands and Pat watched as Peter gestured toward her and she could see his lips form the words, *That's my mother*. Pat thought the professor looked surprised, maybe even pleased, to hear the information.

Pat was used to it. People often commented that it had to be impossible for her to be the mother of a nineteen-year-old. But she'd been Peter's age when her only child was born.

As Pat looked on, she was surprised herself. Seton Hall University must be paying good salaries. Fabergé cigarette cases didn't come cheap. The men shook hands again and Peter came back to join his mother. His face was flushed with pleasure.

"This is great, Mom," he whispered. "Meeting my favorite professor at a Churchill's auction—I think he was surprised to see one of his students at something like this."

Pat enjoyed her son's enthusiasm. Peter was such an earnest kid. She often found herself hoping he wouldn't get hurt.

"I told him about your shop, Mom. He said he'd like to stop in sometime."

"Great, sweetheart," she whispered back; but she was more interested in what was happening at the front of the room.

The numbered treasures continued to fetch small fortunes and Pat felt the electricity building in the crowd as the star attraction slowly made its way closer to the auction block. Then, it rolled into view. The audience sat up straighter in their chairs and a low, reverential roar swept over the tension-charged room. The television news crews stationed throughout the gallery rolled their video cameras.

Pat shivered at the auctioneer's announcement.

"Ladies and gentlemen, the Moon Egg."

❧ Chapter 3

Safe from the curious stares of the eyes below in the auction gallery, there was privacy in the Churchill's skybox. In the skybox, one could see out, but no one could see in.

The bidding on the Moon Egg was heated. From the floor, on the phones, the price went higher and higher.

The auctioneer entered the bids as he received them, and the price rose higher still.

Whatever it took, the skybox bidder was determined to have the egg. It was meant to be.

❧ Chapter 4

"What else should we shoot, boss?"

Tall and lanky, B. J. D'Elia stood poised with his video camera, ready for Farrell's cue.

"Hold on a minute, Beej, I'm thinking."

Farrell stood at the side of the crowded gallery and debated with herself. This was a better story than she had originally anticipated. Should she snag Churchill's president, Clifford Montgomery, for a unilateral interview? What was the point? Range was never going to buy a full piece on the sale of the Moon Egg. He wasn't going to give one minute and thirty seconds of his valuable *Evening Headlines* airtime to this story. Farrell had known this the minute he'd assigned the piece to her.

A voice-over, at best. Anchor Eliza Blake would narrate fifteen or twenty seconds of video of the Fabergé egg and the auction scene, telling the audience that the egg had sold for a record six million dollars.

But it was a far more compelling story than Farrell had first thought. Frustrated, Farrell was certain she could construct a more interesting piece. She'd get some file video from the film and tape library. She remembered some old black-and-white newsreel stuff KEY News had obtained of the Romanovs at play on their royal yacht, the *Standart*. Shortly thereafter, Czar Nicholas II and his family had been forced from the Alexander palace and sent into exile, only to be executed a few months later by the ruthless Bolsheviks. Their royal bodies had been doused with acid and buried in a pit in the darkness of the Russian woods.

She could ask Robbie to pull it for her.

The story of the long-lost Moon Egg and how it had been discovered decades after its creation as an Easter gift for Czarina Alexandra from her devoted husband, was a producer's dream. It had all the elements: romance, wealth, betrayal, tragedy. *I can't miss with this story*, thought Farrell. *It's great TV*.

Farrell pulled out her cell phone and stabbed the numbers that would connect her with the Fishbowl, the *Evening Headlines* command center. Dean Cohen picked up.

"Cohen," he answered crisply.

Swell. The fair-haired boy busy kissing up to Master Bullock. Dean was forever trawling around the Fishbowl. He thrived on hanging out in the executive producer's glass-enclosed office.

"Dean, it's Farrell."

"How'd the auction go?"

"Great. Can I talk to Range?"

"He's on another line."

"I'll hold."

Farrell held on, her eyes scanning the auction gallery. She

saw a tall, pretty woman gathering up her things and rising from her seat. An even taller teenaged boy got up along with her. There was something familiar about her.

Pat! She looked almost the same as she had the last time Farrell had seen her. How long ago was that? Farrell's mind searched. Could it be almost twenty years? And that must be Peter—he had been just a baby when last she'd seen him! *My God*.

"Bullock here," snapped the voice in the earpiece. Bullock's abrupt, clipped manner always caught Farrell off guard.

"Range, it's Farrell."

"I know who it is."

Of course he knew who it was. How stupid of her to identify herself again. When would she learn that, with Bullock, she should dispense with the niceties? He just wanted her to get to the point.

Farrell hated herself as she heard herself stammer, "Well, the Moon Egg just went for six million."

"And?"

"Well, I think we could do a good story on it."

"Why?"

"The whole history of the thing is fascinating."

"Who bought it?"

"A telephone bidder who wants to remain anonymous."

There was a short pause on the line. Farrell pictured Bullock checking his computer screen.

"We're heavy tonight. Best we can do is give it a twenty-second v/o."

The connection was broken.

�֍ Chapter 5

"The Bowl doesn't want it," Farrell announced, shrugging. "Do you mind, Beej? I'm going to take a cab back to the Broadcast Center now."

"Damn, I love the shot I got of that doorman in the Russian cossack getup out front. Cool costume. Oh well, you go ahead, Farrell. I'll see you back there."

B. J. D'Elia continued to pack up his video gear as he watched Farrell walk away, her shoulders slumped. It would only take about ten minutes to break down and stow away the tripod, lights, and wires and load them into the crew car parked outside Churchill's on Madison Avenue. Farrell knew that. And with no story to produce for tonight's broadcast, there was certainly no big rush to get back to KEY. She must want to be on her own, not in the mood for company or conversation. Who could blame her? Farrell couldn't get herself arrested on *Evening Headlines*.

Twenty-eight years old, Bartolomeo Joseph D'Elia loved working in television news. Forty hours a week, plus all the overtime he could get, he was paid for his passion. Going out to cover whatever assignment blew his way, B. J. lived by his wits, his skills, and the seat of his pants.

Was he lucky, or what! He thought of that all the time. Most poor stiffs hated to get up in the morning, dragged themselves to their boring jobs, counting the hours until it was time to go home. Then they ate some dinner, watched a lot of television, and went to bed, only to get up and do it all over again. When he thought about what life must be like for those guys, he shuddered. B. J. knew he was one of the fortunate few who actually looked forward to work each day.

Farrell, on the other hand, was struggling, and everyone at KEY knew it. Gossip was elevated to an art form. Who was in favor, who was screwing up, who was on the rise, who had already seen his or her best days. Career bumps and rough patches sustained the voracious appetites of the news-hounds. They watched with the same fascination of rubber-neckers on the highway who slow down to see if the passengers in a car wreck are going to come out alive— mesmerized and grateful, (perhaps "happy" would be the right word) that they were safe, at least for today.

KEY News was no longer the cradle-to-grave operation it had once proudly been in years gone by. In the past, when a longtime employee had served the company well, the news division would keep him on staff when his most productive days were behind him. *You took care of us, now we'll take care of you.* Not anymore.

Corporate loyalty cut both ways. Employees sensed the company wasn't committed to the workers the way it had been once. Many employees didn't give as much as a result. Why bust your hump for the company when it wasn't going to be there for you?

That's why B. J. was a standout. He always went the extra mile, treating every story he worked on like it had Emmy Award–nomination potential. He paid attention to the details, put thought and energy into each camera shot. Producers loved to work with him. When B. J. had done the camera work in the field, they knew that there would be great material to work with in the editing room. Producers always asked to have him assigned to their stories.

He was also a lot of fun. Quick-witted, well-read, and street-smart, he was able to size up a situation and, when it got tense, diffuse it with humor. In a world where everyone took themselves very seriously, B. J. could be counted on to put things in perspective with some comic relief. But today his attempts at humor had failed with Farrell. She hadn't even smiled at any of his wisecracks.

He finished winding up the last bit of black rubber-coated electrical wire and stowed it in the camera gear case. He forgot Farrell as once more he looked to the front of the auction gallery.

That young Asian woman staffing the telephone bank was a babe. He wondered for about five seconds if he should go for it.

Chapter 6

The auction over, Pat and Peter went downstairs to the Churchill's checkroom to collect their coats. Professor Kavanagh joined them on line. He extended his hand to Pat.

"Let me introduce myself, Mrs. Devereaux. I'm Tim Kavanagh, Peter's Russian Studies prof."

Pat shook his hand, smiling warmly. He had a good, firm handshake. Pat liked that.

"So very nice to meet you. Peter's always talking about your class. It's his favorite."

"Your son has a real enthusiasm for Russian history. It's uncommon for someone his age, especially since I would have to guess he doesn't have much Russian blood in him."

"You'd be guessing right. Peter comes from a long line of Irish men and women. But he's never taken much of an interest in that part of his heritage."

Peter corrected his mother.

"Mom, I'm an American. I know about American history."

Pat nodded. "Of course, Peter. But it doesn't hurt to pay a little more attention to what our forebears went through."

Their turn came to pick up their coats and, buttoning her

camel-hair reefer, Pat turned to say good-bye to Professor Kavanagh.

"It was so nice to meet you."

"Same here. You know, it's lunchtime, and seeing all that beautiful Fabergé has really stimulated my appetite. How about I take you two out for an all-American hamburger?"

Before Pat could decline, Peter chimed, "Great!"

Pat laughed. *Why shouldn't I go?* she asked herself. Often when a man asked her out, she made some excuse about her business or her parental responsibilities. She'd finally admitted to herself that she just didn't want to fall in love again, to be involved with someone who could complicate her life. But this would be safe enough. Peter and his teacher. A hamburger. There'd be no pressure. Professor Kavanagh was looking at her expectantly.

"Sounds good. A cheeseburger would hit the spot right about now."

As they exited to the street through the heavy glass door, Pat felt a tap on her shoulder. She turned expectantly.

"My God—Farrell! Farrell Slater!" Pat reached to hug the other woman. "I haven't seen you in . . . forever!"

ℐ Chapter 7

Tony didn't really mind wearing the cossack costume. It sure worked like a charm on the little old ladies who were the big tippers. He was just grateful that Clifford Montgomery had decided that Russian Season at Churchill's was February and March, not July and August.

He stood before the imposing entrance of the auction house wearing a long, marine-blue wool coat with red collar and cuffs, and slouchy black boots. A sword hung at his waist and slings of bullets crisscrossed his chest. A holster held a fake gun on his hip. He'd even let his beard grow in anticipation of this month. Tony wanted to look as authentic as he could.

What a crowd this Fabergé stuff was bringing in! Montgomery and the board of directors must be pretty happy. Good for business. And what was good for Churchill's was great for Tony.

The more customers who came to the auction house, the more tips Tony made. At about thirty thousand dollars, his salary was meager by New York City standards. But in a good year he could triple his income by charming and pampering the wealthy clientele.

He hailed cabs and checked coats and packages, ingratiating himself to the patrons who expected to be accommodated and were prepared to pay for it. He accompanied old men and women and blind people across busy Madison Avenue; not because he'd get paid for it, but because it was the right thing to do. Many times, though, it did pay off—not because these vulnerable creatures were wealthy Churchill's customers, but because the regular auction-house clients took notice of his good deeds and rewarded him for it. Ten- and twenty-dollar bills added up quickly and it was easy not to declare cash for tax purposes.

Christmastime was the best. People were the most generous then. But when there were special theme months at Churchill's, and the same customers returned to each session in a series of auctions, they soon felt comfortable with the pleasant doorman. Tony took good care of them and, honoring their part of the unspoken contract, they slid the bills into his gloved hand.

"Good morning, Mrs. Busby." He opened the door for yet another attractive, well-groomed woman.

Tony enjoyed his vantage point in front of Churchill's. He saw everyone as they arrived and when they departed. He always made an effort to learn their names. The customers liked that.

✣ Chapter 8

Life was raw in "Little Odessa," or Brighton Beach, as it was named on the map of the borough of Brooklyn. Brighton Beach Avenue, the main thoroughfare, bustled with intense, hardened faces hurrying to their destinations. Only the old and the very young moved at a more relaxed pace.

The avenue was dotted with open-air fruit stands. The Russian immigrants chose their apples, bananas, and pears with a level of concentration and wonder. It had not been like this in the Old Country. Never this abundance of fresh produce, ripe and unspoiled.

At the corner newsstands, the *New York Post*, the *Daily News*, and *People* magazine were displayed alongside Russian newspapers. Along the sidewalks, people set up their own small stands to sell books printed in Cyrillic, the Russian alphabet.

The street signs were in Cyrillic, too. So were the signs that labeled the drugstores, five-and-dimes, and jewelry shops. The markets stocked the traditional Russian foodstuffs: black bread, fish, and pastries. Lots and lots of pastries. After decades of deprivation, the Russian immigrant loved to indulge his sweet tooth.

On the boardwalk that ran parallel to Brighton Beach Avenue and alongside the cold, gray Atlantic Ocean, older men and women took their daily exercise in the late-winter sun. Conversations were all in Russian. Often the discussions centered on the crime in Little Odessa.

Some things would never change. In the Old Country, the government officials were always on the take. In America, the Russian mafia demanded its own pound of flesh. Too many times, the talk on the boardwalk was about some poor, defiant shopkeeper who'd been shot when he didn't come up with the protection money. The criminals wanted a piece of everything.

In a rented room over the Primorski Restaurant, Misha Grinkov bent over his workbench. He had come to the United States so many years ago, heading straight for Brighton Beach. Not speaking a word of English, he wanted to go to the only place in America he knew of where language would not be a problem for him.

But when seeking employment in his new country, he had gone back to the business he knew best. He took a subway to Manhattan and to the sleek world of the Upper East Side, heading straight for La Russie Imperiale, the venerated Fifth Avenue antique store. La Russie Imperiale specialized in the sale of Russian antiquities, artifacts and jewelry from the days before the Communists had seized control of the largest country in the world.

The owner, Konstantin Kaledin, had spoken to him in Russian. Misha had described his work in St. Petersburg, and gingerly unwrapped a black felt-covered bundle that he had carried and guarded carefully on the long journey to his new home. When Kaledin had examined Misha's expert work, he had hired the immigrant on the spot.

The very next day, Kaledin set Misha to work executing his specialty—enameling. There was a constant stream of cigarette cases, letter openers, tea-glass holders, kovshes, frames, and candlesticks that needed to be repaired. Misha mixed the compound of glass and metal oxides and heated it until it began to melt. That was painstakingly applied and fused to a prepared metal surface which had already been engraved. The extremely high temperatures necessary to melt the enamel taxed the skills of most enamel experts, but Misha had always enjoyed the challenge. During his long apprenticeship in Russia, he had spent every minute he could, experimenting with layering enamels, inserting gold-leaf patterns between the layers, and engraving decorations on the metal surface before applying the enamel. Misha lovingly polished the enamel with chamois leather for many, many hours. He did it willingly, knowing that the extra work made for a more beautiful finish.

One day Mr. Kaledin, his face even more serious than usual, approached Misha at his workbench.

"I have a very unhappy customer. The enamel cracked on a very costly piece. I trust you enough to repair it."

So Misha Grinkov had come to see his first Fabergé egg in America.

For the next decade, Misha labored at La Russie Imperiale, repairing the enamel on the beautiful pieces that came into the shop and picking up English from the other workers and the aging Konstantin Kaledin. A job at La Russie had cachet in the world of antiques. A sales position provided one with an opportunity to acquire a better education in Russian works of art than could ever be gained in any classroom or library.

There was one apprentice salesman back in those early years, a salesman who had eventually become Kaledin's right-hand man—a tall, well-spoken black man named Clifford Montgomery. Misha remembered how upset Kaledin had been when Montgomery had decided to leave the shop and go to work at Churchill's Auction House.

⌘ Chapter 9

Jack McCord hated Russian school. He found the language difficult and he had little aptitude for it. But he loved his job, thrived on the investigative work and puzzle-solving, and took great satisfaction in nailing the bad guys. Learning that damned Russian language was the price of admission to his profession.

The Cold War was over, but the Federal Bureau of Investigation still had reason to send select agents to Russian school. Though for decades the FBI graduates had worked in espionage and focused on the Soviet spies in the United States, McCord was assigned to the art-fraud division in the New York office. The spread of forged Russian art objects was virulent.

As he drove out to Brighton Beach in the early-morning hours, he cursed the budget cutbacks at the Bureau. There were never enough agents to do everything that needed to be done. A ridiculously strong argument had had to be made to his supervisor in order to have a surveillance team assigned to his case. Despite Jack's pleading, the boss didn't think Misha Grinkov was important enough to be watched around the clock.

"You'll have to do the best you can," Supervisor Roger Quick said.

Easy for Quick to say as he sat on his can, never having to leave the office. It had been a long time since Quick had been in the field, and it showed. Jack couldn't stand Quick, and it angered him that he had to take orders from the jerk.

But he controlled himself. He knew Quick was egging him on and would love to see Jack lose his temper. Again.

In the foggy grayness of the morning, Jack found a parking space around the corner from the Primorski Restaurant. He parked the car, locked it, and walked toward the coffee shop across the street.

Nothing would make that son of a bitch happier, Jack reflected as he crossed Brighton Beach Avenue. Quick wanted Jack to blow his stack, knowing that one more burst of uncontrolled temper would end Jack's career. The FBI didn't like loose cannons.

He'd be damned if he'd give Quick the satisfaction.

Jack took a seat in a booth that faced out to the street, ordered a cup of coffee, and waited for Misha.

❧ Chapter 1o

At her KEY News desk the morning after the auction, Farrell
sipped her coffee and read the black-and-white account on the
front page of the *Times*.

> The Moon Egg, the last of the Imperial Easter Eggs
> commissioned by the czar Nicholas II for his wife,
> Alexandra, lost for decades in the chaos following the
> Russian revolution in 1917, was purchased yesterday by
> an unknown buyer for six million dollars at Churchill's
> auction gallery in New York. The creation of the egg
> was guided by Carl Fabergé, the best-known artist-
> jeweler of all time.
>
> The Moon Egg, fabricated of milky, translucent en-
> amel over engraved gold, rests on dark blue clouds of
> carved lapis lazuli which rotate on a gold base. The
> design for the egg, recently unearthed in an old cata-
> logue of Fabergé designs, called for the egg to open to
> reveal the Fabergé trademark "surprise"—in this case,
> a spray of diamonds which, at the triggering of a mech-
> anism, shimmers to simulate a comet of shooting stars.

Over time, the diamond surprise has disappeared from the Moon Egg.

The egg was never delivered to the czar since Nicholas, his wife Alexandra Feodorovna, and their five children were taken as prisoners by the Bolshevik revolutionaries. The entire family was executed the following year.

In the tumult that followed the overthrow of the Imperial family, many treasures were lost, stolen, or sold by the cash-poor new government. Carl Fabergé's jewelry-design book, from the St. Petersburg Archives, includes sketches of the planned egg but, until Churchill's announced the sale, the actual whereabouts, or even the existence, of the Moon Egg had been a mystery.

Over the years, varied objects of fantasy and function created at the House of Fabergé have turned up in unlikely places. Churchill's reports that the Moon Egg was discovered and purchased by the consignor at New York's Twenty-Sixth Street Flea Market late last year.

The discovery sent tremors of excitement throughout the art world. It had been expected that the Moon Egg would be purchased by the Forbes Magazine Collection, which retains twelve Fabergé Imperial Easter Eggs. The buyer, who bid by phone, wished to remain anonymous, according to Clifford Montgomery, president and specialist in charge of Russian Works of Art and Objects of Vertu at Churchill's.

Farrell took another sip of coffee, dribbling some on her starched white blouse. Slob! She was on a roll, all right. She stared at the color picture of the Moon Egg that accompanied the *Times* article and wished that Range's dislike of her hadn't clouded his decision. A full piece on the Moon Egg had been warranted on *Evening Headlines*. It was pretty pathetic when a personality clash dictated what the American viewing public saw on the evening news. But Farrell knew that was exactly what had happened.

Even KEY News president Yelena Gregory had taken note. Yelena, who had some Russian blood herself, had phoned to let Range know she wasn't pleased by the omission. Range must be kicking himself, Farrell mused gleefully. The *New York Times* was gospel at KEY—and all the other networks had done full pieces on their evening broadcasts.

But Range could never blame himself. He was going to blame *her*.

Chapter 11

Misha answered the knock at the door of his small, hidden workshop in Brighton Beach, leaving his half-eaten sausage sandwich on his worktable.

"Don't you know you should ask who's there before opening the door? I could be anyone—the police, the Russian mafia . . . anyone."

Misha smiled wryly. "Yes, but I knew it be you. No one else ever comes here."

That's fortunate for me, unfortunate for you, thought the visitor.

Misha turned and gestured to his workbench, cleared of all but the sandwich, his jeweler's tools carefully hung on the wall rack above.

"As you can see, I am having some trouble starting on something new."

"Why do you think that is?"

"I tell you before, I want bigger piece of profits. You making fortune while Misha does all work," Misha said resentfully, staring at the jeweler's tools. "I only ask what fair."

"I know you do. Your work on the Moon Egg was perfection. So perfect that neither one of us should ever have to work on anything else. Six million dollars is a lot of money."

Misha turned to look at his visitor, a relieved smile on his face.

"So. You share with me?"

The hammer came down right in the middle of Misha's forehead. He never knew what hit him. Methodically each limb was hacked off, each fingertip removed, and his head cut off with the double-edged ax.

Chapter 12

If she were mine, I'd never let her go, Charlie Ferrino thought, as he smeared a fresh raisin bagel with cream cheese. Instead he said, "I've never understood how you can make a living selling other people's old junk."

Pat smiled and pulled a crisp *New York Times* from beneath the counter at Choo-Choo Charlie's Coffee Shop. Eagerly she noted the story about the auction was featured on the front page.

"Charlie, Charlie," chided Pat, her green eyes playful as she and her friend began their familiar morning dance. "It's not old junk! You know our slogan: 'The Consignment Depot—Everything of Quality and Character.'"

"Then why don't you just call it an antique shop?"

"Because our merchandise isn't necessarily antique. I've explained it before: I don't own the furniture, crystal, silver, or whatever else we have on sale. I'm selling it for the owners. They bring me their things, I display them in the shop, and when something sells, the owner and I split the purchase price . . . fifty-fifty."

Charlie filled a paper cup with steaming, fresh-brewed coffee, sprinkled the contents from a pink package of Sweet'N Low, and added some milk. He was wearing a blue baseball cap to cover his balding head, which was shaking from side to side.

"I don't know, Pat. I hear some of your prices are pretty steep. Why would anyone want to pay good money for secondhand stuff when they could afford to buy it new?"

Pat grinned. They both knew that Charlie understood the concept of fine things and antiques quite well. He just liked to tease her. Feigning exasperation, she tugged her auburn hair out from the sides of her head.

"Charlie, it's a good thing I'm crazy about you, because sometimes I just want to grab your shoulders and shake you."

Charlie carefully packed the wrapped bagel, coffee, and a napkin into a small brown paper bag.

I wish you would, he thought, admiring her as she walked away.

❧ Chapter 13

Peter didn't know what to do.

He lay on his single bed in Boland Hall, the large Seton Hall University freshman dormitory, staring at the ceiling, his arms crossed behind his head. The gray, rainy day outside the metal-rimmed window matched the college freshman's mood. He was deeply troubled.

Since the auction yesterday, something had been eating at him. The Moon Egg.

It sure was beautiful. The enamel work and all the jewels were awesome. And when it sold for six million dollars, Peter heard the man sitting in the row behind him comment, "Well worth it."

It would have been. Except that it was a fake.

Peter was sure of it.

He rolled over and, closing his eyes, buried his face in his pillow. God, what should he do?

He didn't want to tell Olga. She was so old, and she had already been through so much in her life. Peter didn't want the old lady to have any more problems in her remaining days.

And she had made him swear that he wouldn't tell.

He remembered the afternoon clearly. Olga had set out tea and her homemade eggplant caviar as she did whenever he came to visit. But from the moment Peter entered her little apartment that day, he sensed that something was different.

Olga's eyes had shone brightly as the two of them sat in her small living room, Olga reminiscing about the old days. She told him about her family, now long dead, and about how it had been growing up as a young girl in St. Petersburg after the Communists had taken over. She talked about her father's resigned acceptance of how their comfortable world had changed forever.

Gone was their spacious apartment in St. Petersburg and their charming *dacha* in the countryside. Gone was the well-stocked kitchen with its ample supply of good wine and vodka in the pantry. Gone were the fine dresses and well-tailored suits and the many fur coats in the hall closet.

Then, in the bitterness of another unforgiving Russian winter, her mother died.

A tear had come to Olga's eye as she spoke of her father. She had watched her father eaten away more by the inability to use his gift than by the loss of material wealth. In the Russia of the Communists, there had been no place for the "frivolous" creation of beautiful things.

Then she pulled herself from her chair and slowly walked toward her bedroom.

"Come with me."

Peter followed the old lady as she headed to the closet. She opened the door and gestured.

Peter got down on his knees and reached toward the back of the closet. Beneath a wool blanket, he felt something soft and plush. He pulled the box free, rose, and handed the yellow velvet container to Olga.

"You promise not to tell what I show you? My father make this, but he also take from studio when Communists come."

Peter nodded solemnly. "I promise."

Olga's hands shook as she opened the golden box, and Peter gasped at its contents.

"Imperial Easter Egg. Czar have it made for present for Czarina Alexandra."

Olga held out the box toward Peter. Peter carefully lifted the blue-and-white egg from its yellow nest.

Slowly he turned the egg over in his hands, his breath taken away by its cool beauty.

"Open it."

Peter studied the egg, trying to figure out how it opened. He looked up at Olga, a quizzical expression on his face.

"Here, I do for you."

Olga took the egg from him. She pressed on a gold bead that was part of the design, and the egg split open.

A shower of delicately connected diamonds quivered inside.

"Is made after Halley's comet. Comet appear in Europe before czar overthrown. Was sign—telegram from God."

✖ Chapter 14

The Consignment Depot opened at ten, but Pat liked to get there at least an hour earlier to get organized. Once she opened the doors for customers, she often didn't have a minute to herself until she locked up at six o'clock. Still, she just barely paid her bills each month. She'd never been able to get ahead.

Pat stood, breakfast and *New York Times* in hand, on the wooden porch that rimmed the charming Victorian frame house that was home to the consignment shop. Fifteen years ago she had gone way out on a financial limb to buy the old, run-down house in suburban Westwood, New Jersey. But as always, when she looked at it, now so lovingly restored, she was glad she had taken the chance.

After Allan had died, Pat had missed him so much there were times she didn't think she could keep going. But she had put all of her energy and the proceeds from a small insurance policy into fixing up the old house and starting her own business, and somehow, to her amazement, she'd gotten through the worst. She'd always love this old place. It had saved her. Barely.

The house, the business—but more importantly, Peter—had kept Pat going. Now he was a freshman in college; but then he'd been just four years old . . . a little boy facing childhood and the complicated growth to manhood without a father to stand by him. It was so unfair.

Uneasily, Pat inspected the paint job. The body of the house was a pale apple green, with elaborate gingerbread trim done in an unexpected shade of raspberry. Before selecting the paint, Pat had researched carefully, wanting to be true to the colors used at the time the house was built. She had been surprised to learn that people had been painting their houses whimsical colors at the end of the nineteenth century.

She sighed. The house needed another painting. And that would be costly. All the scrollwork and tiny patterned shingles had to be colored carefully by hand. What a miserable drag it was, worrying about money all these years.

Letting herself in through the beveled glass-paneled front door, Pat knew who would be waiting for her on the other side.

"Emily!" she cried, as she knelt and buried her forehead into the collie's long, honey-colored fur. "Good girl! Good girl! I can see you are taking good care of everything for me. I know I can count on you. Come on, Em. I'll let you out."

The collie followed her mistress to the tiny kitchen at the rear of the house and eagerly made her way through the door that led to the backyard. Insurance regulations called for the Consignment Depot to be electrically alarmed, but Pat always had trouble with the damned thing. Emily was the safety backup and Pat had the feeling the dog liked doing her part.

Pat walked back to the living room and surveyed her shop

with pride. The plum-colored walls were a good foil for just about anything she hung on them . . . paintings, etchings, mirrors, sconces and, sometimes, just empty frames, if they were interesting enough on their own.

Mirrors. We're down on mirrors, and they're always good sellers. She hoped someone would bring one in today.

She switched on all the lamps, both upstairs and down, plumped a needlepoint pillow on a tufted settee that sat beside the fireplace, and straightened a vanilla candle that tilted in the silver candelabra on the mantel. Smoothing the corner of a beautifully woven kilim that Emily had accidentally flipped back from the aged oak floor, Pat was satisfied the shop looked in order.

Back in the kitchen, Pat unwrapped her breakfast and opened up the newspaper. She relished the headline, remembering the excitement at Churchill's salesroom.

MOON EGG FETCHES SIX MILLION DOLLARS.

As she read the article, Pat's thoughts turned to Farrell Slater. How weird to meet again at an auction gallery after all these years.

They'd been grammar-school classmates and had been, at one time, inseparable. But Farrell had gone to parochial high school, while Pat had gone to Westwood High. When Farrell went away to college, Pat married Allan just after graduation.

Too young, too young to get married, everyone had clucked.

She considered that Peter was, today, older than she had been when she'd married his father. Pat admitted that they'd been young. But she didn't regret her decision. Not one single day of their too-short time together.

Her friend Farrell had gone on to the big leagues. A producer at KEY News! What an exciting life Farrell must be leading.

And yet, Farrell hadn't looked very happy at Churchill's yesterday. She'd been friendly enough when introduced to Tim Kavanagh, and seemed genuinely pleased to see Pat and Peter, exclaiming her amazement that the little baby she had known had grown into such a handsome young man. But Pat sensed a troubled air about her.

When Pat had suggested that Farrell drive out sometime to see the Consignment Depot, Pat had been surprised by Farrell's enthusiasm at her invitation. With a job that took her all around the world, that opened doors to interviews with some of the most fascinating people of our time, Pat couldn't imagine why in the world her old friend would be so interested in coming out to visit a consignment shop.

✖ Chapter 15

Peter lingered after his Russian Studies lecture in Fahy Hall. He wanted to talk to Professor Kavanagh.

He hadn't come to his decision lightly. He wanted to tell his mother about his fears about the Moon Egg. He'd often gone to her when things bothered him and she was never too busy to listen. Together they'd always been able to figure things out.

But this was different. This wasn't about a Spanish progress report or being caught smoking with his buddies in the fifth grade. Those things, which had loomed large at the time, were so trivial now.

A six-million-dollar art forgery—that was in a whole other league. And Peter knew this was way beyond his or his mother's depth.

That, and the fact she had enough to worry about. He knew it hadn't been easy for her, raising him alone and always anxious about money. Though she'd tried to keep it from him, many nights when his mother had thought he was asleep, Peter had quietly gotten out of bed and checked on her as she sat at the kitchen table, engrossed in paying bills and going over the Consignment Depot ledger. She'd been unaware as he'd watched her sigh deeply, running her fingers through her hair, her brow knitted with worry.

Yet anytime he brought up the subject of their family finances, she'd always smile and say, "Don't worry, honey. Everything is fine."

He knew her workouts were a way to release anxiety.

No. He didn't want to saddle her with this. He was a man now. It was time for him to take more responsibility, make life easier for her. He would figure out what to do on his own.

Professor Kavanagh was gathering up his lecture notes as Peter approached the teacher's desk. Kavanagh smiled when he saw the young man.

"What did you think of the lecture today, Peter? Those

Romanov czars pulled some pretty atrocious stunts, didn't they?"

"Yeah, it was pretty interesting, Dr. Kavanagh. But I was wondering if I could talk to you about something else."

Kavanagh looked at his student with concern. "Your mother's all right, isn't she?"

"Oh yeah. She's fine. But I don't know what to do about something, and I, uh, was hoping you could give me some advice."

❧ Chapter 16

COME SEE ME AFTER THE BROADCAST TONIGHT.

Farrell's chest tightened and her mind raced as she read the e-mail from Range Bullock.

She could probably get a job over at *Dateline*. Farrell had heard that NBC had two hundred producers on staff to get their news-magazine show on the air five nights a week. But she didn't want to go to NBC or any of the other networks. She liked KEY News. It was home. Despite her problems with Range, she wasn't interested in learning her way around another network's news operation at this stage of the game.

Sure, the mechanics were the same and her knowledge was

easily transferable. A satellite feed was a satellite feed whether at KEY, CBS, or ABC. Videotape was edited the same way wherever you went. Farrell had a Rolodex of contacts and sources that would work for her just as well at any news division.

It was learning a whole new cast of characters that didn't appeal to Farrell. At KEY News, she could pick up the phone and know just who to call to get done what she needed done. She knew personnel history, who was good, who was mediocre. She didn't want to move to another network and be forced to memorize the names and jobs of scores of new people. She could find her way around the maze of the KEY News Broadcast Center with her eyes shut. She didn't want to start all over again somewhere else.

But if something didn't change, that's exactly what Farrell would be doing. She knew Range wanted her out.

❧ Chapter 17

Bunny's back room was crowded at lunchtime, with students from Seton Hall and other village residents and shopkeepers. A short drive from campus on South Orange Avenue, the bar and restaurant was popular with anyone who wanted some good, cheesy, New Jersey pizza. Up front, men sipped midday beers at the old wooden bar, while college students hung out and chowed down at booths in the back.

Peter and Professor Kavanagh sat in a booth in the corner.

"I think you'll have to tell your mother about this, Peter."

Peter helped himself to another pizza slice from the raised metal pie plate in the center of the table. Watching the young man shake red hot-pepper flakes and garlic powder over his pizza, the professor noticed that Peter's worries weren't affecting his appetite any.

"My mother already has enough to worry about. Besides, I promised Olga I wouldn't tell anyone about her egg." Peter looked uncomfortable. "I've already broken my promise by telling you."

Professor Kavanagh considered Peter's predicament as he sipped his cold Budweiser. Before it was over, many people were going to have to know Olga's secret.

"Peter, we're talking about art fraud and millions of dollars here."

"I know. I know." Peter closed his eyes and rested his head on the back of the booth. He heard a loud conversation at the booth behind him, about the Seton Hall Pirates and their March Madness prospects. How he wished he could be concentrating on something as simple as basketball right now. But he knew the professor was right. He should tell his mother about all of this. Then she could decide what to do and how to tell Olga.

Tim Kavanagh peeled several singles from his billfold and tucked them under the pizza stand for the waitress.

"Look. If you want, I'll come with you and we can both tell your mother. Would that make it easier?"

Peter considered the professor's offer. It would be good to have someone there to help figure things out, someone to lean on a little. That might be great for his mother . . . and for him.

"If I decide to tell her, I'll let you know."

❧ **Chapter 18**

It had been a good day, but Pat was anxious to finish up and get over to the American Woman health club to work out. With Emily curled snuggling at her feet, Pat was entering the day's receipts into the Consignment Depot sales ledger when she heard the creaking of the front door opening. She rose from her desk tucked at the rear of the shop and, seeing who it was, Pat smiled with pleasure.

"Olga! I was hoping you'd make it in today."

The wizened old woman looked brittle and worn as she crept toward Pat, but when she smiled back, it was clear that she was pleased by Pat's welcome.

"Here, Olga. Come try out this big wing chair we just got in."

As Pat helped Olga into the upholstered seat, she noted that the aged lady looked thinner and smaller than when she'd seen her just a few weeks ago, when she'd picked up the old woman's brooch to take it to Churchill's.

Churchill's reputation as a first-class auction house was well deserved. Over the last few years, as she had handled the arrangements for Olga to sell her pieces of Fabergé, Pat had been impressed with Churchill's staff and their attention to detail. Each object to be auctioned was inspected, studied, and authenticated by Churchill's experts. The auction house staked its considerable reputation on the fact that Churchill's could be trusted to reveal everything known about works of art, furniture, and decorative objects on the auction block.

That's why Pat had taken the pin into Churchill's weeks ago. Clifford Montgomery insisted on inspecting all Fabergé items himself before they could be listed in the Churchill's auction catalogue.

"Why don't I make us some tea?"

Olga nodded gratefully, and Pat went to the small kitchen and put the kettle to boil on the electric stove. She took some shortbread cookies from a tin canister and arranged them on an old pink-and-white Dresden plate. When the whistle blew, she fixed tea for them both, serving the dark amber liquid the way Olga liked it, in a glass instead of a cup.

"Hmmm, that is good." Olga sipped the hot tea appreciatively and warmed her old, cold hands on the glass.

Pat was happy to see her take several cookies. "The check should be here soon."

Olga nodded. "That is why I come." She slowly opened her worn, brown leather pocketbook, reached in with shaky fingers and withdrew a small blue booklet. Handing it to Pat, she said, "You put in for me."

Pat was momentarily saddened. It was tough to get old.

Olga must really be 'feeling weak if she was handing over her bank savings passbook. The elderly Russian lady was adamant about taking care of her banking herself. Though Pat had volunteered to make trips to Westwood Savings Bank for her, Olga had always declined. Life experience had taught Olga to guard her monies carefully, and she had always wanted to see the deposits made herself.

"Okay, Olga. I'll be glad to take care of it. I'll deposit the check as soon as it arrives and then I'll drop the passbook off at your apartment."

"Good. My Papa, he take care of me again." Olga delicately worked on her shortbread cookie. "How is my Peter?" she asked, changing the subject.

Pat smiled broadly. "Wonderful. He's loving college and, thanks to you, he is most enthusiastic about the course on Russian history he's taking this semester."

"He is good boy."

"Yes, Olga, he is."

Of anything in her life, Pat was most proud of Peter. Her son, her only child. It seemed like such a short time ago that she had watched him ride his tricycle down the driveway, and wondered how he was going to make it without his father. But over the years, the two of them had depended on each other. As a single mother she had worked hard at raising him and at starting her own business. He had worked hard at school and tried to help his mother by not giving her much to worry about. Pat was grateful that in an age of horror stories about drug and alcohol abuse, as far as she knew, the worst Peter had pulled was smoking in the Westwood High men's room. He'd been mortified when he was caught, and she'd been called to school for a conference with the principal.

Afterward, contrite and very upset, Peter promised Pat that he wouldn't do it again. His mother believed him.

Since he had first started going to school, Peter would come to the Consignment Depot at the end of the schoolday. She could still remember watching the little redheaded boy swinging his book bag as he skipped up the sidewalk. Some days her heart felt as if it would literally burst with the love she felt for her child. He'd always be so happy to see his mother, giving her a big, hard hug. He would eagerly head for the kitchen for an after-school snack, and then he'd tell her the details of his day, what his teacher had said, who got yelled at, who had gotten into fights in the schoolyard. For Pat, the best part of having her own business was that it had allowed her to be there for her son after school each day.

Peter had been in the shop when, years ago, Olga had brought in her first piece of Fabergé, a silver letter opener. Not understanding the concept of a consignment shop, Olga had wanted Pat to buy the letter opener. Patiently Pat had explained that she didn't buy things, she only displayed and sold them for other people. Upon scrutinizing the silver piece, Pat had checked a book out of the public library and correctly identified the Cyrillic markings on it to read "Fabergé." Pat let Olga know that the piece was probably too valuable to get the right kind of customer exposure in the Consignment Depot anyway. She urged Olga to take it to New York. Somehow, in her halting but persuasive English, the old lady had convinced Pat to go to New York for her.

Pat had shown the letter opener with its famous markings to her son. She explained the history of the wondrous House of Fabergé and the connection with the doomed Romanov dynasty. Peter was enthralled, later choosing to do a term paper on the Russian Revolution. As part of his research, he decided to approach the old Russian lady and see if she could give him some first hand stories of that historic time.

Olga came to love Peter. At first hesitantly, then more and more openly, she told the young man stories of her early life, and ways of the Old Country. Even after the school assignment was completed, Peter kept going over to see the old lady once a week. She complimented him on his name. "Peter the Great was the father of all Russia. Your name is strong. You be strong man, too." Peter's love for Russian history was born.

But now, turning over the blue passbook in her hands, Pat's thoughts turned from her son back to the Russian woman.

"Olga, what will you do after this money is gone?" she asked gently.

"Don't worry," she answered in a surprisingly firm voice. "I still have one thing left."

❧ Chapter 19

"It's not working out, is it?"

Farrell sat before Range Bullock, and though the door to the office was closed, a sign that the executive producer did not want any interruptions, Farrell knew she was on display for all the newsroom to see. The glass wall that fronted the newsroom was an invitation to gawk at the players inside the Fishbowl. She tried to arrange the expression on her face. Don't let Bullock or any of the voracious busybodies posted in the newsroom see the panic she felt inside. Look confident, or they'll smell blood.

She'd made one last trip to the ladies' room in another attempt to blot out the coffee stain on her shirt, but her rubbing had only made it worse. She saw Range glance at the brown spot on the snow-white field of her blouse, and she supposed her sloppiness would only be another nail in the coffin of Range's opinion of her. She crossed her legs.

As usual, Farrell had felt it necessary to talk first. Why? She remembered the old saying, *He who talks first, loses*. But it was her nature to take things head-on. Most times she liked that about herself. But this time, she should have let Range talk first. Let him bring up the tough subject. Put the ball in his court. Instead, Farrell had served right to him and she sensed his relief.

"We missed a good story last night," Range responded ruefully.

"We didn't *miss* it. A decision was *made* not to do it." Farrell left unspoken the *made by you, Range*.

For a moment Range glared at her, but when he spoke again, he sounded more resigned than angry.

"You're right, Farrell. I did decide not to go with it and now I'm sorry. I misjudged. I take full responsibility for that."

Farrell sat quietly, waiting for him to continue.

Range rose and walked around his desk, taking a seat beside Farrell on the other end of the gray tweed couch. He angled his body toward her and bent forward, staring at his hands.

"Look, I want to be honest here."

"Please do."

"In my thirty years of working in this business, I've learned to trust my instincts. My instincts are telling me that I shouldn't renew your contract."

Farrell had known it was coming. Why, she wondered, did she feel the wind knocked out of her when it actually happened? A blow to the solar plexus. She inhaled deeply, but she'd be damned if she would cry. She dug her nails into her thigh.

"Don't you think you should base such an important decision on fact rather than instinct?"

Farrell thought she detected a tinge of admiration in Bullock's eyes. He seemed to consider her question.

"You're right. True, your work is basically solid. There

hasn't been a story I can point to and say, 'See, Farrell screwed up. She made mistakes, she left out something important.' But you haven't been aggressive, either. I don't see you going after stories, pursuing them vigorously. You don't seem sold on your own work. Case in point, the Fabergé auction."

"Hey, I told you we should do that story," Farrell protested.

"Barely. You expressed no enthusiasm or commitment, no hunger. You could have sold me on it and you didn't. In fact, sometimes I sense you're almost relieved not to have to do a piece."

Farrell snapped. "If there's any truth in that, it's only because I know that you won't go for anything involving me. The cards are stacked against me in the first place."

Range opened his mouth to say something, but stopped. He rose and walked back behind his desk.

"Well, then, perhaps we should write it off to bad chemistry," he said coolly. "And that is a good enough reason for me. The *Evening Headlines* producers are part of a very well-trained, exclusive team. We have to play well together, anticipate and understand each other."

"So. . . ." She trailed off. She was going to make him say it.

"Your contract expires in six weeks. It won't be renewed. You better start looking for another job."

Farrell skulked back to her office, Range's dictum pounding in her head. In a funny way, she was relieved. At least it was out on the table.

What was she going to do now? She should start making

some phone calls right away, start sniffing around to see what was out there. She had connections at the other networks.

What was she going to answer when asked why she was leaving KEY News? She could say that after working at the network for fifteen years, she'd wanted to try someplace new, start something fresh, didn't want to get stale. They might buy that.

Or she could just tell the truth. She hadn't gotten along with her executive producer. Just about everyone in the industry had, at one time or another, an executive producer he clashed with. Personality conflicts were de rigueur in the television news business.

She supposed she might as well go with the truth. Whoever might interview her at the new place could easily pick up the phone and call Range. No point in lying when they would just find out the truth anyway.

Ugh. Looking for a job. The worst. Farrell marveled that some people actually liked it, enjoyed the search, the challenge of the hunt for better employment. She despised it.

But that could be symptomatic of the bigger problem. She hated to admit to herself that Range could have a point. Maybe she *wasn't* hungry enough. Why hadn't she insisted more strenuously about the Fabergé story?

The hallway leading to her office was deserted. She prayed that her office would be empty as well. The last thing she wanted to deal with now was Dean Cohen.

No such luck.

Dean was putting on his coat to go home.

If only she'd been a minute later, she'd have missed him entirely.

Don't look upset, she commanded herself.

"Everything okay?" Dean looked concerned.

Was he sincere? Maybe. But she didn't want to go into it with him.

"Yup. Everything's fine. Just fine."

❧ Chapter 20

Sticky. That much blood was sticky. Despite the rubber gloves, despite the slicker and galoshes, despite the goggles and the cap, Misha's blood found a way to ooze through the plastic, the plasma tacky and thick.

How did those guys in the meatpacking industry do it? Perhaps if you did it enough, it got easier, maybe you got used to it—hacking and sawing your way through skin and muscle, sinew and bones.

And the sound. That was the worst part of all. Joints snapped and popped. Bones broke with a sickening crack. And the saw droned steadily, back and forth, back and forth.

Piece by piece, section by section, Misha went into black heavy-plastic garbage bags. The body was dumped in a local landfill. The head was thrown into the Hudson River along with the fingertips, food for the fish newly returned to the cleaned-up waterway. All part of the plan.

It was filthy work, and exhausting. Funny how a human being could sleep so well after so gruesome an experience. It was the sleep of the deadly . . . and the desperate—

What an idiot! In the haste of disposing of Misha, one loose end had been left dangling. The design plans—they were still out there in Little Odessa.

✣ Chapter 21

The bony fingers of Nadine Paradise rubbed the milky enamel crescent she'd bought at the Churchill's auction. Her eyes, eyes that had watched vigilantly for nearly eight decades, appreciatively took in every detail of the work of art that was meant to be worn.

Life was strange. After eight decades on this earth, she knew this. That she should now own both halves of the brooch, proved it.

There were some things she should cut back on, but the purchase of this pin was a necessity, not a luxury.

Nadine sighed and sat back in the comfortably worn, green velvet armchair, her old eyes falling on the silver-framed black-and-white picture sitting on the mahogany table beside her. A young ballerina in a feathered headpiece was caught in midair in one of a series of whipping turns from *Swan Lake*. Nadine remembered with pleasure that the most famous ballet critic of the time had called her dancing both "astonishing" and "frightening."

The former prima ballerina closed her eyes, remembering how she and her mother had painstakingly inspected the stage to choose the exact spot at which Nadine would perform those notoriously difficult turns known as pirouettes. They prayed over the spot. Nadine's pirouettes never faltered.

Mother. Nadine's fiercest partisan and sternest critic. What a life she'd led. Raising a child alone in Paris after the Revolution, struggling to find a way to let her dark-haired Nadine study the dance.

Over the years, mother had accompanied daughter as she toured the world. Acting as dresser, laundress, cook, and chaperone, Mother had loved to play poker, believed in fortune-telling, faith-healing and, most of all, in Nadine.

"I didn't disappoint you, Mother." Nadine murmured the words aloud. It was a distinguished career. Dancing first with the Ballet Russe, followed by the American Ballet Theater for Balanchine, then dancing and acting in several motion pictures, and then, in an ironic turn of events, marriage to a man who had brought her back to Russia as the wife of a diplomat.

She'd been unable to have children of her own. But they'd adopted a beautiful Russian child. Victor. She wished her grown son was as smart as he was good-looking.

Nadine's had been an interesting life, and though she was all too aware that she was in its final act, she felt an excitement as she held both halves of the crescent brooch. It had been a long time since she'd felt this way.

Life, even at this stage, continued to surprise. There was

satisfaction in the knowledge that things eventually did come around, if one waited long enough.

Nadine knew who had owned the jeweled pin and believed the possessor to be long dead. But perhaps he wasn't. Perhaps her father was still alive!

No, that couldn't be. Her father would be over a hundred years old.

She rose from her chair and walked to the antique walnut secretary. Opening the paneled doors at the top, she felt beneath the shelf for the button. Pushing it, a small concealed drawer on the side of the secretary slid open. Nadine felt among the contents and gingerly lifted a small packet of letters, yellowed and flaking with age.

Yet again, she began to read the fading Cyrillic script.

My darling Nadjia . . .
The days pass—slowly, achingly, and I long for you, my dearest one.
Why did you go? How could you leave me?
And yet I know the answer. St. Petersburg is a bitter, living hell and you were right to get out when you had the chance.
Oh, my Nadjia, how I wish we were together. And how I pray we will be reunited someday.
Until then, my darling, wear this pin. . . . I designed and executed it myself. . . . A big, round moon . . . of enamel and sapphires. Each month, when the moon is full, look up at the vast dark sky and wish upon it. Hope and wish and pray that we will soon be together again.
Know, Nadjia, that I will be here in Russia . . . looking up, too. I have another pin, a companion piece to yours.

Mine is the moon, too, but in its crescent phase. And I will be wishing on the slivered moon.

Between us, the moon is ours, in its waxing and its waning. And when we are together again, we will slip the moons together, a masterpiece to behold.
My love to you for all eternity,
'V.'

Nadine removed the round enamel-and-sapphire pin she had worn almost every day since her mother Nadjia had died. As she lay dying, mother had given daughter the round pin as she whispered the story of her true love, Nadine's father. She had passed away before telling her daughter her father's name.

Now, as she fitted the round moon to her newly acquired crescent, Nadine trembled as she realized that the two pieces did indeed create a masterpiece.

The round, full moon, joined to its crescent, together formed an oval—a miniature Moon Egg.

Chapter 22

Maybe she should think about a whole new career. Flipping hamburgers at McDonald's looked real good right now. You worked your shift and went home. No mind games.

Farrell stood in the tiny galley kitchen of her West Side apartment and twisted the can opener.

"C'mon, Walter. Here, Jane." She put two small ceramic bowls on the floor, one red and one blue. In true anchor style, Walter Cronkat and Jane Pawley didn't share. The cats each demanded, and got, their own.

Four years at Sarah Lawrence, graduating at the top of her class, fifteen years at KEY News, the pinnacle of broadcast journalism, multiple Emmys, and hundreds of thousands of miles logged covering fascinating stories, and now *this*.

What do I have to show for all of it? she asked herself, glancing at the awards collecting dust on the crowded bookcase.

Her personal life was empty.

She thought of Rick and wondered what might have been. What if she had followed him to Atlanta when he had taken the job with CNN? At the time, they had thought a long-distance relationship could work out. How naive they had been.

Now Rick was married to someone else, with a second baby on the way. And Farrell doubted she would ever have a child.

Thursday night, and the March weekend loomed gray and long. Farrell's mind was reeling. The thought of looking for another job depressed her—big time. Nor did she want to dwell on Range's words—or worse, consider that he might be right. Maybe she *wasn't* aggressive enough, hadn't gotten psyched enough about her stories. She had to admit that sometimes she found herself just going through the motions at work. And that wasn't good enough.

Procrastination was always an option. She didn't want to spend the weekend analyzing herself and thinking about her uncertain future. She could call Robbie. But the idea held little solace for her. In the sibling relationship they had, Farrell, as the older of the two, was the comforter. She did not think going to Robbie would make her feel better. She would feel guilty leaning on him when, in her opinion, he could barely take care of himself.

Farrell wanted to get away. She should get out of the city. A change of scenery, that's what she needed. But where?

Someplace close by, but a world away from KEY News.

Chapter 23

Olga lit a fresh white candle beneath the icon of the Virgin and Child that hung in the *krasny ugol*, the beautiful corner of her tiny living room. She closed her eyes and prayed, as she always did.

"Holy Mother, forgive us. Holy Mother, protect us. Holy Mother, pray for us."

The frail old woman reached up to smooth the linen stole that draped the gold-rimmed icon. It was a white scarf on which, so many years ago, she had carefully stitched tiny birds, flowers, and trees with bright red threads. Then, she had been a young girl with good eyes. That was before she had escaped from Russia; before she made it to America.

The embroidery was one of the few things she'd been able to take with her. She'd used it to wrap up the exquisite pieces of Fabergé.

The Fabergé. Pat had gotten seven thousand dollars for the brooch. That should hold for a while. It had to. With the crescent brooch gone, there was only one piece of Fabergé left.

Potted red begonias lined the windowsill, and Olga decided

they needed to be watered. She went to the kitchenette sink, filled a glass with water, and shuffled slowly to the flowers. Olga tended her plants lovingly and she had gotten years of enjoyment from these particular begonias. Especially in the winter, in the gray, dark months, the flowers cheered her.

Olga lived carefully, frugally, and that was fine by her. It was all she had ever known, really. Life was hard, Olga knew that. But she was one of the lucky ones. America was her country. In Russia, she was scared all the time. In America she was free and she didn't live in fear.

Except about the Fabergé.

❧ Chapter 24

Grateful for the increased physical strength she'd developed since she'd been working out, Pat easily moved a walnut writing desk to a spot where it would be shown to greater advantage in the Consignment Depot living room, when a sudden blast of winter air from the opened front door signaled the arrival of Stacey Spinner. Stacey, the owner of Spun Gold Interiors, stopped at the Depot at least once a week, always on the prowl for anything new that came into the shop.

Pat knew that Stacey's interior design business was thriving. Saddle River was only a few miles but a world apart from Westwood and the Consignment Depot. Spun Gold Interiors by Stacey Spinner catered to people who had too much money and too little time. Her clients often lacked the inclination or the confidence to decorate their multimillion-dollar homes. Stacey possessed both qualities in abundance. Pat knew that Stacey bought things at the Consignment Depot and then turned around and sold them to her wealthy clients for many times what she had paid. The clients oohed and aahed about Stacey's "wonderful finds." Pat supposed that Stacey's business was a case study of capitalism in action. Hey, everyone has to make a living.

As usual, Stacey looked terrific. Though not really a pretty woman, she was ever so highly maintained. Her ash-blond hair was expensively cut and blown dry, her makeup expertly applied, her nails freshly manicured. (Pat had always suspected reconstructive surgery.) Her snug-fitting jeans were carefully ironed and creased precisely down the front. She wore ostrich-skin cowboy boots and a sheepskin jacket the same oatmeal color as her boots.

Pat smoothed back her own hair, and tucked in the back of her dark blue turtleneck, which had come loose from her khakis as she'd moved the desk.

"Hello, Stacey. How are you?" Pat asked politely.

"Can't complain, Pat. My business is amazing. How are things for you?"

"Well, spring fever and the urge to either clean up or perk up the home hasn't begun yet, so it's just a little slow. But we did get in a few interesting things this week. Take a look around."

Pat watched as Stacey's radar zeroed in immediately on the

large china pot that had come in two days ago. Decorated with showy peonies in graduated shades from palest to brightest pinks, the pot was a Chinese export and dated from the late 1800s.

"Where did this come from?" Stacey asked, as if she had only a mild interest. But Pat knew from experience that the feigned lack of enthusiasm really meant Stacey would be taking out her Gucci-covered checkbook.

"A local family was cleaning out the estate of an elderly aunt."

Stacey checked the price tag.

"Four hundred? Isn't that a little steep?"

"It's worth it, Stacey."

The decorator moved on through the shop without committing to the Chinese pot, but once the front door opened again and another customer arrived, Stacey made a beeline back to her treasure.

"I'll take it."

As Stacey made out her check to the Consignment Depot, she told Pat, "Don't forget to give me a call if anything else good comes in from that estate."

✣ Chapter 25

The new BMW sedan pulled into the circular drive in front of the stately Tudor mansion. As the driver switched off the ignition, she made the wish she made each and every time she arrived at Nadine Paradise's home. *God, I wish this house was mine.* But unlike so many wishes that people make, Stacey Spinner knew her wish had a very good chance of coming true.

After her trip to the Consignment Depot she had gone home to change, and then headed right to the beautiful old home.

Stacey swung her jodhpur-clad legs out of the car, her shiny leather riding boots sinking into the crushed-stone covered driveway. Those legs had never known actual contact with a horse, but the equestrian look was meant to look elegantly casual. Everything Stacey did was painstakingly calculated.

Carefully she lifted the large Chinese porcelain pot from the backseat and, holding it close, made her way up the wide fieldstone steps that led to the heavy double doors. Nadine Paradise herself answered the bell.

"Mrs. Paradise! As always, so good to see you. You're looking so well!" Stacey eyed the brooch anchored to Nadine's charcoal-gray cashmere dress. "What a beautiful pin!"

Nadine's thin arms reached up and her fingers delicately rubbed the brooch. The crescent of enamel and sapphires preened upon the dark soft wool.

"Thank you, Stacey. Won't you come in?"

Stacey entered the spacious entry hall, careful to appear nonchalant in the elegant surroundings. Her boots clicked on the marble floor as she caught a look at herself in the enormous, ornate gilded mirror that hung from the mahogany wall. Briefly she imagined herself to be the lady of the house, home from a day of antiquing.

"I've been looking forward to seeing this," Nadine said eagerly, reaching for the porcelain pot in Stacey's arms. "Even though I really shouldn't be buying anything," she added.

"It's very heavy, Mrs. Paradise. Let me put it down on the table in the conservatory so you can have a good look at it. The colors are just perfect for the room. I thought it might look wonderful with your orchids growing from it."

As the two women walked across the fine old Oriental rugs on their way to the conservatory, Nadine complimented her interior decorator.

"Stacey, I know why you are so successful. You make your clients feel that you love and care about their homes as much as they do."

Not their *homes, Mrs. Paradise. It's just* your *home I really love.*

❧ Chapter 26

Jackie Kennedy boosted Sotheby's, Princess Diana advanced Christie's, and now, thank God, the romance and history of Fabergé was helping Churchill's, Clifford Montgomery thought to himself, with a mixture of pleasure and relief. He checked the New York Stock Exchange listings in the *Wall Street Journal.* Churchill's stock had gained three points since the announcement of the sale.

In the president's office, Clifford sat back in his red leather chair, momentarily relishing the knowledge that he held options for more than one hundred thousand shares of the auction house's stock. For him, every quarter-point equaled twenty-five thousand dollars—every point rise, another one hundred thousand dollars. If the stock jumped ten points, Clifford would be one million dollars richer—at least on paper.

All the publicity surrounding the sale of the Moon Egg had been a fantastic perk-up for business. Though the Wall Street professionals thought that the price-earnings ratio was too high, the public didn't seem to share their concerns. The market was always susceptible to emotions, and the history of the Moon Egg had captured the imaginations of investors.

If the stock sustained its current rise, Clifford stood to become a very wealthy man.

Clifford shuddered slightly, remembering how upset Churchill's board of directors had been when Caroline and John ultimately had chosen Sotheby's for the sale of their mother's possessions. But that upset had turned to rage when that sale turned into the media event of the decade, with resulting sales of over thirty-four million dollars—so much more than Sotheby's highest estimates.

The next year, Princess Diana had selected Christie's to sell seventy-nine of her dresses because she wanted to raise money for cancer and AIDS research. Three-and-a-quarter million in sales, and priceless goodwill and publicity for Christie's.

Clifford stroked his dark, bearded chin, remembering that miserable time. To add insult to injury, Churchill's had experienced a severe downturn in business after each of those sales. Those with estates to dispose of, or treasures they wanted to sell, chose Sotheby's or Christie's, not Churchill's. They liked thinking their things were being sold by the same people who were good enough for England's princess and America's queen.

It was a vicious circle. The choicest merchandise was consistently consigned to the competition, and that merchandise drew better crowds of bidders, which drew higher prices and more publicity. Churchill's was drowning. Clifford sensed that he was very close to losing his job. As the only African-American to rise to the presidency of a major auction house, he knew that his every move was under the microscope. He didn't want to fail.

Then, a lifeline—Churchill's chance to auction the fabled

Moon Egg. Clifford had seized the opportunity hungrily, and capitalized on it by scheduling the auction at the same time the long-anticipated "Riches of Russia's Romanovs" exhibit was being featured at the Metropolitan Museum of Art. After viewing the Russian treasures at the Met, those with the means and inclination could buy their own souvenir of Russian history and culture around the corner at Churchill's. To keep the excitement going, Churchill's would be featuring auctions with Russian themes all month.

A knock at the office door interrupted Clifford's reverie. Meryl Quan entered, carrying her ever-present clipboard. Now only twenty-four, Meryl had graduated from Vanderbilt University with a fine-arts degree, then packed herself off to London to enroll in Sotheby's Works of Art course. For the next nine months, she'd immersed herself in the study of paintings and decorative art. When she'd moved to New York, she'd found her first paying job as a floater at Churchill's.

Meryl tackled the entry-level job enthusiastically, working the floor, answering telephones, doing whatever anyone asked of her. With her keen mind and positive attitude, she impressed everyone she worked for. When it came time to choose another assistant, there had been general agreement that Meryl Quan, though young, should get the position.

Clifford regarded the woman. Her shiny black hair glowed in the sunlight that streamed through the office window overlooking Madison Avenue. Her dark eyes peered from almond-shaped openings. Clear, smooth skin; straight nose; even, white teeth behind a delicately shaped mouth. All that and brains, too.

God, I wouldn't be surprised if she had my job one day.

"Nadine Paradise called. She wants to know more about the brooch she bought at the Fabergé auction."

Meryl Quan was eager to go over details of the sale with Clifford Montgomery. Clifford half listened, a smile of satisfaction on his face as he perused the rest of the *Journal*.

"That was the enamel-and-sapphire crescent pin, wasn't it?"

Meryl nodded. She admired Clifford's file-cabinet mind. It amazed her how well he could recall the buyers and sellers of so many of the items auctioned off at Churchill's. But then again, Nadine Paradise was a very good customer. Not only had she bought often over the years, the legendary prima ballerina also had name recognition. Churchill's liked having a star-studded salesroom.

"What does she want to know?" he sighed, reluctantly folding up the newspaper.

Meryl had been observing Clifford closely over the last months and wondered if her boss would be happier working on Wall Street than he was managing a major auction house. Clifford was constantly reading the *Times'* business section, *Baron's*, and the *Wall Street Journal*, and watching CNBC on the small television set in his office. She'd never seen Clifford excited until the day a CNBC reporter came to interview him for a piece on the competition among Sotheby's, Christie's, and Churchill's.

"She wants to know who consigned the brooch."

"Pat Devereaux brought that piece in to us, didn't she?"

Again Meryl marveled at Clifford's sharp memory. Wanting to be prepared, Meryl had looked up the sales record on the crescent pin before meeting with Clifford.

"Yes," she answered. "But apparently Ms. Devereaux was

acting as an agent for someone else who wished to remain anonymous."

"Did you tell Mrs. Paradise that?"

Meryl shook her head. "I thought you'd want to explain it to her yourself, especially with her own auction coming up in three weeks."

"You're absolutely right, Meryl. Mrs. Paradise should feel that she is of utmost importance to us. I will call her myself."

Chapter 27

Misha was gone. And just like in the best crimeland movies, it wasn't pretty. Blood covered almost every surface of the small apartment. Special Agent Jack McCord surveyed the mess.

Now it was too late. The crime-lab guys could dust all they wanted, but Jack knew they weren't going to come up with anything. Now he could show that idiot Quick exactly why he should have okayed the round-the-clock surveillance team. It would be fun to rub it in.

Jack studied the workbench. Like surgeon's instruments, the jeweler's tools were carefully arranged above the work-table. With his rubber-gloved hand, Jack examined a piece that looked like a scalpel. As he turned it over, the tool slipped from his grasp, hit the linoleum floor, and slid beneath the workbench. As Jack went to retrieve it, he bumped his head on the bottom of the bench as he pulled himself to his feet. That should have hurt more, he thought to himself.

Sliding his hand along the undersurface of the table, he found taped to it a package wrapped in plastic. Jack carefully and quickly unfastened it and slipped it into his jacket pocket.

❧ Chapter 28

Pat was surprised when Farrell called to say she wanted to come for a visit. Until that day at Churchill's they'd completely lost touch with one another.

Pat replaced the receiver in the cradle.

The last time she'd seen Farrell, Peter had been a baby. It was Christmastime. Farrell, then a college sophomore, had brought over a tiny Santa Claus sleeper for Peter, complete with a little red pointed cap.

They'd dressed Peter up in it, and they'd had a good laugh and agreed that he was probably the cutest baby in the whole world.

But after that, it had been awkward, as their lives went off in different directions. Pat felt that Farrell thought she was stupid to be married and a mother at such a young age. Farrell's talk about what was going on at school was as alien to Pat as chatter about baby teeth was to her friend. By the end of the afternoon visit, both young women were edgy and uncomfortable.

Neither one had followed up after that.

How stupid we were! Pat thought to herself. But her life had been so busy. And the years had just passed.

After Allan's death, Pat heard that Mr. and Mrs. Slater had sold their house on O'Toole Street and moved to a condominium in Sarasota, Florida. She'd assumed that there wasn't much reason for Farrell to come back to Westwood anymore.

From time to time, Pat had thought about her old friend and wondered what had become of her.

What would Farrell think of Pat's small-town, humdrum existence compared to the exciting life a KEY News producer must lead?

❧ Chapter 29

Farrell couldn't remember the last time she'd taken a bus anywhere, much less out to Westwood. Since her parents had moved to Florida, there had been no reason to return to her hometown. She'd completely lost track of her friends from grammar school and high school. Only occasionally, she'd get together with college friends, meeting in the city somewhere for drinks and dinner. But she feared she had become pretty one-dimensional. Work was the main focus of Farrell's life. Big mistake. Because when work went south, there wasn't much to fall back on.

She was surprised at how much she was looking forward to her visit with Pat. They had once been fast friends, walking home together day after day, leaving the nuns at St. Andrew's School behind. They'd stop at the Dinner Bell Deli, buying a couple of Cokes and splitting a package of Yankee Doodles. Cupcakes in hand, they'd make their way past the public junior high, steeling themselves for the predictable scathing comments about their navy plaid uniforms from the kids whose parents didn't force them to go to Catholic school.

They'd been in the same Girl Scouts troop, had had sleepovers, gone to the movies, and taken what were, back then, adventurous trips by bus all the way to the Bergen Mall. Years later, Farrell could still remember Pat's parents' phone number.

But high school had split them up. Farrell's parents had insisted that she go to Immaculate Heart Academy, the all-girl prep school in the next town. Although Pat had passed the school's stringent entrance exam, and was offered acceptance, her parents hadn't had the money to pay for the tuition. It was Westwood High for Pat.

For a while, they'd continued to hang out together. But as time passed, each girl became increasingly involved in after-school activities and made new friends at her respective school. Farrell had worked on the school paper and *Halcyon*, the IHA yearbook. For Pat, her main extracurricular activities had been cheerleading, and the good-looking Allan Devereaux.

Farrell remembered how shocked she had been when she heard that Pat was not going on to college.

"What a *waste*," she'd wailed to her mother.

"Not everyone is made for college, Farrell."

"Well, Pat *is*. She was the smartest girl in her eighth grade class! Or I thought she was. I can't believe that she isn't going to college. I heard she's going to marry Allan Devereaux instead. How can she just throw her life away?"

.   .   .

The red-and-tan bus pulled to a stop at the depot across the street from the flag-festooned gazebo perched in the manicured park, a picture-postcard of life in small-town America. Perhaps Pat hadn't made such a bad decision after all, Farrell thought.

❧ Chapter 30

If Nadine Paradise was the type to give up easily, she never would have accomplished all she had done over her long, rich life. If Clifford Montgomery could not, or would not, tell her where the crescent brooch had come from, Nadine would try a different tack.

"Victor," she called.

Her adopted son appeared in the doorway of the conservatory, wearing a white polo shirt and shorts, a tennis racquet in his hand. Victor was off for another morning at the club.

"Yes, Mother?"

"Please, sit down for a minute, dear."

Victor obeyed, but Nadine knew he was anxious not to be late for his tennis game. He sat on the edge of the chair, fiddling with the strings of the racquet. She didn't know his partner, Stacey Spinner, was waiting for him. Victor didn't want her to know. She didn't have to know everything, did she?

"Victor, I need you to help me with something. I want to find out where the pin I bought at the auction with you came from. Clifford Montgomery at Churchill's says he can't tell me because the seller wishes to remain anonymous."

"Then what do you want me to do?"

"He did give me the name of the seller's agent. It turns out she has some sort of antique shop in Westwood. I would like you to go over to see her and find out who she sold the pin for."

Nadine could tell her son did not care for his assignment. Victor didn't like to be put out, even for her. She halfheart-edly told herself it wasn't because he was lazy, but because he lacked self-confidence. It was safer for him not to try to accomplish anything. But how hard could this be? A shop-keeper in Westwood shouldn't be too much of a problem. Even for Victor.

"What's her name?" he asked, sighing heavily.

"Patricia Devereaux, and I would appreciate it if you would go over and speak to her *today*."

✣ Chapter 31

Farrell entered the vestibule of the Consignment Depot and took in the shop, pleased at how welcoming it was. Pat had a real flair for displaying the objects for sale to their best advantage. Anyone walking in could not help but be drawn to the wonderful treasures that awaited.

She spotted Pat at the back of the store, talking with a customer. Pat saw Farrell at the same time, and waved. "Farrell! I'm so glad you're here. I'll be right with you."

Farrell unbuttoned her navy wool pea coat and hung it on an oak wall rack conveniently placed at the front of the shop. Adjusting her green tunic sweater down over her tan corduroys, she began slowly poking around the gleaming mahogany tables covered with artfully arranged shining sterling, sparkling cut glass, and fine crystal. Hand-stitched pillows perched on a velvet-tufted Victorian settee, delicate lacework draped a cherry card table with ball-and-claw feet. A gold-leafed, pagoda-crowned Chinese Chippendale mirror hung over the old fireplace mantel, lighted candles reflecting in its glass.

Farrell thought of her own apartment and how she had neglected it. She still had most of her books in cardboard boxes stacked against a living-room wall because she used her bookcase as a catchall for junk. Her sofa was a hand-me-down from her parents' housecleaning when they had made their move to Florida. She'd never really liked it, but she hadn't managed to do anything about it. The same was true for the table and chairs in her dining area. She'd barely bothered to hang anything on the walls, and what was there, was haphazardly arranged. A bulletin board, tacked with souvenirs, press releases, and newspaper clippings about favorite stories she'd worked on, belonged more in her office at KEY or in a college student's dorm than in the living room of a Manhattan apartment of a woman who—ugh, she hated to admit it—was pushing forty.

Pat had finished her conversation with the customer, and came toward Farrell with open arms. "It's so good to see you!" she said warmly, embracing Farrell in a big hug.

"What a terrific place!" Farrell gestured sweepingly. "I am so impressed. Do you make house calls?"

Pat laughed. "I'm so glad you like it. I have to admit, I've been a little nervous about your coming and what you would think about my little shop. It must seem so small-time to you."

"Honey, you couldn't be more wrong."

❧ Chapter 32

Peter watched as Charlie made three thick turkey sandwiches. "Heavy on the mayo on mine, Charlie."

"Why three sandwiches today, Peter?" asked Charlie, as he sliced a pale-looking tomato.

"Mom has an old friend visiting."

"Oh yeah? Who?"

"Someone she went to school with a million years ago. She seems pretty cool. She's a producer for KEY News."

Charlie nodded as he cut the sandwiches and wrapped them in white paper. "Chips?"

"Mmm. Barbecue. And a Coke and two coffees."

The deli owner packed a brown sack with the Consignment Depot lunch order. "You know, Peter, you're a good kid. Coming up here every Saturday to help your mom. Most kids wouldn't be bothered."

Peter thought about it a minute. "Yeah, I guess so. But it's been just Mom and me for so long. And she's been such a good mother. She's really devoted her life to taking care of me. The least I can do is help her when I can."

"True. But I hope you're having a little fun, too. These

are good years, Peter. College is a time for you to branch out on your own. I doubt your mom expects you to spend all your spare time with her. For example, what are you doing tonight?"

Peter looked embarrassed. "Having dinner with Mom's friend."

Charlie shook his head. "See what I mean?"

"It won't be so bad. Actually, I'm kinda looking forward to it. Farrell seems really smart and she has a great job. I'll bet she has some great stories, too. Besides, after dinner I'm going back to Seton Hall for a keg party."

"Good. That's more like it. It's the kind of thing a guy your age should be doing now, while you don't have any big responsibilities. You've got to live a little, kid. Although, don't tell your mom I said that. She wouldn't be too happy to know I'm supporting the idea of a little underage drinking."

As Peter peeled off the dollar bills to pay, Charlie asked, "How come you're having dinner with your mother's friend? Why don't just the two of them go?"

"Oh, Mom finally has a date."

Charlie felt his heart sink.

Chapter 33

"I'm very sorry, Mr. Paradise, but I can't tell you. The person who sold the crescent pin doesn't want his or her identity known." Pat was careful not to give a clue as to the sex of the seller.

The man who stood before Pat was clearly uncomfortable. He shifted from foot to foot and he'd already dropped his car keys twice on the hooked rug that covered the office area of the Consignment Depot. Stacey Spinner was with him, having explained her presence there as Nadine Paradise's decorator.

"You know, Pat, Nadine Paradise was one of the most famous ballerinas in the world."

"Sure, Stacey, even I, buried here in little old Westwood, have heard of Nadine Paradise." *Don't try so hard to impress, Stacey,* Pat said to herself.

"My mother *bought* the pin," he pleaded. "She paid a good deal of money for it. She really wants to know where it came from."

"Come on, Pat, I can vouch for Victor." Stacey entwined her fingers in his and batted her baby-blues up at him. *So that was it,* Pat thought. Stacey had her hat set for the beefy hulk. No accounting for taste.

A reference from Stacey wasn't worth all that much to Pat. And it was somewhat distasteful to watch the interior decorator playing up to this guy. He was plainly loving it. Dope.

Pat smiled sadly and shrugged. "I wish I could help you out. But the seller insists on anonymity. I have to respect that."

The implication was clear. *You, Mr. Paradise, should respect that, too.*

But the man wasn't giving up easily.

"Isn't there anything you can do?" he appealed. "My mother will be so disappointed."

Pat was firm.

"I'm sorry."

Farrell had been busying herself inspecting an ornate wrought-iron side table, but had listened to the whole conversation. When the annoyed couple left the shop, she looked at Pat expectantly.

"Who were *they*?"

"I don't know much about him, except that his mother is Nadine Paradise. From the looks of him, that's his only claim to fame."

"And her?" Farrell asked.

Pat shook her head in disgust. "Stacey Spinner. She plays her role as a Saddle River interior decorator a little too much for my taste. She forgets I remember her from years ago— we actually met at an evening seminar at Churchill's auction house. She was working as a department-store salesgirl at the time, but smart enough to know that there was a big world out there that she wanted a part of."

Pat stopped to consider a moment.

"I've got to give Stacey credit, though. She's really built a solid business for herself and, from what I've seen and heard, she does have a certain flair. She knew what she wanted and she went for it. I admire that."

❧ Chapter 34

Olga struggled to lift the heavy carton of Epsom salts and place it in the small wire shopping cart. It would feel good later to fill the old porcelain bathtub with the salts and hot water and sit in the soothing pool. Her arthritis was really aching today.

Slowly she finished her shopping in the aisles of CVS. A box of tissues, some soap powder, a package of butterscotch. She made her way to the cash register at the front of the store.

She waited quietly in line, waiting for her turn to pay. She watched a child cry to his mother for a Milky Way. The mother gave in.

Olga turned her head away from the spoiled child and his weak mother.

And then she saw it. Featured on the counter for the world to see.

On the cover of an American magazine, the Moon Egg glared.

The teenaged girl at the checkout counter watched as the old lady pointed in the direction of the magazines and crumpled to the floor. Instant hubbub ensued as the other customers on line and browsing near the front of the store, gawked and gasped. A strong-looking man bent over the fainted woman, rubbing her hand and talking to her.

For a few minutes, the white-haired woman lay motionless on the pharmacy floor. Then, as she began to come to, she was mumbling.

"Ma ijtso, ma ijtso."

"What's she saying?" a blond-haired woman asked, as her four-year-old tugged at her arm.

"I hope she hasn't broken a hip," another woman said with some alarm.

"Ma ijtso."

Olga's eyes opened and began to dart around, frightened.

"It's all right," said the man who bent over her. "It's all right. You just had a fainting spell."

Olga struggled to get up on her feet. She held tight to the man's arm as she tried to regain her equilibrium.

"Thank you, mister. Thank you."

"Is there someone I can call for you?" he asked.

"No. No one. I am all right in a little while."

"Do you live far from here?"

"Just a few blocks."

"Then, please, let me take you home. You shouldn't walk home by yourself."

Chapter 35

Before closing for the evening, Charlie took the pink ham from the shiny glass display case and shaved off a generous portion. He filled three plastic containers, spooning in creamy potato salad, pickled beets, and rice pudding. He packed everything up in a brown paper bag, along with a couple of seeded rolls.

He switched off the store lights and locked up. Standing out on the sidewalk in front of the delicatessen, Charlie didn't have much to look forward to in the night ahead. Maybe he'd stop on the way home and rent a video.

As he walked in the chilly evening air toward the garden apartments, he realized how much it bothered him that Pat had a date tonight . . . a date *not* with him. He'd be home, sitting in front of the television, and she'd be out with someone else.

Well, it was his own fault, wasn't it? He never got up the courage to ask her out for dinner and a movie. He'd watched her for years, admired her, dreamed about her. But he did nothing about it. Nothing to move his dream toward reality.

So here he was, good old Charlie. Dropping off some food to the elderly on Saturday night.

He knocked on Olga's apartment door and waited. He could hear the faint sound of her slow, shuffling progress to the front door.

"Who is there?"

"It's Charlie, Olga."

He heard the lock slide open as Olga unbolted the door. The diminutive woman's old face smiled with pleasure and anticipation at the sight of Charlie and his package.

"Ah, Charlie. I not know you coming tonight. You good man. So kind to think of Olga all the time."

As Charlie reached out to hand the paper bag to Olga, he looked over her head into the apartment. Before Olga closed the door, Charlie caught a glimpse of something gleaming on the table behind her.

❧ Chapter 36

Pat noticed that she was taking too much time trying to decide what to wear.

Six dresses were strewn across the gaily-flowered quilt on her antique iron-and-brass bed, and five pair of shoes were arrayed on the floor.

It's just dinner, for God's sake. What's the big deal?

When Tim Kavanagh called asking if she'd like to have dinner, she'd only hesitated a moment before saying yes. It had surprised her how much she'd been anticipating the evening all week. Most times she found herself dreading new dates.

Not that there really had been that many of them. She knew that she didn't give out the signals that said "approachable" and "available." Truth to tell, she usually didn't want to get involved. It was simpler that way, which translated into "safer that way."

But it felt different this time. Pat laughed to herself. *You idiot! What makes you think you are exempt from the natural human desire for the companionship of the opposite sex? Admit it. You've missed it for a long time. Too long.*

She'd narrowed the selection down to her black wool long-sleeved dress or her blue velvet cocktail dress. The black was always safe. She could dress it up with her pearl earrings and necklace.

But the velvet was more sensuous and, frankly, sexier. It hugged her well-exercised figure. When she wore it, she felt decidedly more feminine.

Go for it.

On went the velvet. She fastened on rhinestone earrings but chose to wear nothing at the open neckline. She slipped on black suede high-heeled pumps over her sheer dark hose. As Pat turned before the full length mirror, she felt confident about her appearance.

Farrell and Peter applauded when she came out of her bedroom.

"What a bod, Pat! You look fabulous," exclaimed Farrell. "You make me want to get right to the gym."

"Okay, you two. Thanks for the compliments to this nervous mother going out on a date for the first time in a long while. Farrell, you're sure this is okay?"

"Of course it is. *You're* the one doing me a favor, having me out for the weekend after I invited myself. I'd feel terrible if you canceled your date. Go, have a good time. Peter and I will have a little dinner and then I'll let him get back to Seton Hall where he should be on a Saturday night."

Pat went out into the cold March night and slid into the front seat of her eight-year-old Volvo. Tim had wanted to pick her up, but she'd insisted on meeting him at the restaurant. She always felt safer when she had her own car.

She drove the thirty miles into Manhattan and miraculously

found a parking spot on West 58th Street, a half-block from her destination.

Tiny, twinkling white lights glittered, framing the entrance to Petrossian. Even in the dark, Pat could see the architectural ornateness of the building that housed the renowned restaurant. Amid the limestone gingerbread and scrollwork, bizarre little gargoyles perched on the walls, smiling or grimacing upon the people on the sidewalk below.

You guys look like you're daring me to come inside, Pat thought as she went up the steps, where an imposing doorman awaited her. She drew a deep breath as she entered.

Inside, a small shop offered the delicacies for which Petrossian was known. Jars and tins of caviar, foie gras, and pâtés lined glass shelves, while packages of smoked salmon, sturgeon, and eel rested in glistening display cases. Truffles, Russian caramels, and vodka- and cognac-filled chocolates beckoned temptingly.

Pat looked to the right, into the restaurant, and spotted Tim Kavanagh waiting at the art deco-style bar. She saw his eyes sweep over her and she could tell by his expression as she walked toward him that he was pleased. She was glad she'd opted for the midnight-blue velvet dress.

Tim rose to greet her.

"You look wonderful," he whispered.

"Thank you." Pat felt the old tingling sensation, something she hadn't felt in a long time.

A navy-blazered gentleman guided them to their table for two. As Pat took her seat, she noticed that most of the other tables were meant for two as well. The restaurant was smaller and more intimate than she had imagined it would be.

"Pat, would you like some champagne?"

"Mmm. Perfect."

As the waiter, also attired in a navy blazer with the Petrossian insignia on his breast pocket, went to fetch the Charles Heidsieck 1985, Pat enjoyed the loveliness of the surroundings and the allure of her dinner companion. How delicious to be sitting there with a man she was drawn to. God, how she had missed it—the chemistry, the attraction.

"How did you come to love all things Russian?" she asked.

Tim thought a moment before answering. "I guess it was when I read *Nicholas and Alexandra* in high school. The whole thing about the Imperial family and the czarevitch's hemophilia and Rasputin and the overthrow and murder of the Romanovs intrigued me. Also, about the same time, I saw the old Ingrid Bergman and Yul Brynner movie *Anastasia*, about the woman who claimed she was the youngest daughter of the czar and had escaped her executioners. After that, I was hooked."

Pat smiled. "You remind me of Peter. Once he started hearing stories from Olga, an elderly Russian woman who has become a surrogate grandmother for him, he couldn't get enough."

The couple sampled Sevruga, Ossetra, and Beluga caviar, as Tim explained the differences between the Caspian Sea sturgeons that produced the tiny eggs. Pat selected a salmon with lobster sauce as her main course, while Tim chose a sea-scallop soufflé served with truffles and a pressed-caviar sauce. They sampled each other's dishes, both declaring that dinner was fabulous.

Over coffee, Tim reached for Pat's hand.

"I really enjoyed myself tonight, Pat."

"I did, too. The food, the surroundings . . ." She paused. "The company."

Tim smiled. "I hope there will be more evenings like this."

"Me, too."

❧ Chapter 37

Farrell and Peter both ordered the juicy cheeseburgers for which the Iron Horse was famous, and sat back with their drinks.

"I watched you and your mother today, Peter, and I admired you. I guess I should admit it, I'm envious."

"You—envious of *us*?" Peter laughed incredulously. "I can't believe it."

"It's true. You guys have a solid life. Your mom makes a living doing something she likes to do and she does it well. She's raised a good son, and on her own, too. That's a lot to be proud of."

Peter took a drink of his Coke.

"Well, what about you, Farrell? You've accomplished a lot—you're a television news producer."

Farrell looked at the train prints that were scattered along the wall over their table, trying to decide if she felt comfortable taking in so young a confidant. What would it hurt for the kid to hear a little about how the real world worked? "Peter, I think it *sounds* more impressive than it really is. It's a job—or, at least, it has become a job. I don't seem to have the enthusiasm I once did for it. Besides, it doesn't look like I'm going to have a place at KEY News for much longer."

Peter listened intently while Farrell told him the story of what had been going on with her career.

"The Fabergé story was just the final straw. It had been coming for a long time. I just hate to go out on such a defeated note." Farrell finished off her wine and then turned philosophical. "Hey, look at the bright side. At least I ran into you and your mother again at that auction. It was worth going for that."

The burgers arrived. As Peter poured ketchup over his railroad fries, he decided to tell Farrell about the story of Olga's Moon Egg. He'd known that something had to be done with the information. Maybe it was meant to be, that he entrust Farrell with the story. KEY News could investigate as well as the police. That way he didn't have to drag his mother into it.

Farrell listened to the story Peter told. Could she actually be getting a lead to a fascinating story from this college kid? She knew that news often came from unexpected sources, but the tale Peter was spinning for her now was so fabulous that Farrell was extremely skeptical—skeptical that the story would turn out to be true, and skeptical that she would have the good luck to have it fall right into her lap like this.

"Peter, do you think you could get Olga to let us shoot some videotape of the Moon Egg?"

Peter's eyes widened and Farrell saw the Adam's apple dip as he swallowed.

"Are you kidding? In a million years, Olga's not going to allow anyone to see the Moon Egg, much less a television crew."

"Look, Peter, it won't be a big production. Just me and my cameraman, B. J. He's a great guy. It will be very calm and we'll be as unobtrusive as possible. We can do the whole thing in a half an hour."

"She won't go for it."

"I'll need this, Peter," Farrell urged. "I'll need some proof that another, *real* Moon Egg exists. Unless, of course, you could get Olga to turn the egg over to us."

"Not a chance in hell."

Farrell grinned sheepishly. "All right, all right. But if anyone can talk her into letting us have a glimpse of the Moon Egg, it's you, Peter."

Peter looked troubled.

"What's wrong?"

"I don't want to put Olga in any kind of danger."

Farrell's expression turned serious. "I know you don't. But the truth has a way of coming out eventually. And Olga won't be in any trouble, she hasn't done anything wrong."

"What about her taking the egg from the Fabergé studio in St. Petersburg?"

"Her father took the egg. And it was over eighty years ago. Ever hear of the statute of limitations? Who do you think is going to prosecute her anyway?"

"How 'bout the Russians?" Peter offered.

"I doubt the United States government is going to hand over a little old lady to Moscow."

Peter finished off his soda, his face brightening.

"So Olga doesn't have to be scared of going to jail?"

"I'm sure of it."

"She's sure gonna be relieved to hear that."

❧ Chapter 38

B. J had a litmus test: Hogs and Heifers.

If a woman could deal with a night at the biker bar in the heart of the New York City meatpacking district, there was hope that she would be his type. He was past the point of progressing through the series of dinners, movies, and concerts that was the traditional dating routine. That's what he used to do to get his dates ready for the big test.

Now he got right to it. What was the point of beating around the bush? If a woman couldn't deal with Hogs and Heifers, ultimately she wasn't going to be able to deal with him. He loved the wildness of the place, its total abandon.

He watched Meryl's face. It was inscrutable. What was she thinking as they maneuvered their way past the transvestites that strutted the streets leading to the bar? Did she realize that the heavily made-up, long-legged, booted and miniskirted creatures were actually men?

A tall, thin blond approached them and arched a darkly penciled eyebrow. "Want some, honey?" asked the deep baritone.

Meryl looked up at B. J. "You really know how to impress a girl, don't you?"

Outside Hogs and Heifers, dozens of Harleys were parked, their owners openly guzzling beer on the street. Passing through the black motorcycles and the sinister-looking, black-leather-jacketed bikers, Meryl took tight hold of B. J.'s arm.

It's working already, he thought.

The couple entered the smoke-filled bar, the Allman Brothers welcoming them from the blaring sound system. Confederate flags hung on the wall. A long bar lined the left wall and, overhead, scores of bras hung from the ceiling.

B. J. checked out Meryl's reaction.

"Charming," she said sarcastically, but her dark eyes sparkled.

The female bartenders wore bikini tops and short cutoffs, with cowboy boots and hats. Through megaphones, they jeered insults at the customers who left lousy tips.

"Twenty-five cents? That's what your mother gets for making out with the sailors when the fleet's in."

There was nowhere to sit and B. J. was reminded of a packed subway train that stunk of stale beer, cigarettes, and cheap cigars.

"Two PBRs," he called to a bartender over the din.

"Wow, you're a sport, B. J.," Meryl remarked. "Pabst Blue Ribbon . . . mmm."

"Come on, Meryl," B. J. laughed. "Get with the program."

The bartender popped the tops of the two cold cans of beer and plunked them down on the bar. "Now, you gotta get three shots with that, bud." She poured three jiggers of tequila, immediately swallowing her own. B. J. followed suit and grinned at Meryl expectantly.

Without blinking, Meryl put away her shot neatly. "I thought it was illegal for bartenders to drink on the job," she related earnestly.

B. J. answered with an impish shrug of his shoulders, as if to say, *Who cares?*

"What's that over there?" She pointed. A pole with barbed wire at the top stood next to the bar.

"If you can scale to the top, you get a free shot of tequila," B. J. explained.

"Clever." Meryl took a long drink of PBR.

"Come on, Mama," the megaphone called. "Get on up here and drop that bra."

She'd heard about this place, read about it in the newspaper. A lot of young movie stars came down here to party with abandon. The bras of some of the biggest Hollywood box-office draws hung over the Hogs and Heifers bar.

"Come on, now, yo! You, China girl. Get on up there and show off what your Mama gave you."

B. J. was watching Meryl for her reaction. Her face remained passive as she tried to ignore the megaphone's demands.

The bartender wasn't giving up.

"Come on, baby, we're all friends here. Share the wealth with your friends."

Meryl chugged back the rest of her beer and resolutely placed the empty can on the bar. She hoisted herself up on the bar, and before B. J.'s admiring eyes, she began to sway in rhythm to the country-rock music. As the tempo increased, so did the gyrations of Meryl's hips and the cheering of the crowd. From beneath her black wool sweater, she wiggled free of her bra and swung it over her head to the audience's delight.

When they left Hogs and Heifers an hour later, the stench of dead meat hung in the night air, and packs of moldy bacon lay strewn before them on the sidewalk. Meryl seemed not to notice, and B. J. knew this chick had passed the test.

 Chapter 39

First Sunday of Lent

It had been a long time since Farrell had been to Mass at blue-bricked St. Andrew's Church, and she found it comforting this Sunday morning. Things may be unsettled in her life right now, but the church she had gone to growing up was pretty much the same as it had always been.

Farrell crossed herself with holy water from the font at the entrance, said a silent prayer, and took a seat in a pew at the back of the church. As she rubbed and blew on her icy fingers, cold from the several-block walk from Pat's house, she looked around. Nope. The old place hadn't changed. Farrell could picture all those Sunday mornings that she and Robbie, uncomfortable in their good clothes, had been marched in by their parents. They alternately sat quietly and fidgeted, eager for Mass to end so they could get their reward at Purity Bakeshop, Farrell always getting the thick crumbcake, Robbie always choosing the chocolate creme-filled donuts.

Chocolate had been Robbie's passion even back then. Thirty years later, his breakfast of choice was Cocoa Puffs or Cocoa Krispies, cereals which he'd readily accept as lunch or dinner courses as well.

Robbie. He seemed to be doing better, Farrell thought, relieved. Maybe the worst was over. Maybe it had just been an isolated episode. She prayed so.

The purple-shrouded crucifix over the altar would stay that way until Easter Sunday. Then the cross would be uncovered, symbolic of Christ's resurrection from the dead. Six weeks. In six weeks, where would she be?

She'd better start making some plans. Get some interviews lined up. Six weeks went by awfully quickly. She didn't want to think about it. *Hey, girl, you* better *start thinking about it! Your bank account isn't any too full.*

Why hadn't she saved more? She made a good salary. Where had it all gone? What did she have to show for it?

Farrell knew the answer. She lived in New York City. It didn't come cheap.

Perhaps she should give up the city life. Move back out here, get a job on the local newspaper or go work for New Jersey Network. They'd hire her in a flash. KEY News was a great credential, if Range didn't sabotage her.

It would be much less expensive to live out here in suburbia. Rents were cheaper, she wouldn't have to spend so much on clothes or going out to eat. It would be much simpler.

But would it be boring? She'd always wanted to get out

of Westwood because she thought it was dullsville. Funny how appealing it was looking now.

And, hey, things happened in the 'burbs. Look at this whole Olga thing. She wished she hadn't promised not to tell Pat. Farrell really wanted to get her take on Peter's story.

But what if Peter's account was true? What a story! A candidate for the lead on *Evening Headlines*. If she could nail this down, she could hold her head high as she left. And best of all, she'd show that son of a bitch, Range.

The priest was droning on. Farrell was paying just about as much attention to his words as she had done when the nuns had herded all her grammar-school classmates to Mass every morning of Lent to start their days off right. How she'd groaned about having to climb up the hill and sit quietly in God's house, when she'd much rather be secretly making paper dolls in the scarred wooden desk she shared at school with her artistic buddy, Laura Dail. But you wouldn't dare complain out loud. That would be like *asking* Sister Raymond to twist your ear or pull your hair.

Farrell watched to see if she saw any familiar faces as the parishioners lined up to go to Communion. She didn't, but the ones there today looked like decent, hardworking people trying to do the best they could with their situations, playing the cards life dealt them.

I guess that's all any of us can do, Farrell concluded, thinking of Pat. She'd taken a really tough blow and had carried on bravely. She was a real role model.

Chapter 40

Farrell and Pat spent Sunday afternoon eating a roll of raw chocolate-chip cookie dough and poring through the books on Fabergé Pat had collected.

"When Olga brought the first piece of Fabergé into the shop, I got hooked," Pat explained. "Every time I see a new book on the subject, I buy it. Here's one I bought at Hillwood—you know, cereal heiress Marjorie Merriweather Post's estate in Washington, D.C. She was a Russophile and an avid Fabergé collector. She purchased the diamond crown that Alexandra wore at her wedding to Nicholas, as well as two Imperial Easter Eggs."

"Which ones?" asked Farrell.

"See here?" Pat pointed. "This blue monogrammed egg and the Cameo Egg. But the surprises are gone from the inside of each of them. The most valuable eggs are the ones which still have their little unexpected treasures left intact."

Farrell continued flipping through the art book, through the chapters on the history of the great house of design, and artists diagrams of the works that were carefully drawn on paper before they were made into objects of gold, enamels, and precious stones. She stopped at the chapter on the Imperial Eggs and read hungrily.

There is uncertainty about the number of Imperial Eggs produced by Fabergé. This reflects the private nature of their commission and execution. They were not considered to be created for the public's enjoyment, not to be displayed for the world to see. They were, instead, family gifts from the czar, personal tokens of his affection.

Ten eggs were made during the reign of Alexander III and another forty-four were made for Nicholas II. Two more eggs were designed and made in 1917, although they were lost and there is no evidence they were ever delivered to the czarina Alexandra or to the czar's mother, the dowager empress Marie Feodorovna, before the Romanovs were overthrown.

The Moon Egg was one of the last two eggs, Farrell thought, *ordered by the czar not knowing that he and his family would be killed within the year.* She shivered and continued reading.

The Armory Museum of the Kremlin has ten of the Imperial Eggs. America has a richer collection of the precious eggs, twelve of them at the Forbes Museum in New York City. There are a number of eggs in European collections and there are some owners who are reluctant to admit they possess Imperial Eggs, knowing their value and not wanting to explain how they came by the treasures.

Olga.

Farrell wished again she could tell Pat about Peter's story. But she had promised not to tell.

❧ Chapter 41

Unlocking the door to her apartment and switching on the lights, Farrell backed down the little hallway that led to her living room. She held up one end of the wrought-iron side table and Pat lifted the other.

"Well, here it is." Farrell gestured widely. "Welcome to my abode. Is it everything I said it was?"

"That and more!" Pat laughed, looking around the sparsely furnished room.

"Think you can help me do anything with it?"

"Absolutely. By the time we're done, *Architectural Digest* will want to do a feature on this place." Pat took off her coat. "You game for a little moving around right now?" she asked, rubbing her hands together.

"Sure."

Pat directed and both women tugged and lifted and pushed Farrell's furniture into new positions. The forest-green leather couch slid from a side wall to the spot beneath the picture window.

"There!" said Pat, with satisfaction. "Now you can sit here with your feet up, sip your morning coffee with your newspaper, and watch the world go by on the street below."

Why didn't I think of that? Farrell wondered. But when the movers had carried in the sofa, they had plopped it against the wall. There it had remained, all this time.

Farrell admired what their thirty minutes of effort had produced. The lone armchair, now angled toward the sofa, created a more inviting area for conversation. The Consignment Depot wrought-iron table was positioned next to the chair; Pat inspected Farrell's crowded bookcase for something interesting to perch on the top. She selected a hand-painted ceramic bowl Farrell had purchased when she had gone out to New Mexico to do a story on life, or rather survival, on a Native American reservation. Farrell watched with respect as Pat grouped together some candles that lay haphazardly on the bookcase shelves and displayed them on the edge of the coffee table.

"Looks better already." Farrell was getting a kick out of the changes.

Pat nodded with satisfaction. "Next time I come, we'll hang and rearrange the stuff on the walls."

"Deal," Farrell answered enthusiastically.

Pat lifted a small brass frame from the bookcase shelf, studying the picture of Farrell and her brother.

"How's Robbie?"

"Better, now that he's not at Nutman Stein anymore. He

couldn't take the pressures of the brokerage firm. He's working at KEY now, you know."

"And that's less pressure than Wall Street?" Pat asked skeptically.

"Where Robbie works, it is. He has a job in the film and tape library. He catalogues all the KEY News material shot around the world every day. It's interesting, but not much stress."

"He always was a sensitive kid," Pat mused, staring at the picture. "I remember you watching out for him all the time, making sure that no one picked on him in the schoolyard."

Farrell smiled poignantly. "That's what big sisters do, isn't it?"

❧ Chapter 42

Monday

With more enthusiasm than she remembered having in a long time, Farrell pushed through the heavy revolving door into the KEY News lobby on Monday morning. The weekend out in Westwood had given her just what she needed—some perspective. There was a whole world that functioned and was relatively happy and none of the people in it gave a rat's ass about what happened at KEY News.

She stopped for coffee at the lobby kiosk.

"Two, please. Black."

Why not be a sport and bring one for her officemate? It would really throw Dean off to see Farrell smiling and being Lady Bountiful. He'd expect her to be depressed and dragging. Farrell was sure that Dean would know about her termination conversation with Range. Everyone on the *Headlines* staff did by now. Happy news traveled so fast.

She braced herself as she approached her office door.

"You look great for someone who just got the ax."

B. J. was sitting in her chair. Dean was not in the office.

"Whew. That's a relief. It's only you. I thought I was going to have to put on a show. Coffee?"

Farrell offered a paper cup to him. He pried off the plastic lid.

"Ugh. Black."

"Oh yeah, how could I forget? You like it light and sweet."

"Just like my women."

"You're a pig."

"That's what you like about me." B. J. grinned wickedly, white teeth flashing.

She admitted it to herself. She did get a charge out of the irreverent, no-holds-barred banter with B. J. It went directly against all her years of Catholic-school training.

He took a sip of the dark brew and grimaced. "So now what are you going to do?"

"I'm not sure yet. Maybe get out of this nutty business altogether."

"I doubt that. You're hooked."

"I always thought I was, but now I'm not so sure." She

told him about the weekend with Pat at the Consignment Depot. "You know, B. J., there's a big world out there. This isn't the only way to spend your life."

She could tell he wasn't convinced.

"You know, I blame myself somewhat," he said quietly.

Farrell looked at him keenly. "What do you mean?"

"I heard you on the phone with Range the day of the auction. I should have told you to ratchet up the enthusiasm."

"For God's sake, B. J., I'm not a cheerleader. And this isn't high school. I shouldn't have to pump up Range Bullock, or sweet-talk him into a story. News judgment is news judgment. It's pretty pathetic to think that an executive producer of a national news broadcast is swayed by the presentation."

B. J. shrugged. "Pathetic, maybe. But you should hear the way your buddy Dean pitches a story from out in the field. When he describes it, every story he works on has the potential for a Dupont Award."

Farrell considered B. J.'s words. She knew there was something to them.

"You're right," she murmured. "That Fabergé story was a strong one. I should have fought harder for it."

"So what are you going to do now? Finish out your time here with your tail dragging between your legs?"

Farrell thought of Peter's story of the old lady with the allegedly "real" Moon Egg.

"Actually, I do have something I'm going to work on. An exclusive. Want to work on it with me?"

"Shoot."

Farrell filled him in on everything she knew so far. "I guess the first thing I should do is talk to Clifford Montgomery, the president of Churchill's." She made a note on the yellow legal pad on her desk. She looked up at B. J. "Why are you grinning that ridiculous grin?"

"Guess who I had a date with Saturday night?"

❧ Chapter 43

Monday morning. Pat hummed as she waited for her coffee at Choo-Choo Charlie's.

"Nice weekend?" Charlie Ferrino asked.

"Mmmm. Really nice."

"Do anything special?" By the sound of Pat's "mmmm," Charlie had the feeling he didn't want to hear the answer.

"Yes. I went to dinner in Manhattan. The restaurant was wonderful."

"How 'bout the company? Was it a 'date'?" Charlie busied himself fastening the top to the coffee container, trying to act as if his interest was only a friendly one, when in fact his heart was sinking.

"As a matter of fact, it was." Pat looked like she was trying to suppress her smile.

"And?"

"Oh, Charlie, what do you mean, 'and'? It was just a date, no big deal." Pat laughed nervously, shaking her head.

He didn't believe her.

❧ Chapter 44

Tuesday

Meryl Quan poured tea for Farrell Slater as she waited for Clifford Montgomery to arrive. So this was the woman B. J. was so keen about. Lovely.

"Sugar?"

"No, thank you. But I will have some lemon." Farrell squeezed the juice from the yellow slice into the amber brew.

"I'm sorry that Mr. Montgomery is running a bit behind schedule," Meryl apologized. "But he should be here momentarily."

"No problem." Farrell smiled. She was relieved to have a few minutes to collect herself. She was not looking forward to the conversation they were about to have.

As she waited for Montgomery to come in, Farrell wondered how the president of the auction house was going to react to the news. In her research on him, she had learned about the years he'd studied Fabergé as a young man, while working at La Russie Imperiale—probably one among a half-dozen of the finest antique shops in the world, and the main clearinghouse of the Russian enamels and jewelry in this country. Montgomery was regarded as one of the world's top authorities on Fabergé. Farrell doubted he would be happy when confronted with the possibility that he'd made a mistake in authenticating the Moon Egg.

A six-million-dollar mistake.

"I'm sorry to have kept you waiting."

Montgomery strode across the room and offered his hand to Farrell. He was dressed impeccably in a navy chalk-striped suit. A cornflower-blue pocket handkerchief matched his knotted silk tie.

"Thank you for seeing me so quickly. I'll try not to take up too much of your time."

"Well, we make time for KEY News and your phone call to Ms. Quan here, my assistant, was certainly intriguing."

Outwardly Montgomery seemed calm and in control. Farrell wondered how he felt inside right now. Probably a bit apprehensive. In a minute he'd be choking.

"Mr. Montgomery, I'm working on a story about *Faux*-bergé. You're familiar with that, of course."

Montgomery nodded. "Sure, I've come across a piece here and there myself, from time to time. Usually the sellers who brought them here for auction weren't aware that what they owned were fakes."

"You mean, they purchased the pieces thinking they'd bought authentic Fabergé?"

"That's right."

"How do they take the news when you tell them they've been had?"

Picking up a paperweight, Montgomery paused to consider.

"Disbelief, anger, embarrassment. There's not really much they can do but report the deception to the authorities and hope that the forgers are caught. That rarely happens."

"Why is that?" Farrell asked.

"Forgeries in the art world are much more common than most people realize. Even some of the most learned experts have authenticated fakes."

Farrell wondered if Montgomery already realized she was about to confront him with the possibility that he had authenticated a fake Moon Egg. Was he setting up an excuse for himself, that even the most esteemed in their fields make mistakes? Farrell scribbled in her reporter's notebook.

"Mr. Montgomery," she began. "Do you think there is any possibility that the egg auctioned here at Churchill's last week was not a real Imperial Easter Egg?"

"Anything is possible, Ms. Slater," he said coolly. "However, I authenticated the Moon Egg myself. I stake my reputation and the reputation of this auction house on my decision."

He's a smooth one, thought Farrell.

"Now it's my turn to ask you a question, Ms. Slater. What makes you think that the Moon Egg may be a fake?"

"A source says he knows where the real Moon Egg is."

"A reliable source?"

"I think so, yes."

"Have you seen this alleged Imperial Egg?"

"Not yet."

"Nor will you. It does not exist. These are very serious accusations that you are throwing around here, Ms. Slater. I suggest that you be very careful."

✣ Chapter 45

Olga sat huddled on the side of the worn sofa in her small living room, nervously fingering the pearly buttons on her gray cardigan. Her lined face was troubled as she listened to the earnest pleading of her surrogate grandson.

"Really, Olga. This will be all right. You haven't done anything wrong. You won't be in any trouble."

Olga's cloudy eyes searched Peter's young face. What was it like to be so trusting?

"How are you sure I won't be in trouble?" she asked. "The police are everywhere. Even when you cannot see them." She wrapped her arms tight around her torso, trying to warm herself in the suddenly cold apartment. This American boy was so naïve.

"Olga, I'm not telling you that the police are not everywhere," Peter answered, undaunted. "It's a good bet that they are in places and know things we can't even imagine. I agree with you on that. But what I'm trying to say is that you haven't done anything wrong, and you don't have to worry. No one is going to put you in prison or send you into exile because you have the Moon Egg."

Olga slowly lifted herself from the sofa and slowly made her way to the kitchenette. She switched on the electric burner beneath the tea kettle and opened the fridge, taking out a jar. Peter quickly came to her side.

"Mmm. The caviar! I was hoping you'd have some of this for me!"

Olga smiled as she watched Peter spread the sweet eggplant mixture thickly over slices of white toast. He could never get enough of it. Olga's mother's recipe from the Old Country. She loved watching him enjoy it. "I make more eggplant caviar for next time you come. You can bring to school with you."

As Peter ate, with relish, Olga considered his arguments. Maybe it was time to come forward, she thought. Time to lift away the heavy burden that she had been carrying for as long as she could remember. What would it be like not to live in fear?

"You say this woman from the television can be trusted?"

Peter nodded solemnly, wiping his mouth on the back of his hand. "I promise, Olga. Farrell is an old friend of Mom's. She grew up here in Westwood. She works for KEY News now and she's sure you won't be in any trouble. She's in a position where she can find out what's going on. Somebody paid six million dollars for a fake. That's not fair."

Olga smiled ruefully. Ah, Peter was so young. He thought the world was fair.

Suddenly Olga was very tired. Tired of hiding, tired of worrying, tired of covering up the truth. She knew it would not be long before she would pass to the next life. She knew it would be best to go with no unfinished business behind her.

She didn't have the energy to live with the secret any

longer. Perhaps Peter's coming to her like this was a sign, a sign from God to make things right. While there was still time.

"Okay," she said finally, in her thick accent. Peter looked astonished for a moment. He had actually gotten her to agree! "Okay, Peter, you bring television lady to take pictures of Moon Egg."

❧ Chapter 46

Farrell gazed out the taxi window as it crawled across midtown. It was lunchtime, and traffic was in its usual miserable state.

Where to go from here?

Without the actual egg as evidence, Farrell could not advance the story. From everything Peter had told her about Olga, the old lady was not about to bring her Fabergé egg in for any sort of inspection by Clifford Montgomery, or any authority figure, for that matter. Olga was terrified of the police. But without authentication, it could well be that it was Olga who had a fake egg.

Authority. The FBI.

That was the next logical step.

The yellow cab pulled up in front of the Broadcast Center. She gave the driver a very generous tip. Poor guy, he had to drive around in this mess all day.

He didn't say thank you. Typical. No good deed goes unpunished.

Dean Cohen was getting ready to go out to lunch when Farrell arrived back in their office. "What have you been up to this morning?" he asked.

"Oh, a little of this, a little of that. Since I'm a short-timer. I'm pretty well doing as I please." Farrell tried to sound lighthearted.

"Any job prospects yet?"

"Actually, I have a few things in the fire," she lied.

"Glad to hear it." Dean lied, too.

Farrell tapped the number pads on the telephone to check her voice-mail messages.

"Hey, Farrell, it's me, Rob. If you want to have some lunch, give me a call."

She listened excitedly to the next message, a young man's scratchy voice.

"Farrell, it's Peter Devereaux. Olga will let you take pictures of the Moon Egg. Can you do it today, before she chickens out?"

Chapter 47

God, what have I done?

Clifford Montgomery stared from his red leather chair, a stricken expression on his face.

If Farrell Slater proved right. . . .

His reputation would be ruined. Churchill's would be terribly damaged, perhaps irreparably. And the stock . . . Clifford's mind raced and he could feel his chest tighten.

No, it had to be a mistake, some sort of misunderstanding. Slater could be wrong, couldn't she? After all, she hadn't actually *seen* the egg herself. And the egg sold at auction was flawless, down to the Fabergé marking stamped on its golden base.

He had to see this new egg for himself. But how?

Clifford was so engrossed in his worries, he'd momentarily forgotten that Meryl Quan had been privy to the whole unsettling conversation. Word mustn't get out that there was even a hint of a problem with the auctioned Moon Egg.

He buzzed the intercom, signaling his assistant to come back into his office.

"Meryl, you must promise me, nothing that was said here over the last half-hour must leave this room. Until we figure out what's going on here, we can't talk about this to anyone. Understand?"

❧ Chapter 48

"Hey, Jack. What's the status of the Fauxbergé investigation you've been working on?"

"Continuing," Special Agent McCord grunted, not looking up from the paperwork on his desk at FBI New York Headquarters in Foley Square.

FBI press information spokesman Fred Behrends wasn't amused. Why was McCord always so damned difficult? Someone should knock that chip off the big guy's shoulders.

"Well, buddy, KEY News is working on a story about fake Fabergé. The producer who called was asking a lot of questions. Lots of what-ifs."

Suddenly McCord seemed interested. "Like what?"

"Like, what if a fake piece of Fabergé was auctioned off for serious money? And what if someone else had the real thing, but was afraid to come forward?"

"What did you tell him?"

"I told *her* that we'd get back to her."

B. J. adjusted his lights carefully. It wasn't easy to maneuver
in Olga's tiny living room. He tried to think of the various
shots he'd like to get. The old lady's apartment was a trip. It
reminded him of the illustrations in his childhood storybook
of the inside of Hansel and Gretel's cottage, where they lived
before their parents lost them on purpose in the woods. Or
maybe it was the Three Bears' house. Whatever. Olga's place
was visually interesting.

Farrell was busy reassuring the old woman. She was looking pretty shaky. Bet the old gal hadn't had this much excitement in a long time. He hoped she didn't stroke out or
something on them now.

"Olga, it would be great if we could shoot some pictures
of you sitting in front of the icon," Farrell said softly.

*So that's what the little religious painting on the wall was
called. An icon.* It was draped with a carefully starched and
embroidered linen cloth, and a white candle flickered beneath
it. A little shrine. B. J. wondered if the old lady knelt and
prayed before it. Probably, if she could bend those birdy legs
and get down there on those bony knees. He felt momentarily

guilty. He couldn't remember the last time he'd gotten down on his knees to pray.

"Peter tell me you want picture of egg. Not picture of me," Olga protested to Farrell.

God, he hoped Farrell could talk the old lady into letting him tape her. She was straight out of central casting and she'd be a really great element for the piece they would eventually do. *C'mon, Farrell. Talk the old girl into it.*

"Of course, Olga. You don't have to do anything you don't want to do. If you don't want us to take pictures of you, we won't. But I have to be honest with you, it will make the story much stronger if our viewers are able to see the woman who has the real Moon Egg."

Olga considered the producer's request. She looked uncertain.

"How about this?" Farrell continued. "While we're here, we'll take the pictures of you. I'll call you when we get ready to air the story and you can tell me then if we can use them or not. I promise I won't include you in the story without your permission."

Olga looked confused. B. J. didn't like feeling they were taking advantage of her. But he felt that way lots of times on different stories. He felt sorry, if he let himself, for the poor schnooks who found themselves with unwanted notoriety and had to live with the aftermath of their particular circumstances long after he and his camera left.

"Come on, Olga," Farrell encouraged. "Why don't you sit over here? We'll put this little chair over by the icon. There. Sit here, Olga."

Olga obediently took a seat in the wooden chair. She

smoothed out her skirt and then folded her hands in her lap. She looked nervously from the camera to Farrell.

"Tell us a little about yourself, Olga."

"What do you want to know?"

"Where were you born?"

"St. Petersburg."

"Russia?"

"Yes."

"When did you come to this country?"

"When I escape from Russia after Papa die."

"When was that?"

"After World War."

"One?" asked Farrell.

"No, Two."

"How did you get out of Russia?"

Olga was beginning to look frightened. B. J. hoped Farrell would pick up on that and lay off this line of questioning.

"You don't have to talk about that, if you don't want to, Olga," Farrell said gently. "But tell us how you came to have the Moon Egg."

Olga took a deep breath and B. J. zoomed in tighter on her face. The camera was picking up a nervous twitch at the corner of Olga's right eye.

"My father work in Fabergé studio in St. Petersburg. He is famous workmaster. Makes many beautiful things for czar and royal court. The most special thing, he make Easter eggs for czar to give czarina and his mother on our most special holy day. My father work on these eggs."

Olga stopped and her eyes darted from Farrell to the camera and back again, reminding B. J. of a scared rabbit.

"Just look at me, Olga," Farrell instructed gently. "Don't think about the camera. Just relax and talk to me like I'm the only one here."

"When czar and royal family overthrown, there is chaos everywhere in our country. Revolutionaries take over everything. They come to studio and take everything for the new people's government."

"Everything?"

Was the camera picking up a smile in Olga's eyes?

"Well, not everything. Some of the workers hide things. My father, he hide Moon Egg."

"Could you show us the Moon Egg now, Olga?"

℘ Chapter 50

Wednesday

B. J. popped the videotape into the machine, cuing it up ten seconds before the part when the Moon Egg opened and the comet of diamond stars appeared. Then he and Farrell sat back to wait for Range Bullock.

Farrell wondered if B. J. could feel her tension. The moment she'd seen Olga's Moon Egg, she'd known it was the real thing. She was sure of it. It didn't matter that she was no expert in gemology or antiquities, didn't know all that much about Russian history or jewelry design. The power of the work of art overwhelmed her and she knew to her bones that she was looking at Nicholas's gift for his beloved Alexandra.

Would Range be able to see it as well? Or would he dismiss it because she was the messenger bringing it to him?

"Let's see it." The executive producer loomed in the viewing-room doorway.

As B. J. hit the play button, Farrell watched Range's face, trying to read his reaction. Skepticism.

That's his job, Farrell thought to herself. *He has to make sure of the facts. Don't take it personally, he isn't judging you. He's judging the facts of the story.*

"Interesting," he grunted, when B. J. stopped the tape. "So you say it's an old Russian emigré that has this alleged Fabergé egg?"

"Yes. And she's hidden it all these years, afraid to let anyone know that she has it." Farrell waited.

"And the head of one the world's foremost auction houses, and an acknowledged expert on Fabergé, authenticated the egg that was sold last week?"

"I know it seems unbelievable, but yes." Farrell's heart thumped in her chest.

There was thick silence in the room as Range leaned on the doorjamb, mulling over the improbable story. Farrell could feel her pulse pounding in her ears and her face flushed as she waited for his response.

"I suppose anything is possible," he answered finally. "But we need more than this before we can go with the story."

"I have an interview at the FBI this afternoon. I'll see what I can get there," Farrell said, hiding her disappointment.

"Good. Let me know what you find out." As Range left the viewing room, he wondered if he had misjudged Farrell.

⚘ Chapter 51

As Farrell waited for her interview at New York FBI headquarters, she already suspected a few things about her subject. He would be in good physical condition, he would be an expert marksman, and he would probably be a somewhat cynical patriot, with a good measure of control freak sprinkled in for good measure. Acquiring wealth would not be of major importance to this guy. Nobody got rich working for the Federal Bureau of Investigation.

Farrell did not bargain for the fact that she would be instantly attracted to Special Agent Jack McCord.

His eyes. Piercing blue, they locked onto hers the moment he entered the room. He was accompanied by the FBI press information officer, Fred Behrends. Farrell knew that Behrends was there to run interference for McCord, make sure that the investigator did not run off at the mouth too much.

After they all shook hands and took their seats in the metal chairs that graced the spare government office, Behrends asked, "How can we help you, Miss Slater?"

Why did she feel suddenly nervous? She had gone on hundreds of interviews in her career. Usually she could tell the interviewees were far more intimidated than she was. Why did Jack McCord's eyes boring into her make her heart beat faster? She could feel her cheeks grow hot. The foot at the bottom of her crossed leg wiggled and she wished she had worn a better outfit than her gray flannel trousers and navy merino wool turtleneck. Why hadn't she taken a few minutes to freshen up her makeup before she came?

No wonder she hadn't had a date in over a year.

Farrell cleared her throat. "I'm working on a story about art forgery—Fabergé forgery, to be exact. And I want to find out what you can tell me about what the FBI is doing about it."

"Can you be more specific?" Agent Behrends asked.

"Well, it's come to our attention that a recently auctioned Fabergé Imperial Easter Egg may be a fake."

Neither agent's facial expression changed. *Nice job*, thought Farrell.

"Are you talking about the Moon Egg just auctioned at Churchill's?" asked McCord.

"As a matter of fact, yes."

"And what makes you think that it wasn't the real thing?"

"Information that I have from a source who is sure of the real Moon Egg's location."

"Have you seen the alleged real egg?"

Hey, I'm supposed to be asking the questions here, thought Farrell. She did not like feeling grilled by McCord.

"Yes, I have," admitted Farrell.

"Well, Ms. Slater, the FBI would be very interested in seeing this other egg. How do you think we can make that happen?"

"Not through me, you can't, Agent McCord."

"Of course, you realize that, as a United States citizen, you have a responsibility to not withhold information that could lead to the solving of a crime."

"Certainly I do, but my information isn't about a crime," Farrell answered primly. "If what I've been told is true, the real Moon Egg is out there, but that is not a criminal offense. The law that's been broken is that a fake egg was auctioned off as the real thing. That's where you guys come in. What, if anything, is the FBI doing to investigate?"

Farrell could tell she had hit a nerve with McCord, as she noticed his jaw clench. Behrends jumped in before the other agent could say anything in anger.

"We don't comment on ongoing investigations, Miss Slater. But you can be sure, the Bureau is using its considerable resources to track down anyone or any group who is breaking the law."

✄ Chapter 52

"Legal called. The FBI wants a list of our recurring Fabergé sellers and buyers." Meryl ticked off the next item on her list.

Churchill's legal department had a good working relationship with the FBI—all major auction houses did. Both sides routinely swapped bits of information.

But it was the specific type of clients the Bureau wanted to know about that raised the red flag to Montgomery.

He thought quickly. If he didn't turn the list over voluntarily, it would look bad, arousing suspicion that something was wrong. And if he refused, the FBI could just go ahead and subpoena the information anyway.

It was smarter just to hand it over. The name of the egg consignor wasn't on the list anyway. "Okay, fine. Give it to them. We want to cooperate with them whenever possible." Montgomery's voice didn't betray how worried he was.

What the hell was the FBI going to do with that list?

✖ Chapter 53

It was never easy. Never simple. That was just the way of the world. You took care of one problem, and there was always another to take its place.

Misha was out of the way. Now this.

It would be simple to get to her. A defenseless, frail, ancient woman, living alone in a tiny garden apartment. No big deal.

Don't be too cocky, big shot. This *was* a big deal. A very big deal. A six-million-dollars-or-go-to-prison deal. And that wasn't the way this was going to end up. Be sure of it. Not after all the years of hard work that it took to get to this point. Not after all the exacting study and planning.

Maybe Olga wouldn't have to die. After the Misha mess, the thought of another murder was distasteful. Perhaps it could be avoided.

Yes. Actually, it was necessary only to obtain the real egg. That would be enough. No need for killing. Without the egg, she'd be no threat. The timid old soul wasn't about to go to the police.

But if it did end up that she had to be killed, it sure as

hell wasn't going to be like the last time. Getting Misha out of the way had been gross, and too much work, to boot. If it came to it, this time it would be much easier. At least for the one doing the killing.

❧ Chapter 54

Cossack-costumed Tony held the door open for Meryl as she hurried from Churchill's. She was late for her date with B. J.

"How long are they going to make you wear that getup, Tony?" Meryl asked him. As he hailed her a cab, he waited with her at the curb.

"A few more weeks, Miss Quan. But I don't mind. It's good for business and, hey, it keeps me warm, too."

Meryl slid into the open taxi and listened to Eartha Kitt growl at her to make sure to buckle up her seat belt. The smell of curry permeated the air inside the cab and, despite the chill, she cracked the window to let in some of the fresh, evening breeze.

The car cut through Central Park to the Upper West Side, dropping her at the Lincoln Plaza Cinemas. B. J. was waiting just inside the theater door. He kissed her hello.

"Come on. I've got the tickets already. We're going to be late."

˄   They climbed the steps of the escalator, not waiting for the automated stairs to take them to the second-floor theaters.

"Popcorn?" B. J. offered as they passed the neon refreshment stand.

"No thanks. I'll wait."   ,

They found two seats together in the already darkened theater and settled in just as the previews were finishing. The opening credits rolled. Starring Tom Cruise, her favorite.

But Meryl found, try as she might, she couldn't concentrate on what was happening on the big screen. The Fabergé thing was bothering her. First the KEY News producer, then the FBI. Something was wrong, she knew it. And she didn't want to be caught up in it. If something illegal was going on, Meryl didn't want to be associated with it. She'd spent her life so far achieving, always living aboveboard and trying to improve herself. Her young career was going well. She didn't want to be part of any scandal.

"What did you think?" B. J. asked as the lights came up.

"Good."

"You're kidding, right? It sucked."

Meryl wriggled into her coat. "I don't know, B. J. I just couldn't concentrate."

"C'mon. Let's go get some dinner and we can talk."

They walked a few blocks uptown in the frigid February air, and ducked into a small Italian restaurant in the bottom of a brownstone just off Central Park. Some faux frescoes, all in pastels, were painted on the dining-room walls. Votive candles flickered on the white-tableclothed tables.

The ponytailed maître d' led them to a small table near the back.

"La signorina è bellissima stassera." As he pulled out her chair, he complimented Meryl in what she suspected was a phony Italian accent. Probably none of the people who worked here was Italian. The waiters were likely out-of-work actors.

Lately Meryl felt that she lived in a world where things were not as they seemed. She didn't know what to be sure of anymore. Was Clifford a crook? Had he knowingly authenticated a fake Fabergé egg?

B. J. ordered a bottle of chianti. Meryl downed the first glass quickly and set right to drinking another glass of the red wine.

"Hey, slow down," laughed B. J. "If you don't watch out, you'll get plastered and I'll definitely take advantage of you."

Meryl smiled weakly and pulled a piece of Italian bread from the loaf in the basket in the middle of the table. She wanted to talk to B. J. about what was going on, but she was afraid. She didn't want to be disloyal to Clifford in disclosing what was happening in the office. On the other hand, if Clifford had done nothing wrong, there really was no harm in telling B. J.

"You know, I've been meaning to ask you. . . ." She tried to sound offhanded. "Do you know someone at KEY named Farrell Slater?"

"Sure I do. Farrell and I work together all the time. She was the producer I was shooting for the day you and I met at the auction, as a matter of fact. Why do you ask?"

"Well, she was in to see my boss recently, and when she left, he was pretty upset."

"Upset about the Fabergé Moon Egg?" he offered.

Meryl's mouth dropped. "How did you know?"

"After what I saw today, your boss better be upset."

❧ Chapter 55

Now that the television people were gone, the closet didn't feel safe anymore. Her treasure needed to be somewhere else, somewhere safer, somewhere nobody would ever find it.

Olga knew where she would hide it. No one would think to look there.

She lifted the jeweled egg from its golden nesting box. Her withered hands trembling, Olga carefully wrapped the Moon Egg in three CVS plastic bags, the kind that Americans used once and tossed away, but Olga saved.

Round and round she swaddled the egg until she was satisfied that no dampness could permeate the plastic. Then, her arthritic knees throbbing, Olga shuffled across her small apartment and thrust the small package into the cool, dark ooze.

❧ Chapter 56

Friday of the First Week of Lent

Russian Peasant Folk Belief

*"Whoever fasts on this Friday
will not die a sudden death."*

A knock on the door always unsettled Olga.

She thought back to her childhood. When the knock came, she was afraid that the vicious Russian police were coming to drag away her father as they had stolen the fathers of her friends. Leningrad—as St. Petersburg became after the czar was overthrown and the Communists took control—was a treacherous place, a deadly place, full of whispers and the sounds of heavy footsteps in the night. Young Olga knew the terror of the banging on apartment doors, the loud, deep voices that demanded entry. The wailing and weeping that followed the screams.

But her friends had two parents. They had mothers who stayed behind to take care of the young ones when the fathers went to meet their fate. Surely the new government would not take her father.

Her mother was dead, killed by the cruel conditions of their new life. The bitter Russian winter, not enough to eat, and no medicine had seen to that. To Olga, the Communists had already killed her mother. They would not take her father, too.

But eventually the insistent knock in the night came.

Decades had passed, but she still heard the pounding on the wooden door. At night she dreamed of it—fitful, tossing dreams that left her heart pounding and her skin cold and clammy. By day, she dreaded even the lightest tapping on the doors of the other apartments on her hall. And when there was a knock on her own door, she trembled.

But, thankfully, knocks on her door were rare. Pat, Peter, once in a while the landlord. Charlie occasionally dropping off something from the deli. She kept to herself. She didn't want any trouble.

The candle flickered beneath the icon of the Blessed Virgin and her infant Son. *Holy Mother, protect us,* she prayed as she crept to answer the third knock.

"Who is there?"

✣ Chapter 57

Olga's visitor painstakingly searched and examined every nook and cranny of the small apartment, taking extreme care to put things back as they were. It must appear that nothing was amiss.

For a moment, the promise of a satisfying search. The distinctive yellow velvet Fabergé case discovered beneath the blankets at the bottom of the bedroom closet. But as it was lifted, it was too light.

Empty!

Where was the Moon Egg?

Think. Don't panic. Never panic.

The visitor looked some more. The seconds ticked away to minutes. The search turned up nothing. Nothing. Where was it?

It was time to get out. It was too dangerous to stay any longer.

If the Moon Egg couldn't be gotten, at least its owner—the person who could produce it, could attest to its existence—had to be put out of the way. That made sense.

The visitor carefully positioned the old lady on the single bed. It would look like she was asleep when the fire started.

The holy candle was lifted to ignite the white linen stole that draped the gilt icon of Christ and his Mother.

❧ Chapter 58

The shrill ring of the phone cut through Farrell's exhausted sleep. The bedside clock read two A.M.

In the instant it took her to reach for the receiver, apprehension coursed through her body. Most people thought a call in the middle of the night signaled a family emergency, but for someone in the news business, the nocturnal ring could mean anything. A plane crash, a war, an assassination.

"Farrell . . . it's Peter. Peter Devereaux."

Farrell could hear fear in the young man's voice.

"Peter, what is it? What's wrong?"

"It's Olga. A fire. Oh my God."

Farrell struggled into a sitting position and snapped on the bedside lamp, her eyes burning as they adjusted to the sudden light.

"Peter, just take a deep breath and tell me what's happened. First of all, where are you?"

"I'm at Pascack Valley Hospital."

"Where's your mother?"

"She's talking to the doctor in intensive care."

So it was bad.

"What happened?"

"There was a fire in Olga's apartment. I don't know how it started. But she. . . ." His voice trailed off and Farrell could hear he was struggling not to cry. Poor kid.

"How badly is she burned?" Visions of raw flesh, oozing blisters, and painful skin grafts flashed through her head. Burns were the worst. The pain was beyond excruciating. Farrell's bedroom was warm, but she shivered with the thought.

"I don't know. But she's unconscious and the doctor told Mom that it doesn't look good."

At that, Peter couldn't hold it in anymore. Farrell heard his breaking voice.

"Farrell, it's my fault. I know it is. I should have kept my promise."

Chapter 59

The car service dropped Farrell at Pascack Valley Hospital. Pat and Peter were waiting in the lobby.

"Thanks for coming all the way out here," Pat said as she enveloped Farrell in a hug. "Peter told me he called you. It makes us both feel better having you here."

"It's no big deal. How's Olga? How bad are the burns?"

"Thank God, she isn't burned. It's the smoke that was the problem. She must have fallen as she passed out, and hit her head. She's not waking up."

"What are the doctors saying?"

"It doesn't look good. Someone Olga's age doesn't just bounce back." Pat's voice shook.

Peter reached out and put his arms around his mother. She rested her head against her son's shoulder. "Oh Peter, this is so sad." Pat began to weep.

Farrell saw the anguished expression on Peter's face.

"This isn't your fault, you know," Farrell whispered.

Pat looked puzzled. "*Your* fault? How could you ever think this was *your* fault? It was an accident."

Peter nodded silently. Farrell watched the young man and

wished he would tell his mother what was bothering him. Get
it out. He'd feel so much better. Instead, he hung his head
and said nothing.

Pat scrutinized her son's face. "Peter, sweetheart, of course
it wasn't your fault. The fire chief said that the candle that
Olga always kept burning started the fire. You had nothing
to do with that."

✣ Chapter 60

Professor Tim Kavanagh drove up the Garden State Parkway,
compelled to get to Pat and Peter. He hoped Pat wouldn't
think he was too presumptuous. After all, they'd only had one
date.

But when Pat called to say she wouldn't be able to make
their second dinner together, he could hear the worry in her
voice. And knowing Peter's relationship with the old lady,
Kavanagh knew they both could use some moral support.

He wanted to be close by.

He thought of the pile of ungraded quizzes that sat atop
the desk in his study and sighed heavily. They'd have to wait.

This was his life. One semester followed another. Each
new Russian Studies class barely met the minimum enrollment

requirement. With the Cold War over, very few students seemed interested in Russia, past or present. Only occasionally did you get a kid who really loved the subject. A kid like Peter.

Of course, Seton Hall's School of Diplomacy looked very promising. He'd been involved in getting the new school off the ground when the United Nations Association went looking for an academic partner to educate future specialists in international relations. The professor readily agreed to be a faculty fellow, offering courses specifically designed for the increasing number of students who were coming to Seton Hall from around the world and who were now giving the university a more global reputation.

Tim tossed a token into the Hillsdale Plaza toll basket and rolled up the car window against the cold night air. A champagne-colored Lexus LS400 pulled out in front of his maroon Altima, beating him to exit 168. He'd love to buy a Lexus, he thought, yearning, but a tenured professor with a salary of $60,000 a year couldn't very well be driving around in a $50,000 car. It wouldn't make sense. People would talk.

No. He'd have to content himself with his growing Fabergé collection. Knowing that he and the Russian royal family had that in common gave Tim Kavanagh much pleasure and satisfaction. If it was good enough for the czars, it was good enough for him.

❧ Chapter 61

There wasn't much worth saving in Olga's apartment. What the fire hadn't charred, the smoke had blackened and the firemen's hoses had soaked.

Farrell and Tim accompanied Pat and Peter to survey the wreckage.

"It's a miracle she survived this at all." Farrell whispered what was on the others' minds.

Farrell and Peter went straight in the direction of the bedroom. The wooden bedframe looked like the charcoal remains in the bottom of a barbecue pit. A small mirror had managed to stay anchored to the wall, but thick, black soot kept it from reflecting anything.

The bedroom closet was shut tight. Farrell and Peter looked at each other before prying it open. Olga's clothes were carefully and precisely hanging from the rod, some hats and Olga's brown leather pocketbook were lined up on the overhead shelf. Peter bent to rummage under the blanket on the closet floor. He found what he was looking for. He quickly opened the yellow velvet carrying case.

It was empty.

"It's gone!" he whispered to Farrell.

The four continued to pick their way through the scorched debris on the floor, looking for recognizable remnants of Olga's life. The air was thick with the acrid stench of the burned wool rug, now soggy beneath their feet. They didn't say much as they went about their grim reconnaissance. Only an occasional cough broke the silence as their lungs rejected the apartment's toxic air.

Peter opened the refrigerator door. A stick of gleaming, yellow butter on a clear, glass dish. A piece of salmon peeked through Saran Wrap, ready for Olga to prepare for her solitary dinner. Half a loaf of dark, pumpernickel bread waited to be spread with the homemade eggplant caviar that filled three thick Mason jars.

Peter stood staring into the refrigerator.

"Come on, sweetheart," Pat said as she put her arm around her son's shoulder. "There's nothing more we can do here. Let's go." Then she added in true motherly fashion. "Here, honey. Take Olga's caviar with you. She always loved to make it for you and she'd want you to have it."

Looking over at Farrell and Tim, she offered, "You take some, too."

❧ Chapter 62

Jack came in drenched from the cold rain and his double jog around the Central Park reservoir. He loved his Sunday-morning run. It gave him an opportunity to get rid of some tension and organize his thoughts. His thoughts lately were primarily about his Fauxbergé case.

Meryl Quan was an invaluable source of information. She'd provided Jack with a list of all Churchill's recurring Fabergé customers and sellers. She said that her boss had okayed it. Of course, if McCord was going to use it down the line in court, he'd have to get a subpoena.

If it came to that, a court order wouldn't be a problem. Churchill's and the FBI had a good working relationship. It was mutually beneficial. When Churchill department experts suspected stolen property had been consigned for auction, they advised the FBI right away. The Bureau, in turn, called the auction house about property known to have been purloined.

On the one hand, Churchill's had a private relationship with its clients, but on the other hand, it didn't want hassles, didn't want to be receiving and selling illegal merchandise.

And, usually, Churchill clients consigning objects for sale didn't even know that they had unwittingly purchased stolen goods.

It constantly amazed Jack how eager the public usually was to cooperate with the FBI. Sure, the Bureau had taken some serious hits since the days when J. Edgar Hoover had reigned over the agency. Back then, the American people had viewed the Federal Bureau of Investigation with awe and absolute respect. But when Hoover died, and some of the not-so-pleasant realities of how the Bureau conducted its business came to light, the FBI's sterling reputation had gotten a little tarnished. The bungling at Waco and Ruby Ridge had added to the public awareness that the nation's justice force was comprised not of the infallible special agents of the Hoover myth, but mostly of dedicated and well-trained men and women who sometimes made mistakes.

Still, it seemed to Jack that on the whole, the public was eager to believe in the FBI. The average American citizen took comfort in the idea the federal government was doing its best to protect them. And they wanted to help when they could.

Then Jack's more cynical nature kicked in. *Let's face it,* he thought, *no one wants to piss off the FBI.* They were just too scared.

They should be.

Jack thought of Farrell Slater. She wasn't cooperating any. The KEY producer with the big brown eyes didn't seem to care one way or the other if she angered the FBI. From her position with a network news organization, she probably felt secure that the FBI wasn't going to give her a hard time.

Don't be too sure, Farrell.

❧ Chapter 63

It was so easy to get past hospital security. All you had to do was tell them you were a relative and they let you through. *Just act as if it's the most natural thing in the world that you are coming to visit. Tell them Olga's doctor said it was okay.*

Once you got past the front desk, you were home free. The nurses and orderlies, overworked and understaffed, were too busy to question why you were there.

Olga lay frail and thin against the stark white hospital sheet. The blue cotton blanket was tucked neatly around her where it would most likely remain undisturbed until the morning when a nurse would come in to pull it back to tend to the old woman, perhaps giving her a sponge bath, maybe massaging her aged limbs.

Gray-tissued lids hooded Olga's deep-set eyes. Would they ever open?

Chances were that nature would take its course. Olga had lived a long life. It would have ended soon anyway. This was only going to speed things up a little.

But if she did come out of it, if she did pull through . . . It was essential to know when it was time to finish the job.

⚘ Chapter 64

Another Monday morning at KEY News. There weren't that many Mondays left.

Farrell would rather not see anyone in the halls of the Broadcast Center. When she bumped into someone she knew in the cafeteria or the ladies' room, she could tell they were uncomfortable. They didn't know what to say. Farrell was being kicked out of what was, to them, the be-all and end-all. KEY News.

Farrell understood. It was seductive stuff, the television news business. It gave you cachet when it came time to swap occupations when introductions were being made at cocktail or dinner parties.

But how many dinner parties did she actually go to, anyway?

It was more the feeling of being on the inside, knowing what was going on before the public heard it reported, that had always given Farrell a charge. She had that feeling now. The excitement of knowing she was on to something. The urgency of getting her facts straight so she could go with the story, beat the competition.

She was fairly certain she had an exclusive going on this Moon Egg story. She was eager to broadcast it. But she grudgingly admitted to herself that Range was right. She needed more to go on than some videotape of Olga holding her egg. The other part of the story had to be figured out. Had the president of Churchill's authenticated the egg knowing it was a forgery? Or had he simply made a mistake that would cost him his professional reputation and ruin the standing of the esteemed auction house? Where had the bogus egg come from? And who had bought it, unwittingly paying six million dollars for a fake?

Then there was the scariest, saddest part. Olga. Farrell prayed it was just a coincidence the fire had broken out at the Russian woman's apartment when it had. She hoped it was only a fluke, that it had nothing to do with Olga's coming forward with her precious Moon Egg.

Farrell tried to reassure herself. The video of Olga holding the Imperial Egg hadn't been aired on *Evening Headlines*. The public hadn't seen it yet. So the video could not have led anyone to Olga.

The fire had to be an accident. Please, God, it had to be.

Chapter 65

Clifford Montgomery paced the Persian carpet in his Churchill's office. Haggard and worried, he hadn't slept well since Farrell Slater's visit. What was she up to? What was she finding out? He had to know. It didn't help matters that he was absolutely inundated by things that had to be attended to, what with the various Russian auctions coming up. He had taken to falling asleep several nights a week on his office couch, freshening up in the mornings in his small dressing room—one of the perks of being the president of Churchill's. He had a place to leave some clean shirts and a Brooks Brothers suit, and a place to take a shower, right next to his office.

Was he going to switch on *KEY Evening Headlines* some night soon and listen while anchorwoman Eliza Blake announced the biggest scandal to hit the art world in years? Was everything he had worked so hard to achieve going to come tumbling down for all the world to watch on their television screens? Would the audience be fascinated by his ruin?

Better to have the enemy inside the tent, so you could see what she was doing.

Montgomery buzzed the intercom.

"Meryl, would you please call Farrell Slater over at KEY News and ask her if she'd like to be my guest at the lecture I'm giving on art forgery at the Metropolitan?"

"Farrell Slater?" Meryl asked, surprise in her voice.

"That's what I said," he snapped.

If he could befriend Farrell, perhaps he could convince her that the auctioned Moon Egg was legitimate. After all, she'd said she hadn't seen the other egg herself, practically admitting she hadn't any proof.

It was worth a try. If he couldn't persuade her, he'd have to deal with Farrell in another way.

✋ Chapter 66

Dialing the phone number of the Consignment Depot, Farrell glared at Dean Cohen's back as he sat at the desk in front of hers. How she hated sharing an office with him. *Not for long*, she thought. That would be one good thing about leaving KEY News.

Pat picked up on the second ring. "Consignment Depot."

"Pat, it's me, Farrell. How's Olga?"

"Holding on, so far," Pat answered quietly.

"Still unconscious?"

"Uh-huh."

"What are the doctors saying?"

"Not much. Those guys play it so close to the vest. They say we'll have to wait and see."

Farrell heard a bell ring in the background.

"Got to go, Farrell. A customer is here. I'll keep you posted if there is anything new on Olga's condition."

Next, Farrell dialed area code 201 information.

"Westwood, please. I'd like the number for the fire department."

She had the feeling that Dean was listening to her side of the telephone calls. Busybody.

"Hello, this is Farrell Slater with KEY News in New York. I'd like to speak with the fire chief, please."

Farrell doodled on the blotter on her desk as she waited for the chief to come to the phone. *Olga. Egg. Video. Fire.* She traced six question marks after the last word.

The chief came to the phone as quickly as he could. "KEY News" had brought him running in from outside.

"No, Ms. Slater, we don't think there was any foul play here. We're pretty sure the old lady's candle started the fire. It was an accident."

"You're sure of it?"

"Almost a hundred percent sure."

" 'Almost'?"

The chief hesitated for a moment. "Well, the only thing that's bothering us, is that the apartment door was unlocked when we got there. Most of the old people around here keep their doors locked. Even though we like to think ours is a safe little town, we've done a local public-awareness campaign on the importance of home security. And the old lady's landlord told us she was fanatical about making sure her door was locked."

❧ Chapter 67

Victor had found it years ago, when he was just a little kid, though his mother did not know it.

He checked the hidden drawer in the walnut secretary every so often to see if there was anything new inside. Over the years, the drawer had yielded lots of interesting things, bits of information that helped him to figure out his mother, Nadine. The prima ballerina. The legend.

The love letters had always been his favorite secret. The letters to "Nadjia"—a nickname, he assumed, for his mother. Nadjia, Nadine. Close enough.

But who was "V."? Who was the man who signed the heartsick love notes? It wasn't his dead father. His name had been Michael. His mother must have had a clandestine affair with someone. Someone who meant a great deal to her, or she wouldn't have saved the letters, incriminating as they were.

It had always intrigued Victor to think of his mother sneaking around, involved with a man other than his father. She must have met him during her stint as a diplomat's wife in Russia. The letters revealed how lonely her lover was without her in St. Petersburg. Had she been lonely as her husband worked long hours in the American embassy during the Cold War? Was that what drove her to taking a chance like that?

The "V." bothered him, though. Not many names began with that letter. The fact that Mother had named her only son Victor, made him wonder. He'd never asked her about it, though. That would signal to her that he knew about her hiding place.

Victor hadn't checked the drawer in a while. There hadn't been anything new in there for a long time. Not too much happened in his mother's quiet, insulated life anymore. But he was bored today, and it was worth a shot. Nadine was upstairs having a massage that would keep her occupied for at least the next hour.

His thick frame looked out of place in the finely detailed office. Peasant stock. That's what he'd heard a maid whisper about him years ago. He tried to make the most of the attributes he did possess. Physical strength was his long suit and he worked hard to maximize his power. Lifting weights and working out were part of his daily routine. The gym was his passion.

The gym and—lately—Stacey Spinner. She made him feel so good. She complimented him all the time on his physique. Told him how handsome he was. No one, except his mother, had ever done that. And somehow his mother didn't count. Mothers had to praise their sons.

Being with Stacey made Victor feel good in a whole variety of ways, and he wanted to make sure she stayed in his life.

Victor took a seat at the walnut desk, his thick muscles straining against the seams of his trousers. Opening the paneled doors at the top, he felt beneath the shelf for the button. Open sesame.

❧ Chapter 68

Farrell watched Walter Cronkat and his pal Jane Pawley nibble indifferently at their dinners while she dwelled nervously on her conversation with the Westwood fire chief. The fact that Olga's door had been unlocked bothered her. Though she prayed otherwise, Farrell felt increasingly certain that the fire had been no accident. And most unsettling was the idea that Olga lay near death in Pascack Valley Hospital merely because she possessed the Moon Egg. The Moon Egg that Farrell had insisted she reveal.

The television producer paced her apartment, straightening the crooked bulletin board and plumping the kilim pillows she had purchased in Pat's shop, another tiny attempt to spruce up the tired sofa. She thought of Peter, earnest and so young, telling her Olga's story, trusting Farrell to know what to do.

She had let the kid down, letting her own hunger for a good story, a redeeming story for herself, get in the way of being responsible. Hell, she had reassured Peter that Olga wouldn't be in any trouble without knowing for sure what the legal repercussions would be for the old woman with the smuggled egg. And now the fire.

She pulled her thick white velour robe tighter around her and made up her mind.

She didn't really want to do it, but she had to. She had to call Jack McCord at the FBI and tell him about her fears. Before someone else got hurt.

❧ Chapter 69

Wednesday

Farrell stood at the base of the grand steps of the Metropolitan Museum of Art on Fifth Avenue. A bright blue sky framed the massive granite structure, with dun-colored Central Park on both sides. Long, luminously colored banners flapped noisily in the late-winter wind, announcing the special exhibits on display inside. One, in vivid purple, proclaimed, Russia's Royal Romanovs. Farrell made a mental note to take a peek at the exhibit after Clifford Montgomery's lecture.

New York was such a magical place sometimes, she

thought. So alive, so intense. Could she ever really go back to a small-town kind of life?

She climbed the stairs with a bounce in her step, eager to get inside.

The main foyer bustled with museum patrons, checking their coats, conferring with the volunteers at the information desk, studying their programs and deciding what beauties to behold first. There was a palpable energy in the air, the excitement of being able to get close enough to touch some of the most fabulous and famous art in the world.

A gray-haired man at the round information desk directed Farrell to the lecture auditorium. She checked her trench coat and walked through a long hallway full of Greek and Roman statues, past a small gift stand, and down some stairs to the lecture hall. The room was almost full and Clifford Montgomery was already speaking.

"Art forgery has gone on throughout the five thousand years of mankind's creative history. Not a month goes by in the art world without another tale of some new, fabulous fake being unmasked, or someone being royally ripped off by acquiring an expensive, well-executed imitation, but an imitation nonetheless."

Montgomery continued, smoothly and interestingly. Using slides, he showed the audience examples of famous forgeries through the ages. Portions of the Bible were faked. In the fourteenth century, a known forger confessed to having faked the Shroud of Turin, yet it wasn't until the 1990s that this fraud was laid to rest. Renoir was known to have copied some of his better work, selling them as "original" when he needed to keep food on the table. The list went on and on.

"And so, ladies and gentlemen," Montgomery concluded,

"I leave you with the words of Horace who had the whole thing nailed down so long ago when he said, 'He who knows a thousand works of art, knows a thousand frauds.' "

The audience applauded enthusiastically and Montgomery reveled in the praise.

"Are there any questions?" he called to the audience.

"Can you comment on the rise of Fabergé forgery?"

Farrell, standing at the back of the auditorium, knew Montgomery didn't like her question, but she had to admire the showman in him. He took a drink of water and smiled amiably.

"Of course. That's a very good question, especially in light of the increased interest in Fabergé caused by the recent auction of the legendary Moon Egg for six million dollars at Churchill's, and the Fabergé featured in the popular Romanov exhibit that's going on here at the Metropolitan. Fabergé has been copied and imitated for years, the forgers using the photographs in art books as models for their purpose. But serious collectors could usually spot the fakes. The work just wasn't as fine and, since Fabergé's works were usually one of a kind, duplicates must be forgeries.

"Now, with the recent record prices being paid for Fabergé, and the discovery of the actual Fabergé design book, forgers have come out of the woodwork. Current fakes, made in St. Petersburg and New York, are quite ambitious and exceedingly well executed. Many unsuspecting buyers, even some museum curators, have been duped. Forging Fabergé has become a major source of income for criminals."

Was Montgomery taunting her? Farrell wondered. Or, by inviting her to hear his lecture, was he trying to reassure her that he had nothing to hide?

Chapter 70

With no appointments pending all afternoon at Spun Gold Interiors, Stacey clicked the television remote control in the office, eager to watch Joan Rivers on QVC. She wished Rivers' show was on more often. She loved Joan's jewelry.

Of course, it was only costume, but the designs were clever and the workmanship was quite good. Stacey had ordered things from the show, though she really didn't like to admit to anyone that she even watched QVC.

She especially liked the pieces based on Fabergé designs. Joan was a Fabergé aficionado. Her husband Edgar had given her a Fabergé necklace years before, which had once belonged to Empress Marie of Romania. Joan's jewelers had copied it so that Jane Q. Public could have her own version of the tiny, enameled-egg charms in various shades and designs that hung from a gold-plated chain.

Stacey had always wished she could afford the real thing. She resented being a pretender. She was meant to have precious jewelry, not costume. When she'd taken Churchill's fine-jewelry course, she had fantasized about owning and wearing the glittering gems set in gold and platinum.

Like Nadine Paradise's crescent brooch. How royal she'd feel wearing that beautiful pin! But she consoled herself with the thought that if she played her cards right, if she could keep things going with Victor, she would have plenty of her own authentic Fabergé someday. Nadine's Fabergé.

The sound of the front door opening prompted Stacey to snap off the television. She smoothed her hair as she moved from her office to the showroom.

Stacey could see past the woman who stood framed in the large picture window. A silver Mercedes sports coupe was parked out front. Stacey put on her brightest smile.

"Can I help you?"

As the woman explained that she was new to town and had just purchased a colonial on Winters Way, dollar signs danced in Stacey's head. Checking their respective diaries, they made an appointment for Stacey to take a look at the woman's new house.

"Let me ask you something," the new client said, as she stopped at the shop door on her way out. "I've lived in Manhattan all my life—doesn't it get a little scary out here? Everything seems so secluded. So isolated." The woman appeared to shiver.

"No," said Stacey, shaking her head from side to side. "The police are wonderful and patrol like mad and just about everyone I know has an alarm system." Stacey lowered her voice to a stage whisper. "But I'll tell you a little secret," she said conspiratorially, wanting the woman to like her.

"I do have my own personal protection."

Chapter 71

"Farrell isn't in the office right now. May I take a message for her?"

"I'm returning her call."

"Is this in reference to a piece she's working on?"

"Yes."

"The art forgery story?"

"With whom am I speaking?" asked Special Agent Mc-Cord.

"This is B. J. D'Elia. I'm working with Farrell on the story."

"Okay. Would you please tell her that Jack McCord at the FBI returned her call?"

"I'll see that she gets the message." Dean Cohen lied again as he put the receiver back in its cradle.

✣ Chapter 72

Thursday

Farrell figured that shooting some video at the Metropolitan Museum's Romanov exhibit was a good idea. If and when she could piece together enough information to go with the Moon Egg story, elements from the Russian exhibit would really add to the texture of the package she would produce.

While B. J. fiddled with his camera gear, Farrell strode through the airy, high-ceilinged gallery rooms, scanning their contents for the items she wanted shot. She stared at a large portrait of the children of Nicholas and Alexandra: the four lovely Romanov daughters and their younger brother, Alexei, the hemophiliac heir to the doomed throne. Their expressions were innocent, trusting, mercifully unaware of the violent fate that awaited them.

Another painting, one of the czar and his beloved czarina, haunted Farrell. Here was the man who had commissioned the Moon Egg as his wife's Easter gift all those years ago. On the other side of the world, the action of the Russian emperor decades before was now impacting on Farrell's life. And the lives of others.

A large, white ostrich-feather fan, part of a costume worn

to a Winter Palace ball. Satin gowns covered with diamonds, emeralds, and sapphires. Mother-of-pearl opera glasses, bronze swords encrusted with rubies. Religious objects, icons and altar crosses and golden chalices. And jewelry: pendants and brooches and tiaras and bracelets that had adorned the Romanovs as they ruled Russia for three centuries, wearing pounds of yellow and blue and white diamonds, Ceylon sapphires, and blood-red rubies—while eighty percent of their country's people were living in poverty. The peasant farmers toiled in the impoverished countryside, and the factory workers slaved away in miserable city slums. Russia was ripe for revolution.

As Farrell and B. J. made their way around the exhibit, museumgoers watched them, interested in observing what the television people were doing. A tall, well-coifed woman approached Farrell.

"Excuse me. Didn't I see you recently in the Consignment Depot in New Jersey?"

Startled, Farrell studied the woman's vaguely familiar face, trying to place it. It was the woman who had come into the shop that day with Victor Paradise.

"Stacey Spinner," the woman prompted. "Small world, isn't it?"

"Oh, yes. I remember you now. Nice to see you again—although Pat didn't really get the chance to introduce us. Are you a Romanov fan?" Farrell asked politely.

"Well, yes, I am interested in Russian history," Stacey nodded, "but I especially came to see the Fabergé eggs. This is the largest collection of the Imperial Easter Eggs ever assembled, you know."

"So I hear. Which one do you think is the most interesting?" Might as well get some input from the woman on the street.

"My favorite is the Pansy Egg. I think the surprise inside, the tiny, heart-shaped frames with the miniatures of the Imperial children along with their parents, aunts, and uncles, is quite remarkable."

"We'll make sure to get over there and get a shot of it, then," said Farrell.

"I didn't get *your* name that day in the Consignment Depot."

"Farrell Slater."

"And what exactly do you do, if you don't mind my asking."

Would this woman ever go away? "I'm a producer for KEY News."

"Wow! That must be interesting." Stacey was truly impressed. "And you're doing a story on this exhibit?"

"Actually," snapped Farrell, losing patience, "we're doing a piece on art forgeries."

The moment the words were out of her mouth, Farrell wished she had not blurted out her assignment to a woman she did not even know.

❧ Chapter 73

Long after Eliza Blake had signed off, removed her anchor's mike and gone home, and all of the stage crew had cleared from the *Evening Headlines* studio, Range Bullock sat alone at his desk in the Fishbowl and stared at the latest ratings printout. KEY News was down.

In Range's mind, there was one main reason for the ratings slip. Money. Or rather, the absence of it.

At every one of an endless series of budget meetings, news division president Yelena Gregory pounded home the message. Keep down the spending. That meant sending fewer correspondents, producers, and camera crews on the road to cover stories, which meant using videotape obtained from affiliates when you could get it, and it meant having little quality control. It meant not going for that extra element if it meant springing for a news crew staying an extra night in a hotel in a faraway city or town. It meant thinking about what a story would cost to cover and measuring it against the story's importance. Good stories were being left uncovered because they were too expensive to produce.

His mind turned to the Fabergé story that Farrell was

working on. If she could prove what she suspected was true, it would be a powerful *Evening Headlines* exclusive news piece. The fact that it would all be done in New York, and therefore cost relatively little to produce, made it that much sweeter.

Suddenly Range wanted to see that video of the Fabergé egg again, and he didn't want to wait until tomorrow morning to do it. He'd just go up to Farrell's office, check if it was open, look around and see if he could find the videotape.

But when he got there, Farrell's second-floor office wasn't empty. Dean Cohen was inside, sitting at Farrell's desk. When Dean looked up and saw Range standing in the doorway watching him, the younger producer's face reddened.

"I just took a call for Farrell and I was leaving her a message," Dean explained.

Range nodded. He walked to the desk and looked over the tape boxes on the top. Then he checked the tapes that were stacked on the shelves on the wall.

"Can I help with something?" Dean volunteered.

"No . . . I'm just trying to find a videotape Farrell screened for me the other day. . . ." His voice trailed off as he continued his search.

"On what?" Dean tried to sound casual.

"Some art forgery story she's been working on."

Chapter 74

Friday of the Second Week of Lent

Dean Cohen paid for his coffee and bagel at the Station Break checkout. The KEY cafeteria was ridiculed endlessly by the news staffers, yet they ate there frequently. It was convenient, fast, and relatively cheap.

As Dean paused at the condiment counter to grab some paper napkins, he noticed Farrell and B. J. occupying one of the cafeteria booths. Their heads huddled together, Farrell and the cameraman were in the midst of an intense conversation. Dean wondered if Farrell had figured out yet that he had intercepted her message from the FBI agent. He didn't think so.

Dean hurried from the cafeteria and walked quickly to the elevator that would carry him up to the second-floor *Evening Headlines* offices. He wanted to have a few minutes in the office before Farrell returned. When the elevator doors opened, Range Bullock was waiting in the hallway.

"Hiya, Dean. What's happening?"

"Not much yet, boss, but the day is young."

"Isn't that the truth? God knows what today will bring. Another terrorist bombing or another campaign scandal."

Range shook his head. "I'm starting to think I'm getting too old for all this."

Dean laughed. "I wouldn't go around mentioning that to other people here, Range. But your secret is safe with me."

The two men chuckled as Range got into the elevator Dean had vacated. "By the way, buddy, it's about time for you to be coming up with another 'KEYhole,' piece, isn't it?"

"Don't worry, Range. I'm working on something now. I'll let you know when it comes together more."

Range gave a thumbs-up sign as the elevator doors closed. Dean smiled but groaned inwardly. He didn't really have anything he was working on for "KEYhole to America", the lengthy, investigative endpieces that closed *Evening Headlines* each night. With the exception of the lead story, "KEYholes" were the most coveted assignments on the broadcast. All the producers kept a running mental tally of who had come up with the most "KEYhole" pieces. Dean had been on a streak for a while, but lately his mental well had been running dry.

You're only as good as your last story.

Back in his office, Dean headed straight for Farrell's desk. Again he read her doodle.

Olga. Egg. Video. Fire.

Dean reached for the black metal hide-a-key case that he knew she kept magnetized to the bottom of the desk. His hands trembled as he slid open the case and pulled the small, shiny aluminum key from its bed.

By the time Farrell arrived, minutes later, the videotape of Olga's Moon Egg was snug inside Dean's briefcase.

❧ Chapter 75

It was not unusual for Meryl to work on Saturdays when special auctions were coming up. It was unusual for her to get phone calls from the FBI on the weekend.

"Ms. Quan, the list you provided me of Fabergé consignors and customers has a glaring omission," Special Agent McCord said sternly.

Meryl was intimidated by McCord's menacing tone. "How can I help you, Mr. McCord?"

"You can help me by getting me the name of the person who consigned the Moon Egg for sale to Churchill's."

"That wasn't on the list?"

"Ms. Quan, please don't play innocent with me and don't insult me. No. The name wasn't on the list. And if Churchill's doesn't hand it over, I'm going to get paper and force you to."

Meryl's mind raced. A subpoena would be easy enough for McCord to get. Why hadn't Clifford included the name on the list he had her turn over to the FBI? It just looked like he was hiding something. Was Clifford trying to buy time?

"I'll speak to Mr. Montgomery and see what I can find out, Mr. McCord."

"I'd appreciate it if you do it sooner than later, Ms. Quan. I'll expect a call from you."

The phone line went dead, leaving Meryl worried. The FBI usually ended up getting what it wanted. She didn't want to get on the wrong side of Jack McCord.

Meryl knocked on Clifford's door. The catalogue for the auction of the Nadine Paradise Collection was on Montgomery's desk and her boss was flipping through the thick, glossy pages. Leaf after leaf featured the mementos collected over the years of the ballerina's colorful life. The items for sale had been carefully photographed to show them off to the best advantage. Colorful antique posters from the Ballet Russe, programs from the famous Paradise performances, satin ballet shoes in palest pinks and flaming magentas, hand-engraved sheet music and set-design sketches, costumes Paradise wore as Aurora in *Sleeping Beauty* and Odele in *Swan Lake*. . . .

It was a coup to acquire the Paradise collection for auction. It would be worth a small fortune to Churchill's in commissions and publicity.

"We have some beautiful things to be sold for her next week, Meryl. I'm so pleased that we are hosting the Paradise auction of her wonderful ballet memorabilia. It ties in so perfectly with our Russian month. And the publicity department tells me that we are getting lots of calls from the media about covering our celebrity auction. That's great exposure."

Clifford looked satisfied and a lot less worried than Meryl had seen him in recent days. She hated to ruin the mood.

"The FBI just called."

"And?"

"The name of the consignor of the Moon Egg wasn't on the Fabergé list we turned over."

"It wasn't?"

"Not according to Agent McCord. He wants it as soon as possible or he's going to go for a subpoena to get it."

Clifford continued to look unruffled. "I'll take care of it," he said.

Meryl remained standing in front of Montgomery's desk.

"Is there something else, Meryl?"

"As a matter of fact, there is," Meryl began uncertainly. "This Moon Egg thing is really bothering me. First KEY News comes in with suspicions about it. Now, the FBI is clearly looking into this, and I'm being called about it. I'm worried that if there is some sort of problem or impropriety that occurred here, it might look like I'm involved."

Clifford studied Meryl, but didn't say anything.

Meryl summoned up the courage to continue. "What I'm trying to say, Clifford, is that I think . . . well, I don't think we can continue to ignore the media and the FBI. Agent McCord is waiting for a return phone call and I seem to be caught in the middle of all this."

Only a tiny vein throbbing at his temple betrayed Clifford's annoyance.

"I said I'd take care of it," he said curtly. Clifford then made a deliberate effort to soften his tone. "Meryl, dear, please don't worry. You aren't in the middle of this at all. Churchill's guaranteed confidentiality to the buyer and seller, and the entire sale rests on our ability to keep that promise. You will be perfectly safe—as long as you keep out of it."

✦ Chapter 76

Third Sunday of Lent

The sound of Olga's breathing beneath her oxygen mask echoed through the silent hospital room as Farrell and Pat sat quietly next to her bed.

"I try to get here every day," Pat whispered. "I like to think she knows I'm here."

"They say that a coma victim is aware on some level of what is going on around her." Farrell tried to reassure her friend. "I'm sure having your energy here, caring about her, helps Olga."

The two women stared at the frail figure lost in the vastness of the hospital bed. They kept their worried thoughts to themselves as the nurse's aide rustled in to check Olga's vitals and register them in her medical chart.

Pat broke the silence again. "It's so good of you, Farrell, to come out here like this. You've been a real friend."

"It's the least I can do."

"You don't even know Olga."

Farrell wanted to spill out her worries, tell Pat the truth about the Moon Egg and how she had come out and taped it just before the fire. Instead, she honored her promise to Peter. He would have to tell his mother himself.

When they rose to leave, Farrell asked if Pat wanted to go out and grab a bite to eat.

"That would be fun," Pat replied. "But I have a business call I have to make."

"On Sunday?"

"Yep. I'm at the Consignment Depot the rest of the week and on Saturdays. So I have to do my other business at night or on Sundays."

"Well, how about if I come with you and we can get some supper after that? Then I'll take the bus back to Manhattan."

As they walked down the corridor, they met up with Charlie Ferrino. Pat introduced the deli owner to Farrell.

"It's really good of you to come and visit Olga, Charlie," Pat said, reaching out to touch his arm.

"I have a soft spot for the old gal. I'm really pulling for her, but it's not looking so good, is it?"

"Not really." Pat shook her head and smiled weakly.

Farrell and Pat continued down the hallway.

"Did you see the way that guy looked at you, Pat?" Farrell whispered. "He's got it bad."

"Charlie?" Pat laughed incredulously. "He's just the sweet guy at the deli—we've known each other for years."

"I'm telling you, he's crazy about you," Farrell insisted.

Pat's Volvo pulled out of the hospital parking lot onto Old Hook Road, and headed through Westwood, up the steep Washington Avenue hill toward Saddle River. Farrell watched as the more modest houses on small lots gradually led to larger and larger homes on acres of wooded property. When their car pulled into the circular driveway in front of the Tudor mansion, Farrell let out a soft whistle.

"Who lives here?"

"Nadine Paradise."

"The ballerina?"

"Yes. The legend. And the mother of one Victor Paradise who came to the Consignment Depot with Stacey Spinner and so charmingly demanded that I tell him where the crescent brooch that his mother bought at Churchill's came from."

Farrell stared at Pat. "It came from Olga, didn't it?"

Pat nodded silently. "So now Nadine Paradise is going to try to convince me to tell her the pin's provenance. She just about begged me to come to the house today."

"Are you going to tell her?"

"I'm not sure."

❧ Chapter 77

Leading them just past the small library into the conservatory, Nadine waved Pat and Farrell beyond the baby grand piano, toward two Burmese rattan armchairs with brightly flowered cushions that sat at angles to a matching loveseat. In the center of the triangle was an oblong table with brass finishings on which a porcelain tea service took up almost all of the space.

The room was not unoccupied. Farrell observed that Victor Paradise looked distinctly awkward in a room filled with delicate plants and fine china. He stood up and moved toward his mother and the two visitors.

Nadine made the introductions. "You remember my son, Mrs. Devereaux. Victor, this is Miss Slater, a friend of Mrs. Devereaux's." As the women took their seats, Nadine looked in her son's direction and said, "Victor, dear, would you be kind enough to get us some napkins? If there aren't any on the wet bar in the library, you may have to look in the dining room."

Victor knew he was being dismissed. He walked out of the room as his mother began to pour out her story. Although Mrs. Paradise directed most of it to Pat, Farrell listened intently to the aged ballerina's recollections and watched her with a television producer's eye for detail.

"So you see," Nadine finished, "I have to know who you sold the crescent brooch for. I'm convinced that that person has some sort of connection to me. My father, a father I never met and longed for all my life, made that pin for my mother."

Farrell studied the old woman's face, still beautiful in the late-winter sun streaming through the conservatory window. In passing, one would see very little resemblance between the face of this wealthy, artfully made-up legend, and the wrinkled old lady who slept in a hospital bed a few miles away. But as she watched Nadine's expressive hands, they looked familiar, like the delicate ones that lay folded on the blue cotton hospital blanket. Artful hands, hands that could have been part of the genetic code of a workmaster in the Fabergé studio.

Farrell looked over at Pat, who was considering Nadine's appeal. What would it hurt to tell her that the crescent pin was Olga's? Since Olga lay dying, this could be Nadine Paradise's last chance to make peace with her past.

The same thought must have been running through Pat's mind.

"Mrs. Paradise," said Pat gently, "a very sick woman is lying near death at Pascack Valley Hospital right now. The crescent brooch was hers. Her father made it."

Nadine listened silently but wide-eyed as Pat told her what she knew of Olga's history. The early years in St. Petersburg, defined by the revolution and the death of her mother. Her proud father, once a Fabergé workmaster, left brokenhearted and unable to leave his mother country. Olga's ultimate escape from the Soviet Union and emigration to the United States, her quiet life in Westwood financed by slowly selling off pieces of her father's artistry.

"It's all falling into place. Olga may be my half-sister." Nadine's eyes glistened with tears. "I need some time to take this in."

"Of course."

Victor cleared his throat as he entered the conservatory with three white linen cocktail napkins in his hand. "You were right, Mother," he lied. "I had to look for them in the dining room. I hope I haven't kept you from your tea."

"We were just leaving," said Pat. "We need to get going." She and Farrell rose, and Mrs. Paradise escorted them past her son and out to the foyer.

"What a beautiful scarf." Pat admired a luxurious turquoise scarf left casually on the hallway table. Nadine picked it up and pressed it into Pat's hands.

"Please take it, my dear," she urged.

"But I couldn't," Pat protested.

"Please, I insist. Keep it as a reminder of a day you made an old woman deeply happy."

❧ Chapter 78

Monday

Days had gone by since she'd made the call to Jack McCord and still she hadn't heard back from him. First thing Monday morning, Farrell resolved to call him again. She waited until Dean was out of their office.

"Thanks for the call back," Farrell sniffed sarcastically. "I really feel that my country's security is in capable and efficient hands."

"I did call you back," McCord protested. "Your colleague told me he would give you the message that I returned your call. It sounds to me like KEY News is the inefficient organization here."

"I didn't get your message. Did you get the name of the person with whom you left it?"

"Some guy with initials for a name." Jack shuffled through some papers on his desk.

"B. J.?"

"Yeah. That's it. B. J. D'Elia. I have it right here in my notes. He said he was working the Fabergé story with you."

It's not like B. J. to neglect giving a message, Farrell thought. *And he's not usually in my office when I'm not there.* She'd have to ask him about it later.

"Well, what was it you wanted to talk to me about?" Agent McCord asked.

Without naming names, Farrell told him about her suspicions regarding the fire at Olga's.

"So, let me get this straight. You harass some old lady and get her to let you take pictures of her illegal property and she ends up in a coma somewhere after her apartment catches fire."

Farrell winced. "Yeah. That's about it. That, and the fact that the woman lived in fear and, at the same time, her apartment door was unlocked at the time of the fire."

"Don't you think it's about time you gave me her name and address?"

"I can't."

"Can't, or won't?"

Farrell thought quickly. Without too much trouble, Jack could have the FBI computers check every reported fire that had occurred in the country during any given period. As he checked further, eventually he would end up with the Westwood fire chief, who would willingly give up Olga's identity to the mighty feds.

Maybe, by giving McCord the information he asked for, Farrell could buy a little allegiance from the guy. When the

time came he had something to share about his Fauxbergé
investigation with the public, maybe he'd choose Farrell to
share with, seeing as she had helped him out along the way.

She told him.

"Thanks," he answered matter-of-factly.

"Your gratitude is overwhelming," Farrell remarked dryly.
"At least you can help me with this: What are the possible
legal ramifications for Olga once it becomes public that she
has the real Moon Egg?"

"Well . . ." Jack considered. "This isn't a 'spoils of war'
issue. The Russian Revolution was a civil war, not a war
between two sovereign countries. But if the Russians find out
that Olga has an Imperial Easter Egg looted from the St.
Petersburg Fabergé studios back in 1917, they could put a
claim in United States Federal Court. A judge would decide
its ownership."

"How likely is that scenario?"

"Remote. Plus, from what you tell me, that's the least of
the old gal's problems."

❧ Chapter 79

Robbie Slater sat with his sister in a corner booth at the Station Break.

"Man, I can't believe how hard it is for a guy to have lunch with his sister." His cardboard lunch tray held a fat roast-beef sandwich, a package of Fritos, an orange soda, and three packs of Oreos.

"Nice, healthy lunch there, Rob." Farrell nodded as she poked at her plastic salad bowl full of lettuce, tuna salad, and carrot sticks. Farrell noticed with a twinge that his hairline had receded a little more from the last time she saw him. His exposed forehead looked so vulnerable to Farrell.

"You're just jealous. Watching your girlish figure, huh? Somebody new in your life? Is that what's keeping you from returning my calls? Come to think of it, you look especially good today."

"Nah. Same old, same old, but I *have* been busy." Farrell did not want to talk about Jack McCord or fill Robbie in on Olga's fire and the Moon Egg. She especially did not want to tell him yet that she was being let go from KEY News. She did not want him to worry.

"What are you so busy with?" Robbie asked, taking another large bite from his sandwich.

"A story on art forgery. I'd like to develop it into a 'KEY-hole to America' piece."

Farrell wanted to change the subject. "How's it going for you, Robbie?"

"Pretty well. I like my job at the tape library. I can't believe all the material that comes in. It's amazing to me how much is shot on each story and how comparatively little makes air. It's fun to look at the outtakes, too. Plus, no one really bugs me over there. I work at my own pace and that seems to be fine with my boss."

"That's because you're so smart and do a great job, and he knows he's lucky to have you." Farrell always tried to boost Robbie's shaky self-esteem.

"Spoken like my big sister."

"It's true," Farrell protested.

"I think it's more like my boss realizes that for the modest salary they're paying, they can't expect too much, or complain too much."

"Don't sell yourself short, Robbie, please," Farrell pleaded. "I hate when you do that."

Robbie glanced at the large white clock and piled his sandwich wrapper and empty soda can on his tray. He slid the remaining uneaten package of Oreos into his shirt pocket.

"Gotta get back," he said, reaching out to squeeze Farrell's shoulder. "And do me a favor, will you? Stop worrying about me."

❧ Chapter 80

"I was wondering if I could possibly come in for a tour. I've been to the public rooms of Churchill's so many times for exhibitions and auctions, but I'm curious to see what goes on behind the scenes."

Balancing the telephone receiver on her shoulder, Meryl checked her DayTimer. A half-hour of her day was well spent on someone who could help Churchill's. Being polite and accommodating was good for future business at the auction house.

"Of course, I'd be happy to show you around. When would be a good time for you?" Meryl asked.

"I know it's short notice, but you wouldn't happen to have some time tomorrow, would you?"

Meryl scanned her calender. "As a matter of fact, I do have some time open tomorrow afternoon. How would three o'clock be?"

"Wonderful. I'll see you then."

Meryl penciled in the appointment.

❧ Chapter 81

Still, she breathed. In and out. In and out. The clear plastic oxygen mask covered her nose and mouth.

It was surprising that such an ancient, wizened old thing could hang on so tenaciously. You had to give the old girl that much. She didn't want to die.

But there was consolation in the fact that the nurses looked so glum when they came in to check on her, the rueful, understanding smiles they gave to the regular visitor who kept watch so patiently.

"So many of our elderly patients have no visitors. It's nice to see someone on in years get so much company," the blond night nurse said.

Olga, Olga, Olga. Why don't you let go, sweetheart, make the decision to move on yourself? It would be better that way. Go willingly rather than be forced.

❧ Chapter 82

Farrell was more than a little anxious about Jack McCord coming over to KEY News to take a look at the Moon Egg video. She'd taken care putting on her makeup and dressing this morning, choosing her charcoal-colored Calvin Klein suit, sheer black hose, and stack-heeled pumps.

"What's the occasion?" B. J. asked when he saw Farrell in the hallway.

"Can't I dress up a little without it being an occasion?"

"No."

She waved him off and continued on her way. Then she stopped and turned back in B. J's direction.

"Hey, hot shot," she called. "Thanks for giving me my message."

B. J looked puzzled.

"The message from the FBI agent," she prompted.

"Since when do I take messages for you?"

"You didn't take a message for me from Jack McCord at the FBI?"

"Not me, kiddo. Must have been someone else."

Chapter 83

Holding open Churchill's door, Tony greeted the visitor by name.

The coat checked, the visitor was announced by the Churchill's security staffer at the front desk in the lobby.

"Ms. Quan will be right down," he said.

"Thank you."

The visitor paced back and forth. Waiting.

Meryl Quan descended the stairs, her hand extended. "How good to see you again. I thought we'd start upstairs with the various offices, Business Department, Trusts and Estates, et cetera. Then we'll work our way down to the jewelry gallery and the board of directors' conference room. We'll finish up by going backstage, where the storage rooms are. That's where the items that are going to be auctioned are kept. Our security department is also situated back there."

"Great."

Meryl guided the visitor, floor by floor, through the labyrinth of Churchill's offices, explaining the function of each.

"Fascinating," the visitor said, eyes observing the security cameras positioned in the halls and doorways.

"This is my favorite part of the tour," said Meryl. "Backstage where the work is done to ready the items for auction." Meryl led the way through a maze of storerooms where shelves held auction items according to category. Furniture, bronzes, silver and glass, rugs. . . . Each room had cameras peeking from various points in the ceiling. The visitor's heart was sinking.

"My Lord, what's all that?" An opened door revealed an organized jumble of what looked like space suits.

"Those are items for the Russian Space History Sale. It's rather sad, really—they're selling off their history just to survive financially. . . . And here is our security area," said Meryl as they moved on. A guard sat at the console, watching three dozen television screens that covered the wall in front of him. "As you can see, we are very careful here."

The visitor nodded. "Impressive."

"That about wraps up our tour. Is there anything else I can show you?" Meryl offered.

"No, I think I've seen all I was interested in seeing."

"Then let me walk you out." Meryl escorted the visitor from the security room and down the hallway toward the public area. They stopped momentarily, blocked by two moving-men who were unloading a heavy, tiger-oak dining table from an oversized freight elevator.

The freight elevator. It had no camera!

Chapter 84

When Farrell went to greet Jack in the Broadcast Center lobby, she noticed with satisfaction that he thirstily drank in her appearance. Farrell was glad that she'd made the extra effort as Jack shook her hand firmly and his piercing blue eyes locked onto hers.

"I'm glad you've decided to share your information with us, Farrell."

So now it was Farrell instead of Ms. Slater. Good sign.

"Well, the fire at Olga's really changed things from my perspective. I'm afraid someone is playing for keeps here, and I don't want anyone else to get hurt. Let's stop in my office. I'll get the videotape from my desk and I have a viewing room reserved for us."

"I'm surprised big-shot network news producers have to share offices," said Jack, gesturing toward Dean Cohen's empty desk.

"Yeah. I'm not only surprised, but unhappy, too. It's not that I have a need to work alone—most of my work is out in the field anyway. There's just not enough space in the Center for all the broadcasts that are being worked on here.

KEY News has expanded a lot since the time we moved into this building."

Farrell unlocked her desk drawer and reached for the videotape B. J. had shot. At first puzzled, and then frantic, she emptied the drawer searching for the tape.

"Don't tell me," Jack said cynically. "It's not there."

"It's got to be here. Maybe I put it in another drawer."

Soon the entire contents of Farrell's desk were strewn out on the top. No videotape. Where was it? She was embarrassed in front of the no-nonsense FBI agent.

Jack, though, didn't seem overly concerned. "Hopefully it'll turn up. Why don't you just tell me exactly what Olga showed you?"

Farrell described for him the yellow velvet carrying case, inscribed with the Cyrillic letters, enough of which she could recognize as spelling Fabergé. She told of Olga's opening the case and taking from it the milk-colored, enamel-and-gold egg that rested on a cloud of midnight-blue stone.

"Lapis lazuli?" he asked.

"Yes, that's what I think it's called. I was at the Moon Egg auction, Jack. Olga's egg looks just like the egg at Churchill's. Except for one thing. Olga's had the surprise still intact inside the egg. The auctioned one, as you know, did not."

"What was the surprise?"

"A spray of diamonds. Brilliant diamonds. Olga called them a comet. I admit that I'm no expert, but I'd bet the farm those diamonds were real."

Jack made some notations in his notebook.

Farrell folded her arms across her chest. "Well, what do you think?"

"I've seen the design plans for the Fabergé Moon Egg,

Farrell. The surprise called for a comet of diamond stars, signifying Halley's Comet which appeared in the early part of the century. From what you are describing to me, my gut tells me that you've seen the real Moon Egg."

"Now what?"

"Now I think you should leave this case to the professionals. Obviously you are treading dangerous waters here."

Farrell smiled. "Know what I think?"

"I know you are going to tell me whether I want to hear it or not."

"You're right. I think two heads are better than one, and that if we work together, we can solve this thing. You'd get kudos at the FBI, and I would score big around here. Sounds good, doesn't it?"

"If you really want to know the truth, Farrell, I'd be a lot more interested in having dinner with you than in working with you on a case."

"That's what you think now, Jack. You might find out, though, that both scenarios will be mutually satisfying."

ℳ Chapter 85

The Nadine Paradise auction was worth a pitch. Viewers were interested in celebrity auctions, loved the vicarious thrill of peeking into famous people's personal lives. Farrell herself remembered going to the Duke and Duchess of Windsor auction preview at Sotheby's and being mesmerized at finding the Elizabeth Arden recipe for the duchess's black hair dye, the hundreds of gloves the duchess wore because she was self-conscious about her large hands, and a box with a piece of the couple's 1937 wedding cake.

Farrell was certain that she could do a fascinating piece on the Paradise collection. She could shoot the most interesting items for sale at the preview over the coming days, and Friday she could cover the auction itself. The piece would air on *Evening Headlines* on Friday night.

As she tapped out her note to Range on her computer, Farrell was grateful for e-mail. It gave her a chance to compose and express her thoughts without having the uncomfortable pressure of having to pass her idea by Range face-to-face.

Go for it, came the executive producer's e-mailed reply.

Yes! thought Farrell. The Paradise auction was a cool story, but even more important to her, it was another opportunity to get over to Churchill's.

✣ Chapter 86

Thursday

The elegant woman, cloaked in a jacket of brown broadtail fur with braid edging, carried a small matching muff as she alighted from the black Mercedes sedan in front of Churchill's. Though passersby did not immediately identify her, they instinctively sensed that the woman was "somebody."

"I'll park the car, Mother, and I'll meet you inside."

"Thank you, Victor dear."

The Churchill's doorman, a welcoming smile on his face, held the door open wide for Nadine Paradise, who stopped for a moment to talk with him.

"How have you been, Tony?"

"Just fine, Mrs. Paradise."

"Holding up with all the Russian festivities?"

"Yes, ma'am."

Nadine eyed the cossack costume and an idea struck her.

"You know, Tony, I think I'd like to see you inside during my auction tomorrow. Do you think you could come inside and stand in your uniform next to the auction platform? I think that would be a nice touch."

"Certainly, Mrs. Paradise. Whatever you and Mr. Montgomery want."

Nadine pressed a crisp bill into the doorman's hand.

"Good to see you, Tony."

"Thank you, Mrs. Paradise."

Clifford Montgomery and Meryl Quan were waiting inside for Nadine, and welcomed her warmly.

"I hope you will be quite pleased with our display of your wonderful things, Mrs. Paradise," Clifford said solicitously. "We are so happy to have the opportunity to showcase these treasures."

The threesome entered the busy auction gallery, alive with the energy of the interested public inspecting—and television crews filming—the relics of Nadine's ballet career. Mural-sized blowups of decades-old pictures of Nadine dancing *The Firebird*, *Scheherazade*, and *The Rite of Spring* hung on the gallery walls, serving as a backdrop for the carefully arranged items that would soon be auctioned. Spotlights illuminated framed water-colored costume sketches and set-design plans that were works of art in themselves. The jeweled and feathered headpieces that had once crowned Nadine's head as she pirouetted on the stages of the world, now hung on Churchill's walls, waiting to be taken home by the highest bidder.

"Clifford, you've done a beautiful job here."

"Thank you, Mrs. Paradise."

Nadine continued her tour, satisfied with the decision to

divest herself of all these things. It would be that much less for Victor to do after she was gone.

"Excuse me, Mrs. Paradise?"

"Miss Slater! It's so nice to see you here."

"Thank you for remembering me. I'm here covering the auction for KEY News. I was wondering if you'd be willing to be interviewed briefly."

"Certainly, dear."

Clifford Montgomery was clearly annoyed. Meryl tried to hide her pleasure at seeing B. J. approach with his camera, while Victor Paradise arrived at his mother's side.

Farrell started with some questions about Nadine's dance career, asking her if there were any auction items that were of particular significance. Nadine answered eloquently, her French accent giving her responses an almost melodious quality. Farrell knew that, back in the editing room, she would have good material to work with.

"Why now, Mrs. Paradise? Why did you decide to auction these things off now?" Farrell asked.

Nadine smiled. "As one gets older, one wants to simplify one's life. This just felt like the right time to let go of a few things and move on." She failed to mention that the money would be welcome income after living so many years in retirement.

❧ Chapter 87

Friday of the Third Week of Lent

You had to hand it to them. Churchill's really knew how to do it right.

Farrell observed and B. J. shot as the Paradise auction began. Clifford Montgomery made brief opening remarks from the auctioneer's platform. The lights dimmed and a movie screen lowered from the ceiling. As the music of Tchaikovsky and Stravinsky played, black-and-white slides of the prima ballerina flickered on the screen.

When the lights came back up and the applause died down, a Russian cossack appeared to stand guard as the first item for sale wheeled into view on the automated platform. The costume that Nadine Paradise wore in the title role of *The Firebird*. Farrell consulted her auction catalogue to read that the ballet was based on a selection of Russian fairy stories. It was a good selection to start off another auction in Churchill's Russian series.

Farrell was really beginning to feel comfortable at the auction house—not feeling, as she once had that it was a hushed, intimidating place that only the very, very wealthy dared enter. As she looked around the gallery, she saw faces she recognized. Nadine Paradise, of course, and her son Victor. Farrell was interested to see that Stacey Spinner was sitting with them.

Where was Pat? Farrell wondered. She had said that she was going to close up the Consignment Depot and come to the auction with Tim Kavanagh.

Farrell felt a tap on her shoulder, and her spine stiffened.

"We have to stop meeting like this."

It was Jack.

"They really do let just about anyone in here, don't they?" Farrell whispered. Suddenly the auction had become even more stimulating.

✺ Chapter 88

"I'm interested in something that's going to be auctioned at the Russian Space History Sale, and I won't be able to make it to the preview. Can you show it to me?"

"Right now?" asked Meryl.

"I know it's an imposition, but I don't have much time."

Meryl glanced around the auction gallery. Everything was going smoothly. It wouldn't hurt if she slipped away for a few minutes.

Meryl led the way. "I hope you don't mind, but we have to take the freight elevator."

"I don't mind in the least."

Did the costumed doorman look in their direction? Couldn't be sure.

It had to be quick. There was no time for any more bungling.

As the freight elevator doors closed behind them, Meryl drew in a sharp breath as she felt something snap around her neck. She struggled urgently but silently as she tried to rip away whatever it was that was choking her. She fought hard, but the strong hands that twisted the tourniquet around her neck were unrelenting.

When it was over, Meryl's limp body collapsed. Although the deadweight was heavy, the corpse was easily folded and stuffed into the large packing barrel at the side of the freight elevator. Forcefully the barrel was clamped shut, as a Hermès scarf slipped through the narrow opening at the side of the car and wafted down the elevator shaft.

\mathcal{X} Chapter 89

B. J. looked for Meryl before he and Farrell left Churchill's. He had wanted to confirm their date for Saturday night but he couldn't find her. Farrell had been anxious to get back to the Broadcast Center to start putting her auction story together and B. J. had wanted to get back to check the quality of the tape he'd shot.

He thought he'd gotten some good stuff, and his hunch was confirmed as he played the videotapes back for Farrell.

"Nice work," she said. "I notice you got some good shots of your girlfriend as well."

B. J. grinned. "You know what they say—all work and no play. . . ."

"Get out of here, you goofball. I have work to do." Farrell opened up a new computer page to begin composing her story.

"In another of the growing phenomenon known as celebrity auctions, the collection of the renowned ballerina Nadine Paradise went on sale today at Churchill's in New York City, attracting an audience eager to pay to have a piece of a legend's life. . . ."

She typed for the next forty-five minutes, interweaving her writing with sound bites from Nadine Paradise and from three of the enthusiastic auctiongoers she had interviewed today. Farrell glanced at her wristwatch. Five o'clock. She punched the computer keys to send the script down to Range in the Fishbowl.

Fifteen minutes later, the executive producer called.

"Drop the third auctiongoer's soundbite, change the close to read, 'Nadine Paradise, who has spent so much of her life on center stage earning the applause and hearts of her admirers, won their fealty again this afternoon at Churchill's.' Then go ahead and track. Eliza Blake will be ready to record in booth three."

With just over an hour until airtime, Farrell made the script adjustments and hurried downstairs to the editing area. She felt satisfied that Range had changed so little of her script. In the past, she had thought he had taken great relish in ripping her work apart.

❧ Chapter 90

Fourth Sunday of Lent

All day Saturday B. J. had tried to reach Meryl, unsuccessfully. Was she giving him a none-too-subtle message that she did not want to go out with him anymore?

Saturday night, he had left another message on her answering machine at home: "Meryl, it's Beej. Please call me, honey. I'm worried sick about you."

With pages of the Sunday *Daily News* spread out over his bed, B. J. decided to try her at Churchill's. Maybe she had work to catch up on after the auction on Friday. His heart leapt as the phone was picked up on the second ring.

"Clifford Montgomery." The voice sounded anxious.

"Hi, I'm trying to reach Meryl Quan."

"Who's calling, please?"

"B. J. D'Elia. I'm a friend of hers. We had plans for last night and I haven't been able to reach her. I was hoping she would be there at the office."

"I wish she were, Mr. D'Elia. I haven't seen Meryl since Friday afternoon at the auction here. I've been calling her at home myself. It's not at all like her to just disappear like this. Not when we have another important auction we're preparing for. She is really very conscientious."

B. J.'s heart pounded fearfully. "I'm calling the police."

ᔥ Chapter 91

Monday

Farrell walked to work, anxious and tense about B. J.'s frantic call the night before. First Olga; now Meryl. Where was she? She didn't want to admit it to herself, but she was frightened.

Dean was waiting for her when Farrell arrived in their office.

"I was in the Fishbowl Friday night when your piece on the Paradise auction ran. Range loved it."

"That must have made you very happy, Dean," Farrell snapped back sarcastically.

"Whoa. Sorry. I just thought I'd pass on a little good news for a change. I'll be sure not to do that again." Dean turned back to his newspaper.

"Cut the crap, Dean. Let's not pretend that you are rooting for me. You'll be glad to have a new officemate. And now that I'm leaving, may I take this opportunity to tell you what a lowlife, sneaky skunk I think you are."

The color rose in Dean's cheeks and he attempted to mount a sputtering protest, but Farrell pressed on.

"Don't play innocent. I know you've intercepted phone calls and purposefully neglected to give me the messages. I know you sniff around my computer and eavesdrop on my phone conversations. And though I can't prove it yet, I know you are the reason why a videotape crucial to a story that could save my career here is missing from my desk."

"Hey, Farrell, don't blame me if you misplaced something."

" 'Misplaced,' my foot! You took it, and don't worry, I'm going to prove that you did. I wonder what your buddy Range will say when I tell him that his boy wonder is a common thief. So much for journalistic integrity!"

"Be careful, Farrell," Dean warned.

"*You* be careful, Dean."

❧ Chapter 92

"Can you believe it?" the overalled stagehand asked his co-worker. "Now we're auctioning off Commie spacesuits, for Christ's sake. Russian Space History Sale, my ass. I'll be glad when this Russian thing is over. I'm sick and tired of getting here so damned early to set up."

"You and me both," agreed his companion. "You gotta feel sorry for those cosmonauts, though. Having to sell off all their space souvenirs just to get some money to live."

"Ah . . . I don't feel sorry for those guys. They worked against us all those years. Now they're getting what they deserve. Their country is a mess."

The stagehands pushed a large dolly stacked with space-suits, helmets, thick gloves, and parachutes, and stopped to wait for the freight elevator that would carry the merchandise to the gallery above.

"Hey, lookie here, a doggie spacesuit! Those Russians were big on sending animals into orbit."

The stagehand held up the miniature suit for his friend to

see as the elevator doors opened. Instantly both men winced as they inhaled the putrid stench of what they would soon find out was decomposing flesh.

"Oh man, it smells like something died in here."

✣ Chapter 93

Another week gone by, and still no check from Churchill's.

Orchestrating the forgery and the sale of a Fabergé egg was a colossal feat in itself. Now, with the murders of Misha and Meryl, and Olga still to be dealt with, if necessary, that money from the auctioned Moon Egg had been earned many times over. And the work to be done was not finished. Unfortunately, it looked like there were others who were getting in the way and might have to be taken care of as well.

The phone was picked up on the third ring at Churchill's.

"Clifford Montgomery."

"You've taken to answering your own phone?"

"What do you want?"

"My money."

"Listen, while you're sitting safe and sound, I've got the FBI on my back."

"Poor Clifford. If it makes you feel any better, I've been busy, too."

"It doesn't make me feel better. I'm drowning here. Besides, the buyer is having some trouble coming up with the money. And even if I did have it, should I issue a check now, the feds would be all over me."

"Well, you better think of something, bucko. Get the money from that secret buyer of yours or I'll tip off the FBI myself."

Clifford laughed nervously. "You do that, and you'll go down with me."

"You forget, don't you? All I need to say is that I bought the egg at the Twenty-Sixth Street Flea Market and brought it to *you* for authentication. Don't worry, I'll be just as shocked as your buyer that the egg is a fake. There's nothing in the world that can connect me to the forgery."

The auction-house president thought about his career. He was being hung out to dry and he knew it. He wished he had never gotten involved in this. A chance circumstance had led to this nightmare and it was going to take more than mere chance to end it.

"Just get me that money, Clifford. Or you're the one who'll be going to jail. I have the feeling you won't like the accommodations in federal prison. That's where you'll go if I'm forced to make that call."

❧ Chapter 94

"They found Meryl's body." B. J. stood, shell-shocked, in the doorway.

Farrell felt pinned to her chair, dumbfounded.

"Oh, B. J. No. Oh no!"

The cameraman slowly walked to the couch positioned against Farrell's office wall, and sat down heavily. Closing his eyes, he laid his head back against the top of the sofa, and sighed from deep within his chest.

"They found her this morning, in a packing barrel at Churchill's. From the condition of things, they think she was lying there all weekend."

"Oh God, B. J. I'm so sorry."

Farrell sat quietly for a few moments with her friend.

"What are the police saying?"

"The usual. They're investigating, so they aren't saying much. An autopsy will be performed to figure out how she was killed."

Killed. Farrell rubbed the tops of her crossed arms, suddenly cold.

"Do you know anyone who would want to hurt Meryl, Beej?" she asked softly.

But B. J. wasn't listening to Farrell's question. "I just saw her at the auction on Friday. She was so much fun. We were planning to see each other this weekend. If only I had stuck around at Churchill's until I found her, rather than rushing back here to check if my stupid video was good, maybe, just maybe, Meryl would be alive right now."

Farrell rose and sat next to B. J. on the couch, taking his hands in hers.

"Beej, you can't beat yourself up like this. If someone wanted to kill Meryl, he or she would have done it eventually. You couldn't be with her twenty-four hours a day."

"That's for sure," B. J. sneered. "Not the way she lived at that damn auction house, with that boss of hers always giving her *agita*."

"Clifford Montgomery?"

"Yeah. She was worried that Montgomery was into something that she didn't want anything to do with."

Chapter 95

Every month, the elevator maintenance man came to Churchill's to make sure the company's lifts were running well and safely. Liam O'Shea was actually due on the seventeenth of the month, but today he was twenty-four hours early. He wanted to take tomorrow off to go to the St. Patrick's Day parade.

Working in the sub-basement, one by one Liam checked the motors and wiring of the various elevators, getting, at last, to the freight elevator. At the bottom of the shaft lay what he could tell was a very expensive woman's scarf. *Hermès-Paris* was printed prominently in the design.

Liam thought of turning the scarf in to auction house security. They must run a lost-and-found. But temptation lured. Mary had always wanted a scarf like this one. He had even checked out the prices at Christmastime last year, planning to splurge and buy his wife something she would never buy for herself. But with three kids in parochial high school, and with college coming up for all of them, he just couldn't rationalize spending $250 for a scarf.

The women who came to Churchill's probably had drawers

of scarves, Liam reasoned, when his hardworking Mary had never had anything so fine in all her life. Was that fair?

He packed up his toolbox and carefully folded the silken scarf into a small square which he slipped into his jacket pocket. His Mary would get a St. Patty's Day surprise this year. She deserved it.

❧ Chapter 96

The best thing to do was to get rid of the evidence. But how?

Dean dwelled on Farrell's threat. That was the last thing he needed. A bad reputation. He had carefully cultivated his position on Range's good side. Trying to sabotage Farrell's story wasn't worth jeopardizing his standing with the executive producer.

He didn't want to destroy the videotape. At some point it might be to his advantage to be able to get his hands on it. But Dean didn't want to have it in his actual possession anymore.

Then it occurred to him. He knew where to send it. There it would sit, with thousands of companions, undisturbed and undetected.

"If I'd waited for you to ask me to come over for a home-cooked meal, I'd have starved to death. Though I admit, this is some pathetic dinner for St. Patrick's Day. I don't know how to make corned beef and cabbage."

Jack looked at Farrell expectantly, hoping for a flippant answer. But there was none. Farrell twisted the spaghetti around her fork and sipped her wine, unable to stop thinking about the violent death of Meryl Quan.

"Some more merlot?" Jack asked.

Farrell nodded.

"Jack, I've just got this cold, frightened feeling inside. A feeling of impending doom. Someone just walked right into Churchill's and murdered Meryl Quan. Just like I think someone walked right into Olga's apartment and meant to kill her."

"And you think they're connected—how?" Jack prompted.

"Meryl was in the office the day I told Clifford Montgomery my suspicions about the auctioned egg being a forgery. B. J. told me that Meryl said her boss was very upset after my visit." Farrell thought for a moment. "Olga was in possession of the real Fabergé egg that B. J. and I went out to Westwood to shoot just before the fire. Coincidence? I don't think so." Farrell downed the rest of the merlot. "So now we have one murder and one attempted murder."

"Make that two murders."

Farrell looked at him sharply. "How so?"

Jack told Farrell about the vicious murder of Misha in the tiny jewelry workshop in Brighton Beach.

"Did they ever find a body?" asked Farrell.

"Judging from all the blood left behind, if they find anything, it will only be part of a body. Misha Grinkov doesn't exist in one piece anymore."

Farrell stopped to digest what Jack had told her. "Why didn't you tell me all this about Misha before?"

"Before, things seemed fairly removed from you and your safety."

"And now?"

Jack rose from his chair and walked around the table to her. He pulled her to her feet and led her over to his living-room couch. Taking her face in his hands, he kissed her softly, then firmly on the mouth, and he felt her arms circle willingly around his neck.

"And now?" she whispered again.

"It may not be long before things start getting a bit too close to you."

❧ Chapter 98

Every day since Patricia Devereaux had told her the identity of the seller of the crescent brooch, Nadine had had Victor drive her over to Pascack Valley Hospital.

. "Come back in about an hour, dear. I'll be waiting for you in the lobby."

Nadine watched as Victor drove off in the Mercedes. He had shown little interest in having anything to do with the sick woman inside who was his newfound aunt. Nadine was disappointed with her son's indifference.

Nadine walked down the long hallway to Olga's room, smiling at the nurse who staffed the desk outside her room. She sat down and began to talk soothingly in Russian to her older sister.

"Please, Olga. Please, dearest one. You must hold on. I've longed for a sister my whole life. And now—now that we finally have a chance to know one another, we cannot lose that gift. I will take good care of you. You can come live with me. I have a big house with plenty of room. Our papa in heaven will be so happy if he knows that his two girls are together at long last."

Nadine took Olga's delicate hand, so like her own, and held it tightly.

"Please, Olga. Please. You must try."

Nadine felt a weak squeeze.

❧ Chapter 99

Farrell stood before Range Bullock's desk and pleaded her case. The executive producer was unmoved.

"As long as you don't have the real Moon Egg, or at least the videotape of it, I don't see how we can go with the story."

"But Range, B. J. and I both saw it with our own eyes, and you yourself saw the videotape," Farrell pleaded.

Range was shaking his head. He said out loud what Farrell could not bring herself to say. "That's all well and good, but we no longer have any documentable evidence, now, do we?" He paused, and then drove home his point. "With the growing spate of lawsuits against network news divisions recently, you can understand why I am hesitant about sticking our necks out on this story. KEY News does not need a multi-million-dollar defamation suit with Churchill's."

Farrell was not dissuaded. She considered revealing her suspicions about Dean and the missing tape, but thought better of it. Stick to the story. "We're talking about two murders and an attempted murder here."

"Can you prove the murders are related to the Fabergé egg?"

Farrell was silent.

"Look," Range relented slightly. "I'm not saying that this isn't a great story. *If* you can prove it. As it stands now, it's too soft."

"I'm not through with this yet," Farrell resolved as she strode out of the Fishbowl.

Range watched her walk across the studio floor and found himself wishing that Farrell had shown this much tenacity in the months before he had made his decision to let her go.

℘ Chapter 100

Robbie unloaded the latest carton of videotapes that had arrived via the KEY News traffic desk. It contained a dozen tapes shot at the St. Patrick's Day parade.

Stacking the tapes, he carried them over to his video monitor, and one by one inserted them into the machine, taking computer notes on what was recorded on each tape.

Marching bands, ruddy-faced police officers, bagpipes, and

lots and lots of people wearing green. One St. Patty's Day like so many others.

Robbie popped in the seventh tape, fully expecting more of the same. Instead, a very old woman holding a spray of sparkling diamonds appeared on the television monitor.

Chapter 101

Friday of the Fourth Week of Lent

Russian Peasant Folk Belief

"Whoever fasts on this Friday
will be saved from unjust murder."

"Please, Olga. Just try to take a little of this broth. It's important so that we can get you off the intravenous feedings," the night nurse urged.

"My throat is sore. I cannot swallow."

"That's from the oxygen," said the nurse. "But now that you're off it, your throat will get better in a few days."

"That is when I eat, then."

The nurse smiled to herself. Tough old cookie. For weeks,

no one had thought she was going to make it and now, just over twenty-four hours after coming out of her coma, Olga's stubborn streak was shining through. How strong the human spirit is!

"All right, dear. We'll try again tomorrow. Good night." The nurse smoothed the blanket on the hospital bed and left to tend to her next patient.

Olga lay with her eyes closed, drifting in and out of sleep. The intermittent call of the hospital paging system penetrated her fragmented dreams. *"Ma ijtso. Ma ijtso."*

A visitor leaned close over Olga's sleeping body. "Yes, old soul, 'your egg.' Your egg is the reason you must die."

The visitor's back blocked the view from the doorway. The night nurse, coming back into the room with a fresh pitcher of water, could not see the pillow poised in the visitor's hands. "Isn't it wonderful to see her doing so well?" she chirped to the old woman's frequent guest.

Fluffing the pillow, the visitor turned to smile. "I just want her to be as comfortable as possible.

She's been through so much."

Charlie was closing up for the night, locking the front door of the deli. Out of habit he looked in the direction of the Consignment Depot. What he made out in the dusk's light made his heart sink.

Pat was walking down the path in front of her shop, accompanied by that guy she had been seeing routinely for several weeks now. Charlie watched as the man opened the car door for her and Pat got inside. Where were they going? What would they do in their next hours together?

You're a fool to let this get to you, he told himself. *You don't know if she really cares about the guy. She isn't being disloyal to you. She doesn't even know how you pine for her. You've never let her know how much you care about her.*

Why haven't you told her? Because you're afraid, you coward. Afraid that someone like her could never go for someone like you.

Charlie walked to the alley behind the deli and deposited a large, black trash bag into a heavy metal garbage can. He continued to beat himself up. *So now you're going home to spend another Saturday night with the remote control and a six-pack of Budweiser. You've got to do something, man! Make a* stand. *Just see if there is any way that Pat could possibly care for you—could stop thinking of you like a brother and more like a. . . .*

Maybe if she knew that you had wealth. You've never let her know that you could take care of her, give her a wonderful life, let her quit her job if she wanted. She only thinks of you as Choo-Choo Charlie, the guy with the bald spot covered with a baseball cap, slicing salami and liverwurst at the deli.

No wonder she wasn't impressed.

❧ Chapter 103

Fifth Sunday of Lent

There was still time to get Olga. But doing it at the hospital was out.

Misha, Meryl, and, eventually, Olga. And now, unfortunately, another.

Tony, the Churchill's doorman. He could point a finger. He recognized anyone who came into Churchill's with any regularity. He could name names.

It was uncertain that Tony had noticed anything unusual, dressed in his cossack costume, adding color to the event as he stood guard during the Paradise auction. He might not have been watching as Meryl strode across the gallery to exit down to the storerooms. But he could have been. His eyes seemed to be looking in their direction.

No, it wasn't a certainty, but it was a possibility. A strong possibility that could not be ignored.

ℑ Chapter 104

"It's been almost a week, Jack, since they found Meryl's body. What the hell are the police doing?"

"Hey, Farrell, any chance we could just enjoy the first springlike day this year?" Jack popped the other half of his third Krispy Kreme into his mouth.

Farrell and Jack sat on a bench in Strawberry Fields, the Central Park memorial to John Lennon, at West 72nd Street. Across Central Park West, the Gothic Dakota, home to the wealthy, famous, and accomplished, loomed above the trees.

Jack was right. It was a beautiful day, the first tantalizing taste of the spring to come. It had been a rough winter and Farrell was relieved that it was over. But Meryl Quan would not be here to savor the budding trees, the chirping birds, the warm breeze.

Of course, Meryl hadn't expected not to be here, Farrell reflected. She had lived through the previous spring not knowing that it would be her last. Meryl had had every right to think she would have scores of springs to come: riding in convertibles with the tops down; falling in love and watching tulips and daffodils bloom; even getting married and having babies of her own. Meryl had been cheated of all that.

Farrell took Jack's arm and lay her head on his broad shoulder. "God, life is so uncertain," she whispered.

❧ Chapter 105

Tuesday

The treadmills hummed at the coed health spa. Victor and Stacey exercised side by side, Victor running hard, Stacey bouncing at a brisk walk.

"So now Mother wants the old crone to come live with us," Victor puffed.

"Would that be the end of the world?"

"Just what I need, two old ladies to take care of. As it is, there's something creepy about a guy my age living with his mother. Now I'll be there with two old girls, and you know damn well they're only going downhill from here on in. That means good ol' Victor is going to have to play nursemaid."

Stacey rearranged the terry-cloth sweatband that circled her forehead. "If you're so sure of that, why don't you move out now, while you've got the chance? You're certainly entitled to have a life of your own."

Victor finished running his four miles and waited for Stacey to come to the end of her two-mile power walk. They made their way to the Nautilus machines. Victor lowered himself into the leg press and Stacey stood over him as he adjusted the weights.

"You know, Victor, sooner or later, you are going to be a very wealthy man."

Victor grunted. "But when are you and I finally going to have some real fun?"

Stacey looked around. Everyone seemed to be minding their own business. "Don't get so discouraged all the time," she said. "You've got to be patient. You don't hear me complaining."

"My mother doesn't have as much money as you think." He hadn't meant to blurt that out.

Stacey took a swig from her water bottle, trying to appear nonchalant.

"What do you mean?"

"Why do you think she sold all that stuff at auction?"

Considering his words, Stacey responded with a lie. "Stop worrying, sweetheart. We'll be okay. I'm on your side, Victor. You know that money has nothing to do with the way I feel about you."

Even Victor was not dumb enough to believe that.

Chapter 106

Farrell walked across the street from the Broadcast Center to the KEY News garage to track down B. J. She wanted to tell him the news in person. Something like this shouldn't be heard over the phone.

B. J. was lying with his feet up on the couch in the crew room, the spot where the union camera guys hung out when they were waiting to be assigned to a story. Empty paper coffee cups and day-old newspapers lay strewn on tables. A soap opera blared from the television bolted to the wall, but B. J. was not watching. He was staring up at the ceiling.

"Hi."

B. J. sat up quickly, surprised to see Farrell.

"Hey, what brings you over to this side of the world?"

Farrell took a place next to B. J. "The autopsy is back."

"And?"

"It shows that Meryl was strangled."

B. J. was quiet for a moment.

"And?"

"From the condition of her body, they figure that she had been dead two to three days before they discovered her."

"How do you know?" he asked.

"Jack McCord told me."

B. J. bowed his head and Farrell knew he didn't want her to see the tears that had come readily to his eyes.

She barely heard him whisper, "If only I'd been there for her."

❧ Chapter 107

"What should I do with this tape, boss?" Robbie asked. "It came in with the St. Patrick's Day tapes but clearly doesn't belong with them."

"What's on it?"

"Shots of an old lady and some kind of jeweled egg."

"Any markings on the tape box?"

"No assignment number or story slug. No cameraman's name, either."

"When are those guys out in the field going to realize how important it is to mark their tapes?" the exasperated supervisor asked. "Just leave it up at the front desk, Rob. Sooner or later someone will probably come looking for it."

Chapter 108

"What are you doing going through my desk?" Dean Cohen demanded.

Unruffled, Farrell looked up from the desk drawer she was rifling through.

"Turnabout is fair play, Dean, my man. Two can play your sneaky little game."

"What the hell are you talking about, Farrell?"

"Where is my videotape?" she demanded.

"I have no idea."

"The hell you don't."

Farrell yanked open the next drawer, continuing her search.

"Stop rummaging through my drawers or I'm going to call security."

"Call away. And I'll tell the guards and anyone else who happens to be walking by and sees all the hubbub, that you, Dean Cohen, are a liar, a sneak, and a thief!"

"You better watch out, Farrell."

"Of course, they may not be sure they can believe me," she said, pulling open another drawer. "But the seeds of doubt will be planted in their minds. It will be my happy legacy to you, dear Dean, that even after I'm gone from the hallowed halls of KEY News, people will look at you and wonder if you really are the dishonest slimeball I said you were. You know how happy news travels around here."

"You're not going to find your tape in my desk, Farrell," Dean said quietly.

"Well, it sure as hell better turn up soon."

✣ Chapter 109

Friday of the Fifth Week of Lent

Inside the cavernous expanse of the United Nations building on New York City's East Side, Professor Tim Kavanagh leaned over the railing with the students he was escorting from Seton Hall University's School of Diplomacy and International Relations, and watched the giant metal globe sway back and forth on its wire pendulum.

The artist who had designed the moving display had managed to convey a united world.

"Come on, gang. The lecture starts in ten minutes."

Kavanagh led the group of hopeful future diplomats to the auditorium where they were to hear a talk on the history of the UN, and the new trends in diplomacy caused by the re-alignment of global power structures. Once the students had taken their seats and the UN lecturer had begun, Professor Kavanagh slipped out of the room. He had a good hour and a half to kill before he had to come back.

❧ Chapter 110

As Churchill's closed for the day, the killer hid in a locked stall in the downstairs restroom, feet up on the toilet seat. The door to the bathroom opened as a security guard made a cursory check of the room to make sure that it was empty for the night. The killer didn't even breathe.

Hearing the door click shut, five silent minutes went by. Leaving the stall, a quick look in the mirror over the bathroom sink. So that's what a murderer looks like just before the deed is done. Wide-eyed but calm.

Stealthily, up the back stairs to the locker room, opening the door slowly and without a sound. If anyone other than Tony was there, the excuse would be simple: just lost in the maze of Churchill's building.

But no one else was there. Just Tony.

Tony was standing, back to the locker-room door. His furry headpiece sat on the bench next to his locker and he whistled absentmindedly as he pulled off the blue cossack coat. Poor stiff. Whistling one moment, dead the next.

❧ Chapter 111

B. J., you've got to snap out of it, man. You're obsessing over this. Maybe you should get some professional help.

Sitting alone in a darkened editing booth, B. J. played the tape again. At the time he shot it, he had thought it would be fun to play back for Meryl later. But there was no later.

He had made sure to get every shot Farrell could possibly want for her piece on the Paradise auction. Every costume, poster, and set design. He had shot pictures of the audience for Farrell to use later for cutaways. He had taken long shots of the auction gallery for the tape editor to choose as possible openings shots.

But at every other opportunity, when he had felt certain he was not missing something Farrell would need, B. J. had trained his camera on his girlfriend. Meryl, his lovely Meryl.

He watched the video as the beautiful woman with the dark, straight hair stood vigilant as the auction progressed. It was Meryl's job to be watchful, to do her part to make sure that everything ran smoothly.

"Beej, don't torture yourself, honey."

Farrell stood in the doorway of the editing room.

"Come on, let me take you out for dinner. It's been a long week."

"God, Farrell, I can't believe she's gone."

"I know."

Farrell put her hand on B. J.'s shoulder and together they watched the tape.

Suddenly Farrell snapped, "Roll that tape back!"

Automatically B. J. pushed the rewind and then the play buttons, and the producer and cameraman studied the television monitor.

"Look who's following Meryl out of the auction gallery!"

❧ Chapter 112

"Federal Bureau of Investigation."

"Jack McCord, please. It's urgent."

Farrell waited what seemed like an eternity listening to the silence, praying to hear Jack's voice.

The operator came back on the line. "Mr. McCord is not

in the office. But I can reach him. May I take a message for him?"

Farrell's heart sank.

"Yes. Tell him Farrell Slater called. Tell him to get back to me right away. It's very important. He has my numbers. It probably would be best if he beeped me.

✣ Chapter 113

Tony felt something snap around his neck. Instinctively he reached for his throat, trying to pry the band that strangled him. He was choking. He heard the sounds coming from his mouth. Convulsively gasping, gulping for air. *So, this is what dying sounds like.*

It all happened so quickly. Sensing that this action would be his last, Tony dropped his hands from around his throat, reaching down behind his back. He grabbed hold of the killer's crotch and squeezed hard with all that was left of his strength.

The attacker shrieked and Tony felt the band around his neck loosen. As Tony collapsed on the locker-room floor, the killer doubled over, yelping like a wounded animal.

Chapter 114

An hour after her call to the FBI, Farrell's beeper went off and she dialed the displayed callback number.

"McCord."

"It's me."

"What's up?"

She told him about the videotape. He was quiet for a minute but he didn't sound surprised when he responded.

"That makes sense."

"What do you mean?"

"The police were just called to Churchill's. Victor Paradise left the auction house in a body bag."

Chapter 115

Jack flashed his Federal Bureau of Investigation credentials and he and Farrell were able to go right up to to Tony's room at New York Hospital. The doorman lay in his hospital bed, pale, with his eyes closed. The man's thick neck was black, blue, and angry red. Tony opened his eyes when Jack cleared his throat. They introduced themselves.

"How are you feeling?"

"Sore, and I've got a helluva headache."

"Can you tell us what happened?" Jack asked quietly.

"The guy came at me from behind," Tony croaked. "It was terrible, but I managed to grab him in the nuts." He looked at Farrell. "Sorry, ma'am."

"Don't worry about it. I've heard worse," Farrell reassured him.

"Anyway, we both fell to the floor. I managed to reach for the gun I keep in my locker and I shot him. That's all she wrote. I wasn't going to give him a chance to come at me again. Once was enough." Tony winced as he swallowed.

"Do you have any idea why Victor Paradise would try to kill you?" Farrell asked.

"No, ma'am. I've seen the guy lots of times when he'd bring his mother into the house. He always seemed like a nice enough guy."

Tony winced, the sound of his own voice seemed to be making his pain worse. Farrell and Jack leaned a little closer so Tony didn't have to strain.

"Nice," Tony continued, "but not too smart. You know, the wheel was spinning, but the hamster was dead." Tony put his index finger up to his temple and turned it around and around in the air. "We usually ended up talking about working out."

"One more question and we'll let you get some rest, Tony. Did you notice Victor Paradise talking to Meryl Quan the day of the Paradise auction?" Jack asked.

Tony tried to recall. "Can't say as I did."

✠ Chapter 116

Clifford Montgomery opened the door to his office to let his visitor in.

"Working weekends again, Clifford?"

"What in hell are you doing here?" he hissed angrily,

shepherding the visitor inside and closing the door quickly behind them.

"Relax, Clifford. Relax. My being here is not going to be a problem for you. Not unless you fail to do as I say."

Clifford glared sullenly. "Relax, my ass. How can I relax with two people killed here in as many weeks? I'd think you'd be a little more upset than you are."

"Meryl Quan had to go—she knew too much and was ready to tell. I'd think you'd be gratified that I had her taken care of."

"And Victor Paradise?"

"Victor was a stooge. Useful for pruning and clearing away the deadwood—but actually it's cleaner this way. With him gone, there's one less person to trip us up. Victor was no brain surgeon, and sooner or later he might have given something away. He served his purpose, getting rid of Meryl, and I'm sure that the police will be satisfied that her murderer is lying on a slab down at the morgue."

Clifford was stupefied by his visitor's cold audacity.

"Now, the doorman needn't be killed, even if he did see poor Victor walking out with Meryl to the freight elevator."

"You are one cold customer," Clifford observed.

"Yes. And I want my cold, hard cash. Cut me my check now."

"It doesn't work like that."

"Come again?"

"I can't just write you a check for six million dollars. It has to be done through the accounting department. The last time I inquired, they hadn't gotten the money from the buyer yet."

"Who is the damn buyer, anyway?"

"I'm not telling you. I'm more afraid of the buyer than I am of you."

The visitor tried not to lose control. *Keep calm, don't lose your temper.*

"Clifford, you don't seem to understand. Let me explain it to you again. If you don't give me that money, I am going to let the feds know everything. Anonymously, of course. And you and your precious Churchill's will be ruined."

"But you won't have your six million dollars, either." Clifford smiled at the thought.

The visitor decided it was time to take a conciliatory tack. "Look. Let's work together here. We've always been able to work things out in the past. We can figure this out. I don't know who bought the egg, and frankly, I don't care. As I see it, the only real problem we have here is if the real Moon Egg turns up."

"If you knew who bought your fake egg at auction, you damn well would care."

Chapter 117

Farrell spread a flowered cloth over the round table and set it for two. A fresh peach-scented candle perched in a brass candlestick, and a bunch of white tulips stood at attention in a glass vase that she placed in the middle of the table. That was about as Martha Stewart as she got. Take it or leave it.

She surveyed the apartment and realized that it looked inviting now. With Pat's help, the touches they had added created a whole new feel for the room. Salmon and seafoam-green colors lay beneath the coffee table. Her books were now off the floor and arranged with care in the bookcase. Two large brass sconces hung on the wall on either side of the bookcase, apricot candles flickering welcomingly from them. A tiny oil painting of an old man reading a newspaper, a monkey sitting on his shoulder, rested on a wire easel on a mahogany butler's table, another Consignment Depot find. Farrell hadn't spent a lot of money, but the results of the few careful purchases made a big difference.

When Jack arrived, he kissed her and smelled the Pleasures perfume she had sprayed on the front of her neck and behind her ears. As she led him into the living room, he eyed the table in the small dining room beyond, appreciating the effort.

"Drink?"

"You have any scotch?"

"Dewar's on the rocks, coming right up."

Farrell poured the tawny liquid over a glass of ice and added a lemon twist.

"Ah, this hits the spot. Thanks." Jack eased himself into the couch beneath the window. He stretched out his long legs and let out a deep sigh of relief.

"So what do you think, Jack? Did Victor set the fire at Olga's?"

"Don't know. We'll have to get a picture of him and show it to the old lady."

"When will that be done?" Farrell pressed, as she stood over him.

"Hey, you," he smiled, putting down his drink and pulling her down into his lap. "Let's just enjoy each other's company tonight, shall we? I think we deserve a little rest and relaxation."

"Not to mention a little fun, I see." Farrell kissed him hungrily, then pulled away. "But let's not get too distracted. I have a dinner all planned and you've got to realize that, for me, this is a major undertaking. I mustn't be distracted."

Jack laughed. "Okay. I can wait for dessert until later. What are we having?"

"Lamb. Lamb and asparagus and roasted potatoes."

"Farrell, I had no idea I was in the presence of such a culinary master."

"Don't make fun of me. I'm really trying here."

"I know you are," Jack relented. He stood up and walked toward the kitchen. "How can I help?"

"I thought we'd start with some of Olga's eggplant caviar. It's in the fridge."

As Jack went to the refrigerator to take out the mason jar filled with the old woman's homemade concoction, Farrell flinched with recognition, feeling the skin tingle on the back of her neck.

Eggplant—plant the egg!

✣ Chapter 118

Range Bullock caught the late local television news Sunday evening before turning in for the night. The lead story gripped him.

"Double murder at Churchill's," trumpeted the New York anchor, who went on to recount that a female employee, and now, a patron, had both been killed at the exclusive auction house in the past two weeks.

It was time to do the story for national broadcast. As Range switched off the light, he resolved to talk to Farrell about it first thing in the morning. He hoped he hadn't made a mistake in not encouraging her to do the Fabergé egg story sooner.

She could tell she was waking him up.

"Hello," Peter croaked groggily.

"Peter, it's Farrell. I'm sorry to have wakened you. I thought ten A.M. would be a safe time. I forgot what it is to be a college student."

"No, no. That's okay, Farrell. I have to get up anyway. I have one more midterm before spring break and I need to get a little more study time in. I was up late last night cracking the books. What's up, anyway?"

"Just a quick question."

"Shoot."

"Did you get at that jar of Olga's eggplant caviar yet?"

"Are you kidding? I polished that off a long time ago."

"Nothing out of the ordinary about it?"

"No, it was as good as ever. I love that stuff. Isn't it great news about Olga? She's getting out of the hospital this week!"

"Yeah, Peter. Your mom told me. That is great news. Before you know it, she'll be making caviar for you again."

"Can't wait."

"Peter, one more thing. Do you have Professor Kavanagh's home number?"

"Nope. But I think he lives in Maplewood. Maybe the operator has it."

"Thanks, Peter. I'll see you Sunday. Your mother invited me for Easter dinner."

❧ Chapter 120

Farrell took the elevator down to the *Evening Headlines* studio, answering Range's call summoning her to the Fishbowl. She felt nostalgic. This was her last week at KEY News.

The poignant feeling that swept over her, changed to disgust when she saw that old suck-up Dean stationed on the couch across from Range's desk. She couldn't even bring herself to acknowledge him.

Range got right to the point. "Farrell, I think, with the Churchill's murders, there is enough to make a piece now, Moon Egg or no Moon Egg. I see it as 'What's Happening at Churchill's?' You'll have to be careful, have the facts to back up whatever you allege. Do you think you can get it together by Friday? I'd like to pencil you in for the 'KEYhole on America' slot. Two and a half minutes."

Farrell listened to Range's directions. How ironic! Her last story for KEY News would be a 'KEYhole' piece, the coveted slot on the broadcast. It would air on Good Friday. The anniversary of the crucifixion. Perhaps it was a sign she would rise again, another life after KEY News.

She mentally smacked herself. *Cut it out. Don't read anything ridiculous into the timing of this.*

"I can get it together by then," she answered determinedly.

❧ Chapter 121

Farrell remembered she probably wouldn't have to deal with directory assistance to get the number in Maplewood, New Jersey. She called Westwood instead.

"Hello?"

"Pat, it's Farrell."

"Now, I told you already, you don't have to bring anything on Sunday."

"No, it's not about Easter. I should have remembered, I need Tim Kavanagh's number at home. I've been trying to reach him at Seton Hall, but it's Holy Week, and spring break begins on Wednesday."

"What's up, Farrell?"

"Oh, it's just a hunch, Pat, and I'm going to feel pretty silly when it doesn't pan out. I promise to tell you all about it when I see you on Sunday."

After scribbling it down, Farrell dialed the number that would give her the last chance to prove her theory. She listened, frustrated, to the beep of Tim Kavanagh's answering machine. Where was the professor?

Jack had looked at her skeptically when she told him her suspicion about the eggplant caviar as a hiding place. "That's what I'd call a long shot, Farrell," he said dismissively, "especially because the play on words only works in English."

Farrell had explained that she didn't think Olga had chosen the eggplant because of its semantic properties. In any event, Farrell didn't think it was that improbable.

"Tim, this is Farrell Slater. . . ." She began to leave her message. "I know this may sound crazy, but would you please check that jar of eggplant caviar Pat gave you the day we went to Olga's apartment? Let me know if you find anything out of the ordinary inside. Call me back anytime. Thanks a lot." Farrell ended by giving him her office and home phone numbers.

It was worth a shot.

Chapter 122

He made no move to pick up the phone, even as he listened intently to Farrell Slater leave her message.

He had no intention of keeping it. He had just wanted the pleasure of admiring it for a while. Imagine him, Timothy Kavanagh, having the last Russian Imperial Easter Egg! If only for a little while, he wanted to relish having the work of art with him.

Of course, he had told no one what he had found when he'd opened the mason jar. At first he had been incredulous; after all, he had watched the sale of the egg with his own eyes. Then, as he had carefully studied the glittering beauty of the milky-white egg, the treasure became real to him. There were no accidents in life. He was *meant* to have his time with the Moon Egg.

Now, a stack of essays on Russian history to correct sitting menacingly before him, Farrell Slater's message signaled that time was up. He would not call her back right away.

It would be better for it not to look as though Farrell was forcing him to give up the egg, that her call was the reason for coming forward. It had to appear that he was voluntarily giving it up to the proper authorities as he had planned to do all along.

In his darkened den, the drapes drawn closed to guard his secret, Tim had positioned a halogen lamp to warm the Moon Egg in its own special light. He looked at it now, as he had done every night since he had made the discovery, watching the diamonds and sapphires dance and sparkle. He stared at the Moon Egg, his guest for the last eleven days. His delightful, welcome houseguest. How sorry he would be to see it go!

He picked up the telephone. If he hoped to have any real future with Pat, he had to tell her what he'd found.

Chapter 123

Tuesday of Holy Week

The two old women sat together in the lounge on Olga's floor at Pascack Valley Hospital. Olga was able to walk now, and the trip down the hall to the reception room was good exercise for her.

Nadine Paradise, dressed in a beautifully-cut lavender wool suit, talked somberly to her sister.

"Now that I've lost my son, you are all I have left, Olga.

I'm so grateful to God that I've found you. And so glad that you will be coming home in a few days to live with me."

"Do you have a picture of Victor?" Olga asked from her blue Naugahyde chair. "I never had a child of my own. I would like to see my nephew."

Nadine opened her smooth leather purse and carefully took a photograph from the zippered compartment inside. She looked at it sadly as she handed it to Olga.

Olga stared silently. She could not bring herself to tell her sister that the face in the photo was familiar to her. It was the face of the man who had taken care of her when she had fainted in the pharmacy. The man who had come to her apartment the day of the fire.

❧ Chapter 124

"Spy" Wednesday

It was a small group that gathered for the graveside service of Victor Paradise.

His mother stood erect, dry-eyed. Her face did not reveal the torture she felt within. How could she have raised a child capable of murder?

Nadine felt someone gently take her arm. It was Stacey. Her eyes were red-rimmed.

You thought I didn't know, but I did, reflected Nadine. *I know you wanted to be Victor's wife.* She looked up at the taller woman and smiled weakly but gratefully. She was grateful, too, for the few others who showed up. It was very kind of them. Patricia Devereaux and Farrell Slater and a man she did not recognize. He must have been a friend of Victor's. Beautiful, blue, penetrating eyes.

❧ Chapter 125

Farrell and Jack drove back into Manhattan together after the funeral. Farrell was anxious to get back to the office. With just two days until air, she had to work on her script for the Churchill's "KEYhole" piece. She was grateful, with Passover beginning at sundown, that Dean had already explained he would be heading home early.

As they crossed the George Washington Bridge, Farrell gazed over the Hudson River, drinking in the majesty of the New York City skyline. She felt sorry for Nadine Paradise. What a cruel fate, loving and raising a child who turned out to be a cold-blooded murderer. There was no consolation for that.

Farrell was glad, though, that Nadine could have Olga

now, for however long they both had. At least in the immediate future, neither woman would be alone. Farrell made a vow to herself to make sure to keep in touch with the old ladies. Perhaps, later on, she and Pat could be there to help the remaining sister when the other one passed on.

"Penny for your thoughts," Jack fished.

"Oh, I was just thinking about Nadine and Olga. Just when they have a chance to finally know each other, Nadine has to go through the heartache of losing her only child. Life. . . ." Her voice trailed off.

As the car made the turn south onto the Henry Hudson Parkway, Farrell cracked open her window to let in the spring breeze. How cool and wonderful it felt on her face. Spring. A new beginning.

Jack took her hand and held it firmly on the seat between them. Farrell appreciated the gesture, but she could not really enjoy it. Her mind had shifted into another gear as it faced what had to be done. How was she going to construct the "KEYhole" piece without the Moon Egg as concrete evidence?

She had to call Tim Kavanagh again.

❧ Chapter 126

The KEY News producer's arguments made sense, thought Clifford Montgomery, as he hung up the phone. As much as he detested the idea of it, and after worrying about little else all week, he knew it was right to agree to have Farrell Slater come over to interview him about all that had been going on at Churchill's.

"Okay, come over and I'll talk with you. But no camera. I'll give you my statement."

Not talking would look like he had something to hide. He knew that members of Churchill's board of directors, along with millions of other Americans, would be watching Farrell's story. It would look bad to them if the president of the auction house had nothing to say.

So he had agreed to an interview.

"Farrell Slater from KEY News is going to be here within the hour. Her piece is almost finished and she insists it is to my advantage to comment," Clifford told the visitor who sat relaxed in the leather chair on the other side of the president's desk.

"What does it matter, now that we have the real Moon Egg?"

⚜ Chapter 127

On the way out the door, Farrell decided to give Tim Kavanagh one more call. After getting his answering machine so many times, she was surprised to hear the professor himself answer.

"Oh, hi, Farrell. I'm so sorry I haven't gotten back to you," Tim apologized, "but these last days before spring break are so hectic. I just haven't had a chance to call you back."

I've left you at least half a dozen messages, Farrell thought. *Wouldn't it just be common courtesy to take a few minutes from your busy schedule and call me back?* She tried not to sound exasperated as she explained why she was calling.

There was silence on the telephone line, and for a moment Farrell thought it might have gone dead. But then Tim spoke.

"Look, Farrell, I'm going to level with you. I did find the Moon Egg in Olga's caviar."

Eureka! With just twenty-four hours until her "KEYhole" piece, the Moon Egg had turned up! The proof she needed to tell the story of the scandal of the six-million-dollar forgery! She and B. J. could ride out to New Jersey right away and shoot some video of it. She was saved!

"I'm coming right out there," she told Tim excitedly. She would reschedule her interview with Clifford Montgomery for later in the afternoon, after she had her proof in her hot little hands.

"Farrell, I don't have the egg anymore."

"What?" she gasped in disbelief.

"I don't have it anymore."

"Where is it?" she demanded.

"I turned it in."

"Turned it in to *whom*?"

"Clifford Montgomery at Churchill's. Pat and I decided that it was the best thing to do."

Pat? Why hadn't Pat told her? Farrell immediately wondered. But of course Pat didn't know Farrell was working on the Moon Egg story. Farrell cursed that damned promise she'd made to Peter.

She ended her conversation with Tim and immediately called the FBI. Jack was not in the office.

Again!

"Could you please tell him Farrell called? Tell him I've found what we've been looking for, and I'm on my way over to Churchill's."

Chapter 128

Security called Montgomery's office to announce that Farrell Slater from KEY News was in the lobby.

"Send her up."

"Whatever that nosey Farrell Slater comes up with, you can handle her," the visitor assured Clifford. "You don't know anything about the murders here at Churchill's, other than what the police have told you."

"And if she brings up her suspicions about the egg again?"

"Just deny, deny, deny. She has no proof, remember?"

The visitor slipped into Clifford's dressing room and pulled the door most of the way closed.

Clifford opened his office door as Farrell entered the assistant's area outside—Meryl's old spot.

"Come in, Ms. Slater. Come in."

❧ Chapter 129

B. J. sat in a crew car parked on Madison Avenue. There was no need for the car's "NYP" tags, the license plates of the New York press corps that offered a greater selection of places to park than was available to the average citizen. With its being both Holy Thursday *and* Passover, alternate-side-of-the-street parking regulations were definitely suspended in all five boroughs of the city.

He stared at Churchill's across the street and he felt his chest tighten. Meryl.

When Farrell had asked him to come with her, B. J. had agreed, only because it was Farrell. He really didn't want to be here, didn't want to go inside where Meryl had spent so much time—the place he had last seen her.

But Farrell needed him to be close by in case Montgomery changed his mind and would talk before the KEY News camera. If she could convince the auction-house president, Farrell would call B. J. on his car phone. He could be upstairs in minutes, ready to set up and shoot.

He wanted Farrell to get what she needed for her story, but he would not be disappointed if she did not call him from the president's office. He would just as soon never go into Churchill's again.

✣ Chapter 130

"Mr. Montgomery, I know you are a very busy man, so I won't waste your time beating around the bush," Farrell began. "The part of the story I'm most interested in here, is the auctioning of the fake egg."

"I thought you wanted to talk about the deaths of Meryl Quan and Victor Paradise."

"Well, we can talk about them first, if you like. What do you know about them?"

"Only what the police tell me."

"Okay, now we've covered that," said Farrell, eager to move on. "I know what the police tell me about the murders, too. But the police don't tell me what I need to know about this remarkable case of Fabergé forgery. The KEY News audience would only have a passing interest in the murders of two people they really don't know. They'd be fascinated, however, by the sale of a six-million-dollar forgery, perpetrated at one of the most famous auction houses in the world. What, Mr. Montgomery, do you know about the Moon Egg?"

"Ms. Slater, we've been through all this before," Montgomery sighed, with exasperation.

"Yes, but that was before I knew that the real Fabergé Moon Egg had been handed over to you."

Clifford stared at his accuser as the door of the dressing room opened silently behind Farrell.

❧ Chapter 131

Should I go up? B. J. wondered. He sat with the car running, debating whether he should wait for her call.

She'd been inside for almost twenty minutes now. Knowing Farrell, that would certainly be enough time for her to wear Montgomery down, get him to agree to be interviewed on camera. If B. J. went up now, maybe he could help clinch the deal. *Please, Mr. Montgomery. You really should take this opportunity to speak for Churchill's, Mr. Montgomery. We can do this very quickly, sir.*

But he didn't want to go inside.

B. J. checked his watch. He'd give Farrell a few more minutes.

Chapter 132

Farrell felt something cold and hard press against the back of her head. She could feel her pulse pounding in her neck.

Clifford looked, horrified, at the two women before him. "Are you insane, Stacey?" he hissed through his clenched teeth.

"I haven't come this far to have anyone ruin it for me," Stacey snarled.

Clifford rose from his chair behind his desk and walked toward them. "It's too late, Stacey. KEY News is ready to go with the story."

"They only have the murders. Only Miss Big-Shot Producer here is trying to connect it to the Moon Egg forgery."

"You can't get away with another murder," Clifford declared desperately.

Stacey smiled maliciously. "What do you mean, 'another murder'? I haven't murdered *anybody*.

So far. Victor Paradise killed Meryl Quan. And the jeweler, too. It was Victor who tried to kill the old lady, setting her pathetic little apartment on fire. If only he had done a cleaner job. Now, when his mother dies, she'll leave her estate to

Olga. And any chance I had of coming into Nadine's fortune, such as it was, is over. Thank God I had my alternate plan. My exquisite, brilliant plan. Who would have had the courage to pull off a hoax of this magnitude? I must say I'm proud of myself."

"Stop it, Stacey, stop it. Don't say another word," Clifford demanded. "It's over."

"Don't tell me what to do, Clifford. I'm not your eager student anymore. *I'm* calling the shots now."

Stacey poked the gun harder into Farrell's skull. "You, miss, are not going to ruin it for me."

❧ Chapter 133

B. J. watched a blue Crown Victoria pull up. Fed car. Law enforcement types like those big boats. Guess they think that size is intimidating.

Jack McCord got out of the dark blue boat.

"Hey, Jack!" B. J. called from his opened window.

The FBI agent strode over to the car, his raincoat blowing open behind him.

"Where's Farrell?" he demanded.

"Upstairs with Clifford Montgomery." B. J. motioned up-ward with his thumb.

"How long have they been up there?"

"Just short of half an hour," B. J. answered, checking his watch.

"Come on!" Jack shouted, as he sprinted to Churchill's heavy front doors.

B. J. grabbed his camera and followed.

✂ Chapter 134

Farrell tried to keep herself from shaking in terror. *Keep calm*, she told herself. *Keep calm. Look for your opportunity.*

"Stacey, now I can make it right," Clifford pleaded sooth-ingly. "I can make a swap. The real egg for the fake egg. Nobody will be the wiser."

"And just how do you think you will be able to do that?" Stacey demanded angrily.

"Stacey, you forget. The egg hasn't been paid for yet. If you don't pay, you don't get. The buyer doesn't have the egg yet. It's still here. Look, I'll show you."

Clifford went over to the wall and slid back an oil painting, exposing a safe. Quickly he spun the combination and the metal door opened, revealing the two breathtakingly beautiful Moon Eggs. They were identical.

Farrell sensed that Stacy Spinner was momentarily distracted as she viewed the treasures side-by-side. Now was the time! Now!

Farrell twisted around and grabbed the gun Stacey had at her head. She caught hold of Stacey's wrist, preventing the desperate woman from aiming. Using her head as a ramming post, Farrell butted into Stacey's chest, pushing her backward. Stacey fell back against the wall, but managed to get off a shot.

Chapter 135

Jack and B. J. heard a booming shot as they rounded the corner of the hallway outside Clifford Montgomery's office. Jack pulled his gun and motioned for B. J. to stay back. He positioned himself in front of the president's door, raised his right leg, and kicked with all his might. The wooden panel exploded away from the jamb, and Jack entered as another shot rang out.

"Jack! Watch out!" screamed Farrell.

✒ Chapter 136

B. J. shot all he could of it. Jack tackling the off-guard Stacey, wrestling her to the floor and expertly handcuffing her hands behind her back. Farrell writhing in pain, gripping her left shoulder. Blood covering the floor. Clifford Montgomery lying motionless in front of his desk. The Moon Eggs sitting side by side majestically on their blue-stone thrones in the opened wall safe.

Farrell suspected how close Stacey's bullet had come to her heart, and she was grateful. *Thank you, dear God, thank you,* she prayed. Her gratitude, though, could not eclipse the sheer joy of knowing that she had the pictures necessary to tell the most exciting story of her career.

❧ Chapter 137

Russian Peasant Folk Belief

*"Whoever fasts on this Friday
will be saved from robbers."*

Farrell mustered all her mental and diminished physical strength as she one-handedly tapped her script into her computer. Her stomach growled, but there was no time to eat. Frustrated at the interruption, she answered her ringing telephone.

"Farrell Slater."

"It's me."

"Hi, Robbie, what's up?"

"What's up with *you*? I haven't heard from you in days."

"I'm on a deadline, Rob. I'll tell you all about it later. But I'm glad you called. Can you pull some old black-and-white footage of the Romanovs for me? I need it for this piece."

"Okay. Sure. What's the piece about?"

Unwilling to take the time to tell him, but not wanting to brush her brother off, Farrell decided to read Robbie the script she was working on.

"What do you think?" she asked, when she had finished.

"Big sister, do I have something for you!"

✣ Chapter 138

Farrell sat in the Fishbowl Friday evening to watch *Evening Headlines*, as Range's invited guest. Her shoulder, draped with a white sling, throbbed intensely. Her brown eyes were bloodshot and tired. But she sat regally, her head held high.

For two and a half intense minutes, Farrell's eyes, and those of the KEY News staff—and, she would later discover, the eyes of nine million American viewers—were trained on their television sets.

For the dozenth time, Farrell watched the piece that she had put together over the last twenty-four hours. Eliza Blake narrated in her trained, well-modulated voice.

"KEY News has learned that the Fabergé Imperial Easter Egg auctioned last month at Churchill's auction house for six million dollars was a fake."

Up popped a sound bite from a spokesman from the Metropolitan Museum of Art. "Art forgery is much more common than people realize," he said.

Eliza appeared on camera again in a bridge, shot earlier in the day in front of Churchill's. "It's a story that's rocking the art world, a story that began in the St. Petersburg of czarist Russia, wended its way across the world, and came to an end at Churchill's, New York's famous auction house. A story that mixes the human emotions of greed and fear, and the all-too-human deeds of deception and murder.

"KEY News producer Farrell Slater began following this story last month when Churchill's auctioned an enamaled egg purported to be the last Imperial Easter Egg commissioned to famed jeweler Carl Fabergé by Czar Nicholas II, shortly before the emperor was overthrown during the Russian Revolution. Known as the Moon Egg, it was never delivered to the czar and his wife Alexandra who, along with their five children, were executed by the revolutionaries."

Farrell had chosen some archival, black-and-white footage of the Romanovs that Robbie had pulled for her and interspersed it with material that B. J. had shot at the Russian exhibit. The large oil paintings of the emperor and empress worked well here.

"In the chaos of the Revolution, much of the contents of the St. Petersburg House of Fabergé was seized by the new government, who sold the jeweled treasures simply for the value of their precious metals and stones, unaware of—or caring little for—their artistic value. Some pieces were smuggled out of the country. Many treasures were lost completely. Some have turned up from time to time over the years."

More video of the Fabergé pieces at the Metropolitan Museum were just right there.

"That was allegedly the case of the egg that Churchill's auctioned. It was said to have been discovered at a New York City flea market. Churchill's vouched for the authenticity of the egg."

Video of the auction appeared, leading to a sound bite from Clifford Montgomery's opening remarks that day.

" 'We've had many beautiful Fabergé items that have been our privilege to auction over the years,' " said Churchill's president, " 'but none of them has matched the magnificence of the Imperial Moon Egg.' "

Eliza continued narrating the story. "On Wall Street, Churchill's stock rose on the ensuing publicity and record purchase by an anonymous buyer. But KEY News has learned that the egg Churchill's auctioned was a forgery and that the real Fabergé Moon Egg had been in the possession of the daughter of a Fabergé workmaster, the man who actually made the egg in the Fabergé studio in 1917."

Everyone in the Fishbowl listened intently as the video B. J. had shot that day which seemed so long ago at Olga's apartment, appeared onscreen.

Thank God Robbie had found it. Farrell silently resolved to give Jack the videotape box and ask him to have it dusted for fingerprints. *Dean, you're not off the hook yet, my man.*

Faithful to her promise, Farrell just used the video of the old woman's hands holding the Moon Egg; she did not show Olga's face.

"And, in another bizarre and deadly twist, police are investigating the murders of Churchill's employee Meryl Quan, and Misha Grinkov, a Russian emigré and jeweler in the Brighton Beach section of New York. Investigators now believe Grinkov made the fake Moon Egg and that both murders were committed by Victor Paradise, son of ballet legend Nadine Paradise.

"But Victor Paradise is not available for questioning. He was killed by a Churchill's doorman as he defended himself against Paradise's attack. In police custody is Stacey Spinner, an interior decorator from Saddle River, New Jersey. Authorities close to the investigation say that Spinner is the mastermind behind the forgery and the murders, and that Churchill's president Clifford Montgomery knowingly authenticated the Moon Egg forgery. Montgomery, too, is in police custody at New York Hospital where he is recuperating from a gunshot wound.

"Churchill's held an emergency meeting of its board of directors today, as the price of Churchill's stock plummeted on the New York Stock Exchange.

"Eliza Blake, KEY News, New York."

As the closing credits ran at the end of the broadcast, Range rose from his seat.

"Good work, Farrell. That's an award-winner, for sure. Thank you."

✼ Chapter 139

Farrell popped another miniature milk-chocolate Easter bunny into her mouth.

"Keep it up," Jack warned, "and you'll have no room for Pat's dinner."

Farrell stuck out her tongue playfully. "Don't bug me. I've barely eaten in two days, and I'm starved."

"Here. If you want to try something heavenly, have one of these," Tim Kavanagh offered. "I picked up this Belgian chocolate at a little shop near the UN when I was in the city with my class last week."

Farrell chose a rich candy from its golden box and bit into it appreciatively.

"Dinner is served," called Pat, carrying a large, honey-roasted ham to the dining-room table. Emily followed along behind her mistress, eager for any table scraps that might come her way.

Farrell took a seat at the end, so that her sore arm could face out, safe from possible pokes from a dinner companion. Jack sat next to her. Across from them, Tim Kavanagh and Choo-Choo Charlie eyed each other competitively. Farrell got the feeling that Pat was enjoying having both men there, vying for her attention. Peter took his place at the head of the table and Pat seated herself at the other end, nearest to the kitchen door.

"This looks wonderful, Pat," Farrell said, observing the feast spread out before them.

At his mother's urging, Peter said grace. Finishing the prayer, he remembered to be thankful for his surrogate grandmother's recovery.

"Eat up, everybody. But save a little room. There's a big strawberry shortcake for dessert. I thought we could all take a ride up to Nadine's after dinner and share it with them. Olga came home from the hospital yesterday, you know."

It seemed to Farrell that everyone was making a concerted effort to keep the dinner conversation light. When they finished eating, they wandered into the living room and Peter switched on the television as the fanfare of the Sunday edition of *KEY Evening Headlines* began to play.

"Can't get away from the place," Farrell remarked, as she settled in to listen to the weekend anchor.

"The Kremlin announced today that the last Imperial Easter Egg, created for the doomed Russian czar Nicholas II, will be returning to St. Petersburg, the city in which it was created over eighty years ago. Russia anonymously purchased the Moon Egg for six million dollars at auction last month, withholding announcement of the acquisition until Easter, traditionally the country's most important day."

"So *that's* who bought it!" Farrell exclaimed. "But what about Olga? The Moon Egg is hers!"

Peter smiled. "When Mom and I drove Olga home to Mrs. Paradise's house yesterday, Olga told me that a nice FBI agent had come to see her. She told him that she didn't want to make any claim on the egg. She said it's the right thing for the Moon Egg to go back to Russia."

Farrell turned to Jack. "Did you know all this?"

Jack nodded, smiling.

"And the six million dollars? Who gets that?" asked Farrell.

"No one," Jack said. "Russia isn't going to have to pay for the egg at all, which is a good thing, considering the financial mess they're in. Olga said she doesn't want the money. And Churchill's board of directors is waiving any commission that may have been earned. Smart move if they want their auction house to have any kind of future."

"Come on," called Pat, pulling on her blazer and carrying a covered cake plate. "Let's go over to Nadine and Olga's."

As the group rose to leave, Farrell took Jack's hand and pulled him aside.

"I have a surprise of my own," she whispered.

Jack waited expectantly.

"Range told me he made a mistake. A mistake he says he wants to correct. He asked me if I want my job back." Farrell tried, unsuccessfully, to wipe the smug smile off her face. It had been so satisfying to watch and listen as the executive producer admitted he was wrong.

Jack's blue eyes crinkled at their corners as he grinned down at her.

"Don't keep me in suspense Farrell," he urged. "What did you tell him?"

She shrugged, feigning indifference she did not feel. For all the arguments she'd made to herself to the contrary, Farrell knew she was not ready to leave KEY News and the world of broadcast journalism. She was relieved, grateful and thrilled to have her job back. At the same time, she wasn't about to let Range think his was her only option. Let him worry for a while.

"Come on, hot shot," Jack insisted. What did you say?"

"I told him I'd think about it and let him know."

DO YOU WANT TO KNOW A SECRET?

For Elizabeth Higgins Clark and David Frederick Clark

❦ MY GREAT LITTLE MOTIVATORS ❧

✣ Acknowledgments

I tried to keep this book a secret, wanting to reserve the right to fail in private.

But I am weak, and the road from idea to publication is long and lonely. I needed moral support. So I told a few people . . . or now, as I list them, I realize, more than a few people . . . people who were there, pulling for me during a very rough period of my life.

It is my sincere pleasure to thank Louise and Joel Albert, Regina Blakely, Beth Boyle, Joy Blake, Eileen Winters Chiocchi, Bunny Colburn, Pat Cunningham, B. J. D'Elia, Elizabeth Demarest, Roberta Golubock, Amy Guttman, Cathy White Haffler, Randi Hagerman, Cathy and David Holmes, Caroline Leiber, Katharine and Joe Hayden, Elizabeth Kaledin and Jon Dohlin, Judy Keegan, Linda Karas, Hal Leibowitz, Walt Leiding, Susie Marshall, Tina McEvoy, Jim McGlinchy, Marcy McGinnis, Norma and Norman Nutman, Louise Ryan, Steve and Susie Simring, and Frances Twomey. I am truly blessed to have you as friends and confidantes. You guys are much better at keeping a secret than I am!

Dan Rather, you probably had no idea what an emotional boost you gave me each time you asked how the book was coming.

Joni Evans, you were the first to make me believe that my dream could come true. Thank you for your nurturing energy; you made me feel very special.

Liz Mullen, you rooted for me, hoped with me, and led me to Laura Dail, my wonderful agent. Laura, I'm convinced, wanted this to be successful as much as I did . . . and believe me, that's saying something!

Acknowledgments

Thanks to my editor, Jennifer Weis, and her editorial assistant, Kristen Macnamara, for believing in this project and for skillfully shepherding it along the path to publication.

Thanks to George Condouris, M.D., of the University of Medicine and Dentistry of New Jersey Department of Toxicology for his expert advice on what would and wouldn't kill somebody.

Very special thanks to Father Paul Holmes, brainstormer extraordinaire, who asked all the right questions, had a great sense of fun, and knew that genius lay in the details. Thank God for Paul.

And finally, Doris and Fred Behrends, my parents, and my sister, Margaret Ann Behrends. Without your support I couldn't have done it. Thank you for helping me and loving my children.

❧ Prologue

He turned the key in the lock beneath the shiny brass door-knocker and let himself into the townhouse, a triumphant smile on his face. He had made it all by himself.

Daddy will be so happy, he thought.

He stood for a while in the hallway and tried to collect himself as he had been trained to do. He was excited from the trip. Calm down. Calm down.

The grandfather clock ticked loudly to his ears. The car horns blowing out on the street outside sounded angry. The phone was ringing over and over again, but he made no move to answer it.

He felt his arms begin to move up and down in a strange rhythmic pattern. He squeezed his hands into tight fists, trying to concentrate, trying to organize himself. Slowly, he could feel himself calming. Good.

A worried feeling came over him. Would Mom be happy that he had made the trip by himself? She always wanted to know where he was. She might not like what he had done.

He slowly made his way upstairs toward Dad's library. He called out for Millie, Dad's housekeeper. No one answered.

At first he did not see the man sitting in the corner of the library. He unzipped his jacket and took it off, dropping it on the couch. He walked over to the huge window and looked over at Central Park. When Dad came home, they would play one of their favorite games, identifying the special places in the park. Landmarks, Dad called them. He smiled in anticipation.

He slowly turned from the window. It was then that he saw his father in the chair.

"Dad?" His innocent face smiled openly.

His father didn't answer.

"Daddy?" He walked over to the man he loved. Dad's head was tilted to the side and his eyes were open, so he wasn't sleeping. Why didn't he answer? Something was wrong. He began to get that feeling. His hands began flapping, slowly at first, then faster and faster.

Hummingbird. Mom said it reminded her of a hummingbird when he flapped. Stop flapping, stop flapping.

He took his right hand and put the crook between the thumb and the index finger into his mouth. He bit down as hard as he could. He felt no pain. It helped him concentrate.

The grandfather clock began to chime, loudly. Bong, bong, bong, bong, bong, bong. The phone was ringing again. Why didn't his father get up to answer it?

"Daddy, Daddy! What's wrong?" His gentle facial expression turned to one of puzzlement and then fear as he reached out and insistently shook his father's arm. Dad's face didn't move.

None of Dad moved.

✣ Chapter 1

The vague tingling sensation started at her polished toe and quickly crept up her shapely calf.

"Damn!" Eliza Blake exclaimed as she opened the bottom drawer of her desk, fingers shuffling through the jumble of Band-Aids, dental floss, hair spray, makeup and tampons until she found the clear nail polish to stop the run in the second pair of designer pantyhose she'd gone through in what had already been a fourteen-hour day.

Putting her long, well-defined leg up on her desk, she applied the sticky liquid as her mind replayed the day's mishaps. The satellite difficulties on this morning's show were then followed by the first lady's office's abrupt canceling of a long-sought interview scheduled to be taped that afternoon. Scrambling, the *KEY to America* bookers had called around for a replacement to fill the time allotted for Angela Grayson on the following morning's broadcast. They performed admirably, coming up with the starlet du jour, the latest overnight sensation. The actress, however, didn't want to be questioned on live television so early in the morning. And she didn't want to come to the Broadcast Center either. Eliza would have to go to her hotel suite to tape the interview this afternoon.

On the ride to the Plaza with her camera crew, Eliza hurriedly scanned the research packet provided by an associate producer, framing the questions she would pose. She and her gear-laden videotape team were met in the hotel's opulent lobby by the star's apologetic publicist who claimed his boss had suddenly come down with some sort of bug. While the crew resignedly reloaded the camera and lighting paraphernalia back in the car, Eliza spotted the actress and her latest handsome co-star, holding hands, smiling and skipping out the side exit of the hotel toward Central Park.

"Should we take this personally?" Eliza asked her crew wryly, gesturing toward the oblivious lovebirds.

"Nah," came the response from Gus, the senior man on the *KEY News* camera staff, who squinted at the pair and shook his head. "Raging hormones'll win every time."

Now, back in her *KEY to America* office, Eliza had just screened the piece on a popular author that would ultimately fill the minutes originally planned for Mrs. Grayson. The writer had been eager to come in for a last-minute interview. Nothing like a chance to market a few more books and stay on the *New York Times* bestseller list for another week or two, thought Eliza, smiling to herself.

She was tired and eager to get home to Janie but the orange-wrapped Butterfinger called to her from the desk drawer. Aching for the sweet pick-me-up, she debated for all of five seconds and gave in. Guiltily, she relished the candy bar. There had been a time when she never had to worry about what she ate. But no more. The last few years, since John had died and Janie had been born, weight came on more easily and was harder to take off. Stop it! She shook herself. If you're going to sin, at least enjoy it.

As she crinkled up the candy wrapper, the tiny oval locket hanging from the delicate gold chain on her wrist caught Eliza's eye. She took it between her fingers and began to play with it. The locket was her grandmother's gift to her on her tenth birthday. Her grandmother, who had spent her working life scrubbing and cleaning one of the big "cottages" in Newport, had saved to buy the locket. As a kid, Eliza had thought it magical, and she rubbed it and made wishes on it. When things went the way she wanted, she gave the locket credit. When she didn't get what she desired, she ignored the possibility that perhaps the locket didn't have all the powers she wanted to believe it had.

Now, rationally, she knew that a tiny golden oval couldn't really have any force. But that hadn't stopped her from rubbing the yellow charm, dented and jammed unopenable, as she prayed through the long hours at Sloan-Kettering. She hadn't gotten her wish.

Tossing her head to clear the painful memories from her mind, Eliza began to straighten the papers on her desk. She wanted to go home. She thought of how she planned to give Janie the locket on her tenth birthday, in six years. Meantime, Eliza would wear it, still savoring its specialness. Eliza knew it was ridiculous, but when she rubbed it something always happened. Sometimes good, sometimes bad, but something. Silly. What would the *KEY News* viewing audience think if they knew her foolish little superstition?

She was stuffing the last of her homework in preparation for the next morning's broadcast into her canvas tote when her co-anchor Harry Granger appeared at her office door. He was gripping a rolled-up newspaper and by the expression on his face, Eliza could tell he wasn't happy.

"What's up?" Eliza asked, fully prepared for some vintage Granger moaning about *KEY News* management.

But Harry, usually so straightforward and unreservedly opinionated, was hesitating.

"C'mon Harry, what gives? What have they done now?" Eliza found herself smiling. They had played this scene many times before, using each other as sounding boards, venting frustrations about the workings of *KEY to America* and *KEY News*. But they knew they were just blowing off steam. They weren't going anywhere. They loved their jobs.

"I wanted to show you this before someone else did." Harry slowly unrolled the newspaper. Eliza saw the blazing masthead of *The Mole*, the most popular of the nation's supermarket tabloids. At the side of the front page sat an inky black rodent with oversize teeth; next to it was the slogan "We dig it all up."

Beneath that was the gigantic headline. Eliza stared at it, feeling her chest tighten. She let her telephone buzz insistently as she scanned the story about the most painful period of her life. Harry rambled on in outrage.

"Everyone knows these tabloid stories aren't worth the paper they're written on! Oprah just won a lawsuit against one last month. Nobody really pays any attention to them."

"You did," she said.

ℋ Chapter 2

"Eliza, thank Christ you're still there! What the hell took you so long to answer?" Not waiting for her response, Range Bullock pushed on. "Bill isn't in yet and I need you to stand by. I don't know what's with him lately. He hasn't called, Jean doesn't know any of his appointments, and we're forty-five minutes from air. He's making me nuts. Anyway, Eliza, can you get down here and start to go over the copy?"

Bullock, executive producer of the *KEY Evening Headlines*, hung up the phone, sighed heavily, and reached for the economy-size bottle of Tums which sat next to the large container of aspirins he kept on his desk at all times. As he popped the chalky tablets into his mouth he thought, This job is aging me. Quickly.

Where the hell was Bill? An unexplained absence just wasn't like him. At least, not until recently.

Bill Kendall, who had been anchoring the *KEY Evening Headlines* for twelve years, was reliable, dependable and predictable. Range and the hard-news people knew his routine and admired his discipline. At precisely 6:30 every morning, Kendall called the network assignment desk for a briefing by the overnight assignment editor. After getting a rundown of the mostly foreign stories that happened while the nation slept, Kendall would say invariably, "Okay, I'm going for a run. I'll be on my beeper."

Like clockwork, an impeccably dressed Kendall would appear in the newsroom at 9:30, full of amiable small talk for the newsroom staff as he made his way to his office. Once there, he checked with Jean, his secretary, regarding the phone messages and his schedule for the day. Next he finished going through the *New York Times* and the *Washington Post*, which he had begun in the limousine on the way to work. At 10:30 he listened to, but never spoke on, the national conference call, a multiline conversation between the domestic news bureau managers and the *Evening Headlines* producers. Bill Kendall and Range Bullock always had a closed-door powwow after the conference call, Bill venting his views on the stories of the day and what he thought KEY coverage should be.

At their meeting that morning, Bill had seemed a bit preoccupied again. Bill's mind seemed to be elsewhere more and more lately. Range tried not to dwell on it. A guy was entitled to an off day once in a while, even Bill Kendall.

Range looked at his watch. He couldn't stall any longer. He had to call Yelena Gregory, the *KEY News* president, and tell her that Eliza Blake would have to fill in for Bill. If Bill couldn't make it, Range much preferred Eliza to that idiot from the Washington bureau, Pete Carlson. For some reason he couldn't understand, Yelena was high on Carlson. She had agreed to a terrific contract for the guy, including the provision that Carlson was Bill's first-choice replacement. Range was happy that there had been no time to fly Carlson up from Washington that evening.

Range wondered if Eliza had seen the *Mole* story yet. If so, he hoped to God that it wouldn't affect her performance tonight. What a lousy break! He remembered how hard they'd worked to keep Eliza's hospitalization confidential. That was four years ago. Why was someone raking the whole bloody thing up now?

Where the hell was Eliza? He wouldn't need those damned Tums if she was sitting at the anchor desk going over the copy. He had a show to get on the air.

This job was killing him.

�֍ Chapter 3

Judge Dennis Quinn stood in the express checkout at King's, his cart containing cooked shrimp with cocktail sauce, poached salmon, roasted red potatoes and a large salad. Bad enough he didn't have a woman to take care of the menial task of grocery shopping, he sure as hell wasn't going to cook for himself, too.

As he waited, he pulled a copy of *The Mole* from the display rack. He enjoyed reading about other people's misery.

If you could believe what was in *The Mole*, Eliza Blake, the beautiful network anchorwoman, was a big-time cocaine addict and had been forced, a few years back, to check in as a patient at the Carrier Clinic in Belle Mead, New Jersey. The story spent a lot of time describing the various psychological problems and alcohol and drug addictions treated at the hospital. The article wound up by quoting an unnamed *KEY News* source who said, "The public depends on the mental stability of those entrusted with reporting the news," and went on to question Eliza Blake's ability to do her job.

Dennis Quinn threw the paper into his cart. He would read the story to his mother later. She was such an Eliza Blake fan. He didn't think she knew about this.

He carefully counted out the money to pay for his order and carried his grocery bag out to the parking lot.

"Hello, Judge Quinn."

Oh, no. It was Amber. Dennis cringed as he watched the smiling woman with the heavy thighs hurrying across the macadam toward him. Why did she persist in wearing those short skirts? Didn't she know how gross it was to see her legs rubbing together?

Of course he hadn't thought her so gross every Tuesday night after the Westvale municipal court sessions. He'd been only too happy to get some of those chubby thighs. But that was two years ago when he'd just been a town judge, before he had moved on to the Bergen County Superior Court. Amber had been convenient, but she wasn't classy enough for his larger aspirations.

"How ya doin', stranger? Long time no see." Amber was grinning. Bad caps. God, she was chewing gum, too. The cow.

"Hello, Amber. How nice to see you again."

"Haven't you gotten my messages? You never call me anymore. A girl would think you didn't care." She looked up at him in a pathetic attempt at coyness.

A girl would be thinking correctly, he thought. "Oh, you know how it is, Amber. I'm so busy trying to keep up with all my cases. The courts have such a backlog. I have no time for a social life anymore."

"I liked it better before."

"Well, it certainly was simpler then."

"I was wondering, could you use any help in your office?" Amber asked hopefully. "You always said what a good secretary I was."

I'd say anything to get what I wanted. "Unfortunately, Amb, there's a hiring freeze on." Seeing her mouth begin to turn downward, he hurried on. "I wish I could stay and talk but I have several briefs I have to get to tonight. You know how it is."

"Yeah, I know how it is." Amber stood watching as he got into his black Lincoln Continental with the JUDGE decals on the license plates.

Craning his neck, he preened before the rearview mirror as he drove off. Just twelve years out of law school, he was the youngest judge on the Superior Court bench. If you had the funds, anything was possible. The Superior Court was great, but he had bigger plans. He reminded himself he wanted to call Nate Heller again. It wasn't too early to set up the next step.

As he pulled into the driveway of his long, white ranch, he felt good. And then he remembered. Another payment to Bill Kendall was due.

❧ Chapter 4

Eliza replaced the receiver in the cradle after Range's call and wondered if he had seen the *Mole* article yet.

Drug addiction! Cocaine! Dear God!

She felt her heart pounding and her cheeks grow hot. This horrible story could ruin everything! Everything for which she had worked so hard. For herself, for Janie.

Janie.

Thank goodness Janie couldn't read yet and was still young enough that her classmates wouldn't be teasing and embarrassing her.

You've got to get a grip, Eliza told herself. Everyone is going to be watching you for your reaction. Get a hold of yourself. Hold your head up. Do what you have to do to get through tonight's broadcast. Take one thing at a time.

She called home and asked Mrs. Twomey to stay with Janie for another two hours.

"I know I'm already late, Mrs. Twomey. I'm sorry."

"Not to worry, Mrs. Blake. My little faerie and I are havin' a grand time. She's just finished her supper and I'm after pourin' the Mr. Bubble into the tub."

Eliza smiled weakly to herself. "My little faerie." Mrs. Twomey, born and raised in Ireland, was unaware of the connotation of the expression here. Eliza delighted in the woman's affection for Janie.

"Go on with ya," the housekeeper went on. "Do what you have to and stop your worryin'."

Next, as usual, Eliza thought of John. Whenever anything of moment happened, she thought of John, wished she could still share it with him. She felt the loss, the persistent tug of missing him. She was almost used to it now, four years later. But just because you were used to something didn't mean that it didn't hurt.

She held the inside of her wrist to her nose and remembered one of the last nights in the hospital. John was dozing as she entered the room and she had watched him, loving him so. All the painful treatments had not worked. He was very thin and flushed with fever. Eliza could see his chest laboring slowly up and down under the thin cotton hospital blanket. She heard his wheezing breath.

John opened his heavy eyes, and his gaunt, pained face cracked into a weak smile of pleasure as he saw her standing there. She straightened, smiled bravely back and went right to his bed, leaning down to kiss him. She felt the heat coming from his emaciated body as he held on to her. Please God, don't take him from me. Not yet. Not ever.

Then, in his rasping voice she heard him whisper, "Oh, you smell so good."

She knew she would never forget it. John had known he was near death. Yet, as sick as he was, he had taken pleasure in something as simple, as basic as her perfume.

She would never wear another fragrance.

Stop it! Stop replaying everything!

Eliza rose determinedly from her desk, replacing the gold button earring she had snapped off to call Mrs. Twomey. She walked the few steps to the mirror on the pale gray office wall and looked into it. A thirty-four-year-old face gazed back. It had a look of honesty and intelligence, though most of the written critiques of Eliza Blake's face had used words like attractive, pretty, engaging. The face that stared back was the face that greeted millions of viewers every morning on *KEY to America*.

She looked into dark blue eyes which Harry Granger, her morning co-anchor, said "never missed a trick." Right now, the white parts were tinged ever so slightly with pink. She reached back and grabbed the small, ever-present bottle of Visine from the top of her desk, tilted her head back, and squeezed.

She forced a smile she did not feel and gazed into the mirror. Her top teeth, the ones that showed, were white and straight. The ones that didn't show were white and crooked. The orthodontist had never given her a retainer for the bottom ones. Nor had she ever asked for one, she admitted ruefully. As it was, she had only grudgingly and sporadically used the uncomfortable mouthpiece for the upper teeth. She thought of her parents, who hadn't had that much money but did have plenty of problems of their own. She was grateful that they had found the funds for those teenage braces.

Eliza lifted her chin, jutting it out in the direction of the mirror and considered the thin scar, a vestige of an eleven-year-old girl's too deep a dive into a cement-floored swimming pool. Luckily, the scar fell just beyond the camera's watchful eye.

She knew that she had been genetically fortunate in many aspects of her life. A noted cosmetic surgeon had once told her that people paid him thousands of dollars to make a small, straight nose like hers. The shiny brown hair, now resting freshly trimmed on her shoulders, was kissed with natural highlights, though no one around the jaded *KEY News* broadcast center believed it. At five foot seven, she was tall and thin, the baby pounds from Janie's birth having come off with some concentrated effort.

Yes, in the general scheme of things, she had been physically blessed. But as Eliza looked at the crow's feet crinkling insistently at the corners of her eyes and the furrows that had become decidedly more pronounced at her brow line, she knew that the events of the last few years were taking their toll.

Don't start thinking about all that now, she told herself as her adrenaline started to pump.

✺ Chapter 5

The KEY press information officer called. *The New York Times* wanted a statement from the president of the news division regarding the *Mole* report of Eliza Blake's cocaine addiction.

"Tell them it's ridiculous," snapped tired Yelena Gregory.

What else could go wrong?

✺ Chapter 6

In the six years Eliza Blake had been with *KEY News* in New York, the professional gods had certainly been with her. Hired away from the Providence affiliate, where she had anchored the six and eleven o'clock broadcasts, her first job at the network was general assignment reporting. Just a few months into her new position, the vicious winds of Hurricane Anthony had smashed into southern Florida. Mispredicted by the weather service, the malevolent storm had caught Floridians and the network news division unprepared. The end of August found most of the seasoned correspondents vacationing and news management hastily assigned Eliza to the story. She had been on the air around the clock, face wet, hair blowing, raincoat flapping furiously, many times shouting to be heard over the roaring wind. Her reporting had been authoritative and controlled, and yet Eliza had also managed to convey a human reaction to the enormity of what was happening as the hurricane devastated the homes and hopes of thousands of people. She, like too many others in South Florida, had huddled in a bathtub with a mattress over her head as the walls shivered and the roof of her motel began to collapse. Eliza talked herself through the horrific night, making spiritual bargains as the hurricane winds raged. When the senior correspondents arrived the next day to survey the destruction, the story had clearly stayed hers.

Surveys showed that the audience liked what they saw. Executive Row had been impressed. Sensing star potential, *KEY News* president Yelena Gregory decreed that more of the stories likely to make air were to be assigned to Eliza Blake. Eliza appeared with increasing frequency and her audience popularity and identification ratings rose. The scores told KEY management that viewers recognized, liked and tended to believe Eliza Blake. When the female anchor of the morning show, *KEY to America*, departed for another network, Eliza got the job.

That's when the migraines had started. It had all happened within a year. The anchor job, the new baby, John's death, checking herself into Carrier. Now, four years later, the ache of losing John had become so much a part of her life that some mornings she noticed that she almost forgot the pain.

Any other time Eliza would have enjoyed filling in for Bill Kendall. Anchoring the *KEY Evening Headlines* was one thing, but filling Bill Kendall's shoes, even if only once or twice, was heady stuff. But not tonight. Tonight she just wanted to get home.

As her heels clicked down the long corridor from the elevator to the studio, her mind turned to Kendall. Recently, Bill had been arriving late quite often. It was the subject of much staff speculation and now Eliza was concerned, too.

When *KEY News* wooed Eliza away from Providence, Yelena Gregory had suggested that Eliza spend some time observing the anchorman. Bill had been an amiable and charming tour guide of the network news operation. Eliza watched as he filled the morning with telephone calls, script reviews and narration recordings. Lunch varied, Bill explained, but more often than not, it was a notable meeting with some influential type at '21,' San Pietro or the Four Seasons. He said he made it a point to be back in the news center by 2:45 to go over the copy for the 3:00 radio hourly. Kendall loved radio, he had gotten his start there. He never wanted to let the radio guys down.

Another check with Jean, another consult with the executive producer and Kendall would start to go over the contents of that evening's broadcast. Kendall took his title of managing editor seriously. Few things were more important to him than *The KEY Evening Headlines with Bill Kendall.*

Thoughts of Bill Kendall were pushed from Eliza's mind as she mounted the anchor desk platform and slipped into Kendall's chair, sliding her shoulder bag out of sight under the desk. The atmosphere was charged in the studio. Each of the people allowed in at this time of day had a specific function for which they were well trained and well paid. The stage manager, the floor crew, the Teleprompter operator, the makeup woman and the directorial and editorial staffs hurrying back and forth knew well their individual and collective responsibilities and executed them precisely. It was the collective one, the total product, which was called *The KEY Evening Headlines*, from which some got a charge and others derived their entire identities. They worked in rarefied air.

Range Bullock came out to the anchor desk from his glass-walled office which abutted the studio. Dubbed the Fishbowl by KEY staffers, the office was the nerve center of the broadcast's operations. Producers and correspondents conferred with Bullock in his glass office throughout the day and all final decisions about the editorial content of each evening's show were made there. Disgruntled employees had been known to gripe about the piranhas trawling the Fishbowl.

The executive producer was all business. "The lead tonight is the typhoon in India. At this point there are an estimated three hundred thousand people dead and damages could run to a billion dollars. Not much by U.S. standards, the money, I mean, but the video is unreal and Roberts has a two-minute package. We'll follow that with another minute-thirty from Snyder on the fouled-up relief effort. From there we go to commercial.

"Next we do Washington, two pieces in that section, the president's day and the Supreme Court." The producer paused, studied the lineup he had planned and ran his free hand through his thick red hair. "The third section will feature the latest shuttle snafu and more dirty linen in the House of Windsor. Fourth section is two pieces on the candidates today, one on the Republicans, the other on the Democrats, and where they all stand after yesterday's primary. We'll wrap up with 'Here's Looking at You, America.' McBride's done a piece on the state of the American funeral industry that will make their toes curl."

Range Bullock looked over his bifocals and his jawline rippled as he bit down and swallowed. "Of course, all of this is in place until something changes. But you're used to that, right?"

Eliza knew the observation was made as much for the producer's sake as it was for her own. She was surprised she was being called for the fourth time in six weeks to fill in for the unusually absent Bill Kendall. She also knew that Range Bullock did not enjoy last-minute scrambling to fill the anchor chair. It was unsettling for all concerned when the regular anchor was absent unexpectedly.

She hoped that nothing was really wrong with Bill. She made a mental note to call him tomorrow and invite him to lunch. Maybe there was something she could do to help him. He had been so kind to her when she needed a friend. She also wanted to get his take on the *Mole* article. Bill had such a good sense of perspective.

Looking at Range, she speculated again. Had Range seen the story? She couldn't tell. His demeanor was brusque, but that was usual.

"Right," she answered.

Bullock nodded and patted the pile of papers on the anchor desk. "Go get 'em," he urged and he walked back to the Fishbowl.

As she read over the copy, first silently and then out loud,

Eliza noted the broadcast was packed full tonight. Of the half-hour show, eight minutes were always commercials. That left twenty-two minutes of air time. Tonight there would be almost nineteen minutes of packaged reports, leaving the anchor a grand total of three minutes in which to appear on camera. Eliza knew that Kendall got more than three minutes. Okay, okay, the inner voice told her. Just do your part right and be grateful for this opportunity.

Yelena Gregory walked across the studio to the Fishbowl, acknowledging Eliza with a casual wave. Had Yelena seen the story yet? If not, it would only be a matter of time until she did.

Yelena wore her authority as she wore her fine dove-gray silk blouse bowed at her neck and the low-heeled black Ferragamos, with a quiet, understated dignity. There was nothing flashy about Yelena. She was a large woman and both her size and the expression on her solemn face left the impression that no one forced Yelena to do anything she didn't want to do. She and Bullock watched the show together almost every evening.

Lucille, the makeup woman, appeared, signaling that it was ten minutes until air. Eliza continued voicing her copy while Lucille contoured, powdered and lipsticked. A last spray to Eliza's brunette head and Lucille disappeared.

"Ten seconds!" shouted the stage manager.

Eliza thought of Bill Kendall one last time as she heard the *KEY Evening Headlines* fanfare begin to play. Raising her head and looking into the camera in anticipation, she felt the run zip the rest of the way up her thigh.

ℋ Chapter 7

In an expensively decorated library in a brick colonial in suburban Washington, D.C., an impeccably dressed, flawlessly manicured and coifed woman sat sipping a San Pellegrino. On the TV screen a hair coloring commercial proclaimed, "Forty isn't fatal." That's the truth, thought forty-one-year-old Joy Wingard. And if I have my way, fifty, sixty and seventy are going to be all right, too.

Wife of Senator Haines Wingard, Joy had good reason to believe that she would get her own way. She was tall, blond, thin, beautiful and well-maintained. Penciled into her weekly calendar were standing appointments at the hairdresser, manicurist, facialist, personal trainer and masseuse.

She watched intently as President Grayson and his wife, Angela, appeared on the large color television screen. The Graysons stood and congratulated outstanding American volunteers being honored in the White House Rose Garden.

Joy Wingard observed every shot of the first lady. She noticed Angela Grayson's well-cut suit, what she did with her hands, the way she gracefully brushed back a loose strand of hair. Joy had studied Angela Grayson for years and her fascination had not faded.

She remembered she had seen the first lady just last month. Congressional families were routinely invited to the annual White House Easter egg roll. Though their husbands were on opposite sides of the political spectrum, Joy had recognized empathy in Angela Grayson's brown eyes. On her way back into the White House, Mrs. Grayson had stopped, smiled warmly, squeezed Joy's hand and said, "Good luck to you."

God, I need it, thought Joy. She hadn't had any idea how grueling this race would be. And what really worried her was that the tough stuff was only just beginning. The making of President Haines Wingard was a long, hard battle.

By any standard, Haines Malcolm Wingard Jr., the forty-six-year-old senator from Michigan, had experienced an impressive rise. Though from a wealthy family, Wingard, as his campaign biography was quick to point out, paid his own way through college, Wingard Sr. believing that it would build his son's character to be responsible for his own schooling. Eighteen-year-old Win had taken the news in stride. Athletic and bright, he had secured a partial scholarship to Michigan State University. Blessed with good looks and welcomed into one of the most prestigious fraternities, Win's social ascent at college was assured. The four years passed quickly, Win managing to keep up an impressive grade point average while waiting tables at Dooley's twenty hours a week without missing a frat party.

Family tradition had dictated that he follow his father and grandfather, and go on to law school. Good grades and excellent scores on the LSATs led him east, to Yale. In New Haven, a new world opened up to Haines Wingard. He quickly caught on to the fact that for many of his fellow law school classmates, attending Yale Law was the fulfillment of long-held dreams. Even before enrolling in their first courses, they understood that the degree awarded them in three years would define the balance of their professional and, often, personal lives. In addition to the education and pedigree of the institution, Yale graduates were rewarded with the access without which little else mattered.

Until Yale, Win had busily lived in the moment, enjoying school, friends, sports. He had taken for granted the country club his family had played and socialized at throughout his growing-up years, in fact he had groaned at having to spend so much time there as a kid. The piano lessons, the sailing lessons and the dresser drawersful of expensive sweaters and polo shirts were givens as far as young Win was concerned. He had taken for granted the summers spent at the family's vacation house on Lake Michigan. Though he grew up less than thirty minutes from Detroit, Win just hadn't really noticed what went on outside of affluent Bloomfield Hills. When he went to Michigan State, he had been rushed by a fraternity of young men who also came from well-to-do families. They did not spend very much time pondering the problems or inequities of the world. Their immediate world was just fine.

What really opened Haines Wingard's eyes was another Yale law student named Nate Heller, a young man from a background much different from Wingard's, a man who, some twenty years later, would become campaign manager of the Wingard presidential effort. Physically small and often picked on as a boy, Heller was a scrappy, driven young man whose father had deserted his family when Nate was eight years old. His mother had struggled, poor and alone, raising Nate and his brother.

Nate lived his early life as an underdog. By sheer force of will, through endless part-time jobs, merit scholarships, and study at every available moment, Nate had had to work his way through Yale. Win listened, wide-eyed and fascinated, to Nate's stories, astounded by his own ignorance of the consequences of poverty and powerlessness.

Nate, in turn, idolized good-looking, popular Win. His friendship with Win opened a new world for him as well. Always an outsider in the past, Nate, by association with Win, was permitted grudging entry into his study partner's crowd.

It wasn't long before Win realized that Nate was a little too needy of their relationship, a fact that he came to use to his immediate advantage. Through the grueling law school years, Win leaned increasingly on Nate to help him with the enormous work load. Nate was willing to help, eager to maintain and strengthen their tie. Though the future presidential candidate would put his name to them, he had not written every graduate school assignment himself. Both men also shared the secret that they'd gotten an advance look at the essay questions for the bar exam, Win having wooed the secretary in the law office of a bar examiner. Getting the questions ahead of time insured the study partners had thoroughly researched the cases before the exam.

Nate wasn't about to be telling the press that.

The friendship had lasted through school, law clerking, private practice and into politics. Wingard had the attributes, Heller had the drive. Win, after one congressional term, had run for and won an open Senate seat. Nate, who plotted, coached and rooted every step of Win's successful way, was the one who had convinced the junior senator that he could win the presidency.

By April Fool's Day, with a win in February's New Hampshire primary and a strong Super Tuesday outcome, Haines Wingard was his party's front runner. And the party was very pleased to have him.

Wingard was intelligent and good-looking. Though he was lacking somewhat in the wit department, the party regulars felt that was only a minor debit. Best of all, he did not fool around. Politics was his mistress, and he could not get enough of her. There were no worries of "bimbo eruptions" during the campaign.

Joy was staring intently at the television set tuned to the *KEY Evening Headlines* when she heard voices in the front hall.

"Mrs. Wingard is in the library," drawled Trudy, the housekeeper.

Moments later Wingard appeared in the doorway, closely followed by his bantam campaign manager.

"Have we been on yet?" asked Win urgently as the two men took their seats in butterscotch leather armchairs, the same color as the Dewar's in the glass waiting untouched beside Joy.

No hellos, no how-are-yous, no polite kisses on the cheek, noted the candidate's wife. "Not yet."

"Great," said Nate Heller, leaning forward eagerly in his chair, his eyes riveted to the screen. "I really want to see how KEY plays yesterday's results. How 'bout a beer?"

Make yourself at home, thought Joy as she walked over to the mahogany butler's table. The ice cubes clinked in the crystal glass while, on the screen, the space shuttle *Endeavor* displayed missing tiles on its underbelly. Joy poured Win's usual cranberry juice and club soda. From the tiny, built-in refrigerator, she pulled a green bottle, uncapped it and handed it to Nate. She knew from experience he wouldn't want a glass.

If Win had tried, he couldn't have cast a more predictable type for campaign manager, Joy reflected. Heller was all business, all energy, all let's-get-it-done attitude. He also had a keen mind, and strategy was his passion. He took pride in the fact that while other students were reading *The Catcher in the Rye*, he had devoured Machiavelli's *Prince* and Plato's *Republic*. To this day, he referred to them, borrowing and amending ideas for his purposes. He approached politics as ground battle.

Nate was boasting, "JFK Jr. himself called me today. Wants to do a feature article on me for *George*. We're on a roll, Winboy. Semanski's really our only threat, and I only say that because I don't want to take anything for granted. We can't be too cocky, but God, I'm feeling good about the nomination. Then we'll only have Grayson to beat in November and the White House is ours. We're already getting calls from people wanting jobs in the Wingard administration."

The senator listened and nodded, barely looking up as his wife handed him the clear red drink. He was engrossed in the television images of the young royals.

Eliza Blake appeared on the screen and teased to the upcoming candidate status reports. Both men silently admired the good-looking face that stared out at them, but it was Heller who asked, "Where's Kendall tonight?"

The senator's wife felt her throat tighten and she inconspicuously clasped her hands in front of her to steady their trembling.

✥ Chapter 8

Eliza felt her muscles tense as the stillness of the studio during the fourth commercial break of the *Evening Headlines* was shattered by the red phone buzzing urgently at the anchor desk. The angry ringing of the direct line from the Fishbowl during the broadcast could mean anything, from the notification that a piece of videotape was not ready, to the announcement that a head of state had been assassinated. Whatever the reason, a call on the hotline signaled that some fast changes were going to be made in the show.

Her pulse quickening, she reached for the receiver with trepidation, uttering a silent prayer that whatever it was wouldn't be too horrible, too brutal, too ghoulish. She was still reeling from a story she had reported on the previous week about a man who strangled children and ate them. Please, not another nightmare.

She instinctively swiveled her chair around and looked in the direction of the Fishbowl. Range was not looking at her. He was bent over his desk, one arm holding the phone to his ear, the other arm hugging his stomach. She could tell it was bad.

"Range?"

He didn't answer her. He kept staring down at his desk. Through the glass wall, Eliza could see Yelena Gregory rise from her seat and lean over the table toward Range. Yelena shook his arm.

"Range! What is it?" Eliza demanded in hushed tones, feeling her heart beating through her chest wall and the color rising in her cheeks. In the weeks to come she would remember the fear that she felt in those moments before Range told her, the anguish she felt afterward.

Yelena was still shaking Range's arm. The executive producer looked up at Yelena and suddenly seemed to snap out of it. He turned in Eliza's direction and their eyes locked across the studio.

"Eliza . . ." Range Bullock paused.

"Tell me. *Tell me.* What's happened?" She was trying to stay cool. She knew that whatever Range would tell her, it was going to take all of her professional skills to deal with it live on national television. The sooner she knew what it was, the better.

Range tried again. "Eliza, it's Bill," he rasped. "Bill's been found. Dead."

"What!" She gripped the phone in her hand.

"He's dead. That's all we know. God, he's my best friend." The producer's voice cracked and Eliza watched as his free hand pushed his hair back from his temple. His face was contorted, the face of someone who had taken a body blow.

"Oh, my God. Range, no! This can't be." Even as she was uttering her unbelieving response, she knew that, yes, it could happen. Unfathomable things, tragic things, terrible things happened quite often. She had learned that firsthand. You didn't get used to the big losses in life but, with experience, your brain assimilated them more rapidly and efficiently. And the pain set in quicker.

Even as she took in the enormity of Range's words, she was aware that the seconds were passing, the commercials were rolling to a close and the camera would be coming back to her. She had frequently marveled that human beings were able to go on a sort of automatic pilot during emergencies, focusing on the immediate task at hand, temporarily pushing aside the magnitude of a giant event in order to deal with what had to be done at that moment. She wanted to cry but she could not allow herself that luxury. Not yet. Everyone there tonight was depending on her to carry this off. Later there would be time, too much time, to take in and feel the pain of what had just happened. Right now, and quickly, there were decisions to be made.

The executive producer knew that, too. Eliza watched and appreciated a real pro as he pulled himself together.

"Here's what we'll do," said Bullock, his words precise, deliberate. "We come out of commercial, you lead to the Democrats today followed by the Republicans. That will give us four minutes to grab some video of Bill that you'll have to ad-lib over after you make the announcement. We're sure we're not competitive on this. We are the only ones who know, so none of the other nets will beat us. We can spare the four minutes to get organized."

"Fine." Eliza didn't say anything else.

"Five seconds," boomed the stage manager.

Oh God, help me.

Eliza led to the political pieces. When the video package began to run, Bullock came out to her desk. Eliza felt that she was watching the whole scene, not a part of it. Herself sitting there, the monitor showing first the candidate reaction to the primary outcome, next the graphics illustrating the delegate votes garnered, then the citizens making their observations on the presidential hopefuls. The studio was dead silent save for the click of the computer keyboard of the writer who sat on the side and beneath her, quickly typing some copy for the announcement of Bill's death.

Focus, she thought. Focus.

Eliza heard the executive producer's voice. "We've sent McBride, a crew and a microwave truck over to Bill's apartment, so we'll have a live shot for the West Coast update. But as far as this broadcast is concerned, the file tape we're pulling will be the only visuals we've got. In the meantime, read this."

Bullock pushed a copy of the company biography of Bill Kendall in front of Eliza. She quickly read that the KEY anchorman, the man who lunched with presidents, arrived for dinner in millions of American homes and made more than seven million dollars a year, was born in Omaha and graduated from the University of Nebraska with a double major in journalism and history. His work on the campus radio station led to a first paying job at a Lincoln, Nebraska, station. What the bio failed to mention was that Bill Kendall had done triple duty there as a reporter, weather forecaster and commercial seller. KEY biographies only focused on the appropriate activities of KEY correspondents. Selling commercial time at any journalistic juncture was not a plus. Kendall had mentioned his weather and commercial selling days to Eliza at the correspondents' Christmas party. She thought of him now, his eyes smiling when he considered how far he had come. She felt her throat tighten. Don't think about Bill now. Don't think about how much you cared for him. Don't think about how wonderful and comforting a friend he was. Don't think about how he helped you when you most needed it.

Eliza forced herself to focus on the outline of Bill Kendall's life. It listed a succession of radio jobs, each time in a larger market, bringing him to Chicago. It was during the coverage of a mass murder case there, a case that permeated his life and the news for months, that Kendall made his break into television. The Chicago station's television news reporter assigned to the story had suffered a heart attack twenty minutes before air. Kendall was called from the radio department to fill the local anchorman in on what had happened, and a quick decision was made to have Kendall tell the audience the developments in the case himself. Kendall performed admirably and an offer on the television side presented itself soon thereafter.

Kendall developed star quality. He was observant, a quick study. His looks were of the basic, clean-cut, all-American sort common to most of the TV reporters of that time. But Bill Kendall's best physical quality was his eyes. As the directors were fond of saying, Kendall's eyes held on and didn't let go. They connected through the television screen and grabbed the audience. They were eyes that could be trusted.

The networks took note. Within a few years, Kendall received offers from all of the networks' news organizations. He had chosen KEY.

Range Bullock and Mary Cate Ryan, one of the show's brightest producers, stood before Eliza, their faces gray and strained. Range was twisting the red hair on his right eyebrow.

"Tell Eliza what you've got," Range said tersely.

"Thank God for Jean," Mary Cate began nervously. "She's

been gathering video for a surprise reel for Bill's fiftieth birthday this summer. We've got Bill reporting from all over the world, Bill at the fall of the Berlin Wall, Bill riding into Kuwait City during Desert Storm, Bill in Russia, in China, in Somalia, in Haiti, in Israel, in Egypt, in Bosnia, Bill holding a retarded baby in a Romanian orphanage. We've got some stuff from the early Chicago days, Bill at every major natural disaster this country has seen over the last dozen years, Bill standing chest high in flood waters, Bill picking his way through earthquake devastation. We've got Bill interviewing President Grayson and each of his two predecessors, video of Bill at a White House dinner last year honoring the Special Olympics—"

Range broke in. "There's more, but let's save it for the special report tonight. When you close, Eliza, tease to the special following local news. Good luck."

Eliza heard the correspondent of the Republican report closing as Range and Mary Cate stepped back, just out of the camera's view. The stage manager signaled for her to begin. She opened her mouth. No sound came out.

Eliza cleared her throat and swallowed, trying to start. Usually so erect, she looked almost shrunken in the chair. She could feel the eyes in the studio, along with those of millions of Americans, watching her. She pushed back her shoulders, straightening her spine.

When her voice finally came, it quivered. "It is with shock and great sadness that we report that Bill Kendall, anchorman and managing editor of the *KEY Evening Headlines* was found dead in his New York City apartment early this evening. The cause of death is unknown."

Eliza looked at the monitor and concentrated on what she and the audience were seeing, and pulling from her memory bank the montage of clips from Bill Kendall's life. Eliza watched and identified, where appropriate, what the viewers at home were watching. She recounted the biography information. Just as important, she paused instinctively and let the video carry itself at the correct times.

Eliza was back on camera. She felt her eyes fill and her usually direct gaze into the camera was diverted as she stared off toward the back of the studio and tried to collect her thoughts. She stumbled again as she began to ad-lib.

"We here at *KEY News* are stunned. Bill Kendall was a valued colleague, a beloved friend and a fine and generous human being. It's impossible at this point even to begin to imagine life around here without him." Her voice trailed off and she swallowed hard. Eliza took a deep breath attempting frantically to compose herself. The image of Bill smiling suddenly filled her head. She tried to sit up taller in her chair, but her body felt leaden.

"Police have been called to the scene. *KEY News* will air a special report on Bill Kendall tonight at eleven-thirty eastern, ten-thirty central, following your local news. I'm Eliza Blake. For all of us at *KEY News*, good night."

There were tears in Eliza's eyes and on her face as the director faded to black.

❧ Chapter 9

In Washington, Pete Carlson watched excitedly as Eliza Blake signed off.

"Get a driver to take me to National. Now," he barked to the desk assistant stationed outside his office door.

He marveled at how quickly things could change in his life. A half hour ago, he was smoldering with anger, jealous that Eliza Blake was filling in for Bill Kendall when it should have been him substituting in the anchor chair.

Now he, Pete Carlson, was the next anchorman of the *KEY Evening Headlines*.

He pulled his cellular phone from his briefcase, not wanting to use an office line, yet knowing that the portable phone could be easily tapped. He'd be careful with his wording.

"It's finally happened. I'm getting the big job. But remember, I don't want to be in New York forever, Washington is my home."

"Don't worry. It'll be taken care of," came the grunted response.

When the earnest young desk assistant went in to tell Pete Carlson that the driver was ready to take the anchorman to the airport, he swore he heard Carlson humming.

❧ Chapter 10

The ailing space shuttle and the Prince of Wales did not make the West Coast update of the *Evening Headlines*. Instead, Larry "Mack" McBride reported live from outside Bill Kendall's East Eighty-eighth Street townhouse on the death of the anchorman. Details were sketchy.

After taping the update, Eliza, her head pounding, walked into the Fishbowl. Jean White, the treasured assistant whom Kendall had affectionately called "Coach," was crying. Jean had taken the call from Kendall's housekeeper.

"I just can't believe it," she sobbed, red-eyed. "And you know what really bothers me? When I took the call, my ridiculous KEY loyalty kicked in. I didn't want any of the other nets to have the story before we did. I told Millie not to call the police until she talked to Louise." Jean rubbed a balled-up tissue across her eyes. "Can you believe that I'd be thinking of being competitive at a time like this? I must be really sick."

The others in the room looked at her sadly with weak smiles of recognition. They each knew that the same thoughts most likely would have gone through their own minds. It was second nature to them. How embarrassing it would be if another network scooped *KEY News* on reporting the death of their own anchorman! How it would have defiled Bill's dignity and memory to have another network report his death before his beloved KEY!

Eliza took a small plastic bottle from her shoulder bag and emptied a green Fiorinal capsule into her palm. Pouring a glass of water from the pitcher on Range's desk, she reflected for a moment on the nature and competitiveness of television news. She doubted that people watching at home noted which station broke a story minutes before the competition. But within the profession it was viewed as significant.

As Eliza swallowed the prescription headache medication and sighed deeply, a feeling of sadness swept over her. What did it really matter that *KEY News* had reported it first? Bill Kendall was dead. Who told the world first wouldn't change this miserable fact one damn bit.

An ashen-faced Yelena Gregory was on the phone barking instructions to the KEY press information office, about how to respond to the calls already coming in from the wire services, newspapers and other networks. Yelena's large frame somehow looked fragile as she sat in the gray barrel chair and concentrated on the latest crisis before her. Eliza thought that she saw Yelena's hand, the one not steadied by the telephone, tremble.

Range Bullock was on another phone listening and staring up at the ceiling.

"Hold on a minute, Mack. I'm going to put you on speaker."

Eliza heard McBride's voice. The voice sounded calm, authoritative, in control.

"Bill was found by his son," the voice from the speaker explained.

"*William?*" asked Bullock incredulously. "What a horrible thing for that kid to see and go through."

It was fairly common knowledge among *KEY News* staffers

that Bill Kendall's son was mentally retarded. Eighteen-year-old William had begun a mailroom job at a corporate headquarters in northern New Jersey and had just started living five days a week in a sheltered group home. He spent every other weekend with Kendall.

Bill adored William.

"He's very shaken up. The housekeeper has him up in his room to keep him away from looking at his father. She let me in before the police had a chance to close things off. Poor kid. He was biting his hands like crazy and jumping up and down. Really out of control. I told William that I worked with his dad and he seemed to relax a little." McBride hesitated. "If I had pushed maybe I could have gotten him to talk for the camera, but I just couldn't bring myself to do it."

"Thank God for that!" Jean exclaimed. "That would have been reprehensible."

"Bill was always so gentle with that child," murmured Yelena.

Either McBride didn't hear or he pretended he didn't. He went on.

"The housekeeper is with him now and his mother, Louise, is on her way. She's now left word that no one is to speak to William, not even the police, until she gets here."

"When will that be?" asked Bullock.

"Should be any time now. We'll get the pictures of her arrival and I'll continue to schmooze around here."

"What are the police saying?"

"Not so much so far. They are up there now going over the townhouse. The body hasn't been taken out yet. One of the police told me that Kendall was found sitting, slumped over in a chair, the current issue of *Newsweek*, on the floor beside him. Eerie. They're talking heart attack. Obviously, the autopsy will tell more. All I can get from the police is 'Depends' when I ask when the autopsy will be finished. What are you looking for tonight?"

Range sighed heavily. "Oh Christ, I don't know." He rested his head on the back of the chair and closed his eyes, tears burning behind the lids. The others in the room watched him and thought for an instant that they were about to see something with which they would be very uncomfortable. But he straightened himself in his seat and swiveled around to his computer screen.

"Figure on a two-minute piece, Mack. You'll lead. Just let us know what you need, Mary Cate will be your producer on this end. In fact she's right here and you can talk to her."

Mary Cate picked up a phone at the other side of the room and McBride was switched off the speaker phone.

Range continued to type into the computer terminal as he talked aloud, assigning the other producers in the room the pieces he envisioned in the special. Each producer would be responsible for his or her own piece of the half-hour pie. Each would coordinate and mix all the ingredients: the correspondent, the editorial information and the all-important video elements to make up the individual package explaining a bit of the story.

When he had finished giving out assignments, Bullock asked that the room be cleared, except for Yelena and Eliza.

"You did a good job tonight," he started.

Yelena nodded in agreement. "Very professional."

Eliza thanked them. She was waiting for it and it came.

"Peter Carlson is on his way up from Washington to anchor the special report."

"Would it make any difference if I told you that I wanted to do it?" Eliza asked, looking from Range to Yelena, knowing the answer to come.

"Unfortunately, no," Yelena replied. "You know the pecking order, Eliza. Carlson's got it in his contract to do the special reports when Bill isn't able."

Uneasily, Eliza considered Yelena's response. Instantly, she decided it was best to just get it out on the table. If Yelena and Range hadn't seen it already, they would shortly. "Does this have anything to do with the story about me in *The Mole*?"

There was no look of surprise on either face. So they both knew. Good news traveled fast.

Yelena answered firmly. "Eliza, please. Give us more credit than that. Give *yourself* more credit than that. We know you, we know your work. Don't feel threatened by some sleazy article in a trashy tabloid. It's beneath you. And, to answer your question specifically, no. The decision to have Carlson do the special has nothing to do with the *Mole* story. Pete Carlson really does have it in his contract to be Bill's first-choice replacement."

Range was staring at a spot on the textured carpet. "God, he is the next anchorman, if you can believe that. Is this all really happening?" the producer asked plaintively, putting his head in his hands.

"I'm so sorry, Range," offered Eliza. "This is so tough for you. I know how close you two were."

Range looked up gratefully. "Thanks, Eliza. I know you cared about him, too."

Eliza nodded and averted her eyes downward. On the chrome and glass table in front of her, the faces of Haines and Joy Wingard smiled up at her from a *Newsweek* cover. She shivered, remembering a recent conversation with Bill about this election year. He had confided that he was having a hard time getting the drive and enthusiasm up for the primary season. He admitted that he wondered if he could be impartial in reporting on the election this time. He didn't like Haines Wingard, he'd said, calling him a "cold fish." And he had hinted that he had been wondering lately if perhaps it might be time to reassess his role at KEY, perhaps retire, maybe write a book. Then he had laughed a little, assuring her that the thought of Pete Carlson as his successor was enough to keep him from moving on.

She had never seen Bill so down, but Eliza had been flattered that Bill trusted her enough to confide his vulnerability and she admired his truthfulness. Not many around *KEY News* wanted to admit to anything that could be perceived as weakness.

❧ Chapter 11

Somehow Joy got through dinner.

Win and Nate heartily consumed Trudy's veal roast, mashed potatoes, asparagus and a mountain of her special herbed biscuits. They speculated on Eliza Blake's announcement. Both men had seen Bill Kendall the week before, when the anchorman interviewed the senator on the upcoming primary and Wingard's position in the pack of presidential hopefuls.

"God, that guy was on top of the world," Nate said. "I know his ratings have been terrific. He's first in most of the major markets and extremely strong in the medium and small ones. Those are the ones I always think reflect more accurately the way America thinks. That's why I always care so much how we look on KEY. There was something very trustworthy about that guy as far as the viewing public was concerned. I guess it didn't hurt that he was a good-looking s.o.b."

Win speared another mouthful of salad. "Disarming. That's how I'd describe the man. Even though I knew he was going to try to stick me with some tough questions, I always felt he did it in a charming, almost seductive sort of way. Unfailingly well mannered. As a matter of fact, Joy, he asked me how you were surviving the campaign."

Joy looked up from her untouched plate and nodded but did not comment. Neither man seemed to expect a response.

Instead, Nate Heller wondered out loud, "What do you suppose happened? Awfully young and in damn good shape from what I could see. Remember that member-guest we played at Congressional last fall, Win? Kendall was in excellent form. He shot a seventy-six, for God's sake. A heart attack?" Nate shook his head in disbelief. "That's what it usually is when it's quick like that. If ever there was a stressful job, his was it. It's right up there with mine in the tension department. You know, boss, I deserve a raise, don't you think?" Nate grinned, the uncomfortableness with the death of a contemporary quickly replaced with his particular brand of protective, self-centered humor.

Win mumbled something about the campaign manager's reward coming after November. That led into the latest campaign strategy session, which was interrupted by the ringing of Nate's pocket phone.

Joy half listened as he barked "Nate Heller" into his phone. Why couldn't he say hello like everybody else, she wondered. He said, "Don't worry. It'll be taken care of." She wanted to be anywhere but at this table, feigning interest in yet another campaign talk, listening to business-as-usual. Nate was so rude, taking a phone call at the dinner table. When Trudy had cleared the table and brought in fresh-brewed decaf in the silver coffee service, Joy excused herself, saying that she had some papers to go over.

"Great, hon," said Win. "I'm really glad that we'll be doing that campaign trip together next week. You're a real asset to me, isn't she, Nate?"

"You bet. America still loves a healthy, good-looking, charismatic couple. And you two certainly fit that bill. Photogenically, we definitely have the advantage. But being easy on the eyes is not enough for a potential first lady. Now the candidate's wife has to be well informed, a mover and a shaker in her own right. That's why the preparation you do for our road shows can only help. Unless, of course, you were to say something stupid. But that would never happen, would it, Joy?"

"Never," answered Joy with a tight smile. "And that's why I've got to get in there and hit the position papers. Good night, gentlemen."

Exiting the dining room, she paused on the blood-red Persian rug in the hallway as she listened to Nate continue his speculating. "Man, I wouldn't want to be running *KEY News* tonight. Not only was Bill Kendall the network's big draw, but there's a real smear job running on Eliza Blake in *The Mole*. KEY has some big-time damage control to do."

She hurried up the staircase, wanting to escape Win, the campaign and gossipy Nate Heller. Though Joy didn't think that most people would want to admit it, Nate bragged that he read *The Mole* faithfully, along with *The Star, The Enquirer* and *Spy*. Nate said that a lot of the dirt had an element of truth somewhere.

Joy closed the bedroom door and locked it. Surrounded by the calming sea of textured off-white silk which padded the walls of the bedroom, she walked over to her dressing table, sat down on the tufted chair in front of it and looked into the mirror. The keen blue eyes assessed the face. A straight nose, a shapely mouth, a long, graceful neck. The kind of physical package which had learned early on its power to get what its owner wanted. As a child, a face adults had difficulty saying no to. As an adolescent, a face that teenage boys were attracted to. An animated face which the high school and college cheerleading squads had recruited. A face that had been selected as college homecoming queen. That face had worked in attracting the promising Haines Malcolm Wingard Jr. And, according to Nate Heller, that face was still working for her, this time in attracting the American voting public.

Tonight, the eyes were very sad.

The brass clock on the fireplace mantel read 9:15. The special would be on at 11:30. Joy undressed and went into the bathroom, turning on the shower full blast. She stood there and let the hot water rush over her. It always made her feel better.

How am I going to get through this?

She dried herself, carefully patting a spot on her upper thigh where she had recently had a mole removed. She wrapped herself in a silk robe and twisted a monogrammed towel around her hair. Another look in the mirror and she applied a creamy moisturizer to her face. Only 9:40.

Joy pulled back the heavy coverlet on the king-size bed and climbed in. Two thick folders were on the bedside table. The first was labeled CRIME. Ugh, she thought. Although an extremely important subject, influencing in one way or another almost every man, woman and child in the United States, crime and violence in America was debated ad nauseam and Joy was not in the mood to grapple with it tonight.

The other folder was marked AIDS. Nate Heller had come up with a plan which Win was going to announce in New York during the primary campaign there. Something called the *AIDS Parade for Dollars*. Joy scanned the papers.

Not tonight, I can't deal with this tonight, she thought. Instead, she got out of bed and went over to her closet, which was the size of a small bedroom. Inside, grouped according to color, were dozens of blouses, skirts and slacks. There was a separate rack of suits, beginning with a white wool Valentino and, traveling through the color spectrum, a camel-colored Calvin Klein, a yellow Sarah Phillips, a red Bill Blass, all the way to several black Donna Karans. Joy had been sticking to the American designers lately, not choosing to wear any of the foreign ones at campaign appearances.

Daytime dresses were another sizable grouping. A collection of short and long evening frocks had a wall to themselves.

If we don't win, I can always open a clothing consignment shop, Joy thought, shaking her head. She loved beautiful, well-made clothing. It provided her with confidence derived from the knowledge that she was cared for. Yet tonight, as she looked at the rows of neatly arranged leather shoes and tried to decide what she would pack for the trip next week, Joy couldn't concentrate. None of it seemed to matter.

Bill Kendall. That last time she had seen him was three months ago. Win had just finished out front in the New Hampshire primary. The press coverage intensified unbelievably when Wingard distinguished himself from the rest of the pack. It was then that Joy had realized that Win had a very good chance of becoming the next president of the United States.

The morning after the primary, Win was interviewed by each of the network morning programs. The KEY location had been in front of a covered bridge. She remembered Win complaining before the interview about being outside. It was freezing. Nate Heller reminded Win of the importance of KEY coverage. "Just be glad you're the guy they want to talk to out in the snow this morning," Nate had remarked.

Eliza Blake had conducted the interview for *KEY to America*. Bill Kendall arrived at the bridge location while Win was on the air.

Joy remembered Bill coming up behind her and saying softly, "Looks like you're in the big leagues now."

"Looks like it, doesn't it?"

"How does it feel?"

"It changes some things. And other things have to end."

Joy didn't get a chance to say more. Win's interview was over and he and Nate Heller were walking toward them. Bill had smiled and congratulated Win. There had been some small talk and mild laughter and then Nate reminded the Wingards they had a plane to catch. Hands were shaken all around.

The rest had been done on the phone.

There was a knock on the bedroom door.

"Joy, it's me."

She unlocked the door. Win stood there smiling. "How's the homework coming?"

Joy shrugged. "Not too well, I'm afraid. I just couldn't get into it tonight."

Win took off his tie and started to unbutton his shirt, still crisp at the end of a long day. Joy watched the man and wondered, How does he do it? The long hours, the media attention, the pressure of always being on. Win was unfailingly even tempered, steady and calm. He never lost his cool, even when they were alone. Joy reflected on those qualities—ones that would probably make for a good chief executive.

She thought of the last miscarriage. She had been a wreck. Win had been a rock. He'd carried on with his schedule, making all the meetings, giving the speeches to which he was committed, dutifully making a point of spending some time each evening with Joy. She had cried and Win had told her it would be all right.

He'd leave her tearfully falling asleep, eager to get downstairs and prepare for the next day's senatorial work.

That had been two years ago. After that, they stopped trying to have a baby. Joy had come to accept finally that she would not have a child of her own. But it still stung when she encountered other people's babies and small children.

"How did you and Nate do?"

Win carefully lined up the creases of his pinstriped trousers. "More of the same, just sticking to it. I feel good about the way it's going, but God, I'm tired."

"No wonder. You never stop. You've got to pace yourself."

The senator went into the bathroom. "Are you planning to watch the Bill Kendall special?" he called over the running water.

"I was, but I can watch it in the den, if you want to get right to sleep."

"No, that's okay. Let's watch it together. Gives us a chance to spend some time with each other."

But halfway through the Washington local news, Win was sound asleep. Joy watched the *KEY News* special report anchored by Pete Carlson with the presidential candidate breathing evenly beside her.

Joy viewed the highlights of Bill Kendall's career and listened to his colleagues' reactions and observations on the man. The final piece on the show had no narration. It was a montage of short pieces of video showing Kendall walking with different world leaders and then shots of him volunteering with kids at the Special Olympics all set to the theme music of the *Evening Headlines*. The last shot showed Bill with his arm around the shoulders of his son, William, both of them smiling happily. A touching piece of work.

Joy got out of bed, careful not to wake her sleeping husband. She walked down the carpeted stairway, through the living room and out to the veranda and the cool night air. Joy pulled her robe close around her, sat down on a heavy wrought iron bench, looked up at the stars and sobbed.

❧ Chapter 12

Judge Quinn sat in his paneled den drinking a third glass of chardonnay when he heard Eliza Blake's announcement of Bill Kendall's death. At the close of the show, Dennis switched off the set, stretched out on the plaid sofa, closed his eyes and smiled.

He was off the hook!

The nightmare that had begun when Kendall started demanding those damned payments was over. Now Dennis would not have to worry about Kendall making any sort of waves when the federal judgeship came up, and he'd have $5,000 extra in his pocket each month. How nice that would be.

It had been tough putting the money together each month—it really cramped his style. After all, a Superior Court judge only made about a hundred twenty grand a year, and after taxes took away a large chunk and he paid Kendall $60,000, there wasn't much left.

A guy had to live—and a judge had appearances to keep up. Of course, there was the money he'd told Kendall was gone, the money he'd stashed away. But he tried never to touch that. That had to be saved—for the bigger goal. After all, half a million didn't go as far as it used to. He'd already used $100,000 to contribute to the county political chairman, leading to Quinn's appointment to the Superior Court bench. Before that, contributions had gone to the president of the town council to insure Dennis's appointment to the Westvale Municipal Court. All money well spent.

There was still some left, a lot of it. And it had been gathering interest. It couldn't be used to pay back the debt; it was earmarked for Nate Heller and the Wingard campaign. Then after the election, the federal appointment was going to come through.

He'd have the respectability he deserved. His mother was going to be so proud!

And now he didn't have to worry. When the federal appointment came through, Kendall wouldn't be around to get all patriotic. The FBI vetting was going to be a breeze now. No one who'd taken the payoffs would be volunteering any information to the feds.

Dennis lifted himself from the couch and surveyed the room.

Now he'd be able to afford to get some things done around here. The place had become tired-looking. He'd call in a painter right away, maybe order some new wall-to-wall carpeting. On second thought, oriental rugs. Yes, orientals would be more fitting for a federal judge.

Having Bill Kendall out of the picture was going to make life a lot more pleasant.

❧ Chapter 13

Pete Carlson wondered if he had appeared appropriately subdued as he anchored the special tonight. It had been a real performance to seem somber on the happiest night of his life. He groaned inwardly that he still had more faking to do in the hours to come.

Yelena Gregory and Pete were the only ones left in the Fishbowl, the rest of the production team having wearily headed home after the trying evening. Yelena was on the phone with the overnight producer of *KEY to America*, going over some plans for tomorrow morning's broadcast.

"Yes. I do think we should devote a segment in each hour to Bill, but no more than that. After all, he wasn't the Pope."

Impassively, Carlson observed the large woman as she mentally weighed situations and gave directives. Professionally, she was impressive. At one time that had been enough. He needed her power and position to get to where he wanted to go. But now, it was getting harder and harder to psych himself up to perform with Yelena.

Eliza Blake. Now, that was another story. As much as he resented the competition she increasingly created for him, Pete wished he was going to Eliza's apartment tonight. That would be a fitting way to celebrate his victory.

Yelena hung up wearily and turned to him. "You ready?"

"Yup." Pete opened his leather briefcase to toss in his earpiece, which he had forgotten to remove at the close of the special. Yelena caught sight of a copy of *The Mole* resting on top of the papers in the case. She groaned and shook her head.

"What are you doing with that piece of garbage?"

His cheeks seemed to redden. "I'm embarrassed that you caught me with it, Yelena. It was circulating around the bureau in Washington today and I just threw it in my bag to read on the flight up. I probably should have left it behind on the plane, but you know I just didn't want to give that filth about Eliza a chance to spread further."

Sure, thought Yelena, nodding expressionlessly.

She buys it, thought Pete.

❧ Chapter 14

Four A.M. came too soon. Eliza forced her eyes open, rolled over and quickly switched off the alarm, ever conscious of her young daughter sleeping in the bedroom next door. Eliza knew there was something major to recall before she remembered what it was. In an instant it came to her. The death of Bill Kendall. She felt a wave of heartsickness roll in.

A few hours of fitful sleep, full of troubled visions. She tried to remember her dream. Bill was walking down a hallway. Pete Carlson was coming menacingly up behind him. Eliza was trying to warn Bill . . . of what? That was all she could recall.

She willed herself out of bed and walked barefoot down the hall to the kitchen. She switched on the flame under the kettle and poured a glass of orange juice. She cracked open the kitchen window and then lit a cigarette.

As always, the first inhale and exhale felt great, the second left her feeling guilty. All those health stories she had worked on, all the public awareness, all the accusatory, distasteful looks and remarks of nonsmokers sure took away a lot of the pleasure. But not enough to make her quit.

She blamed some of it on the stress of her profession. Newsrooms were traditionally filled with smokers. Eliza had started to smoke during an internship at a local television station while she was in college. One or two cigarettes during the course of the afternoon quickly escalated to a pack a day by the end of the semester. And over the years since college graduation, Eliza had continued to smoke as more and more of the people she knew gave up the habit. Never buying a carton at a time because that would mean she was a hard-core smoker, Eliza always meant to quit but didn't quite get to it.

She knew she could. She had stopped, cold turkey, the moment she had learned she was pregnant. Through John's deathwatch and funeral she hadn't dared one drag, knowing that if she took just one puff she would never be able to stop. But once Janie was safely delivered, Eliza had gone back to the cigarettes. Consoling herself that she never did it around the baby, telling herself that her life was very stressful and she would quit one day. At Carrier, she had really smoked up a storm.

Carrier. Something caught in her throat as it came back to her mind. The *Mole* story. Having her privacy invaded like this was sickening, having that chapter of her life viciously distorted was terrifying. What if it hurt her at work? What if the ratings slipped? Although perversely, she knew the ratings would probably go up, people would be curious about the "cocaine-addicted anchorwoman." Wonderful.

The kettle whistled and she whisked it from the burner. She stubbed out a second cigarette, halfway smoked. As she stirred the instant coffee, Eliza turned her thoughts back to Bill. It was Bill who had recommended Dr. Karas.

The anchorman had come to see her in her office. She was eight months pregnant, John's funeral had been just two weeks before. She had forced herself to come to work, knowing she would go mad if she stayed in the apartment. Bill took one look at her and gave it to her straight.

"Look. I read once about a ranking of life's big stress events. Buying a new house earns points, so does getting a new pet. But some of the biggest stressors are having a baby, starting a new job, an illness in the family and"—he hesitated, looking into her pained, makeup-less face—"the death of a spouse."

She'd said nothing.

"Eliza, listen to me. You're having everything come down on you at once. You should be talking to someone about it."

"I'm not getting on that psychiatric merry-go-round. I know people who have been 'in therapy' for decades. Not me. I just need some time to work all this through."

Bill hadn't given up. He wrote down Dr. Karas's name and phone number on a card. "I saw Karas when William was young and I needed some help," he confided. "He's good and he can help you."

But Eliza wasn't ready. Then. She put the card in her wallet.

It was two months later, after Janie was born and she found herself staring at her baby daughter in her bassinet, afraid to pick her up and crying more than the baby did, that she pulled out the card Bill had given her.

Dr. Karas had seen her though the worst of everything. Sensitive to her need for privacy, he'd steered her out of the city, tucking her away at the Carrier Clinic, an hour and a half from

Manhattan. She'd stayed for twenty-one days. Three weeks of antidepressant medication, counseling and relaxation techniques in a peaceful environment. Though he wasn't her attending doctor while she was at the hospital, Dr. Karas had driven out to see her three times each week. When she came home, she'd continued seeing him on a weekly basis for almost two years. She thought now of making another appointment. Bill's death, the *Mole* story, she needed to talk.

She had cared for Bill, cared for him very much. It always impressed her that he seemed remarkably open for someone whose life was under constant scrutiny. Eliza guarded her privacy fiercely. She had been ambivalent about all the stories done since she landed the *KEY to America* anchor spot. It seemed the public had a voracious appetite for tidbits about all the morning shows' anchorwomen. Katie, Lisa and Jane lived with it. But, at first, Eliza had not been prepared for her turn. There had been a big media focus on her status as a widowed, single mother. Story after story dramatically recounted the details of John's sickness and untimely death. Some of the stories got the details right, others went to great lengths to play up any fascinating, gruesome elements. Untimely death. They all got that part right. A bright, funny, virile, handsome, thirty-nine-year-old man is not supposed to die. Until now, nothing had been published about her hospitalization. It had all happened while on her maternity leave and not many people even at *KEY News* knew about it.

Eliza freely admitted that she loved the recognition and some of the perks that went with being on a pedestal. She despised invasions of her privacy. She had gone to Bill Kendall for some advice. "It goes with the territory," he told her, smiling.

"Do you ever get used to it?" she'd asked.

"Probably not. But you will learn how to handle it. How to take care of yourself and make parts of your life that are completely your own, which no one can touch except those you choose to let in. It takes time to learn to say no, to be firm, not to worry so much about what people will think. But you'll learn.

Because if you don't, you won't be able to survive in this business."

After that, when she had seen him in the hallway at the broadcast center or on a remote, Bill would ask, "How's the learning coming?" Eliza would smile and wink back.

She wished she could go to Bill now and talk over this *Mole* thing. She remembered vaguely some references to Bill making the tabloids at various times, but she couldn't recall exactly what they were about. See? Maybe Harry Granger was right. Nobody paid attention to those stupid stories.

I'm going to miss him, she thought. Eliza took pride in her affiliation with *KEY News* and Bill Kendall was its figurehead. It occurred to her that everyone on the staff in some way identified with Bill Kendall, even if they never worked directly with him. He was *KEY News*. She knew the impact of his death would be far reaching.

Eliza showered and washed her hair. She dressed quickly, selecting a well-cut navy suit and large pearl earrings. No bright, perky colors this morning. Her hair and makeup would be done at the studio. A driver was waiting downstairs.

She heard Mrs. Twomey let herself into the apartment and gave yet another silent prayer of thanks for the warm Irish woman who took care of her little girl. Each morning at five o'clock Mrs. Twomey arrived and Eliza left for the studio. Mrs. Twomey straightened the apartment and had breakfast waiting for Janie when she woke up at 6:30. Janie liked to watch her mommy on TV at seven, but usually tired of *KEY to America* by the first commercial. A Barney tape was the preferred alternative. By eight o'clock, Mrs. Twomey had the little girl washed, dressed and ready for the three-block walk to preschool. Then the housekeeper returned to the apartment to do whatever cleaning or laundry needed doing and prepare some sort of easy dinner for Eliza to slide in the oven. It was important to Eliza that Mrs. Twomey be at the apartment while Janie was in school, available to drop everything if an emergency call came. At 11:30, Mrs. Twomey, often with a sandwich and juice box packed in her bag, waited patiently on the sidewalk as Janie came swaggering proudly out of her morning session. They headed right to the park, for lunch, fresh air and a ride on the swings. Then it was home for a nap and, on the days when it was possible, Eliza could be home by 2:30 when Janie awoke, warm, quiet and sleepy-eyed. Once Eliza was safely back, Mrs. Twomey went home to her own place.

Though most of her counterparts had nannies and housekeepers who lived in, Eliza was happy with the situation she and Mrs. Twomey had worked out. Mrs. Twomey stayed whenever Eliza needed her. Mrs. Twomey made it possible to go to KEY and concentrate on her work. Mrs. Twomey made it possible to make a living. Mrs. Twomey made it possible to leave Janie without too much guilt. Eliza supposed that she could somehow survive without Mrs. Twomey, but she couldn't imagine how.

Mrs. Twomey was standing in the kitchen doorway.

"I was thinking about that poor Mr. Kendall all night. Such a shame, it is. Him so young and all. I remember that cocktail party you gave that he came to. I don't mind telling you it was a real thrill to meet the man after watching him for so many years on television. He stood and talked to me like I was the most important person in the whole world. Imagine! Him so grand and all! I told all my relatives about it."

"You *are* the most important. . . . I don't know what Janie and I would do if we didn't have you."

"Ah, go on with ya." Despite her protestations, Mrs. Twomey was pleased.

"You're right, Mrs. Twomey. It is a shame about Mr. Kendall, a real shame. When someone dies in the prime of life, it seems so unfair." She stopped, the inevitable thought of John creeping into her mind. Protectively, she rose from her chair. Keep moving, she thought. Don't think about it now.

Eliza went into Janie's 101 Dalmations–decorated bedroom and kissed the head with hair the exact shade as her own. It was amazing how much Janie looked like John as she slept. Like everything else Janie did in her life, the little girl even slept purposefully, getting her rest for another busy day of nursery school, lunch, Riverside Park and the merry crew of preschoolers who played there in the afternoons. With a little luck, by the time Janie and Mrs. Twomey got back from the park, Eliza would be home.

The driver had the car radio on. Shock-jock Howard Stern was in full throttle. "What the hell's going on over at that place? *KEY News* is falling apart. First Kendall bites the dust. Now, you're telling me, Robin, that Eliza Blake is loony?"

Robin Quivers, Stern's on-air sidekick, laughed. "No, Howard. It doesn't say *loony*. It says that she spent some time in a hospital that treats substance abusers and people with mental problems."

"So what is she anyway? A junkie?"

The driver snapped off the radio.

When she arrived at the *KEY to America* offices, the day's newspapers were already piled on her desk. The headlines all trumpeted the anchorman's death.

Harry Granger handed her a cup of coffee.

"Unreal, huh?" he shuddered.

Teaming Harry Granger with Eliza Blake had been the network's attempt to break the morning co-host mold followed by the other networks. KEY took a chance that viewers would want an alternative to the thirty- and early forty-something teams on the other shows.

Granger was in his late fifties and on first impression would be described as craggy. He had a way of saying what others were thinking but hesitated to say aloud. This tendency had, on more than one occasion, gotten him into controversial situations. On any given morning viewers, as well as the show's producers, were never quite sure what Harry would ask or respond in an interview. It lent an excitement to the show.

There had also developed an interesting tension between the two on air. They genuinely liked each other. Granger sometimes came across as paternalistic toward Eliza. Sometimes she went with it and enjoyed it, other times she bristled at it. Always there had been a mutual admiration and stimulation and it came across to the audience. The ratings reflected that the viewers liked what they saw.

"God, I just saw him Tuesday," Harry continued. "In fact, we had coffee in the commissary together. We talked about the usual . . . company politics, the ratings, the campaign. . . ." Granger paused for a moment, his eyes focused on the pen he was twisting in his hands. "It's such a short damned ride. I can't believe he just dropped dead."

"Neither can I," Eliza sighed. She lifted her mug and carefully sipped the bitter black brew. "Bill was always so kind to me. I remember when John died. . . ." Eliza's voice trailed off. She bit the inside corner of her mouth. She didn't want to start crying now. She looked down at the papers on her desk.

Granger patted her hand. He knew her well enough to know that she would talk when she was ready. "Go ahead, read on," he said. As he walked slowly away, Eliza heard him grumbling to himself, "There's no way in hell that Pete Carlson can fill Bill's shoes."

Eliza was unaware that Harry's eyes followed her as she turned to her Newstar terminal and typed in K-E-N-D-A-L-L. He watched her fiddling with the little charm on the bracelet she always wore as a long list of stories slugged for the anchorman popped on the computer. Poor kid. She'd been through a lot. John was a nice guy and she had been crazy about him. She had taken it hard. Now, to have the hospitalization brought up in such a scabby way, casting doubt on her ability to do a job she clearly excelled at, no, she didn't need that. She didn't deserve it.

Harry could not know that Eliza was turning her dream of last night over in her mind and the biting comments she'd just heard on the radio as she highlighted the latest entry and punched the button to make the editorial information appear on the screen.

Much of the data was a repeat of what she had learned from Mack McBride's report on the special. The only new information was what Mack had not been able to pin down from the police last night. The autopsy on Bill Kendall's body was being done today.

✣ Chapter 15

The *KEY to America* morning show televised from a ground floor glassed-in studio. During the live broadcast, outdoor television monitors allowed those who showed up each day a chance to see themselves on national TV.

The man noticed that the crowd gathered outside was larger than usual this morning.

He never went too near the crowd. The voices told him not to. Instead, he watched the monitors from a distance. It didn't matter that he couldn't hear what was being said because Eliza Blake spoke to him directly. Sometimes she told him where to go and sometimes she even told him where to find the animals for his beloved brass menagerie.

Something was wrong today.

Eliza looked very serious and sad on the monitors. She usually smiled a lot.

Now a news story was playing in the monitors. There was a closeup picture of a handsome man on the screen and then a reporter was standing in front of a townhouse with a big black door. A big elephant doorknocker gleamed from the center of the door. At the bottom of the screen flashed the reporter's name and his location.

The homeless man recognized the townhouse. He had passed it many times on his rounds. He had always admired that knocker, but the voices had never told him to take it.

Until now.

❧ Chapter 16

Louise Palladino Kendall stepped into the marble foyer. In the few months she had been living there, she had grown to love her condominium at Bears Nest. Her generous divorce settlement from Bill Kendall allowed her to have a very comfortable lifestyle.

She had purchased the multilevel, luxury condo in Park Ridge, New Jersey, when William moved to the supervised group home where he lived with five other mentally retarded adults. Louise had no longer wanted the house with its accompanying worries. Everything from security to snow removal was now included in her monthly maintenance fee. It made her life much simpler.

Her neighbors were mostly executives employed by the corporations headquartered in the northern New Jersey area, successful private businessmen, lawyers and doctors. There had also been famous residents. Former President and Mrs. Nixon had made their home at Bears Nest. That certainly had not hurt real estate values.

Louise was more aware than most of the market prices of condominiums, and most of the other residential real estate in the Pascack Valley as well. Louise Kendall sold real estate. She was quite good at it.

When Bill had gotten the New York network job, they had decided to live in the suburbs. Better for William, they decided, to be somewhere where he could freely roam around the backyard than life in the city. Both William and they had enough to contend with. Making day-to-day living as pleasant and easy as possible had been a high priority for the Kendalls.

That was before they had finally gotten a diagnosis for William's developmental delays, before they had ever heard of Fragile X syndrome.

At first, Louise had frantically occupied herself with getting William settled in his special school and immersed herself in the therapies, teaching theories, specialists and constant worrying that went along with having a child with "special needs." It was the constant worrying that sent her way down.

Bill was new at KEY at the time and the network seemed to think they owned him. He was away quite often, many times for long stretches. Alone at the end of the day, when William was finally sleeping quietly, Louise had too much time to think.

She thought about her son and his future. She thought about the cruelty of other children and the ignorance of some adults. She cringed at the thought of William being made fun of by anyone. She thought about the looks from other mothers at the Grand Union, their eyes quickly averted when caught staring at her little boy as he flapped his arms and bit his hands in the supermarket aisle, or bit holes in the neck of his shirt while he bounced up and down on his toes at the checkout counter. She thought about what kind of life William could expect and what, in turn, that would mean to her life. And finally, she thought about what her son's life would be after she was gone. These thoughts consumed her.

Finally, her doctor had told her that she had to get some sort of work out of the house. Real estate had fit the bill. She could make her own schedule, was always in the area, easily accessible to either home or school if William needed her. The fact that she enjoyed her work was an unanticipated bonus.

The work served her well and she was grateful for it. When her marriage ended, she was thankful that she had her real estate career on which to force her concentration. It was work that provided her with a social outlet as well as a sense of purpose.

But tonight, as she walked across the freshly vacuumed carpet and switched on the light, real estate and its values were far from her mind.

Bill dead.

William's father, her ex-husband, the man she had lived with for fourteen years. No warning. Gone.

The last twenty-four hours could not have really happened. The frantic call from Millie, the maddening ride into New York, crazed at the thought of William being there, needing her. The frustrating traffic, even going toward the city at evening rush hour, crawling across the George Washington Bridge. She had listened as the radio announcer talked about the death of the KEY anchorman. Bill, her Bill.

William had run to her, eyes swollen. Limited though his mental capacities may have been, William understood that his father, the man he loved more than any other, had died. He sobbed like the child that he was.

The police had been polite but there really wasn't much they could tell her beyond what she had already heard on the car radio. The autopsy would tell more.

Louise had appeared calm. Icy, a policeman would later describe her to his celebrity-struck wife. Louise remained in the townhouse until the body had been taken away and the police had completed what they had to do. She instructed the badly shaken Millie to go home, pressed some crisp bills into the housekeeper's palm and told her that she would call her about what to do next. Louise and William left through the rear to avoid the television cameras out front. Ironic, she thought. Bill made his living in front of those cameras, and in his death we were trying to escape them.

On the ride home, Louise fought back the tears as she listened to her son recall a conversation about the Yankees that he'd had with his father.

Louise could always tell when William was trying to make sense of something. He would do a replay of a conversation with the person involved. Amazingly, she'd known him to be extremely accurate in his recall. He was a wonderful mimic.

Now he was trying to somehow make sense of the fact that his father, who'd promised they'd go to some Yankee games, was gone and wouldn't be taking him.

William had stayed with her last night. Surprisingly he fell asleep quickly and he slept through the night. Louise knew that while it was easier for those around him to think that the young man really didn't have the same emotions as "normal" people, William did have feelings. He felt things deeply. William idolized his father. This was a profound loss.

There had been a few phone calls last night, friends wanting to connect. But she was exhausted and hadn't really wanted to talk. The phone had continued to ring today. Neither she nor Bill had ever remarried. Bill's parents were dead and there were no brothers or sisters. As the mother of Bill's son, Louise was the one they called with condolences and questions about arrangements.

By late afternoon, William, who had spent most of the day in the den playing video games on the computer, approached her in the kitchen.

"I want to go to my house," he said.

Louise was surprised. "You do? Why?"

"I'm used to it. I want to go."

Knowing how important order was to him and knowing that he had never really considered the condominium his home, Louise had driven William back to the group home a few miles away. She herself would have preferred to have her son with her tonight, but she always remembered what a friend who had long taught special education told her: the children who do the best are the ones whose parents let go the most. She encouraged acts of independence. She wanted William to function as well as he could on his own, to have some measure of self-confidence. The counselor had reassured Louise that he would call if William seemed to need her.

Now, home again, she sat in the crewel-covered Queen Anne wing chair and began to flip absentmindedly through the mail. A department store flyer, a couple of bills, mail order catalogs, the order form for the tickets for the New Visions for Living fundraiser in June. Tired, she rubbed her forehead round and round with her fingertips. God, Bill was scheduled to be the featured speaker at the fund-raising dinner. He did it every year. It was a big draw. Now what would they do? Maybe she could get someone else from *KEY News* to fill in for Bill and make a speech. But who could do it nearly as well as Bill with all the experience he brought to the subject? Louise didn't want to think about that now.

The familiar handwriting on a long white envelope caught her up short. Her name and address were written in Bill's distinctive scrawl.

Louise sat for a few moments, staring at the letter. She pictured Bill licking a stamp and sticking it on the corner of the envelope. She wondered if he had walked to a mailbox himself to deposit it, or if he had just given it to Jean to mail for him. She thought of him doing a common, everyday task, oblivious of what was just ahead.

Briefly, she thought of calling someone to be with her while she read the contents of the envelope. She reconsidered, knowing there was no one with whom she wanted to share the intimacy of Bill's last message to her. Louise bit her lip as she carefully tore open the flap. Inside was a letter on heavy paper, and a gray computer diskette.

Dear Lou,

By now, you've learned that I am dead. I'm so sorry that it had to be this way. I'm sorry, too, about leaving you to take care of William all alone.

Leaving you? She stared at those words and reread them over and over again, afraid to continue. How did Bill know that he was dying? She tried to think of how he looked that last time she had seen him. She forced herself to read on.

William's the best thing about us, Louise, and you've been the greatest mother he could have ever had. I've put all my financial affairs in order, as best I could, and you and William will be taken care of.

You know how much I've always hated wakes, so please,

just a Mass. I know how strange it may sound, but I want to be buried from Sacred Heart Cathedral in Newark.

Newark?

There's a young priest there, Father Alec Fisco, and I've already let him know that I want him to give the eulogy. Please make the arrangements, Louise. Maybe a donation's in order, as I'm not a regular parishioner there. If you would, have my body sent back to Nebraska—there's a plot next to my parents'.

It's always amazed me how the experts seem so sure that suicides are angry, wanting their loved ones to know that their love was not enough.

Oh my God! *Suicide*. But that's impossible. Bill would never take his own life.

I'm not angry, Louise, especially with you. You were a good wife. I want you to know that what we once had was very precious to me. I failed at being the kind of husband you deserved, and though I've seemed like a success to the rest of the world I've failed at facing life—failed, I guess, at the most important thing there is. I just can't go on, knowing what I know.

I've enclosed a diskette for William. He so loves that computer. I want him to have a goodbye note from me. I know that I've left you with the impossible job of explaining this to him. Again, I'm sorry, Louise. Please forgive me. LOVE, BILL.

Louise sat alone, stunned, listening to the sound of the ticking clock. The phone rang three times before she even heard it. Range Bullock was on the other end of the line.

"Louise, it's about Bill. The autopsy results are back. I'm sorry. . . ."

"I know," she whispered, not bothering to wipe the mascara running down her cheeks.

❧ Chapter 17

"This is the Bill Kendall autopsy results narration in three, two one. . . .

"New York City coroner Ben Calducci announced the jolting results of the *KEY News* anchorman Bill Kendall's autopsy."

McBride paused. "Insert Calducci's soundbite on the Prozac overdose causing death.

"Pickup narration in three, two one. . . . Bill Kendall, forty-nine, was found dead in his apartment last evening by his son, William. Louise Palladino Kendall received a suicide note in today's mail. According to his ex-wife, Kendall gave no specific reason for the suicide. Speculation is widespread as to why the anchorman would take his own life.

"Here's where the soundbites from KEY staffers will go."

Mack cleared his throat and continued. "Pickup in three, two, one. . . . *KEY News* correspondent Eliza Blake was substituting for the anchorman when word came of his death. It was she who announced it to the nation.

"Drop in Eliza's s-o-t here.

"Three, two, one. . . . Today *KEY News* Washington correspondent Peter Carlson took the *Evening Headlines* anchor chair.

"Insert Carlson's soundbite on his feelings.

"Three, two one. . . . Memorial services for Bill Kendall are still unconfirmed. This is Mack McBride, *KEY News*, New York."

McBride came back into the editing booth. "You want me to stay in here while you edit?"

"No, we should be okay," said Range Bullock. "But hang around until we feed this out. God only knows if something else will happen before feed time."

McBride left for the commissary and a cup of its trademark thin, bitter coffee as Bullock and Joe Leiding, a topnotch video-tape editor, began putting the piece together. It was rare that an executive producer would piece-produce but, as Range pointed out to the night news manager, this was not a usual situation.

Leiding carefully laid the video of the coroner's news conference over the opening sentence of McBride's narration and then popped in the soundbite from Calducci. The doctor estimated that Bill had taken seventy to eighty 40-milligram fluoxetine tablets. Calducci explained that fluoxetine was the generic name for Prozac.

"How the hell could he do that to himself?" an anguished Bullock asked the television screen. "I didn't even know he was taking Prozac."

They screened the pictures of Bill's covered body coming out of his townhouse the night before. They looked at some file video of Bill very much alive and looking fit. The blanketed body shot they used to cover the part of the narration recounting Bill being found by his son. The alive-Bill file tape they used to cover the part about Louise receiving the suicide note and widespread speculation.

They put in Jean next. Poor, bewildered Jean. God, she'll be lost without Bill, thought Bullock. He watched Jean on the television monitor, puffy-eyed and holding a handkerchief under her nose, her hair slightly awry.

"I hadn't noticed anything," she was saying. "He was just as he always was. If only I had known. I don't know what I would have done, but I would have done *something*. He was always so good to me." Jean dissolved in tears.

Bullock looked at Leiding. First judgment call. Did they go for the emotion and let the whole thing run, or edit it down and just take the first two sentences? The producer decided to do something in the middle.

"Let's take 'I hadn't noticed anything. He was just as he always was,' cut out the next part and skip down to 'He was always so good to me.' When she starts to cry, just take a beat or two of it. It's moving stuff, but let's not drown ourselves."

Leiding pushed the incue and outcue buttons on the editing console, expertly executing Bullock's directives.

Next came a soundbite from Yelena Gregory.

"Let's listen to her again," said Range.

The two men watched the interview, which had been taped in Yelena's office within the last hour. She is almost homely, thought Range as he watched her on the monitor. Yet she did have a presence. An intimidating presence which came from her position. Vague rumors circulated at KEY about some sort of Russian royalty in Yelena's background. Range reflected that she looked more like she came from good solid peasant stock. He knew that Yelena had attended all the "right" schools, had gotten her law degree and worked her way up in corporate law at KEY before being tapped to lead the news division as its first female president. She had built a strong legal reputation and was respected by her colleagues. She dealt firmly but fairly and set high standards for herself and for those who worked under her command.

On the screen, Yelena was giving the official view. Kendall was a first-rate journalist, he would be sorely missed. Then she looked down at the blotter on her massive glass-topped desk and began to fiddle with a paper clip. "You know, I played golf with Bill a few weeks ago at the company outing. He seemed"— Yelena groped—"like *Bill*. Nothing was amiss. If anything, he played better than usual." She rambled on, angrily distracted. "Of course, it was on his membership at one of those dinosaur, yet unfortunately not extinct, clubs that only allow male members. But that's a different issue." Yelena took a deep breath and let it out. "I don't know, I just don't know. You name it, I thought I'd seen it. Nothing much surprises me at this point. But this . . . this hits you in the gut."

"Pick up from 'I played golf' and let it run to 'in the gut,' " Bullock instructed Leiding. "Take out the part about the sexist golf club. How're we doing on time?"

Leiding looked at his counter. "A minute fifteen."

"Good. Use some setup video from last night's broadcast to cover Mack's sentence about Eliza's substituting and announcing the death. Then lay in her reaction today."

The two men watched as a misty-eyed Eliza Blake soundbite was edited into the news story. "It just strikes me as incredibly sad that Bill was so overwhelmed that he felt there was no other way than to take his own life," she said. "Bill was well liked and respected around here. It's a big, big loss for all of us. I am going to miss him very much." Eliza wiped the corner of her eye with the tip of her little finger.

Range stared at the video image of Eliza. Some thoughtful soul had made copies of the *Mole* article and tacked them on bulletin boards around the broadcast center. Eliza must feel horrible. He silently admitted to himself that, as a result of the *Mole* article, he was scrutinizing her, watching for weakness. It probably wasn't fair, but that was the way it was. And he'd bet that, despite her protestations to the contrary, Yelena was watching for soft spots, too.

"Okay," Range continued. "Now, wallpaper the sentence about Carlson taking over with some video from tonight's broadcast, then drop in the Carlson bit about feeling like LBJ after Kennedy was assassinated and wanting to do his best, cover the last part about the memorial service with some more pictures of 'Bill looking great' file tape and freeze the last shot."

God almighty, Pete Carlson is the new Bill Kendall. How am I going to deal with that pompous ass, Bullock wondered.

❧ Chapter 18

There must always be an exchange. The voices told him so.

He had waited all day—waited for night to come. The homeless man pushed his cart into a dark alleyway between buildings on East Eighty-eighth Street. He ripped through the plastic garbage bag at the bottom of the cart, feeling the smooth, cool animal heads inside. Finally, he came upon the thin steel rod of the screwdriver and the roundness of the can of spray paint.

Poking his head from the alley entrance, he looked up and down the block. Once the lone person walking a dog disappeared around the corner, the man crept from his hiding place.

The shiny doorknocker came off easily.

"Tit for tat, tit for tat. Spray them an elephant, this for that."

❧ Chapter 19

The yellow cab let Eliza out in the rain on the corner of Eightieth Street and Lexington Avenue. She walked quickly toward Dr. Karas's office, her trenchcoat flapping against her legs, whipped by a wind that felt more like March than May. She pulled her collar up around her face, eager to get to cover.

When she first came to see him, Dr. Karas, with his shaven head, had reminded her of the Great Oz in *The Wizard of Oz*. A giant brain with no body, godlike, possessing all the answers.

That was when she'd been at her weakest and neediest. As therapy went on and Eliza progressed and became stronger, she realized that Dr. Karas was human. He still had that big brain, though, and she trusted him. Completely.

She sat in the straightbacked armchair and stared for a few moments at the green rug with black flecks that carpeted the austere office. Dr. Karas was seated in his customary place across the desk. He waited for her to start.

"Thank you for seeing me on such short notice. But I needed to talk." She lit a cigarette.

"I'm glad you called. Of course, I know about Bill."

"It just seems like some sort of bad dream. One minute, everything seems to be going pretty well. I have my life basically on track again. I'm feeling good, Janie is healthy and happy, work is going really well, John is popping up in my mind less and less. Even the dreams are stopping. I'm feeling as though I've weathered the storm. That I've survived. Then, bang!" Eliza snapped her fingers. "Bill's dead and I'm announcing it to the entire country. And then not only is he dead, but it turns out that he killed himself. And, at the same time, the intimate details of my life are smeared across a national newspaper for anyone who wants to take a look."

She pulled a copy of the *Mole* story from her bag and handed it to Dr. Karas. She studied his face while he scanned the article. She noticed the corner of his mouth twitch slightly. Finishing, Karas looked up through his wire-rimmed glasses, expecting her to continue. He didn't have long to wait.

"Nice, huh? What in hell is going on? Bill was one of the most decent men I've ever known. It makes me sad. No, it makes me angry that he was so depressed or so desperate about something that he would choose to end his own life. Why?"

Leo Karas knew why but could not answer. Not waiting for a response, Eliza reflected, "You know, for protection, I have a gun, well hidden, at the top of my closet. But no matter how bad things got, and they got pretty bad after John's death, I never once seriously thought of killing myself. Poor, poor Bill."

Karas listened.

Eliza shook her head slowly back and forth and took another drag on her cigarette.

"And why did this article on me come out now, of all times? The whole thing happened four years ago. Four years ago! Why is somebody digging this up now?

Leo Karas had his suspicions.

At the end of their session, Eliza asked, "By the way, the show wants to do a piece on suicide. Not Bill's specifically, but suicide in general. Would you mind, terribly, if I brought a crew over and interviewed you?"

❧ Chapter 20

Detective Bob Colburn had twinkling eyes, an easy smile and a receding hairline which he was not crazy about. He also had a job to do. Catch the graffiti artist who was scarring up some of the most expensive real estate in Manhattan.

The 19th Precinct had been deluged with angry calls. Townhouse owners were enraged over the vandalism. Though all the affected property appeared to be in the same Upper East Side neighborhood, no one outside of police circles had put together the common denominators. The graffiti always reflected the animal doorknocker stolen from the nearest townhouse.

At first, Colburn had been less than sympathetic to his wealthy callers.

"What did you say he painted on your wall, ma'am?"

"It looks like a unicorn."

"A unicorn? Like a horse with a horn on its forehead?"

"Yes, like the one on the Bloomingdale's bag."

Now, this.

Last night, someone had taken the brass knocker from Bill Kendall's townhouse door. In its place, the thief had spray-painted a primitive version of an elephant.

Detective Colburn picked up the phone. It could be just a coincidence. After all, the *KEY News* anchorman's death had been ruled a suicide. But just to cover all bases, Colburn wanted to fill in the guys in Homicide about his search for the thief/graffiti artist.

ℰ Chapter 21

"It's going to be a media field day! Win has to be in Washington for the Senate vote. He's the sponsor of the goddamned bill. You have to be our representative. We need a presence there." The campaign manager's voice burned in Joy's ear.

Bill Kendall's funeral. Joy closed her eyes, holding the receiver tight, imagining Nate Heller pacing around his office, puffing furiously on his Camel.

"Everyone and his mother will be there. You can bet your life it will be the lead story on all the network evening shows. You've got to go. I want you to show up in the videotape. Most likely they'll mention you by name as one of the participants. Joy, we need all the positive exposure we can get."

Joy knew she could not win this one even if she wanted to. "Okay," she answered resignedly. "When and where?"

"Monday morning, eleven o'clock, in Newark, New Jersey, of all places. Go figure. Bill Kendall, the premier anchorman, closes out the show in that armpit."

Joy pictured Nate shaking his head and grimacing on the other end of the phone. The conversation concluded, Joy rose and instinctively went over to the closet and walked inside. She did not turn to select from among the daytime suits appropriate for a funeral. Instead, she went to the evening dresses. She pulled out the simple black Ralph Lauren evening sheath, the one she had worn that night. She held the dress close and caressed it. She pressed it to her nose and inhaled. The scent of Jean Patou's "Joy." Bill had commented on it that first night. She could remember it all so vividly. Seventeen months ago. December in Washington at the Kennedy Center.

There had been a private reception prior to the Kennedy Center Honors. Joy knew there would be many beautiful women dressed in elaborate and expensive dresses at the prestigious function. She had opted for the black sheath.

Bill had used it as his conversational gambit. "Understated elegance," he'd said, nodding toward her in appreciation. "You look lovely tonight, Mrs. Wingard." He stood before her, dazzling in his tuxedo.

"Thank you, Mr. Kendall." Joy smiled.

"Call me Bill, please," said the anchorman. He took a sip of his drink. "I suppose you must be busy now, with the race starting to heat up."

Joy thought before answering. "To tell you the truth, Win and his team are busier than ever. And, yes, I suppose I am more tightly scheduled than usual. But so far, so good. I'm not overwhelmed. Actually, the occupied time is good for me." She leaned toward him and finished softly. "Less time to think."

Bill had looked back at her with recognition in his eyes. It was not the first time she had seen the anchorman in person. In fact, she had smiled at him across a round table at a White House dinner just a few months earlier. But each had concentrated on conversation with their respective dinner partners and that had been that. Joy had been relieved at the time. She was extremely wary of the media, and by saying nothing to the man she had no chance of misspeaking.

But at the Kennedy Center that night, she found herself wanting to talk, wanting to connect with this attractive man with the deep brown eyes.

"Before we go a word further, is anything I say on or off the record?"

"Whichever you prefer."

"I think off would be best." She had a feeling she could say things to this man that she wouldn't normally say. There was something about Bill Kendall that made her want to let her guard down.

"Politics acquires a life of its own, doesn't it?" Bill said. "I suppose every field is like that. I know TV news is. Even though I am the figurehead, the one around whom the troops rally, there are many times rather than feeling I am calling the shots, that I feel controlled by events and other people."

"Yeah, but at least you don't have to deal with a campaign manager." Joy spoke unthinkingly and wished that she could take the remark back. She was always so conscious of presenting a united front. Why did she just say what popped into her mind with this man?

But Bill had laughed heartily. "Oh yes, Nate Heller. He is a character, isn't he? Determined, focused, driven. Look, better to have him on your side than on the other guy's. And since Heller is a born worrier, let him do that for you."

"If only it were that easy," she said quietly.

Bill looked hard into her face. She didn't even know this man. Why was she opening up to him? Why did she feel she could trust him?

The chimes rang, signaling that it was time to proceed to the theater and honor five of America's best and brightest.

"I've enjoyed talking with you, Mrs. Wingard."

"Joy, please."

He took her hand and shook it, holding on a moment too long, and smiling warmly.

"Joy," he repeated.

The next week *KEY News* had called and said that *Evening Headlines* wanted to do a segment on prominent Washington wives. Mrs. Wingard was one of the women who Bill Kendall would like to interview. Win and Nate had loved the idea.

The KEY entourage had invaded her office. A cameraman, a soundman, a producer named Mary Cate Ryan, and Bill Kendall. Nate Heller and Kathy, Joy's secretary, were also there to watch. Immediately, Bill had put Joy at ease. He told some self-deprecating joke, they had all laughed and the tension was broken. Joy was fascinated watching Bill, the professional, in action. Obviously having done his homework, he asked insightful questions. He drew her out, following up on her answers with other, more probing inquiries. At the end of the half hour she felt exhilarated.

A few days later, Kathy had buzzed her on the intercom. "Bill Kendall is on the line." Joy found herself smiling as she picked up the receiver.

"Just wanted to let you know personally that you're on tonight."

"How'd I do?"

"We're always our own worst critics, so you'll have to make your own judgment. But I thought you came across very well. Anyway, I'll be in Washington again next week. I was wondering if you'd like to have lunch?"

Then, like politics, TV news and other fields of human endeavor, their relationship had acquired a life of its own.

℀ Chapter 22

He didn't know how many more Saturday nights he could stand to spend with her and yet he didn't know how to break things off. He needed her. Having Yelena as his ally was as essential now as it had been all along.

Just last night as they lay together, she'd told him of the call she had gotten from the corporate office. The chairman of KEY had a thing for Eliza Blake. He loved the way she had come across the night of Bill's death. The public was crazy about her, too. Viewers were asking for more of her.

"What about the *Mole* article, isn't that hurting her?

"Well, it's pretty hard to ignore. The powers that be are watching to see how it plays out with the public. In our business, perception is reality."

The early morning light seeped from the crack at the side of the window shade. Pete looked at Yelena sleeping beside him. Everything about her was bothering him now. At least during the day, with her makeup on, she was more appealing. Now she looked washed out and tired. Her body was soft, but it held no comfort for him. The hysterectomy scar on her loose abdomen was, to his mind, another turnoff.

His mind switched gears. No wonder the chairman was gaga for Eliza Blake. She was young and firm and beautiful. Too bad she was such a threat.

Maybe he had to turn up the heat a little more.

✣ Chapter 23

When Mack asked her if she and Janie would like to go out for brunch on Sunday, Eliza suggested Tavern on the Green. Even though it was one of the top tourist stops in New York City, Eliza unabashedly loved the restaurant. It was a place where the eye was deluged with pleasures. If the food didn't quite live up to expectations, it didn't matter. It was beautiful and just noisy enough to bring kids.

They were seated in the Crystal Room next to a large window looking out at the garden filled with banks of pink and white azaleas that blazed in the May sun. As the white-jacketed waiter placed tall Bloody Marys in front of Mack and Eliza and a Shirley Temple with double cherries in front of Janie, it was Mack who began to reminisce.

"I remember the first time I came here. It was September 1976, and Warner Leroy had just redone the whole place. I had been at KEY for about two weeks in my first job out of college, a desk assistant working the four to midnight shift on the TV assignment desk. You know, a real entry-level job, answering phones, distributing wire copy in the days before computers, doing some errands. Anyway, one night an assignment editor on the radio side organized a group of newsroom people to come over here after work."

Mack stirred his drink with its celery stalk and smiled. "When we walked in, there was a huge sheet cake. It must have been sixteen feet long. On top of the cake, in icing, was an intricate replica of Central Park. I'll never forget it. It was all there, the skating rink, the children's zoo, the carriage drives, the boating pond, Belvedere Castle, the Obelisk—even little miniatures of the Alice in Wonderland and Hans Christian Andersen statues. I was fascinated by the artistry of it and by the magical quality of this place."

Mack went on, acquainting her with facts about Central Park, the backdrop for Tavern on the Green. The 840-acre masterpiece in the middle of New York City was larger than the principality of Monaco. The Sheep Meadow had real sheep grazing on it in the days before it was used for big concerts. The sheepfold became Tavern on the Green.

Mack looked up at the Baccarat and Waterford chandeliers. "Did you know that those two over there came from the Jaipur palace of the hemp king of India?"

"Why, no!" Eliza answered in mock seriousness.

"Okay, okay, I'll stop with the guided tour." Mack grinned sheepishly. "How ya doin', kiddo?" He smiled down at Janie who was happily licking the first cherry off the plastic swizzle stick. The four-year-old nodded in approval.

Eliza's gaze wandered to the fantasy mural of colorful birds, flowers and butterflies. Her eyes traveled up to the molded plaster ceiling, hand-tinted in shades of light mint green, birthday-candle pink and the palest yellow.

"I'm glad we came. It's good to get away, even if we haven't left the city." She sighed. As whimsical as this place was, it seemed a lot more real than the events of the past week.

"I know a joke," Janie volunteered.

"Good. Let's hear it," said Mack.

"Knock, knock."

Mack played along. "Who's there?"

"Annie."

"Annie who?"

"Annie body ready to eat?" Janie giggled, quite pleased with herself.

"Janie!" the adults laughed approvingly.

Plates of eggs benedict for Eliza and Mack and a hamburger with french fries for Janie were presented on the silk-screened tablecloth. For a time, they ate in a comfortable silence that Mack finally broke.

"You know what I remember most about that first night here? I remember feeling so privileged. Here I was, a kid straight out of a state school, and I was working for *KEY News* and coming to a place like this. I was awed by it all. I must admit, I still am sometimes." Mack paused, studying the flowers on the tablecloth. "KEY without Bill Kendall. It's hard to imagine." In a whisper Janie wouldn't hear, he said, "And he did it to *himself*." Mack continued, "But as the saying goes, no one is indispensable and KEY will go on without him. KEY has already gone on." Mack took a large drink of his Bloody Mary.

Eliza filled Janie's request for more ketchup, spooning it all over her fries. If there was such an animal as a sentimental realist, Eliza thought the description fit Mack McBride. He had worked his way up through the ranks exclusively at KEY, an unlikely scenario for an on-air type at the network. Nowadays, most correspondents had honed their television skills at smaller markets before making the jump to network news. Others had come from the radio side, writing and reporting the news hourlies on the KEY Radio Network until, rarely, an offer to try out on television came their way. Mack, instead, had worked himself up the editorial ladder always in television. After his stint as a TV desk assistant, then broadcast associate, assistant producer, assignment editor, associate producer. After he had been writing the scripts while acting as a producer on pieces that the correspondents voiced and signed off with their own names, Mack had decided that he wanted to be the one doing the reporting. Through some wrangling, a lot of hard work and some patience, he had reached his goal. Mack McBride had been a KEY correspondent for eight years and he had made a solid name for himself.

Eliza watched Mack as he read the dessert menu to Janie. As the two debated the merits of chocolate fudge cake and ice cream sundaes, Eliza considered that Mack was the first man she had felt really good about since John's death. Yes, she'd gone out on dates, but she'd always been forcing herself, urged on by well-meaning friends. But with so much time taken up by work, Eliza was content to spend her off hours with Janie. Besides, she didn't want to fall in love with anyone else again.

"You know what I just don't get?" Eliza swallowed the last of her coffee and was conscious of Janie sitting beside her. "How could Bill have done that, knowing that William would find him?"

"That's just it," Mack said. "He *didn't* know. According to Louise Kendall, William's visit was totally unexpected. Apparently, he had been making such good progress in the self-sufficiency department that without consulting his mother or his counselor, he had decided to make his first journey alone from New Jersey to New York. He planned to surprise his father. Instead, well, William got the surprise."

Eliza thought about William bravely concentrating on making the trip, taking the right bus into the Port Authority, going out to the street to hail a cab and give proper destination instructions to the driver. Not terribly difficult for most people. For young William Kendall, a major undertaking. And when he proudly arrived and let himself into his father's townhouse to have found his dad that way . . . how cruel!

Eliza reached over and wiped the red rim around her daughter's mouth with her napkin. She noticed that two of the three rabbits appliquéd on the front of Janie's yellow pinafore were now wearing ketchup coats. Janie was noticing the mess, too. "Mommy . . ." She pointed to the offending bunnies, her eyes brimming. Eliza could see the beginning of an upset. Janie was already showing signs of being a perfectionist.

"Don't worry, sweetheart. We'll wash that out as soon as we get home."

It was so easy to satisfy the child. Or maybe Janie was just very willing to be satisfied. Whichever it was, Eliza was suddenly profoundly thankful that she was sitting beside a healthy little girl whose biggest problem at the moment was a dirty dress.

After brunch, they stepped into the early afternoon sunshine.

"Walk or ride?" Mack gestured toward a hansom cab.

"As much as I love those horse and buggy rides, I think I'd rather walk. We need some exercise and fresh air. And today, I think you could almost call it fresh."

The three made a handsome picture as they walked through the park with hundreds of other New Yorkers enjoying the May Sunday. Some strolled, some jogged, some rode bikes, some rollerbladed, purposeful even in their pursuit of leisure time. Eliza and Mack admired the detailed stonework of Playmate's Arch, appreciated the Victorian lampposts embraced by budding pink and white magnolias, smiled at lovers walking hand in hand. Janie was intrigued by the spinning pinwheel Mack bought her from a vendor. Some heads turned and a few people whispered to one another and smiled as they recognized Eliza.

She hated what she was thinking. She turned to Mack.

"Do you think they've all seen it?"

"Who's 'they' and what's 'it'?"

"These people," Eliza made a sweeping gesture. "Do you think they've seen *The Mole?*"

"I wasn't going to bring it up, but now that you have, yes, some of them have seen it or heard about it. But I'd wager that most paid little or no attention. People are more concerned with what's happening in their own lives than with what they read about somebody else's in a scandal sheet. Try not to worry about this, Eliza."

"Easy for you to say."

"You're right. It is easy for me to say. But I happen to believe it."

Eliza considered his words. "You're probably right. I *hope* you're right. It really bugs me, though. I keep wondering who the *KEY News* source was who so nobly proclaimed that, quote, the public depends on the mental stability of those entrusted with reporting the news, end quote. That backstabber threw my ability to do my job into question! What a low blow! Can you imagine anyone being that vicious?"

"Yes, Pollyanna, I can."

Eliza ignored him, continuing on. "I'm going to find out who is behind that article. I've already called *The Mole*, but of course they won't reveal their source. Journalistic privilege and all that. But don't worry, I'm going to find out who did this."

Mack couldn't help but grin. "I have no doubt."

Eliza smiled back, the first genuine smile of the past several days. "Forget it. Let's not waste this glorious day!"

They continued on their way deeper into the park. Mack turned to Eliza. "Okay, where does 'Eliza' come from? A family name?"

Eliza looked at him, a half smile on her lips. "Ready? The first Broadway show my mother ever saw was *My Fair Lady*. She vowed that if she ever had a little girl, she'd name her Eliza. How do you like that?"

"On you, it somehow fits."

"It gets better. Guess what the middle name is?"

"What was the Professor's name . . . 'Higgins'?"

"Funny, very funny. Nope. Scarlett."

"She was a *Gone with the Wind* freak, too?"

"You got it."

They laughed.

"And Blake? Is that your real last name?"

Mack watched Eliza's happy grin fade and he thought he saw her blue eyes cloud over. The Eliza that America saw every morning was beautiful, bright and in control. The Eliza that he stood with in Central Park today was beautiful, bright and vulnerable.

"Blake is my married name. I was already using Blake professionally when John died. My maiden name was Gallagher."

Though tempted to ask more about the marriage, Mack sensed that Eliza was not interested in talking about it at that moment. She was watching Janie hop up and down, pointing excitedly to the jumbo merry-go-round up ahead.

"You game?" Mack asked when they reached the carousel.

"Why not?"

As the three of them rode up and down on the gaily painted horses, Eliza Scarlett Gallagher Blake closed her eyes and felt the refreshing spring breeze blow across her face. It felt good. She thought of Bill, still unbelieving that the man she had admired so much would have taken his own life. She wished she had reached out to him more, wondered if it would have made any difference. But she hadn't even had any idea that anything was really wrong. Bill's suicide was so sad, such a waste of a wonderful human being. His death squeezed her heart and she wagered that just about everyone who knew Bill felt bruised.

Eliza looked over at her glowing, healthy Janie gleefully riding her wooden horse with the flowing mane and the big white teeth. She was more keenly aware than ever of the fragility of life and was extremely grateful to be there, with her precious little girl, alive.

❧ Chapter 24

Daddy.

William had a sad feeling when he thought of his dad. He missed his father. Mom said today was Dad's funeral.

William went to his dresser, opened the top drawer and began rummaging through the computer diskettes inside until he found the one he was looking for.

He turned on his computer, and put the diskette in the opening where it was supposed to go, and pushed the buttons he knew he had to push to make the letter appear on the screen.

Dear William,
You are a very good person.
You are a very good son.
I am very proud of you.
I am proud of the way you always try so hard.
I am sorry to leave you.
Keep doing a good job.
I love you very much and I always will, even in heaven.
DAD.
P.S. And remember, William, an elephant never forgets.

He had known all of the words. He knew that heaven was the place people went after they died. Daddy was there now. It made William feel a little better to know where his father was and that he still loved him.

✣ Chapter 25

The black limousine carrying Louise Kendall, her son William and Range Bullock pulled up into the brick yard in front of Newark's Cathedral of the Sacred Heart. Louise's first awareness was of the crowds gathered outside. Police barricades had been erected to cordon off the inquisitive onlookers. Television news crews pointed their cameras in the direction of the limousine carrying Bill Kendall's ex-wife and son.

The limousine door opened and the three alighted. Louise adjusted her sunglasses, grateful for the protection against the bright sun and the penetrating stares of the curious spectators. She looked up toward the soaring granite towers. Their carved, gargoyled spires loomed imposingly. Turning to Range, she declared, "It's breathtaking! It's amazing something like this exists in Newark."

It took fifty-six years to build the cathedral. Upon its completion, a group of renowned architects had put their heads together and declared the Cathedral of the Sacred Heart to be the most perfect expression of the French Gothic in the western hemisphere. The cathedral itself covered an area of forty thousand square feet, an area almost equal to that of London's famed Westminster Abbey. Its towers were higher than Notre Dame in Paris. The Cathedral of the Sacred Heart was a world-class cathedral, but until Pope John Paul II's visit, the world hadn't known about it. So taken with its splendor, the pontiff granted it the special title, "cathedral basilica," to acknowledge its rank among Christendom's greatest churches.

At the massive bronze front doors, a flock of clergymen in white vestments waited to welcome the physical remains of Bill Kendall and commend his spirit to God. The turnout of the religious was impressive. Louise recognized Thomas Gleason, the cardinal archbishop of New York, resplendent in his red cassock, white lace rochet and red mozzetta. On his head was a simple red skullcap.

Next to the cardinal stood another man, smaller in stature, wearing a white chasuble trimmed in black and gold, and a high white arch of the miter, the official headdress of a bishop in the Roman Catholic Church. Obviously in charge, the archbishop of Newark stepped forward and extended his hand to Louise. "Mrs. Kendall, I am Theodore Sweeney." He smiled sympathetically and murmured a few words about what a wonderful man Bill had been. Archbishop Sweeney turned toward William, reached out and put his right hand on the young man's shoulder.

Louise looked at their son. William was running his fingers under the collar of his shirt, uncomfortable in his tie. Poor kid. Maybe she had made a mistake in having him come today. *She* was having a difficult time being here. How the hell would William process the elaborate ritual?

Classified as functioning mentally only as a nine- or ten-year-old, William sometimes amazed his parents with a special insight or observation. Louise was convinced that William's brain itself was strong. It was his connective ability that was weak. People with Fragile X lacked a protein essential for making connections. Researchers were trying to figure out the protein. She prayed that someday there would be a manufactured protein for her son, like insulin for a diabetic. Gene therapy was also very promising. For now, though, the Ritalin he had been taking helped him focus a bit better.

So far, his eyes didn't have that panicked, overwhelmed look. Louise summoned up her trusty inner voice which told her again that she couldn't control what her son would do, she could only deal with whatever came.

Standing behind the bishops, among a group of other priests dressed in simple white chasubles and matching tapestry stoles, Louise saw Father Alec Fisco, the earnest, young associate pastor of the cathedral. Father Alec had come to see her over the weekend. Louise had gone along with most of what he had suggested about the funeral plans. She just didn't care much about the details. She was too stunned.

She looked around and thought of the day she married Bill. They had been so young, the future so promising. They were going to have it all. And they did, for a while.

Louise watched as the archbishop sprinkled holy water over the dove-gray casket. "I bless the body of William with the holy water that reminds us of his baptism." The pallbearers then placed a white pall, with black and gold trim, over the casket.

The procession began down the marbled main aisle of the cool, majestic place. First, the incense-swinging thurifer leading the way for the cross flanked by two white candles carried by college seminarians dressed in their white albs. Next, a deacon carried the Gospel book, then Father Alec who would give the homily, followed by a large gaggle of concelebrating priests. The bishops from Brooklyn, Paterson, Metuchen, and Camden walked in pairs, followed by Archbishop Sweeney. Behind him were his crozier and miter bearers. Cardinal Gleason and the cardinal archbishop of Philadelphia, both in their red choir dress, came next. This was Sweeney's cathedral, and he would be the celebrant of the funeral Mass.

Bill's draped casket, escorted by the six honorary pallbearers, five men and one woman who had been part of Bill Kendall's life. Louise had at first been touched when Yelena called and asked if she could be a pallbearer. Louise didn't really like herself thinking that Yelena probably got a charge out of being the only woman. Well, it was fine with Louise. Yelena certainly had the size to pull it off. Besides, Bill had liked her.

Louise, William and Range walked together slowly down the long, white and green aisle, bringing up the rear. Louise spotted faces from *KEY News*. There was Eliza Blake. She made a mental note that she wanted to get hold of Eliza and ask if she'd consider pinch-hitting for Bill at the New Visions for Living fund-raiser. Louise almost smiled, amused that her brain was tending to details even at Bill's funeral. Bill had always kidded her about being so organized.

The three took their places in the carved white-oak front pew. Louise was aware of thousands of eyes upon her. She stood erect, fixing her eyes on the altar ahead. The clergy had taken their carefully orchestrated positions on the elevated sanctuary. The funeral ceremony started.

Archbishop Sweeney began the opening prayer for one who died by suicide. "Almighty God and Father of all, you strengthen us by the mystery of the cross and with the sacrament of your Son's resurrection. Have mercy on our brother, William. Forgive all his sins and grant him peace. May we who mourn this sudden death be comforted and consoled by your power and protection. We ask this through Christ our Lord."

Fifteen hundred voices answered, "Amen."

What would Bill, the former altar boy from a small town in Nebraska, have thought if he could see what was happening now? Louise stared at the marble angel with the open hands affixed to the altar rail in front of her, and wondered about the man who had come so far only to end like this.

Why, Bill? Why?

✵ Chapter 26

What a sendoff this was! He wondered how many would turn out for his own funeral.

Judge Dennis Quinn watched Bill Kendall's casket glide down the main aisle of the cathedral. He stood among the weepy troop from New Visions for Living. Dennis, before everything had happened, had acted as treasurer of the organization, which raised money to buy group homes for the mentally retarded. He'd even played a clown at parties for the residents. Kendall, until his death, had served on the board of directors. Generous with his money, Kendall was also generous with his time. Those associated with New Visions for Living were not only proud to be connected to Bill Kendall the famous anchor, they valued knowing Bill Kendall the man.

Dennis watched Louise Kendall and her son take their seats in the front pew.

Bill worried so about that kid. Dennis remembered going out with Bill to approve the first group home that New Visions bought. After they had thoroughly inspected the five-bedroom colonial with the fenced-in yard, Bill had remarked, "Maybe my William will live here someday." Back then, Dennis's heart had gone out to the guy. All that dough, and he still couldn't make everything all right for his kid.

That was then.

But Bill had discovered that Dennis had been siphoning off funds from the charity and threatened to turn the judge in if he didn't repay the money.

Kendall really was a sucker, though, Quinn thought, suppressing a smirk. When the judge said the money was gone and that disclosure of the embezzlement would kill his poor twice-widowed mother—to have her only son felled by scandal—the sap fell for it.

But Kendall had come up with that miserable payback plan. It had been agony.

As everyone listened to the first reading from Scripture, Dennis reached into his pocket, took his handkerchief and dabbed at the corner of his dry eye. It was important that none of the others sitting all dewy-eyed and sniffling alongside him this morning suspect his true feelings. They, who were such Bill Kendall worshipers, must think that he, too, was mourning the loss of Bill.

But he wasn't.

❧ Chapter 27

During the second Scripture reading, Yelena Gregory sat in the front row on the left-hand side of the cathedral with the other pallbearers. It had been a long walk escorting Bill's casket down the aisle.

She cast a glance to her left. The *KEY News* team sat in the pew beside her. Pete Carlson, Eliza Blake, Mack McBride, Harry Granger. She took some solace from sitting next to them, united in paying their respects to Bill.

Pete looked ill at ease. That was understandable. He probably felt awkward as the guy taking Bill Kendall's spot. Relax, Pete. No one can really take Bill's place, so don't even bother to try. You'll be better off if you are your own person.

Of course, Yelena had to admit to herself, the pressure was really on him. Gone were the days when management waited patiently for on-air talent to catch on with the audience. The pressure would come from corporate and Yelena wouldn't be able to protect Pete. If he didn't deliver the ratings in short order, someone else would be brought in. Yelena knew that the someone would be Eliza Blake. Viewer calls and letters were running high in support of her. There had been a few negative opinions expressed about the *Mole* article, but not enough so far to raise any real worries.

She'd reassure Pete later. She hated to see him hurting.

Pete, her lover, her own. She still marveled at the fact that he found her so desirable. No man had ever wanted her the way Pete did. It was a precious dream come true.

But what if people found out? If they knew, she'd be unable to push for Pete in executive meetings. And then what? Pete wouldn't like that. She knew it made him happy when she boosted his career. And she so wanted to make Pete happy.

Again, Yelena thought of Bill. Just last week, he had come to her and told her to watch out for Pete, that Bill suspected Pete was too close to the Wingard campaign and wouldn't be able to be objective in reporting on the presidential race.

Yelena looked over at Pete. She wasn't going to confront him. And with Bill dead, she didn't have to make that choice.

Yelena was paying no attention to the Scripture reading. Instead, she looked across the aisle at Louise and William Kendall. Bill had loved that kid so. This whole thing was sad. But she wouldn't cry, not here, not in public. The president of *KEY News* had to appear strong.

❧ Chapter 28

He had agonized over what he was going to say. According to the Church, his must be a spiritual discourse to the congregation, not just a recap of the man's life. Father Alec was well aware that the funeral was not really for Bill Kendall. It was for the people left behind, for family and friends in mourning. It was for the people attending, reflecting on life and death and what Christians believe about the meaning of life and death. Bill Kendall no longer needed to be consoled.

From his position on the altar, Father Alec looked out at the nave of the cathedral. It was full. He recognized many faces. He supposed that the highest ranking would be the vice president of the United States, though there were others sitting there today who had more power. He noted male and female TV personalities and anchorpeople, show business faces, political types and even some foreign dignitaries. He had seen the secretary general of the United Nations arrive. There were hundreds of others he did not recognize. Father Alec could only speculate on who they were and what they did. Try to remember this, he thought. You won't see an assembly like this again.

When the cathedral had been planned, it had been thought that it would be a worshiping place for wealthy Catholics. But Newark's fate had dictated the cathedral's. Its primary use now was for large ceremonies such as the ordination of new priests. The elite lay population which sat there today was an anomaly.

Archbishop Sweeny loved it. His cathedral . . . showcased on national television today. For once, not the innocuous second fiddle to Saint Patrick's. Father Alec looked over at the cardinal archbishop of New York, sitting across from Sweeney in the sanctuary. He wondered just how bugged Gleason must be, watching Sweeney sitting in the cathedral, the throne of marble with the crest over it, the bishop's chair.

So far, so good. The bishops had taken off their miters and readjusted their skullcaps. Sweeney's beanie was the violet of the bishop, Gleason's the cardinal's red. The deacon was proclaiming the Gospel.

Father Alec was nervous. Bill Kendall had requested that the young priest deliver the homily. Archbishop Sweeney hadn't been thrilled. That would normally have been his domain. Though Father Alec didn't like the idea of stepping on his superior's toes, and he was nervous at the prospect of addressing this daunting group, he wanted the chance to speak at the funeral of the man he had come to know and respect. Father Alec was keeping his promise.

The time came for Father Alec to mount the steps of the ambo, the elevated marble pulpit on the right side of the altar. The ambo's marble had come from the same quarry as the marble for Michelangelo's *David*. At the bottom of the curved staircase leading up to the speaking platform were two statues, St. Francis de Sales and St. Cyril of Alexandria, the patron saints of wisdom and brevity, respectively. His hands briefly touched the feet of both saints as he began his climb. Please God, let me do this right.

He looked out at the sea of faces. Some of them stared expectantly at him, others were looking around at the marvels of the cathedral, some fiddled with hemlines and handkerchiefs in breast pockets. He knew that some—in fact most—of his audience was not Catholic. But one of his goals this morning was to have as many as possible leaving the cathedral wishing they were.

Father Alec swallowed and began.

"Many of you here this morning make history. Some of you report it. All of you, for one reason or another, have chosen to come here today to pay your respects to Bill Kendall, a man who made his living telling the public what went on in the world each day. Explaining today tomorrow's history."

They were listening.

"So I thought it would be appropriate to begin with a short history lesson. And I do promise to keep it short."

Many in the audience smiled. He could feel them being pulled in.

"We sit here today in a magnificent setting. The Cathedral Basilica of the Sacred Heart. Majestic, awe-inspiring, a tribute to man's imagination and his ability to implement and execute his ideas, and even his dreams.

"What most people *don't* know is that cathedrals were built to house a treasure. The French cathedral in Chartres was built after Charles II presented that tiny town with the tunic worn by the Blessed Virgin at the Annunciation. The cathedral was built to house that tunic, that treasure. The Cathedral of Notre Dame holds a nail from the True Cross.

"But the Cathedral of the Sacred Heart is a modern cathedral; it was not built to hold any particular relic. This cathedral was built to commemorate the treasure of the immigrant spirit here in Newark. The Irish and English and Polish and Italians and Germans came here to Newark, all in search of a better life. They worked hard and prayed hard, and their hard-earned money was earnestly donated to build this structure. The altars in the semi-

circle behind this sanctuary stand in testimony to Newark's immigrants. Saints Patrick and David and Lucy Filipini and
Boniface: the saints of the old countries standing benevolent guard
in the cathedral of the new. The treasure of the hopes and dreams
of the people of Newark is the treasure of the Cathedral of the
Sacred Heart."

Archbishop Sweeney sat a little taller on his throne. Father
Alec's hands gripped the marble pulpit tightly and went on. He
knew that this would be the place he would most likely lose them.
Up to this point they had followed him, comfortable with facts.

"Most of us believe that we are given life for a purpose. Whatever our faith, we believe that we are here to *do* something with
our lives. I would like all of us to imagine that, in a way, we are
all meant to build a cathedral with our lives, to find our treasure
and build a beautiful cathedral to keep it safe." Father Alec
paused and looked out at his audience.

"What was Bill Kendall's cathedral like?"

He stopped and looked directly out to the front pew and into
the eyes of Louise Kendall. He waited for her to realize that he
would be speaking directly to her. Her eyes engaged his.

"God gave Bill 17,233 days to build the cathedral of his life.
We watched as Bill Kendall reported triumphs and tragedies, told
the stories of heroes and villains, covered space shots, stock market ups and downs, coronations, inaugurations, wars, other people's lives and deaths. He shed light on the events of the world
as we know it. And for many of us, that was the Bill Kendall
most of us knew.

"You didn't have to know Bill long, however, to discover the
treasure of his cathedral, what meant the most to him, what sat
at the heart of the cathedral of his life.

"For Bill, his son William was his greatest treasure."

The priest saw Louise take William's hand.

"Bill was a loving and devoted father to William and was
known to have remarked on more than one occasion that, he had
gotten much more from his son, than he had given. Bill told a
friend that because of William, he had really learned how to pray

and he was grateful for that. But Bill, the realist, knew that not everything can be solved by prayer alone. He became very active in fund-raising and, through his efforts, there are more group homes for 'special' people, more places for them to have dignity and independent lives. Bill Kendall tried to make a difference. He illuminated the need for people to do something to try to make the world a better place, a place closer to God."

Father Alec couldn't, wouldn't, use the word suicide in the homily, but he had to address it. Everyone here knew the anchorman had killed himself. There could be no getting around it. He caught sight of Eliza Blake. Her eyes were filled, the corners of her mouth turned downward.

"What some considered problems, Bill Kendall counted as challenges. And that's why, gathered here in this holy place, so many of us feel lost, bewildered at the events of the past week.

"I think it is fair to say that many of us have felt desperate at some point in our lives. We've felt alone. Far and removed from everyone, even God. This is where belief in God can help us through, help us make our peace with what is, help us accept and go on.

"Did Bill Kendall get the chance to finish his cathedral? I think the answer must be yes. Bill Kendall now stands before Christ in heaven—Christ his Savior, who loved Bill every minute of every one of those 17,233 days. He loved him, most of all, at the last moment of that last day. Bill's final legacy to us may be in shaking us, reaching us, reminding us by his startling death that, whether we make history, or report it, all of us still have a chance, still have some time to build cathedrals of our own."

✣ Chapter 29

An earnest expression fixed on his face, Pete Carlson listened as the young priest rambled on. He hated to hear this babble about how wonderful Bill Kendall was. It only made things harder for him, more for him to live up to.

The fact that Eliza's thigh was brushing his as they sat next to each other in the packed pew was the only pleasant part of this whole spectacle. He could feel the warmth of her leg through her silken dress and his fine wool slacks. He was drawn to her at the same time he was threatened by her.

He saw Mack McBride take Eliza's hand. It annoyed the hell out of him.

From the corner of his eye, he observed the somber faces around him. He had arranged his expression accordingly. It was difficult to feign sorrow, when he was actually pleased. It was even more difficult to keep his mouth shut as everyone had been speculating about why Bill had taken his own life. He chose to keep what he knew to himself, at least for the time being.

Like any newsman, Pete had his sources. He knew why Bill Kendall had wanted to die.

❦ Chapter 30

Range Bullock watched as the gray casket slid into the back of the hearse.

He'd never thought it would end like this. In all the time he and Bill had spent together, Range had never once imagined that his friend was the kind of man who could take his own life.

How close Bill had come to death a few years before! Bill had barely pulled through after that accident they'd had while doing some stories in Eastern Europe.

Range remembered waiting in the pathetic hospital in Bucharest, worrying that he'd be shipping his best friend's body home. He'd tried to prepare himself psychologically as Bill fought for life.

This time there had been no such mental preparation. No warning.

The hearse door snapped shut and Range turned to join the limousine already carrying Louise and William. He wanted to accompany the body at least to the airport. He wished he could go all the way to Nebraska with Bill, but Yelena had insisted that Range stay and produce the *KEY Evening Headlines*.

Bill would have understood.

❧ Chapter 31

Just as Nate Heller had predicted, Joy Wingard, the candidate's wife, appeared in the evening news reports of the funeral of Bill Kendall. Nate and Win had been pleased, Win calling from his Senate office just after the story aired.

"Thanks a lot for going today, Joy. I know you weren't particularly keen on the idea. But your presence there was good exposure for us. You looked great, by the way. I'd also like to think that those journalists noticed you paying your respects. That can't hurt in the cause of having them on our side."

"I'm glad I went," Joy responded quietly. "But don't think those newspeople could be swayed merely by the candidate's wife going to the funeral of one of their own. I'm afraid they are a bit too cynical for that."

"You're probably right. Still, I'm glad you were there. I caught the evening news. That was quite an event."

"Oh, Win, it was so sad," sighed Joy, desperate to let out the emotions of the morning. Bill's son had looked so lost and bewildered. Joy had ached to go over to the boy.

"I'm sure it was. Joy, I have another call I have to take. I have a few things to wrap up here, I'll be home around ten." He was eager to get off the phone.

That's right, Win. Just tune it out. Don't let anything in that might hurt a little. You have to give the guy credit, Joy thought as she poured herself a drink. He protects himself. He knows what works for Haines Wingard.

The depression that followed the last miscarriage had been a time of deep introspection. Joy had raked herself over the burning emotional coals. Though it had been an excruciating journey, she had analyzed her life, her motivations and what had led her to that point. She came to realize consciously what she had done and why she had done it.

When she selected Haines Wingard as her husband, Joy had expected that they would have a true partnership. Though she had known going in that Win was focused on his political aspirations, Joy had thought that they'd have a private life as well. Years of repeated excuses, canceled personal plans, and promises made and then broken had left Joy feeling betrayed and alone.

She had gone to Win, telling him that she was unhappy and dissatisfied with the marriage, that she felt a lack of emotional closeness between them. He had looked at her, politely concerned. "Look, you've just had a miscarriage. Give it some time. When you get over the mis, you'll feel better about us," was his answer.

Joy had immersed herself in charity work and community projects. She spent long hours wandering through Washington's National Gallery of Art, soothed by the beauty and wonder she found there. Eventually, she did begin to feel better about life. Her thoughts were not always mired in the sadness of losing the baby. She began to feel hopeful about the future. But she still felt estranged from Win. Equally frustrating, Win did not acknowledge her remoteness.

Then she met Bill Kendall.

She went to the back of her closet and pulled out a well-used leather suitcase. From an elasticized compartment inside, she took out her journal, opened it and wrote down her feelings. Then, she braced herself to read Bill's last letter again. The one that had arrived two days after he died.

Joy shivered. She undressed and took a warm robe and wrapped it around herself. She walked over to the bedside table where her handbag rested. She rummaged through it until she found Bill's Mass card. She held it, thinking of the funeral. It had been incredibly moving in that place of the Sacred Heart. She wondered how the Cathedral had been selected for Bill's final ceremony. Had it meant something special to him? He had never mentioned it to her. They hadn't talked much about religion in their hours together. She concentrated, trying to think back and remember anything he had said about religion or God.

She lay curled on her side on the ivory silk bedspread thinking of Bill, haunted by his suicide. She knew he had been hurt by their breakup. But what else could she have done? It was just too dangerous to continue when her every move was being constantly watched. And Bill himself was not exactly low profile. There had been no choice. Perhaps she and Win had long since lost their emotional connection, but she was not going to blow his chances for the presidency. Or, for that matter, her chance to be first lady. She didn't love politics, but being the wife of the president of the United States was not something to which many women would say no.

Joy heard the front door close. Moments later, Win was in the bedroom. She answered his questions about who was at the funeral and responded with queries of her own regarding the progress of the day and its effect on the campaign. Win was unaware of her eyes watching him closely as he undressed, so engrossed was he in his recap of the vote on the floor of the Senate. He would remember who had backed his bill and who hadn't come through for him. But the main thing was, the bill had passed and Senator Haines Wingard had gotten a lot of positive media exposure today.

"And then you showed up in the funeral reports tonight. It was a good day for the Wingard team."

Win got into bed and immediately put his arms around her, burying his head between her breasts. She stroked his precisely barbered hair. As his mouth covered her nipple, Joy felt a tightening in her throat. She braced herself for what she knew the next few minutes would bring.

Chapter 32

The morning sun forced him to squint to see the monitor.

There she was, talking to him again.

She was standing with a microphone in her hand in front of a building with steps leading up to it.

The homeless man moved a little closer.

Yes. He recognized that building. But it had no knocker.

Why was Eliza Blake telling him to go there? Puzzled, he edged closer still.

Now, Eliza was talking to a man who sat in some sort of office. He concentrated on the man's face.

Oh. That was it. Eliza told him: "Go and watch this man."

Chapter 33

"Good piece on suicide this morning, Eliza."

The day after the funeral, Eliza was summoned to the Fishbowl. Range Bullock sat behind his cluttered desk. Eliza noted that the producer looked beat. The lines around his eyes were deeper, the skin was paler against his red hair.

Range got right to the point.

"Eliza, the decision's been made that you will take over Bill's Presidential Personality Profiles assignment. As you know, these longer pieces are time intensive. I think it would be too much to expect Pete to work on the Triple Ps as he is getting used to the anchor job. At the morning meeting, I made my case for handing the reins over to you. The Front Row gave its stamp of approval."

Eliza's heart pounded. This was especially gratifying after the *Mole* mess! Maybe Mack was right. People weren't paying any attention. She anticipated the executive producer's next words.

"So you'll be a regular contributor on the *KEY Evening Headlines* . . . at least through to the election. Your star is on the rise, Eliza. I can't tell you how pleased I am to have you with us!"

"Range, thank you, thank you very much. It's a terrific assignment and I promise I'll give it my best shot. I only wish that what's led up to it hadn't happened."

"Me, too. But don't let Bill's death diminish your satisfaction. Bill would be happy for you."

Eliza smiled. Range's words rang true.

Bill's takeout pieces got four to five minutes each week. The exposure would be wonderful. Pete Carlson was not going to like this.

Range was going on. "Your first Triple P will be on Haines Wingard. He'll be a good way to break in since most of the shooting can be done right here in town as he campaigns here next week. With all the shooting here, there shouldn't be any conflict with your *KEY to America* duties. Of course, the future stories will require that you travel, but the field producers will do most of the legwork and advance shooting before you get there. So what I'm telling you is, this assignment does not mean that your *America* work is lessened. We're expecting you to do it all."

Eliza smiled. "I get it. I get it." All the hard work would be worth it. It occurred to her immediately that, unfortunately, it would mean more time away from Janie. Part of her believed that it was good for Janie to see a mother who was accomplished and self-sufficient. Another part prayed that the child wouldn't be hurt by her absences.

Range was continuing. "Wingard is planning to spend a lot of time and money here. New York has so much to offer peoplewise, issuewise and videowise, you'll be sure to get a good story. Let me put it to you this way—if you don't come up with a winner, you're going to look like crap."

"Tell me something I don't know, Range."

Bullock cracked a weak smile. "Eliza, level with me. Are you sure that you're up to this? We all have been under a lot of pressure with Bill's death. You've had the extra pounding of that *Mole* article."

"Surely, Range, you don't believe everything you read in the papers." Eliza tried to joke but it sounded hollow to her ears. "I don't know," she continued. "Do you think I should clear it up?"

"What do you mean?" he said.

"I'm not quite sure," Eliza mused out loud. "Maybe I should talk about it right on the show in the morning. Air the whole thing out."

Range shook his head. "Eliza, I think you're making too much of this. Let's ride it out for a while and see how it goes." He peered over his bifocals. "But promise me, if it gets to be too much, you'll let me know."

"I promise."

Range nodded. "Go see Jean. She'll give you Bill's political notes. As usual, Bill's work was well researched. God, that guy did his homework. True pro. Never lay back and let it come to him. As big as he got, he never let anyone down as far as I could see. He kept his edge." The corners of Range's mouth turned down. Eliza read the melancholy in his eyes.

"I appreciate this, Range."

"Go do what you have to do." Abruptly, he swiveled around to his computer terminal.

Eliza wasted no time in getting to Jean and explaining what she was after.

"Life sure does go on around here, doesn't it?" The secretary shook her head. Opening her desk drawer, she pulled out a gray diskette. "Range told me to expect you. I've been downloading Bill's files for you. This has the ones regarding the campaign."

Jean slowly rubbed the diskette, then handed it to Eliza. "I hope this has everything you need."

Eliza reached out and touched the secretary's arm. "I'm so sorry about everything, Jean. If there is anything I can do for you, will you please let me know?"

Jean nodded, unable to speak and busied herself with the papers on her desk. She didn't like Pete Carlson taking Bill's anchor chair and she didn't like Eliza Blake taking Bill's confidential notes. It was an invasion of his privacy, leaving his personal thoughts and observations exposed for Eliza to read and interpret. Bill made those notes for his own use, not Eliza's. He had talked of writing a book someday. His story.

But there were those other files on Bill's computer, files Jean couldn't access. They were password-protected. She felt somewhat miffed that Bill hadn't entrusted his secret password to her.

The secretary watched resentfully as Eliza left the office. Jean didn't like the new order of things around *KEY News*. Her king was dead.

✠ Chapter 34

If only they were all that easy. Father Alec smiled at the elderly couple who had stopped him to ask about the history of the west rose window. It was easy to recite facts, pure and simple.

The deep shades of the window were shown to their best advantage in the last afternoon light. The window was called "The Coming of Christ," and it was thirty-two feet in diameter. It always reminded him of the kaleidoscope he used to play with as a kid. The kaleidoscope had given him hours of enjoyment, often becoming his focus as he tried to block out the sounds of his parents fighting about money again and again. He would go up to the room he shared with his older brother, sit on the floor in the corner and hold the kaleidoscope toward the glaring ceiling light fixture. Deep, rich colors and unfailing symmetry. Beauty and order. All was right with the world.

Twenty-five years later, the rose windows in the cathedral served for Father Alec the same function as that old five-and-ten-cent-store kaleidoscope. When he was troubled or discouraged, he could sit in the deep quiet of the cathedral and study the three rose windows. He had never admitted to anyone that sometimes, when prayer failed, his thirty-two-foot kaleidoscope could do the job of calming and soothing.

Beneath the massive west window there were smaller windows depicting the likenesses of seven saints. John Chrysostom, the preacher with the golden mouth who had ended up a martyr. Monica, the model of Christian motherhood. John Bosco, the founder of the Salesian order. Lawrence, a martyr. Anastasia, another martyr, and Agatha, whose excruciating destiny was to have both breasts lopped off. Agatha was also a martyr. The seventh saint was Nicholas, who died in ecstatic joy, but alas a pious thief had cut off dead Nicholas's arms.

The distinguished white-haired man in his Burberry jacket and his carefully coifed wife listened politely as Father Alec recited what he knew about the windows. He sensed they wanted to ask him something.

"Is there anything else you'd like to know about the cathedral?"

The silver-haired woman cleared her throat nervously. "Were you here for Bill Kendall's funeral yesterday?"

Before the priest could answer, the husband hurried on. "We've lived in New Jersey all our lives, in Ridgewood, just about twenty miles north of here. Until the Pope came, we had no idea this place existed. And then last night we saw the report on the funeral here. We've been watching *KEY News* for years . . . Bill Kendall was familiar, almost a friend. Heck, since the kids left, Margaret and I have watched him while having our cocktails just about every night. We just couldn't believe what happened. Just goes to show you never know what is going on in someone's life."

"No, you never do," the priest agreed.

"Now that Frank is retired, and we are always looking for things to do, I said to him this morning, 'Why don't we drive down and see the cathedral?' And here we are." Margaret paused and looked around the massive church, her mouth slightly opened. Father Alec noticed the good false teeth.

"Well, we're glad to have you here. If there is anything I can help you with, please ask."

The young priest made his way around the cavernous, empty chamber and stepped into the pew in front of the small altar at the side of the church. He knelt and bowed his head. If someone had been sitting behind him, they would have noticed his shoulders rise and fall as he heaved a large sigh. Father Alec was thinking about the day he had met Bill Kendall.

Less than two months ago. Sitting just about here, in front of the thirteenth station. The priest had noticed a man dressed in jeans and a navy ski jacket. The man stared up at the vaulted ceiling, an anguished look on his face.

Father Alec had seen many torn faces in his few short years as a priest. Anonymous faces. This time the face had a name and the priest knew it. As he approached the man sitting alone in the pew, Father Alec hoped that his presentation would be just as it always was when he reached out to someone in pain.

"Is everything all right?"

At first, Bill Kendall had just stared at him. Father Alec recognized the look. It said, Yes, I do want to talk, desperately. But the look also asked, Can I trust you?

Instinct told the priest not to say anything. Give the man time to size me up. It was uncanny how someone in pain could make gut decisions very quickly. Moments passed.

"Father, I have AIDS."

✣ Chapter 35

"That *KEY News* crew is sticking to us like glue. I hope they don't catch me blowing lunch."

In two hours Haines Wingard had devoured fried chicken, yellow and white rice and fried bananas in the South Bronx, spaghetti with garlic and oil and a cannoli at Angelo's in Little Italy, and a hot dog followed by a large kosher pickle at the legendary Katz's Delicatessen. Now Senator Wingard and his campaign manager made their way by car over the Brooklyn Bridge.

"Look, boss, you know the drill as well as I do. Campaigning in New York City requires ethnically and demographically balanced photo ops. Eating the local chow goes with the territory. As for the TV crew, I want them to catch you smacking your lips over every spicy mouthful. I hear KEY is working on a big piece featuring you, scheduled to run the day after the primary. We want you to look good."

"Who's doing the story?"

"Eliza Blake."

New York . . . the city of contrasts. Only forty blocks separated the nation's poorest (South Bronx) and the wealthiest (Upper East Side) congressional districts. New Yorkers themselves took pride in being a tough audience. They had opinions on everything, which they didn't hesitate to express. Often, those opinions were expressed right to the candidate's face at various campaign rallies and appearances. Candidates had to stay on their toes.

So, as the Wingard entourage made its way that balmy May afternoon toward McKinley Junior High School in the heavily ethnic middle-class section of Brooklyn known as Bay Ridge, the candidate and his manager were on their guard even more than usual. New York was a very complicated playing field of ethnic, racial and political considerations. The two men wanted to finesse the game.

"How you handle New York will be viewed as how well you'll handle the country. You know, like the song says, 'If you can make it there . . .' If you bomb here it will be tough to get over."

Winning the primary had been only the first step.

Win unsuccessfully suppressed a burp. "Okay, let's go over this next stop quickly."

"Drugs—Q and A with junior high school students. It's been done and done and done. I know. Yet I'll bet you it makes all the New York local stations and at least two of the network shows tonight."

Heller lit a cigarette, took a deep drag and exhaled out the half-opened window before continuing.

"Remember, Win, keep it general. If you have to refer to a specific drug, use crack as the example. Crack scares parents the most and, after all, they are the ones who will be doing the voting for the hero who is going to make the nightmare go away. If some kid asks you about booze, speak about how troubled you are by the increase in teenage drinking. Then get off the subject. Liquor is not illegal and most of the mommies and daddies want it to stay that way."

Win smiled, listening as he checked his teeth in the mirror fastened to the headrest in front of him.

"Keep your answers short. The TV people are all looking for soundbites. So respond in statements of about ten or fifteen seconds that sum it all up. And be prepared to fill in if there are any lulls in the questioning by the kids. Here are some questions you can turn around and ask the students if they run out of questions to ask you."

Nate handed Win several index cards. The candidate perused them. How many kids do you know who use drugs? Does anyone know anyone who was killed by drug use? What suggestions do any of you have on what to do about drugs? Senator Wingard slipped the cards into his jacket pocket.

"I know it by heart, but let's go over it again. I favor drug education starting in kindergarten, an end to foreign aid for governments that refuse to cooperate in attempts to stop drug smuggling, and I'd increase support to the DEA, coast guard and customs service. Do I or do I not favor immediate treatment for any addict seeking it?"

"You do. Yes, it's extremely costly and the federal government is in tough economic shape. But you believe that these people need help."

The senator smiled. "Thanks for clarifying for me what I believe."

"Don't mention it," returned Nate as he flipped his half-smoked cigarette out the window.

"I'm also against pollution, aren't I? When are you going to give those things up?"

"Yeah, yeah. I know. Don't worry about me. I'll stop after you're in the White House."

The car pulled up in front of McKinley Junior High. Officials and school personnel were standing in front, waiting to greet the candidate. Wingard turned to Heller. "Thank God we've got Pete Carlson on our side."

"It *is* helpful, isn't it?" smirked Heller. "It's so nice to have our own highly placed source in the *KEY News* ranks. That Yelena Gregory keeps blabbing all sorts of interesting tidbits to Pete. But I'll tell you one thing, boss. We're going to have to provide for Pete after we win, he says. He's making himself sick by sleeping with her. He doesn't know how much more he can take." Nate chuckled.

"Remember, think soundbites," hissed Nate as a beaming Senator Wingard stepped out of the car and extended his hands toward the well-wishers milling on the sidewalk.

✣ Chapter 36

His face almost purple with rage, Pete Carlson burst into Yelena Gregory's office.

"What the hell is going on?" he demanded. "I should be doing the Presidential Personality Profiles. Not Eliza Blake!"

Yelena rose from her desk. "I've been expecting you," she said quietly, as she walked to the office door. "Hold my calls," she said to the uncomfortable receptionist stationed outside the office. Closing the door softly, she hissed at him, "Don't ever do that again!"

It was not the reaction Pete had expected from her. He began to sputter, but Yelena held up her hand to stop him.

"Don't even start with me. I go to bat for you as much as I can, but there are negative vibes about you around this place, Pete. I didn't make them, *you* did."

"But this is such an insult! Bill always did the Triple Ps, along with his anchor duties," he implored.

Yelena was unmoved. "Why don't you just act like you go along with the official explanation? That it's too much to ask you to do the presidential candidate takeouts while you're getting used to anchoring."

"But everyone knows that I should be able to fit both in. Bill did it. Now Eliza's doing it, combining her morning anchoring with the responsibility of working on the Triple Ps."

Yelena took a sip of her herbal tea while she contemplated his words. Pete was right. He should be able to handle both jobs. But Range had been adamant at the morning meeting. He wanted Eliza Blake reporting on the *Evening Headlines*. Yelena could have overruled him, but she didn't. She, too, felt that the *Evening Headlines* would benefit from Eliza's input.

Pete took Yelena's silence as an indictment. "So, you don't think I can *handle* it, do you?"

"That's not what I said, dear."

"You didn't have to."

He quickly turned to leave, but Yelena held out a hand to stop him. "Pete, please, wait."

As an executive she was unmoved by Pete's rantings. But as a woman she didn't want to lose the man who made her feel desirable for the first time in her life.

Pete read Yelena's ambivalent expression.

I guess I'll just have to sleep with her more, he thought. And get more dirt on Eliza Blake while I'm at it.

✖ Chapter 37

"You made it, thank God. I didn't know how much longer I could hold this seat."

Eliza slid into the metal and plastic chair next to Mary Cate Ryan.

"Thanks, M.C. I appreciate it. What's the deal? This wasn't on the schedule yesterday."

"Yeah, I know. The assignment desk got a call from Wingard's people after midnight. Apparently Wingard wants to make some AIDS-related point. Could be interesting. So far all any of the candidates have done is tsk, tsk and wear little red ribbons in their lapels."

The din subsided as Nate Heller walked up to the podium in the Miracle House conference room.

"Ladies and gentlemen, thank you for coming, especially on

such short notice. Senator Wingard will make a short statement after which he will take your questions."

Mary Cate discreetly elbowed Eliza as Haines Wingard strode to his position at the front of the room. Without turning her head toward her partner, she muttered, "Hunk, big time."

Eliza half smiled in response. She wasn't sure what she thought of the candidate. Everything she had seen and read about him was so politically correct, so perfect. There hadn't been anything that she had found in her research that she felt gave her any real insight into the man. No personal stories about how he had coped with a hardship or setback. Nothing so far that had given Eliza a gut feeling about the man himself. She hoped she'd be able to get something beyond the surface when she interviewed him.

"Members of the press, this is a condom." Haines Wingard stood in his $1,300 navy pinstriped Brooks Brothers suit, held up a small blue square packet, opened it and displayed its contents. Cameras whirled and clicked and the audience twittered nervously.

Eliza leaned over to Mary Cate and whispered, "Guess who's going to lead everyone's show tonight."

"Now that I have your attention, many of you have already guessed my reason for calling you here this morning. Acquired immune deficiency syndrome. AIDS. It's spreading at an astounding rate in the United States and the rest of the world. Projections of worldwide AIDS cases at the start of the new millennium are estimated to be somewhere between 38 and 110 million. *Thirty-eight to 110 million!*"

The audience was quiet.

"It's not a waste of time to go over the basic facts. AIDS is caused by a virus. The human immunodeficiency virus—HIV. But unlike a cold virus or a flu virus, HIV doesn't die after it has done its damage. HIV makes itself at home, combining its genetic material with the body's cells. The HIV uses those cells to make copies of itself, our cells becoming tiny virus factories."

Wingard looked around the room, his eyes daring anyone not

to pay attention to what he was saying. He took a drink of water before continuing.

"HIV primarily attacks T cells, the critical part of the body's immune system. Once T cells are destroyed, the body's delicately balanced immune system is upset and can't protect itself against disease. The result is an excruciatingly painful death.

"We've heard ad infinitum that the main methods of transmission are unprotected sex, shared needles or syringes and contaminated blood transfusions. Blood screening has been implemented to test for HIV. But there are a few other points worth noting.

"Surveys have found that the average age for a girl in the United States of America to have sexual intercourse for the first time is sixteen. The average age for a boy is fifteen and a half. It is also estimated that two and a half million teenagers are infected with sexually transmitted diseases each year."

Eliza thought of Janie, thankful that her daughter was so young. She hated these scary stats.

"Studies have also shown that sixty percent of American high school seniors have used illegal drugs. Some of those drugs are injected."

Wingard paused to let his words sink in.

"We needn't be rocket scientists, ladies and gentlemen, to figure it out. We have got to do something. Individually, like the people here at Miracle House who help those infected with AIDS and their families get through the most difficult of times. And we have to do something, collectively, as a nation. That's why today I am announcing the formation of the AIDS Parade for Dollars.

"The AIDS Parade for Dollars is modeled after the March of Dimes, which Franklin Roosevelt established in 1938 to combat the scourge of that day—polio.

"Though just pulling out of the Depression and immersed in the effort of the Second World War, Americans sent what they could. Many times a quarter or a dime. But the dimes marching to the White House added up. Eventually $675 million was collected.

Those dimes paid for the research that led to the Salk and Sabin polio vaccines in the 1950s. Polio has been virtually eliminated.

"We have to make this a national priority. If every man, woman and child donated just one dollar, we'd have over 250 million dollars, and be that much closer to finding a way to rid ourselves of this terrifying plague.

"When I get to the White House, I will do all I can to increase federal funding for AIDS research. But we have no time to waste. Scientists continue their search for a vaccine, but researchers agree that developing a vaccine is much tougher than originally thought. We must get busy on it today. Each of us can make a difference."

Wingard looked out at the news crowd. "I might add that all of you are in particularly strong places to make impacts. I hope you will use your positions to do some good. Any questions?"

"What will be the mechanism for the collection of donations?" asked the Associated Press reporter.

"At this point, a simple mailing address, which will be handed out at the end of this news conference."

"Senator, why are you coming out for this particular cause at this particular time?"

Eliza thought she detected a trace of annoyance in Wingard's face as he glanced down at the podium and fiddled with the edge of his note paper. "Because as I've traveled this country, I've been very moved by some very personal stories of individuals with AIDS and the pain and suffering it is causing them, their families and all those who love them. We are seeing AIDS babies, the offspring of AIDS-infected mothers and fathers. These babies lose their parents and then face the prospect of dying of AIDS themselves. The statistics spotlight the potential magnitude of this thing. The teenage stats in particular are frightening. We've already had too many lives cut short. I don't want to see any more lost promise in America.

"We can't stand by and assume that the government is going to make it go away. We've got to take matters into our own hands, too. We've got to do *our* part. AIDS is pressing. AIDS is urgent. Finding a cure must be a national priority."

The questions went on for a while. After Senator Wingard left the podium, aides distributed the press releases with the Washington, D.C., post office box address for the AIDS Parade for Dollars donations.

"Smart or stupid?" asked Mary Cate as she and Eliza rode back to the studio.

"I say smart. It's an important issue. Even those who are disgusted by the subject are realizing that it isn't going away and they can't keep their heads in the sand."

"But he's already out in front. Why risk the controversy?"

"Think about it. At this point, it really isn't all that controversial. Wingard comes out and tries to do something constructive about a horrible disease. Who is going to fault him for that? Actually, it's a pretty damn smart thing to do. He looks like a leader, willing to take up something that no one has had the guts to really take on before."

"Yeah, you're right. Notice the FDR tie-in?"

"Yup. I can see the stories tonight. Wingard talking about the AIDS Parade for Dollars, followed by a little video history lesson on Roosevelt and the March of Dimes. The very presidential connection is made to the viewing audience. Masterstroke."

❧ Chapter 38

Eliza prepared for Senator Haines Wingard's interview, knowing that she would be questioning a sure candidate for the presidency.

She sat at her computer terminal in her *KEY to America* office. Bill Kendall's diskette was inserted into the machine. She wanted to find something that she might be able to use to elicit an emotional response from Wingard, but Bill's notes were not providing what Eliza needed.

She searched the computer screen reading what Bill had written.

Aside from politics, Wingard's passion runs to sports . . . He is a crazed Michigan State basketball fan, and tries to attend as many games as possible each season. Summer vacations are spent at this family's home on Lake Michigan, where sailing and golf are his favorite pastimes.

While Joy has tried to get him interested in subtler theater and art, Wingard prefers popular show tunes and Grandma Moses paintings. (Not to put down Grandma.)

In fact, most of the Wingards' free time (what little there is of it) does not appear to be spent together.

Childless, after several miscarriages, the couple's main focus has been Wingard's career. Joy attends all obligatory events, conducting herself appropriately, eyes on the candidate, nodding at the right times, applauding, smiling, etc. A certain lack of spontaneity and enthusiasm detected at times.

Just great. I'll ask him, "Senator, what's the deal between you and your wife?" That should really get him to open up, thought Eliza.

Ask about the mole.

Eliza caught her breath. The mole? What did Bill mean by that?

Bill had gone on to list congressional bills that Wingard had been unsuccessful in getting passed. The list was short.

The guy was a dream candidate. There didn't seem to be anything to get him on. No miscalculations, no misspeaks, no apparent skeletons.

Eliza switched off the computer, uncrossed her long legs, stood and stretched. Wingard was scheduled to come to KEY this afternoon. Rarely had she been this anxious about an interview. She so wanted to get this right, to have her first Triple P be a standout. She knew she was being watched and it was important to show she was up to the job.

She had decided to focus first on Wingard's history, the theory being that you can tell a lot about a person by what he has been through and how he has responded. Not that people who had it relatively easy couldn't accomplish great things, but it seemed to Eliza that adversity was a great motivator.

She would ask about the childlessness.

Then Eliza thought she would concentrate on Wingard's hopes and aspirations. Her colleagues were already grilling him well on the issues and following his every campaign utterance. Eliza enjoyed discussing the less concrete. She would, to a large degree, take her cues from the candidate, picking up on what he expressed as most important to him, pulling out more when she could.

She had her questions typed on index cards which she took with her into the makeup room. She wanted to go over them one more time before the candidate arrived. Lucille was waiting for her and complimented Eliza on her cream-colored suit, which was elegant in its simplicity. Eliza wore it well, her tall, willowy frame a designer's dream. Eliza sat patiently as Lucille painted the canvas of Eliza's face. Her wide-set blue eyes were fringed with dark thick lashes. Her straight, delicate nose was already sprinkled with a few freckles, the result of time spent with Janie in the park in the spring sun. Her mouth was full enough that Lucille did not have to pencil it larger.

When Lucille finished with the blush, lipstick and eye pencil, Eliza felt even better prepared to take on Senator Wingard. She looked good and she knew it.

Eliza had decided to meet Wingard in the KEY lobby, greeting him as he arrived. She was well aware that some correspondents might play the head game of showing up after the interviewee, flexing some mental muscle by keeping the subject waiting. Eliza felt that didn't play. It could create adversarial tension right away. Instead, Eliza had found the old adage to be true. When she could, she used honey.

Wingard's black limousine pulled up in front of the broadcast center. Secret Service agents were in place on the sidewalk and inside the lobby. One agent opened the car door and out popped the balding head of Nate Heller followed closely by the senator.

Presence. He's got it, Eliza thought, observing the usually unimpressed KEY workers clustered in the lobby craning for a look at the handsome candidate. She inhaled as she walked over to the heavy revolving door. Wingard pushed through, his spare hand buttoning his jacket.

"Eliza! It's great to see you. I saw you in the audience at Miracle House the other morning."

She extended her right hand and the senator shook it firmly, his white teeth flashing in a disarming smile.

"Yes, and the time before that was when you came on our show the morning after you won the New Hampshire primary. Things have certainly been going your way, haven't they?"

Wingard nodded with just the right touch of humility in his face. He gestured to his campaign manager. "You remember Nate Heller."

"Yes," said Eliza, smiling and shaking Nate's hand. "We met in New Hampshire."

As they walked, Eliza proceeded to explain that the taping would be done in the interview room. The room would look to viewers to be a cozy, well-stocked library, but was in fact a large closet with two chairs and fake wooden bookshelves full of discarded books. Camera angles could do amazing things.

Nate stood wedged in the corner of the tiny room and watched Win and Eliza as they sat and the soundman clipped tiny microphones to their suit jackets. Eliza glanced at her index cards. Wingard got a quick powder and spray from Lucille.

They began.

"As the saying goes, Senator, tell me about your childhood."

"Well, Eliza, as you already know, I was born and raised in

Michigan. My family was financially secure and I've come to realize that I had many advantages. Advantages that I took for granted as a kid."

"What kinds of advantages?"

Win didn't have to stop to consider. He reeled off his answer. "Unlike so many kids growing up in America today, not only did I have the necessities of life, a place to live, enough to eat, clothes to wear, but my parents were able to afford things like vacations, educational travel, entertainment, private music lessons, things that I would like all American children to have."

"Surely, no one is going to disagree with you on that." Eliza's voice softened. "Senator, you and Mrs. Wingard have been unable to have a child of your own. How would you say that has affected your outlook?"

"You know, Eliza, it really hasn't been that big a deal. Yes, we wanted children of our own. But Joy and I have accepted the fact that it's not to be. I choose to use the energy that would have been given to a child to further the cause of children in our country. I want American children to have every possible advantage."

An alarm went off in Eliza's head. Not a big deal? That didn't make sense. She knew from a series on infertility that she had worked on that not being able to have children of your own if you really wanted them was extremely painful for men as well as women. It made sense that it would hurt. A lot. Psychologists said the loss of the idea of having a biological baby had to be mourned, like a death. That's what it was, a death of a dream. People who had been through it said it caused pain for years. They went on, but they never got over it completely. Not that big a deal?

"Senator Wingard," Eliza continued, "people say they are tired of business as usual in Washington, fed up with lawyers-turned-politicians running this country. You, sir, are a graduate of Yale Law School and have practiced for many years. How would you respond to people who say, 'Enough with the lawyers, let's get someone in the White House who has some real life experience?' "

Wingard's eyes twinkled.

"I don't know, Eliza, but I'd say going through the whole law school process is pretty good preparation for life. I've often felt that if I could make it through the intense and grueling preparation for the bar, I could make it through anything—even"— he smiled broadly—"a presidential race."

❧ Chapter 39

"Nice job." Range liked the Wingard piece.

The executive producer, Eliza, Pete Carlson and Yelena Gregory sat in the Fishbowl and viewed the Triple P one more time before air.

"It's fairly and insightfully done," offered Yelena. "Good work." She looked over at Pete for his reaction.

Pete just nodded.

Range checked the broadcast lineup on his computer screen. "There's time for Pete to ask you two questions after the piece. You and he work that out. Thirty seconds worth."

Eliza and Pete left the glass office and walked into the studio. "Any ideas?" asked Pete.

She considered for a moment. "Well, viewers always seem to be interested in the candidate's personal life. Why don't you ask me what Wingard likes to do for fun? But don't ask what the Wingards like to do *together*—there doesn't seem to be much going on in that department."

"Okay, what else?"

"Ask me how the AIDS Parade for Dollars is impacting on the campaign."

"Fine."

Eliza went off to the makeup room at the side of the studio as Pete made his way to the anchor desk where Lucille was waiting for him. After finishing Pete's makeup, she came over to apply Eliza's. The lipstick was matted as the *Evening Headlines* fanfare began.

Eliza watched from the side of the studio as Pete read the top stories of the day. Her piece was scheduled to run after the first commercial break. During the Geritol ad, Eliza climbed the steps to the anchor platform and took her seat beside Pete, careful to tuck the bottom of her pale green blazer beneath her so that the jacket would not appear rumpled to the camera's critical eye.

Pete led to her piece. "Haines Malcolm Wingard is the front runner for his party's nomination for the presidency. Eliza Blake has been following 'Win' Wingard and talked with him this week for our Presidential Personality Profile."

Eliza watched the monitor as her story began. She had three minutes until the camera would come back to the anchor desk. She noticed that Pete wasn't bothering to watch the piece. He was busy scribbling some notes to himself.

The package ran smoothly and she noted with satisfaction that it seemed shorter than three minutes. A sure sign that it was interesting. Three minutes was considered an eternity on the *Evening Headlines*.

"Ten seconds," boomed the stage manager.

Pete was looking down at his notes.

"Five seconds."

Pete looked up into the camera and then at her. "Interesting piece, Eliza. Tell me, what does Haines Wingard like to do when he's not running for president?"

The camera cut to a smiling Eliza. "Well, Pete, 'Win' Wingard *loves* sports. He tries to attend as many basketball games as he can each season at his alma mater Michigan State. He's also an avid golfer, although he told me that lately he's only been able to fit in nine holes here and there. Running for president is taking up just about every waking minute."

"And what about the Wingards as a couple? What do Senator and Mrs. Wingard like to do together?' Pete waited expectantly. Eliza saw a slight smirk on his face, a glint in his eye.

Bastard! He had set her up. Pete was sabotaging her.

She kept a pleasant expression on her face and thought fast. She had to be truthful but what could she say? Bill's notes, Bill's notes. The camera watched her hesitation.

"Joy Wingard is very interested in theater and art, Pete," she began falteringly. "Ah, in fact, Mrs. Wingard is an active member of the National Gallery and the Kennedy Center. She has tried to expand her husband's interests in the arts. But so far, his preference is for popular show tunes and simple paintings." To her ears, she sounded like she was babbling.

Mercifully, the stage manager motioned that time was up.

Fuming, Eliza knew she had to call Pete on what he had done. She waited and pulled him to the side of the studio after the show. The staffers in the Fishbowl could hear, but Eliza didn't care.

"That was low!" she declared angrily.

"I don't know what you're talking about." Pete's face was arranged in puzzled lines, but his eyes blazed.

"You know exactly what I'm talking about! I deliberately told you *not* to ask me about the Wingards together and you went right ahead and did it anyway! What are you trying to pull?"

"I'm not trying to 'pull' anything, Eliza. There must be some misunderstanding."

Yeah, right.

❧ Chapter 40

Louise Kendall was coming into the office today to pick up the last of Bill's personal things and Jean was dreading it.

It had to be done. Two weeks had passed since the funeral, and the office was being turned over to Pete Carlson. Yesterday afternoon, after another pleading phone call from Bill's secretary, Louise had agreed to come and get it over with.

"Jean, I know it's hard for you, but thank you for packing up Bill's things. I couldn't stand going through them myself."

That's me—good ol' dependable Jean. Sure, Jean will do it. It wasn't that she really minded. Instead, Jean resented that, given her station in life, she was just expected to agree. Sure, her job description was assistant to Bill Kendall. Sure, she had done lots more than type letters and make restaurant and airline reservations. Sure, she really had been his "coach," always rooting for him, always keeping him organized, always protecting him. All of that was true, but the bottom line was Jean was considered Bill's secretary, his "girl."

Working for and with Bill was worth it. He had treated her with such respect. He considered them a team, he told her. He was very much aware that a good assistant could make his life hum, a bad one could make his life miserable. Bill appreciated Jean and he showed it in lots of ways, big and small. She remembered the first Christmas that they worked together, he gave her a pair of gold earrings from Tiffany's and an envelope containing a generous personal check. Every birthday and Christmas for the next twelve years, it was the same: the little blue box with some small treasure, a silver pin, an ivory bracelet, a gold chain, accompanied by a check. For Jean, living alone and with no one else in her life to give her gifts of this sort, Bill's presents were cherished.

He was stimulating, too. Always making quick observations, commenting on the events of the day on the national and world scene, Bill kept Jean on her toes. Jean looked forward to coming to work in the morning.

Let's face it, Jean thought, you had it made. You're never going to have a boss as good as Bill Kendall. Jean brushed back a tear. Don't start. You've been doing so well, not crying at work, holding it in until you get home. Come on now.

"Hello, Jean."

"Hi, Jean."

Louise Kendall was standing in the doorway, looking cool and stylish in a navy spring suit. William was standing just behind her.

"Mrs. Kendall, it's good to see you," said Jean, shaking Louise's hand cordially. "And, William, I didn't know that you were coming, too! I'm so happy to see you!"

The young man withstood Jean's hug, his eyes cast down. He liked Jean. She was always nice to him when he visited Dad. But he didn't like it when people came right at him.

Jean picked up on the discomfort and directed herself to Louise. "How have you been, Mrs. Kendall?"

"Oh, about as well as can be expected. And you?"

The voice in Jean's head said, "For Christ's sake, you've been divorced from the man for years. How hard can it be?" But the voice that answered said, "Fine." What was the use in complaining?

"What are you going to do now?"

"In the long run, I'm not sure. In the short run, I'm going to take a vacation. I want to get away from KEY for a while."

"What are you planning to do with your time off?"

"Well, at first, I'm going to just take a little time and get my house in order, literally. I have lots of little things I've wanted to do to my apartment. In between waiting for workmen, I'm going to do something that I've rarely done in all the years I've lived in New York. I'm going to enjoy the city. There's so much to do here and I've never really bothered. I've always meant to, but other things have a way of coming up. You know how it is."

"Of course," Louise answered.

Jean was suddenly overwhelmed with a feeling of sadness over the unfairness of life. She had been with Bill, day in and day out over the last twelve years. Not a day had gone by that she hadn't thought of him, worried about him, cared for him. During his divorce, Bill had confided to her that there was nothing left between him and his wife but a mutual love and concern for William, and a respect for one another as parents. Yet here was Louise, prosperous, pretty and the mother of his child. Louise was getting all the respect due Bill's widow, even though they had been divorced for years.

The two women made their way from the elongated reception area outside of Bill's office into the spacious room that was the anchorman's. Louise immediately walked over to the glass wall that looked down at the *Evening Headlines* studio below. She could see Range in his see-through office. He was leaning back, feet up on his desk, talking on the telephone. She wanted to stop down later and ask him to her barbecue this weekend.

"I've packed pretty much everything now. The cartons of books are being shipped to the Omaha Library as you requested. I separated out the ones that were autographed. Those I've shipped to your New Jersey address." Jean turned to Bill's son. "William, you're going to have quite a collection of books signed by lots of famous and important people!"

William did not look up. He had followed the women into the room and headed straight to his father's desk. He was busy now at the computer.

Louise smiled. From the first time her son had sat down at a computer terminal, it had been instant fascination. One of the dozens of therapists who'd been consulted over the years had suggested that William might do well with computers. That was ten years ago, before everyone got so electronics savvy. She and Bill had both been skeptical but, never wanting to feel that they had left some stone unturned in helping their son realize his potential, they had gone out and bought one. All three of them learned to use it. It became a family project.

William had taken to it immediately. He loved the electronic noise and the colors and the instant gratification. In time, he proudly mastered some of the simpler programs. None of the other kids in their neighborhood had computers yet. William had felt very special. He had found something that he could be good at. Bill and Louise considered the purchase one of the best investments they had ever made.

Jean shook her head, a smile on her face.

"It never ceases to amaze me, how well he does with that thing. It was such fun to watch him engross himself at Bill's screen when he came here for visits."

"My dad played games with me on the computer." The young man with the brown eyes so like his father's was looking at Jean.

"I know he did, William. I know how much he liked playing with you."

"I liked it, too. Do you know how to play any games?"

Jean laughed, "No, William, I'm afraid not. I just learned what I had to learn to do my job. I haven't really been too interested in learning anything else."

"You should. Then you can have fun, too."

Jean felt the sting of tears. What a dear boy. She would not let herself cry in front of him. She busied herself with taping up the last of the cartons and explaining to Louise how she had sorted out Bill's things, plainly marking all the boxes. Bill's early years of files alone had filled twenty-five cartons. She had shipped them to New Jersey where Louise could decide what to do with them. Thank God that they had gone to computers. Volumes could be saved on those little diskettes.

William scanned his father's empty desk.

"Where's the elephant?"

Jean went to the locked cabinet in the corner of the room.

Opening the doors, she pulled out a heavy bronze statuette, an elephant, trunk up.

"Here you are, dear. I've been keeping it in a safe place for you. I knew you'd want the elephant that always sat on your father's desk."

Tentatively, the young man took the metal animal and rubbed it softly.

"An elephant never forgets. An elephant never forgets," he repeated.

"Okay, William, let's move on, honey," directed Louise. Turning to leave, she asked Jean if she'd like to come out to a Memorial Day barbecue out in New Jersey. "I thought it would be a way to thank some of the people Bill cared about."

Jean called the attendants to carry the few remaining boxes containing the contents of Bill's desk out to Louise's car. After Louise and William had left the office, the secretary sat alone in the anchorman's tufted leather armchair. She looked at the empty bookshelves and the walls stripped of their first-edition prints and framed journalism awards. The room, once alive with Bill's energy and vitality, was quiet and bare. Tomorrow, the painters would spackle and color. Then Pete Carlson's books would fill the shelves, his awards would hang on the walls.

She went to the glass and looked down. Louise and William were in the Fishbowl with Range. Louise and Range looked very pleased to see one another. William had a puzzled expression on his face. Jean couldn't believe Louise was having a party so soon after Bill's death. Had that woman no shame? She felt that she had to go, though. What would it look like if she had said no?

She turned back to Bill's computer. She didn't like the idea of leaving Bill's personal notes on the hard drive that Pete Carlson would now be using. Jean wished she could figure out Bill's password.

❧ Chapter 41

Eliza shook hands with Louise Kendall. "I'd be proud to give the speech this year, Louise. I'm flattered that you'd ask me to fill in for Bill. Thank you." Turning to Bill's son, she said, "Will you be at the New Visions dinner, William?"

The young man was looking down at the floor. "Yes," he answered shyly.

"Good. I'll look for you."

Louise piped up, "We'll all be sitting at the same table."

"I look forward to it."

"Wonderful. I'm so relieved. If you hadn't said yes, I don't know what I would have done. So, we'll see you next month. I'll call you with the details." Almost forgetting, Louise added, "The other thing I wanted to do was to invite you out to a barbecue on Monday. I know it's short notice, but I thought it would be good for Bill's friends to get together. So much has happened."

"I'd love to come. Thanks for including me."

"Of course, bring your little girl, too. We have a pool, so don't forget to bring your bathing suits."

"Great, Janie will love that."

Another voice chimed in.

" 'So don't forget to bring your bathing suits. Great, Janie will love that.' "

Eliza looked at William uncertainly.

Louise reassured her. "Oh, don't worry, William is a terrific mimic. He's like a little tape recorder. He repeats conversations he's heard just once—sometimes even weeks or months later."

Eliza laughed. "Well, now that I know anything I say in front of William is being recorded, I'll be very careful."

No sooner had Louise and William left, Mack McBride appeared at Eliza's office door, a large brown paper bag in his hand and a grin on his face.

"Don't you look like the proverbial cat."

"Better. We've got something to celebrate and I've brought something to celebrate with." Mack put the bag on Eliza's desk and rubbed his hands. "Two hot fudge sundaes, coming right up."

Eliza couldn't help but laugh. "Ah, finally, a man after my own heart. Hot fudge sundaes before noon." She dug into the gooey concoction, savoring the luscious combination of frozen vanilla cream and warm, thick fudge. "And just what, may I ask, are we celebrating?"

"This." Mack pulled a rolled-up newspaper from the bag and unfurled it. It was a copy of *The Mole*. The glaring headline read MYSTERY SUICIDE OF ANCHORMAN ROCKS NETWORK. Eliza took the scandal sheet from Mack and quickly thumbed through, searching for the story. She found pictures of Bill, Pete Carlson and herself. The story underneath recapped Bill's suicide, Eliza's taking the anchor seat that evening, Pete Carlson's succession to the anchor throne. She read with interest the quote from an anonymous network source who said that Pete Carlson was under hard scrutiny and his ratings would be evaluated constantly. He would be given a limited amount of time and if he didn't deliver the numbers he would be, in the source's word, "toast."

"Pete's not going to like this."

"Tough. He's an ass. He deserves to be embarrassed."

"Mack, such anger," Eliza clucked. "What did Pete ever do to you?"

It's not what he did to me, thought Mack. It's what he did to you.

Mack leaned over the desk and kissed Eliza, long and hard.

"Oh, you smell so good," he whispered.

Eliza stiffened.

❧ Chapter 42

Dennis reread the letter on the heavy bond paper embossed with the letterhead LEO KARAS, M.D. He closed his eyes and uttered, "No, God. No." Not now, not again. Not when I thought it was all over.

> Your Honor:
>
> Before his death, Mr. Kendall told me about your arrangement.
>
> Future checks should be made out to me. Five thousand dollars is, however, no longer sufficient. Monthly payments of ten thousand dollars are now required.
>
> You can be assured of my discretion in this matter.
>
> LEO KARAS

An East Eightieth Street address was listed as the place where Dennis should send his monthly payments.

God damn it! Still on the hook! Bill Kendall's death hadn't ended the nightmare.

He pulled a bottle of Dewar's from the liquor cabinet, poured a generous amount and took a long swallow.

How the hell was he going to come up with $10,000 a month? Karas was a thief. This was blackmail, pure and simple.

Dennis felt a tightening in his chest. The federal judgeship! When Nate Heller came through and got future President Wingard to appoint him—there was still the confirmation process to go through. What if Karas got wind of it? Karas wasn't going to give a rat's ass about protecting Quinn's dear old mother. Karas wasn't the soft touch Bill Kendall was.

Leo Karas was going to make his life miserable. Leo Karas picking up where Bill Kendall left off.

He looked at the telephone hanging on the kitchen wall and debated. He had to get help. He would go crazy if he didn't get some relief. He pushed the speed dial. On the third ring, a familiar voice answered.

"Hello?"

"Thank God you're there."

"Where else would I be?"

"I must talk to you."

"What's wrong?"

"I can't live like this. Help me."

✣ Chapter 43

Leo Karas locked the office door and walked down the carpeted hallway to the elevator. One of the lights was out in a polished brass sconce on the corridor wall. As he noticed that fact, he wondered how many other thousands of observations the human brain made each day. What made some people notice details while others were oblivious? The human brain and how it operated fascinated Dr. Karas.

He pushed the button marked Lobby and the elevator doors slid quietly shut. He looked at his watch—11:30. Another late night. Private practice and work for the state of New York as a court-appointed psychiatrist made for long, tightly scheduled days. Tonight he had spent several extra hours at his desk laboring over the outline for his third book, the working title of which was "The Breaking Point."

Juan, the pleasant, gray-haired doorman, was standing in the vestibule, his uniform jacket neatly buttoned and pressed. "Another late one, Doctor?" he asked politely.

Dr. Karas smiled. "Yes, Juan. See you tomorrow." Karas liked the unfailingly courteous doorman. Word had it that Juan had been a member of the intelligentsia who had gotten out of Cuba by the skin of his teeth when Castro took control. The psychiatrist often contemplated the unpredictable circumstances that influenced human lives. Juan was a good example of uncontrollable conditions impacting a human destiny.

Leaving the building, Karas turned left onto Eightieth Street. It was just a few blocks to his apartment. He enjoyed the walk home. It helped him wind down.

At the corner of Eightieth and Park Avenue, he waited for the light to change. As always, when he looked down the length of Park Avenue at night, he had a feeling of well-being. The expanse exuded success and security. The lights on the MetLife Building twinkled brightly, though, to him, it would always be the Pan Am Building. Azaleas still decorated the planters in the middle of the avenue. The cars and taxis that whirred by shone under the streetlights, the dents and dirt apparent by day, hidden in the semidarkness.

He crossed the wide boulevard and continued on his way. It was abnormally quiet. The street was deserted. Rare that no one was walking a dog or parking a car. Dr. Karas was almost relieved when he saw the homeless man come around the corner. He had noticed the man in the neighborhood before. The police were diligent in moving vagrants along in this area but some, like this man, kept coming back.

The man pushed a shopping cart filled to overflowing with clothing and black plastic garbage bags containing God-knew-what. The man could have been thirty or he could have been fifty, it was hard to tell. He was walking slowly, swaying from side to side, his dark hair sticking out from under a Yankees cap. Even in the warmish May night, the man wore a quilted ski jacket, the reward for foraging through someone's trash or sifting through the clothing deposit box at the homeless shelter.

The doctor briefly wondered what had led that particular individual to his life on the streets of New York. What had been his "breaking point"? Might be a good idea to do some research for a chapter on the homeless in the new book. Actually, that could be a book in itself.

As he got closer, Dr. Karas looked into the man's face. The man did not meet his eyes.

"Hello, Doctor," he said, looking down at the ground.

Karas was startled. How did the man know he was a doctor?

Still looking down at his old sneakers, the homeless man asked, "Do you have any animals?"

What did he mean?

Karas pulled out his wallet and gave the man five dollars.

The homeless man watched silently as Karas continued on his way.

Making a right when he reached Madison Avenue, Dr. Karas walked another few blocks and arrived at his imposing pre–World War II apartment building, stopping by his lobby mailbox. On a heavy manila legal-size envelope, he noted the return address of Albert, Hayden and Newsome, Counselors at Law.

As he rode up the elevator, Karas read the letter.

Dear Dr. Karas:

This is your notice that you have been named a beneficiary under the Last Will and Testament of William D. Kendall. A copy of the will is enclosed herewith for your review.

The Executrix of the Estate is Louise Palladino Kendall, 14 Ashley Place, Park Ridge, New Jersey.

Due to its complexity, I estimate that it will take between twelve to eighteen months to administer the Estate and make distributions to all beneficiaries. Any questions regarding the Estate proceedings may be directed to the Executrix.

VERY TRULY YOURS,

JACKSON HAYDEN

Karas perused the will.

Louise Palladino Kendall and William Kendall were set for life.

Range Bullock was to receive $100,000.

So were Jean White and the Reverend Alexander W. Fisco.

The National Fragile X Foundation, the Special Olympics and New Visions for Living all received large bequests. So did the AIDS Parade for Dollars.

So did Leo Karas.

✱ Chapter 44

Eliza was feeling very pleased with herself. She was becoming quite proficient at using her computer and she hadn't had a cigarette in six days. She wasn't sure which was the bigger accomplishment.

The computer had become her friend, the assistant that helped her work smarter, as the saying went. It was like having a giant brain sitting on top of the desk, a brain that followed Eliza's bidding if she just entered the right instructions. In the beginning, figuring out how to enter those instructions had been a challenge. The computer language was confusing. Fortunately, the techies at KEY were all happy to answer Eliza's very basic questions. Their tutoring, Eliza's trials and errors, and just plain time spent working at the computer was paying off.

She supposed it was a mixed blessing, being able to do more work at home, as she was this Saturday afternoon, Janie sitting on the floor beside her. Janie was doing a pretty fair imitation of Dr. Burke, her pediatrician. Zippy, Janie's stuffed chimpanzee, was being commanded to open and say aah, and Janie was jamming a pencil into the monkey's open mouth. Eliza observed that while Zippy continued to smile gamely, Janie's favored tea-party and bed companion was beginning to look a little bedraggled. Zippy had to last a long time; there could be no replacing him.

Eliza subscribed to an information service that enabled her to punch up newspaper and magazine articles so she could do basic research without leaving her apartment. She knew how to transfer information from floppy diskettes onto the computer's hard drive. In fact, she liked to do that the best, recognizing that she was filling the giant brain with information selected specifically to benefit herself. She had uploaded Bill Kendall's files from the diskette Jean had given her, wanting to make Bill's input part of her computer brain.

She was trying to get ahead of the game, working on the speech for the New Visions dinner well in advance. She wanted to do a good job of it, not rushing at the last minute to come up with something to say. She'd learned from experience that it was smart to use free time to get a leg up on her commitments. She never knew when a big story would break that would require her attention.

As Eliza sat down to write, she ached for a cigarette. Once she had taken a museum course on the American Indian. The instructor had explained that Native Americans, when puffing their pipes, had thought that the smoke traveling upward carried their energies and thoughts to the gods. The smoking process was a form of communication. That idea appealed to Eliza. She could swear that her writing was better when she smoked.

Come on now! Don't be a wimp! The urge to smoke allegedly lasted somewhere between five and seven minutes. If you could tough it out, the desire would pass.

Concentrate on the speech.

She wished she'd heard one of Bill's talks to the group. That would give her someplace to start. Eliza had called Louise, but she hadn't any of Bill's old speeches or notes.

Perhaps Bill had kept computer notes for the speech. It was worth a shot. Eliza decided that it would be as good a time as any to try out the new feature she had just learned. By typing in the subject she was looking for, the computer would search its memory and create a listing of each time the subject appeared.

She typed in N-E-W-V-I-S-I-O-N-S. A big 2 popped on the screen.

She hit the Enter button. The first entry read DENNIS QUINN. The name was followed by a long series of monthly dates. They went back two years. That wasn't what she was looking for.

She hit Enter again. Paydirt! Bill's speech. She read his words, moved by his eloquence. He had obviously spoken from the heart. She particularly liked one passage directed at the parents of the children with special needs:

> A wise man named Leo Karas once told me that I needn't make a career of having a handicapped child. That it was important to go on with my life and that, in cultivating my own strengths, I could best help my son. I've never forgotten that. And I pass that on to all of you. It's a long and arduous haul. You have to take care of yourselves in order to be there for your children.

Eliza smiled. It made sense. Karas made a lot of sense.

She wondered. Had Bill used Karas's observations anywhere else? Just for fun, she typed in K-A-R-A-S.

Up popped 21.

Twenty-one entries? Enter.

First, the New Visions speech came up. She hit the Enter button again.

LEO KARAS, FEB. 23, 1:00 P.M.

LEO KARAS, FEB. 26, 10:00 A.M.

LEO KARAS, MARCH 1. There were twenty entries with Karas, a date and a time.

Eliza took her day-timer out of her purse and turned to the calendar at the front. The dates entered next to Leo Karas's name were alternately Mondays and Fridays. She noticed that the first date was the Friday after the New Hampshire primary.

Eliza grabbed the computer mouse and steered its arrow to the upper left-hand corner of the screen. When the arrow reached File, Eliza clicked the button on the mouse. The menu provided several options. Eliza selected Open. SCHEDULE appeared, indicating that the Leo Karas entries were in the Schedule file. Eliza had supposed that the Schedule file had been the campaign schedules of the presidential candidates.

Jean must have thought so, too, Eliza realized. Jean would never have knowingly handed over Bill's personal schedule.

Bill Kendall had been seeing Dr. Karas twice a week right before his death. Karas hadn't mentioned it to her when she saw him. Did he feel he would be breaking Bill's confidentiality by telling her?

Eliza shivered and checked the final Karas entry. Bill's last appointment had been on Monday, April 29, only three days before he committed suicide. Next to it was a notation. MAKE NEW DQ ARRANGEMENT.

❧ Chapter 45

Maybe she wanted him to know. She hadn't destroyed the letter. Win came across it, tucked inside her journal. The journal she kept hidden at the back of that enormous closet of hers. The journal he had made a practice of reading to keep tabs on her.

The letter was written on a sheet ripped from a yellow legal pad. In scrawling handwriting, Bill Kendall had begun in a businesslike way and then, halfway through, the tone changed:

I have AIDS.
You have been exposed. I'm so very, very sorry, my darling.

You have most likely exposed Win, a fact I don't even like to contemplate. The odds are in his favor, though.

Win closed his eyes and groaned.
Kendall's letter continued:

I can't face life with AIDS and have no curiosity in learning what dying from AIDS is like.

I also know about Heller's arrangement with Pete Carlson. Exposing their connection would be satisfying. Especially since Carlson has been base enough to try to blackmail me into giving up the anchor chair, in return for his keeping quiet about my AIDS. That connection would sink Win's chances for the White House. I have no problem with that, except that I don't ever want to hurt you.

I've been writing a book for the last two years or so. It's all stream-of-consciousness at this point, and I had every intention of staying alive until I finished it. But I've been diagnosed with a runaway cancer, so "my story" will probably never get told.

I don't want to be *the* story, not *this* story, anyway. Professionally, I am probably bowing out of one of the biggest stories of my time. It can be argued that I am taking the coward's way out. If I chose to go on, I think I'd feel duty-bound to report that Win has been exposed. Ironically, had I not been part of the story, I might have decided to keep quiet about the exposure and just wait and see the whole thing played out.

Privacy. What little we've had would be completely destroyed. Everything precious between us would be cheapened and dragged through the mud. I am not going to close my life, or leave you, in disgrace.

I never meant to cause you any harm. I love you, Joy.

It was signed "B." And there was a postscript, urging Joy to get the mole on her upper thigh checked out.

Nauseated, Win put the letter back in the journal.

Where was the bastard's book now?

❧ Chapter 46

In May, the month of the Blessed Virgin, Father Alec liked to spend extra time in the Lady Chapel. Located behind the main altar, it was the most popular and most visited chapel in the cathedral.

Today, the young priest sat and studied the three chandeliers suspended from the chapel's vaulted ceiling. All hand-cut crystal. They must have cost a pretty penny. At one point in his life, Father Alec had questioned the validity of the Catholic penchant for ornate and expensive decorations in their houses of worship. After all, weren't there more humanitarian destinations for Church funds? He had finally decided that the rococo adornments had their purpose. They were scene-setters, creating a mood of solemnity, awe and power.

A middle-aged woman entered the chapel, walked up to the altar, knelt down and bowed her head. Another one. God, there were so many. Day after day they came, all with variations on a few basic themes. A death, sickness, estrangement from a loved one, economic worries, disappointment with the cards dealt, fear of the unknown. They came looking for strength, direction and peace of mind. Some found what they were looking for, others were too overwhelmed by their agony to find consolation.

The priest's thoughts turned to Bill Kendall. The letter from the attorney's office had come today. One hundred thousand dollars! Father Alec smiled wryly, remembering one of their conversations.

They had been sitting in his office. Kendall had admired an Italian tapestry hanging on the wall behind the desk.

"Not bad. I'm glad to see the Church pays for the appropriate accouterments for a promising young cleric's office."

Father Alec smiled sheepishly. "That doesn't belong to the Church. It's mine. I bought it when I was studying in Rome."

"What happened to poverty?"

"That's a common misconception. Not all priests take a vow of poverty. Obedience, yes. Celibacy, always. Poverty, no. I've got the outstanding Visa bills to prove it."

They had both laughed, mercifully forgetting for a few moments why they were sitting there.

One hundred thousand dollars. That was damned generous of you, Bill. After reading his copy of the will, Father Alec knew well that Bill Kendall had been generous to quite a few people. In addition to Louise and William Kendall, he recognized the name of Range Bullock, having met him the day of the funeral. Bullock had been understandably preoccupied, barely acknowledging their introduction. Bullock would soon be a hundred thousand dollars richer also. So would Bill's psychiatrist and his secretary.

Father Alec considered what a compliment he had been paid, finding his name among Bill's loved ones. The priest thought back to their many conversations, how Bill Kendall had been so open, so candid about his life. The priest noticed that one "particular" loved one's name was missing from the bequests.

But a dying man would never subject the woman he loved to such public scrutiny. The scandal to her husband would end his career.

Did she know? Father Alec had tried to convince the anchorman to tell her. Had Bill told the wife of Senator Haines Wingard that he had AIDS?

The troubled middle-aged woman got up from her knees and made the sign of the cross before turning from the altar. Father

Alec looked up at her face. A definite survivor. But Father Alec was beginning to distrust his own instincts. After all, he had thought Bill Kendall to be a survivor, too.

✣ Chapter 47

The messenger placed the flowers on Jean's desk. It was the type of arrangement she had ordered on Bill's behalf for other people many times. Though Jean was extremely practical and careful with her own salary checks, she did enjoy an extravagance once in a while. The white roses, lilies and lilacs in the beautifully woven basket qualified.

Jean opened the small pale blue envelope that bore the mark of a well-known East Side florist. If anyone had been watching they would have seen the secretary's eyebrows rise in surprise as she read the inscription on the card.

"In appreciation. Range Bullock."

Range, though always courteous, hardly spoke to her. Of course he always said hello and asked politely how she was whenever he came to the office to see Bill, but unlike most of the people visiting Bill, Range hadn't tried to engage her in conversation. Others went out of their way to make Jean a friend. They knew that being on the good side of the big man's secretary was a smart place to be. Jean had always suspected that Range Bullock hadn't cared if he was on her good side or not. He and Bill were tight and Range was secure in that knowledge.

Jean closed her eyes and inhaled deeply the fragrance of the flowers. He couldn't have known that lilacs were her favorites. She smiled with pleasure.

Rather than call him, she decided to walk down to the Fishbowl and thank him in person. Range was sitting alone at his desk as Jean knocked cautiously on the open door.

"Come in, come in." The executive producer waved his arm toward a chair.

Jean took the offered seat, placing herself gingerly on the edge of the chair, making it clear that she did not intend to make it a lengthy visit. She was uncomfortable with this man, with all men, really. Except for Bill.

"I just wanted to thank you. The flowers are beautiful."

Range fiddled with the tack on his silk tie. He looked uncertain for a moment as he considered what he wanted to say and Jean found herself wondering why she had been so intimidated by this guy. Clearing his throat, he began.

"I can only imagine how hard it's been for you, Jean. As I'm sure you know, Bill valued you very much. He always said he didn't know what he would do without you."

Jean nodded silently, biting the corner of her lip.

"Anyway, last night when I got the letter about Bill's will, the letter you must have gotten, too . . ."

Jean nodded in affirmation.

"And I was going over in my mind what has happened, and I got to thinking about you and what you must be going through. I just wanted you to know how much I appreciate everything that you did for Bill. I feel certain that Bill would agree wholeheartedly if I told you that I sent them on his behalf as well as mine."

That did it. Jean's tears began to flow.

Range walked out from behind his desk, took out a snowy, freshly pressed handkerchief from his pocket and handed it to Jean. He pulled a chair next to hers and sat patiently as she cried brokenly.

"I think it's fair to say that you and I miss him the most around here," he said quietly.

She looked up at him, gratitude in her eyes. He understood.

"I miss him so much," Jean said. "He was so good to me. And I keep feeling that there must have been something that I could have done, something that I could have said, something that I should have picked up on. I feel so guilty. I should have protected him." She blew her nose.

"Jean, everyone knows what good care you took of Bill. Yelena Gregory herself was commenting on it just last night. Please, don't do this to yourself. I know you miss him, I know that there is a big, gaping hole where Bill should be, but you've got to look to the future. Have you given any thought to what you want to do next?"

"I don't know what to do now," Jean sniffed. "I can't stand watching life go on around here with others coasting right in to fill Bill's shoes. It's tough to watch Pete Carlson sit in Bill's chair, see Eliza Blake doing Bill's favorite assignments. I've been offered a job in the KEY corporate offices, but that isn't the news division and that's what I know best. Yet sometimes I think maybe it would be a good idea to start somewhere totally new. Somewhere where everything doesn't remind me of Bill. I'm very confused."

She had stopped crying and was considering aloud her options. She leaned toward her newfound ally and whispered, "I'm thinking of leaving KEY altogether."

If she was expecting a reaction, she didn't get one.

"They say not to make a major life move after a tragedy," Range said. "The experts say to wait at least a year before making any big change."

"Range, I've lived my whole life doing what everyone else said I'm supposed to do. I've been very careful with my money over the years. With what I've saved and now with the money Bill's left me, I can afford to take a very extended vacation. In fact, I don't know if I want to come back."

"A hundred thousand dollars doesn't last forever," said Range gently.

"I know, but for me, it's more than two years' salary. In fact, since Bill provided that the estate taxes be paid before the money is distributed, that hundred thousand gives me the equivalent of three years of income."

Range nodded. She could afford to take some time off.

"Okay, maybe it does make sense for you to get away from here for a while. But don't burn any bridges. When the pain eases, you may find that you miss us."

As he watched Jean leave, Range found himself wishing that he too could take a long, long vacation. He had said as much to Yelena on the phone last night. He had called her, moved and upset after reading Bill's will. He had forcefully insisted, after two very dry martinis, that Yelena listen to how generous his best friend Bill had been. Not just to him, but to others as well.

Yelena listened patiently and answered soothingly. She missed Bill, too, she said. But they had to carry on without him. It was important that Range be around for the next several months providing stability until Pete Carlson was more at ease on the *Evening Headlines*. She wanted Pete to be happy.

✄ Chapter 48

"What's up, Joy?"

"Nothing."

"Don't tell me 'nothing'!" Nate yelled, slamming his fist on her desk. "How did it come up that Bill Kendall left $100,000 in his will to the AIDS Parade for Dollars—a will he wrote *before* the AIDS Parade for Dollars had even been announced?"

Joy stared up at him, unaccustomed to Nate's anger being directed at her.

Nate settled himself in the armchair across from Joy's desk and tried to readjust his tone. "Listen, if you know something, you've got to level with me. I want to know everything and anything that could affect our campaign. I know Win would never have told Kendall about our campaign, so before I start imagining the worst, please tell me I've got this figured out all wrong."

As much as she detested Nate Heller, she had to give the guy credit. His antennae worked. Should she tell him? Actually, it would be a relief. She had been living with the secret for a long time. The month since Bill's suicide had been especially unbearable. Sooner or later the rumors would fly. It would be better if she told Nate now than if he heard it from one of his myriad connections. Obviously, the will was public, or one of the beneficiaries had already made a call to Nate.

Joy had stood on the sidelines of too many Washington scandals. They all had something in common, she reasoned: the coverups made things worse.

She told Nate about the affair, and braced herself for his reaction.

"Does Win know that you were involved with Kendall?"

Joy shook her head. "No."

"Christ."

The campaign manager let loose with a string of obscenities. How could Joy have done it? She was going to ruin everything. How selfish! How stupid! Did she have a death wish? That was fine with him, but why did she have to bring the campaign down with her? Joy did not even try to interrupt.

Nate looked down at the piece of paper in his hand. He had jotted down the names of everyone who'd be getting rich off of Bill Kendall's last-minute generosity.

"Well, congratulations," he spat out. "Your loverboy was quite a guy."

"Spare me the sarcasm, Nate. That's not going to help things one damn bit."

"Listen, Joy. Kendall's obvious little 'dying gesture of love' might have all the world cooing over what a kindhearted guy he was, but I'm not the only one who's going to figure out that the country's foremost TV anchorman had advance notice of the Wingard campaign strategy. How do you suppose we explain that little phenomenon?"

"Maybe we've got some time, maybe we'll figure something out before the will is made public." Joy's mind couldn't focus, and then it occurred to her to ask, "How in God's name do *you* know the contents of Bill Kendall's will, anyway?"

"That should be the least of your worries. If I know, others probably know, too. It's my job to know. By the way, our little march of dimes wasn't the only charity he named. A hundred thousand dollars each goes to the National Something X Foundation, the Special Olympics and something called New Visions for Living—God, that sounds like some goddamned Communist organization!"

Nate was still angry. He looked down at the list of beneficiaries. "Okay. We've got three very happy charities, plus our own. His wife and son are set for life. Fine. Range Bullock gets a hundred thousand, too. That's just great! The executive producer of the *Evening Headlines* knows that Kendall left money for a parade that hadn't even started marching! And who's this woman, Jean White?"

"Bill's secretary."

Nate whistled softly through his teeth. "A hundred thousand to the secretary! What did he do, throw her over when he took up with you?"

Joy just glared at him.

Nate paid no attention. "I don't suppose you know this Father Fisco. Good little Catholic boy that he was, maybe Kendall confessed his adultery to his priest." He paused only a second and then added venomously, "But then again, maybe he just couldn't live with his sins, even *after* absolution. Is that it?"

"Stop it, Nate! Stop it!"

He'd gone too far and he knew it. "I'm sorry, Joy." He got up and started walking toward the door. He turned to her just before leaving. By the end of his tirade, Joy felt awful but she could see that Nate was thinking. The wheels were turning as he tried to figure out how to proceed.

"Maybe there is some way to salvage this situation, though God only knows how. I need time to think. I don't want you to tell anyone, not even Win, though eventually he has to know. I just want to have a little time to think about what to do." He walked out the door.

One more name on the list. Leo Karas, M.D. As Nate made his way down the corridor, he asked himself out loud, "Now, what the hell did a *doctor* do to deserve a hundred thousand dollars?"

�֎ Chapter 49

Yelena told her secretary that she did not want to be disturbed for a while, closed her office door and lay down on the leather couch at the side of the room.

When Range, somewhat anesthetized, had read her the will over the phone last night, she was glad he couldn't see her face. She was glad he couldn't see anything.

Pete had seemed very annoyed when the phone's incessant ringing interrupted their lovemaking. Why couldn't he understand that she was perpetually on call, that at any moment the world could be coming apart and that she would have to attend to it? Day or night, Yelena Gregory, president of *KEY News*, didn't have the luxury of ignoring the phone.

More than once, she had to place her hand over the receiver and tell Pete to hush up. As much as she lived for these nights of romance and pleasure, she wasn't going to let her executive producer know that she was sexually involved with anyone, let alone the new anchor of the *Evening Headlines*. She thought Pete was only kidding when he frowned at her attempts to keep him still until she was off the phone. But then he threw off the sheet and stormed out of the bedroom.

Was it her imagination? As Range had just droned on, intent on a solemn reading of every beneficiary enumerated in William Kendall's last will and testament, she distinctly heard a click on the telephone line. When she was finally able to get Range off the phone, she called out to Pete. He appeared at the bedroom door, the shadows cast by the lamp on the nightstand falling across his muscular form.

God, I'm so lucky, she thought. So what if Bill Kendall had left money to both Range and Jean White, and not to her. Bill and Yelena were hardly friends. She was happy for Jean, though. The poor soul had nothing going on in her life. Bill had been it.

But Yelena had Pete Carlson. He might have his faults, but he certainly made her feel alive and, sometimes, even loved.

"Come on back to bed, darling," she said in her best Lauren Bacall intonation.

"So, now you're ready," he sneered. He got into the other side of the bed and presented his back to Yelena. "Well, I'm no longer in the mood." He punched his pillow with his left fist and buried the right side of his head into the indentation. "Good night."

Yelena could tell from his voice that there'd be no changing his mind. She'd never known him to be so sensitive. Reminding herself that she had done nothing wrong did not keep her from feeling rejected. She leaned over with resignation and turned the light out.

An hour later, she felt him move. Yelena closed her eyes and pretended she was asleep. She listened in the darkness as Pete crept out of the bedroom, trying not to make a sound. A minute later, straining over her own breathing, she heard Pete's muffled voice. Yelena silently got up and tiptoed to the bedroom door. The combination of moonlight and streetlamps shed enough illumination into her living room. Pete had his strong, bare back to her as he talked in hushed tones into the living room phone.

All she could make out was his last sentence. "That's fine for you," he whispered. "You don't have to sleep with her."

Oh God, no. It's coming. By now it was easy to recognize,

one of those dreaded attacks. Panic attack, that's what the doctor had called it. Damn those know-it-all doctors.

Suddenly, it was hard to breathe. This must be what it feels like to be smothered. Hurry. Catch your breath.

Yelena ran into the bathroom. You're going to die if you don't catch your breath. Breathe, breathe. Take a deep breath. There goes the heart, it's flipping over and beating, pounding, pounding through the chest wall. She opened the bathroom window.

Air. Fresh air. That will work. It's not as if it's the first time you had one of these things. Rushing to the hospital like a damned fool. That young doctor so smug in his diagnosis. You know it will pass. The tingling sensations of your nervous system run amok.

Breathe, breathe. There, it's passing. Yes, it's getting better. The heart is slowing down. Thank God, it's passing.

A knock at the bathroom door. "Are you all right?"

Yelena couldn't find her voice. She stared at the door, swallowing hard.

"Yelena. What's the matter? Open the door."

She reached for the handle and turned the lock. In a second, he was inside with her. As Pete put his arms around her, he murmured, "I'm sorry, I'm sorry, I don't know what came over me when you were on the phone with Range." As he kissed her cheek, and then the side of her neck, he kept lying. "Everything's going to be okay. Don't worry. Pete's here, everything's going to be all right."

Now, at 4:30 in the afternoon, lying on the couch in her office, Yelena was filled with self-loathing. Why hadn't she confronted him in the bathroom last night? What came over her, that she would let him guide her back to bed like that, let him have sex with her? Had she no pride or self-respect?

Yelena felt desperate. She had to find out who Pete was talking to last night. Maybe he wasn't talking about her after all. But what was so important that he had to get up in the middle of the night? She hoped he had been stupid enough to dial direct instead of charging it to his private number. When she got her bill next

month, she'd be sure to check for a number dialed that night—
the night all the fragile illusions of her desirability were destroyed.

❧ Chapter 50

"So there you have it. The whole sorry tale."

Dennis crossed his arms in front of him on the kitchen table
and laid his head down into them, trying to block out the story
he had just told his mother, the only one he could really trust.
He was so ashamed!

"Denny, oh Denny," she was clucking.

He hadn't wanted to unload his worries, but he needed to vent
the desperation he was feeling. So he confessed to her the story
of the funds embezzled from New Visions and how Bill Kendall
discovered the thievery. Dennis was annoyed when she praised
Kendall for making good on the money that was supposed to be
in the New Visions treasury and allowing Dennis to pay him
back monthly.

"How much did you take?"

"All together? Five hundred thousand dollars."

"Denny!" She was aghast. "What did you do with all that
money?"

He ignored her question. "I've been paying the money back,
five thousand a month for the last two years. I have no funds for
anything else. Do you have any idea what a strain that is?"

Dennis looked around his mother's modest kitchen and wished
he hadn't asked the last question. Things looked a little strained
at her house, too.

"Couldn't you make more money at work?"

Why had he come here? She didn't get it. She didn't understand. As a judge, he was well paid compared to the average Joe, but he wasn't really making big money by Bergen County standards, and he wasn't going to be getting any raises.

"No."

"Couldn't you have asked Mr. Kendall if he would understand and ease up a bit?"

"I did. I went to him a few months ago and begged him to let me off the hook."

"And?"

Dennis shook his head. "It was awful. The bastard wouldn't give an inch. Right in front of his retarded kid, he gave me this pious sermon about stealing from the weak. Tried to make me feel this big." Dennis pinched together his thumb and index finger.

"But Bill Kendall is dead now," she said hopefully.

"I know, I know. I thought my problems were over. But he instructed someone else to take over collecting from me. I shouldn't be surprised, really. He told me that if anything happened to him, there would be a record of the money I still owed. And sure enough, he left one. Now I'm on the hook to some doctor named Leo Karas. He's blackmailing me, and it's even worse than with Kendall. He says I have to come up with ten thousand a month. Where am I gonna come up with dough like that? I don't have that kind of money."

He didn't tell his mother about the money still in his safe deposit box. That was earmarked to buy the federal spot. God, if Karas made public what he knew—Judge Quinn would not only become Citizen Quinn, but probably Convict Quinn.

"I do have some money," he finally admitted, "but even if I pay, it's never over. With Kendall, at least there was an end in sight, even though it would have taken forever to get there. I'm beside myself. Something's gotta give. I've worked too hard."

And spent too much, he thought.

"My poor Denny. What are we going to do? If anyone ever

found out about this, your reputation would be ruined. The family would be so ashamed! Maybe you should have another cup of tea."

❧ Chapter 51

"Dr. Karas's office."

"Hello. I'm calling from Mr. Hayden's office at Albert, Hayden and Newsome. We represent the estate of William Kendall. We're going over Mr. Kendall's finances and want to make certain that Mr. Kendall's bill with Dr. Karas is all paid up. Can you help me with that?"

"Certainly. Hold on a moment, please."

Greedy bastards, those doctors.

The receptionist came back on the line.

"Yes. Mr. Kendall's bill is entirely paid up."

"Thank you very much."

So, Karas wasn't Bill Kendall's friend. He was his doctor.

Nate Heller put down the phone.

❧ Chapter 52

"Pete Carlson is trying to trash me. I think he's the one responsible for the *Mole* story on my breakdown."

"That's a pretty strong allegation."

Eliza stared at the books that lined Dr. Karas's office wall and went over events in her mind. She knew Pete wanted to bring her down. He'd deliberately asked her a question on air that would embarrass her. He was obviously trying to make himself look good while making her look bad. Eliza was sure Pete was low enough to plant the *Mole* story if he thought it would help his career. She told Dr. Karas her suspicions.

Karas listened. His face showed no reaction but inwardly he seethed. Pete Carlson was despicable! He'd tried to blackmail Bill, saying that he was going to go public with the knowledge that Bill had AIDS if Bill didn't resign from the *Evening Headlines* anchor post. That had been tearing Bill up in the weeks before he committed suicide. That and the painful end of the love affair with Joy Wingard.

Now, as he viewed Eliza's strained face, he had little doubt that her interpretation of events was on the money. Carlson would consider her a threat and it wouldn't be beyond the snake to discredit Eliza and ruin her reputation.

Dr. Karas considered telling Eliza what he knew about Pete Carlson.

If things went any further, he would tell her. But he was still hoping that Eliza could handle this herself and that Pete Carlson would hoist himself by his own petard.

"What do you think? What do you make of what I'm telling you?" she asked urgently.

He had to give her some warning. "Sounds to me like you could be on the right track. Be very careful of Pete Carlson."

Chapter 53

Nate spent the Memorial Day weekend holed up in his Washington apartment feigning an intestinal virus. He just couldn't face campaigning this weekend.

The small space was conducive to planning major strategy as there were few distractions. Just three basic rooms: an L-shaped living-dining room, a kitchen and a bedroom. It was an apartment like many others in the eight-floor building.

No paintings or decorations hung on the standard rental off-white walls. There was a large wall unit filled with scores of history books and four small television sets. On the rare occasion that he was home to view the network evening news shows, Nate liked to watch the broadcasts simultaneously. He'd sit on the couch with four remote controls, raising and lowering the sound on the Panasonics as his interest level warranted.

A pile of magazines, *Time*, *Newsweek* and *U.S. News and World Report*, was stacked on the floor next to the large brown leather sofa.

The kitchen looked the same as the day he moved in, stark and neat. A cleaning service came in biweekly.

Nate spent most of the weekend in the bedroom, finding refuge on the queen-size mattress atop a box spring that rested on the floor. He had never gotten around to buying a frame. On the rare occasions that he brought a woman to his room, he knew that his companion for the evening was not impressed with the accommodations. .

At first, he had been overwhelmed, huddling underneath the down comforter with the shades drawn and the lights off, absorbing the shock of what Joy had revealed. All that he had worked for in jeopardy. Joy and Bill Kendall. What a nightmare!

Could it get any worse? He jawed that over for a while, literally saying out loud the names of men who would have been even more devastating. After he came up with Saddam Hussein, Manuel Noriega and the grand marshal of the Ku Klux Klan, Nate decided to stop. He could stay in bed for six hours, six days or six months and when he got out, it would still be the same. He had a huge problem. He had to deal with it.

Shuffling into the kitchen to make coffee, Nate began to review his options. As always, there were only three.

Option number one: *Tell the truth.* Tell the world before the world finds out on its own. Where would that leave them? An electorate that might admire the candor of such an admission by the candidate himself most likely would not admire a candidate who, for whatever reasons, couldn't, wouldn't or didn't satisfy his wife. If he didn't give his wife what she wanted, how was he going to give the country what it wanted?

So that ruled out the truth option.

The whistle on the kettle blew. Nate poured water on the coffee granules.

Option number two: *Deny, deny, deny!* But denying that there was any relationship at all between Joy Wingard and Bill Kendall would keep the press snooping around to find out how the KEY anchor knew about the AIDS parade before it was even announced. And what if the two idiots were seen by somebody? Washington was a strange town. The Manhattan Project you could keep secret, but let someone unzip his pants in the wrong bedroom and the whole world knew about it! And as Richard Nixon could tell you, "plausible deniability" was rarely plausible and always dangerous.

That left option number three: *Spin it, and spin it hard!*

Nate did not notice that he had forgotten to put sugar into his coffee. He was too busy patting himself on the back for being one of the best spin doctors around. Hadn't he convinced Haines that focusing on AIDS was not the political risk everybody thought it was? Not only that he'd convinced the media, too. After Win's speech kicking off the Parade for Dollars, the print media had had a field day and television anchors across the country had rushed to underline the rectitude of the crusade with their usual self-important approval.

Yes, they'd have to put their own spin on Kendall's bequest.

Joy would indeed acknowledge that their mutual attendance at various Washington functions, and Kendall's interviews of the candidate and his wife, had provided opportunities for discussion on subjects of mutual interest. They had talked at length about various subjects, including AIDS.

Would they buy it? Probably not totally. Maybe not at all. Much would depend on how good an actress Joy could be. If she was unflustered and convincing, they just might be okay.

But Win couldn't be told the whole truth. Bad enough that Joy was going to have to fake it. Nate didn't trust the candidate to carry off the lie. It would just be better if he didn't know. He didn't want Win to have to deal with the news that his wife had been unfaithful. Win shouldn't be distracted now. His total focus had to be on the campaign. Nothing else.

If Nate, the forever cynical and skeptical campaign manager, appeared to believe the explanation of the bequest, then Win would most likely go along and accept it also. If the whole scandalous truth came out later on, of course Win would never trust his campaign manager again. As much as Nate loathed the idea of withholding the truth from his friend, he knew that it was his job as the general of the campaign to make the hard decisions. Everything that they had worked toward over the past two decades was at stake. Yes, option number three was their only chance.

After all, Nate was good at secrets. Admittedly, it would be hard to keep Joy's affair private because it was so close to home. It was no bother at all keeping the secret about the half-million-dollar payoff he was getting from that joke of a judge in New Jersey.

The decision made, he was suddenly famished. Nate went to his closet, pulled on some jeans, grabbed a sweater from the jumbled mess on the top shelf and found a pair of loafers in the shuffled shoes on the floor. As Nate jammed his feet into his burgundy Florsheims, his mind raced ahead. At least they could count on Pete to do whatever he could to squelch any *KEY News* snooping about the Kendall bequest. But the campaign manager was still surprised that Carlson wanted a White House job. Carlson was full of himself, claiming he wanted to make the news, and not report it. "I want to be a newsmaker," he had said, "not a news reader."

Nate had to give Pete credit. The power-hungry bastard had worked out a pretty good situation for himself. If Wingard went to the White House, Carlson was going to get the chief of staff job. If Wingard lost, Carlson still anchored the *Evening Headlines*. Pete won either way.

Then it occurred to him. There was a way that Nate could get that payoff money from Judge Quinn whether Win triumphed or not.

Heading out of the apartment door, he knew what he wanted. Chinese food, and lots of it. He ate Chinese food before every battle. It was good luck.

℈ Chapter 54

Top down, the rented red convertible cruised up the West Side Highway, over the George Washington Bridge and north on the Palisades Interstate Parkway. It was the beginning of a glorious Memorial Day weekend, the kind that begs for a ride to be taken.

Eliza was enthusiastic when Mack suggested that they rent a car for the day and get out of the city. They ached for a little relaxation before another work week began.

"When I was a kid starting out, I didn't care how much I

worked," Mack said. "Six, seven days a week, that was fine by me. I didn't want to miss anything, I was so engrossed in KEY and the news."

Mack spoke loudly, making sure he was heard over the radio and the open air. The breeze tousled his thick brown hair, the sun accentuating its clean shine. He wore a pair of faded, nice-fitting Levi's, a blue and white striped oxford and a good-quality, though well-worn, navy blazer. Eliza recognized the name engraved on the side of Mack's sunglasses and she could guess the brand of the brown leather dock shoes he wore. The yuppie uniform.

"But now," Mack continued, "I treasure my time off and guard it ferociously. I really need the downtime to recharge."

Eliza listened, her head back, enjoying the sun's warmth on her face. It felt so good, so liberating in the open car. She felt a sensation she hadn't felt in a very long time. It was the feeling of having fun.

In the rearview mirror, she checked on Janie in the backseat, who had a smile on her face, her eyes squinting as the rushing air blew at her. Eliza suppressed thoughts of work and stories and deadlines, and luxuriated in the moment. A convertible, a sunny May day, a smart hunk sitting beside her, and her treasure in the back. What could be bad?

"Where are we going anyway?"

"A little town called Piermont. Ever been there?"

"No, but I've heard it mentioned."

"I think you'll like it. It's a quaint little village sitting along the Hudson River. It has a 1930s kind of feel. Woody Allen used Piermont for the street scenes in one of his movies. Over the past few years, it's become more and more popular. The small stores have been leased by boutiques, art galleries and antique shops. Somehow Piermont has managed to retain its charm. There are also a couple of really fine restaurants, and a few fun places to eat, too."

"Good. I'm starving."

It wasn't long before Mack maneuvered the car into one of

the limited spaces along Piermont's short main street. Eliza took in its charm and was hooked.

"And this is only a half hour from midtown?" she asked incredulously.

He grinned. "I knew you'd like it. How 'bout some brunch? We can walk the street later."

The three took their places at a table on the upstairs porch of an informal restaurant called Terri's.

"Vegetarian?" Eliza read the menu, a look of uncertainty on her face.

"Don't panic. You're going to be pleasantly surprised."

Eliza and Mack ordered Terri's omelette special. Janie wanted pancakes. They sat back and relaxed. From their raised position, they watched others strolling beneath them, and savored the atmosphere of the little town. The Hudson River and the Tappan Zee Bridge could be seen not too far in the distance. Weekend sailors guided their tidy white boats on the river. The clean smell of the water permeated the air.

Fresh-squeezed orange juice arrived along with a basket of small whole wheat and oat bran muffins and bagels. A carousel of little glass bowls full of jam was set on the table. The young clean-scrubbed waitress identified them as strawberry, blueberry, boysenberry, grape and citrus marmalade, no sugars or preservatives added, of course. Janie set right to spinning the lazy Susan.

"So far, so good," said Eliza as she spread thick strawberry jam on her second muffin.

Terri's vegetable omelettes arrived. They were fluffy and full. Slices of cantaloupe and honeydew melon garnished the sides of the plates. A bowl of fresh strawberries and blueberries accompanied the meal. Janie was satisfied with her pancakes, insisting on pouring the maple syrup herself. "I'll do it," she declared determinedly.

"I didn't know eating healthfully could taste this good," Eliza admitted. "In a world where it seems everyone is more and more into wholesome eating, I still enjoy the hell out of a quarter pounder with cheese and an order of fries. Of course, I order a Diet Coke with that, so it's not so bad."

Mack looked at her, smirking. "What about all those health style segments you do on the show. If America only knew."

"If America only knew, they'd probably like me better and our ratings would go up. You've just given me a good idea for a segment. We'll call it 'Do as I say, not as I do.' Harry and I could report the sound medical and expert advice pertaining to good health and then we could confess to the audience what we really do. For example, Harry could explain the latest findings on the benefits of oat bran and then he could close by telling the viewers that he himself plans to go down to the commissary for a Pepsi and two jelly donuts after the broadcast."

"I like it." Mack segued to his next subject. "Not to ruin the mood, but since you brought work into this, did you see that the ratings for the *Evening Headlines* were down again this week?"

Eliza nodded as she took a sip of coffee. "I saw them."

"And?"

"To tell you the truth, there's not much satisfaction in it. Pete may be a sneaky creep, but I don't relish any *KEY News* dip in the ratings. That's bad for all of us."

"Well, if Pete's slide does continue, the rumor has always had it that you are next in line for the throne."

"That may have been true once, but with my recent history, I'm not so sure now. I just hope that the *Mole* story didn't do any permanent damage. Otherwise, Pete's in like Flynn, bad numbers or not."

Mack reached over and took Eliza's hand.

"Look, you could always go public and tell what really happened."

"What do you mean?"

"Do it on *Here's Looking at You, America.* You couldn't have a better forum. You can explain everything. Get it all out in the open. That is, if you think that America wants to know."

Eliza felt the warmth of Mack's touch, saw the look of tenderness in his eyes.

"Is America curious, or are you?"

"Both."

"I'll tell you all about it," she promised. "But not now." She looked down at Janie. Mack nodded.

Janie chirped, "I'm going to a pool tomorrow and Mrs. Twomey's coming with us so she can see me swim."

"I wish you could come to Louise's party, Mack."

"Well, somebody has to work and I have Memorial Day duty. So, ladies, today will be our holiday."

Mack settled the check and the three walked along the street, wandering throughout the stores, poking around in antique shops, browsing through the art galleries. After having her face painted like an Indian by a sidewalk artist and eating most of a double chocolate ice cream cone, Janie fell asleep on the ride back to Manhattan and didn't awaken when Mack carried her up to Eliza's apartment.

"That's what I love about Janie," said Mack as Eliza came back from tucking the child in her bed. "She's such a cooperative kid."

Eliza felt a tightening in her chest. She'd been thinking about it all day. But she was afraid. Afraid to get close to someone else again. Afraid of letting herself love someone else . . . Afraid of letting go of John. She knew she had to get over it, knew she had to move on. But she just still wasn't sure that she was ready.

"Do you want some coffee?" she asked, trying to delay things.

Mack came toward her and slipped his hands around her waist, pulling her near.

"No. I don't want any coffee."

He bent forward and his lips touched her neck. Eliza felt their warmth on her soft skin, felt a tingling that moved down her entire body.

"I don't know."

"I do," he said.

"But Janie's just down the hall."

"Don't worry," he whispered.

Then his mouth was on hers and he pulled her closer still. Slowly, she felt herself letting go.

Eliza unbuttoned Mack's shirt, at first tentatively, and then urgently. John was nowhere in the room.

❧ Chapter 55

Janie splashed contentedly in the sparkling water of the Bears Nest swimming pool. As the only child at the Memorial Day barbecue, she was getting lots of attention.

Keeping her eyes trained on her little charge, Mrs. Twomey pulled a deck chair to the pool's edge. Jean rolled up her white slacks and dangled her feet, clapping as Janie, holding tight to the side, gave her pounding rendition of a flutter kick. Even William took a break from offering gooey nachos to watch Janie gingerly put her head under the water.

Close by, Eliza, Yelena, Range and Louise sat in a cluster of lounge chairs, sipping their cold drinks and enjoying the clear late afternoon.

"I love it out here," Eliza said aloud to no one in particular. "I think Janie and I should move out. It only took us a half hour to get here."

"That's because there was no traffic today. During normal rush hour, it's double or triple that," Range warned.

"That wouldn't be a problem for me. Not with my hours. I doubt many people are on the road at four in the morning."

"Bill never seemed to mind the commute much. He said it gave him time in the morning to get his thoughts organized, and it was a chance to decompress at the end of the day." Louise's face grew solemn. "Poor Bill."

The group was silent.

Louise went on. "I hate when people say things like this, but it was a beautiful funeral, wasn't it?"

Everyone nodded in agreement and, from poolside, Jean spoke up.

"You know, I thought that Bill should have been buried from St. Patrick's. I go to eight o'clock Mass there every single Sunday morning and it's just so magnificent. But the cathedral in Newark was beautiful and all, and if that's where Bill wanted it, I guess that's all that counts." She looked like she would cry.

"Okay, everybody." Range clapped his hands. "Buck up. Bill wouldn't want us moping around. I'm going for a swim."

"You're right." Louise stood up. "I'm going to put the chicken on the grill."

"Oh let me help. I love to barbecue." Eliza rose eagerly. "Want to come, Yelena?"

"Sure, but I'm just an observer. Don't ask me to do anything too hard."

"Think you could husk some corn?" Louise teased.

"That I could probably handle. But I should tell you, it comes in cans nowadays."

The grill was ready. Louise placed the chicken and Eliza brushed on the tangy orange sauce.

"How are you really, Louise?"

"Not great. I keep wondering if Bill was thinking about this for a long time. I wish I had known, maybe I could have done something."

Eliza put her hand on Louise's shoulder. "I think we all wonder that."

Yelena came out from the sliding glass doors onto the deck carrying a large salad bowl.

"I was thinking of calling Bill's psychiatrist," Louise admitted to Eliza. "Maybe he could give me some answers or at least some peace of mind."

Eliza considered. "I'm sure Dr. Karas would be glad to talk with you. He's very understanding. I should know, he's my doctor, too. When I needed help, Bill gave me his number."

❧ Chapter 56

There it was. The inlaid mahogany box. It had no lock.

The box was opened and its contents extracted carefully . . . contents that were smooth and cool to the touch. Funny, that something so small could be so lethal.

As soon as the job was done, right back the gun would go.

It was too bad, but there was no choice.

A little knowledge is a dangerous thing. Karas knew too much.

June

❧ Chapter 57

The man pushed his shopping cart into the small space next to the staircase leading up to an elegant brownstone townhouse. The freshly painted black front door sported a heavy brass door-knocker. A lion's head, the homeless man noted. Good enough. Another animal for the menagerie.

He opened up one of the plastic bags in his cart, rifled around inside and found what he was searching for. Looking over his shoulders from side to side, he surveyed the quiet East Side block. Seeing no one, he pulled out his weapon and aimed at the brownstone wall. The outline of the head, the curly mane, the eyes, nose and whiskers appeared.

Tit for tat, tit for tat. Spray them a lion's head, this for that.

The man quickly capped the spray-paint can and shoved it back into the bag, stuffing it deep into the middle of the cart. Then he eased the shopping cart out of its hiding spot and continued walking down the street. Easy, not too fast, that will attract attention. Homeless people shouldn't look like they are hurrying to or from anything.

He felt good. He would take the time to observe his creation more carefully tomorrow night when he made his rounds to check on his pets. Tomorrow night, when he planned to talk to Dr. Karas again. He'd been watching Karas long enough.

Now it was late and he wanted to find a place to doze. He chuckled to himself.

A catnap.

❧ Chapter 58

Louise Kendall sat in her shiny white kitchen sipping a second cup of coffee and reading the *Record*. Haines Wingard and the New Jersey primary were in the headlines.

Today was the final voting day of the primary season. At this point it was a foregone conclusion. Haines Malcolm Wingard would be his party's candidate for president. It had been decided that on primary night Wingard would make his victory statement in densely populated Bergen County.

Louise noted with interest that the Park Ridge Marriott was to be Wingard headquarters for the evening. That was where the New Visions for Living fund-raiser would be held later that month. She felt a twinge of wistfulness, a mental picture forming of the organized chaos that must be going on there as the newspeople set up to broadcast from the ballroom. She had accompanied Bill on enough remotes to have become fascinated with what went into making live TV. She missed the excitement of being there as events unfolded. Even in the role of an observant guest, she had felt a part of history.

Louise finished reading the first section and was turning to the classifieds to check the real estate ads when the phone rang. Range Bullock was on the line. After the usual pleasantries, he got to the point of his call. He was down the road at the Marriott and was wondering if she felt like taking a ride over.

Louise fairly jumped at the chance. In the weeks since Bill's death, she hadn't felt like doing much of anything. Of course, the barbecue had been the first real opportunity to be with people again, to laugh and enjoy herself. She was glad that Range had been there.

"Why don't you come over as soon as you can," he was saying now. "We'll do a quick tour and then grab some lunch."

Louise gulped the last of her coffee and stowed the cup and saucer in the dishwasher. Louise remembered her Italian grandmother, a seventy-six-year-old widow when she sold her home of fifty years and moved into a small apartment. Nana was stubborn in her refusal to use the new dishwasher—the sink was always good enough for her, thank you very much. She used her first dishwasher as a liquor cabinet and washed her single plates and utensils by hand after every meal. Louise smiled a little. Now I am like my Nana, alone and dirtying just a few dishes a day, but at least I used the damned dishwasher.

She bounded up the stairs in a burst of energy, heading straight to the luxurious pale rose master bathroom. The Jacuzzi tub with its heavy brass fittings sat on a raised marble platform. Next to the tub stood the separate stall shower, complete with a marble bench providing a spot to sit and let the steamy spray pound down therapeutically. She opted for the shower. It was quicker. Leaning into the stall, Louise twisted the hot water valve on full, knowing that as top-of-the-line as this townhouse was, it still took a little while for the water to run hot. She turned toward the wall-length mirror over the double sink and took a hard look at her face. Taking a pair of tweezers from the vanity drawer, she plucked the stray hairs that broke the line of her well-formed eyebrows. Running her hands through her hair, she searched for those gray invaders that the colorist at the salon had missed. The tweezers pulled out those little buggers, too.

As she lathered her hair, she felt as if she had been given a gift, a chance for pleasure. Such opportunities had been rare lately. She grabbed the razor from the shower wall pocket. Might as well do the whole job. Louise bent down and lifted her leg, propping her foot on the marble bench, shaving carefully. She noted the condition of her feet and wished she'd had a more recent pedicure. That brought her up short. What are you worrying about? No one is going to see your feet.

She toweled herself dry with a thick pink bath sheet and slathered moisturizer on her legs, arms and torso. She smoothed a more expensive cream on her face and neck. After tieing on a cotton robe, she combed out her hair and began planning what she would wear. Beige slacks, white blouse, navy blazer, all linen. Her faux crocodile Belgian loafers. That would be safe.

Half an hour later, hair blown, face made up and body perfumed, Louise Kendall was easing her green Jaguar out of the garage beneath the townhouse. As she pulled out of the complex, she noted with satisfaction the approving look in the eyes of the guard at the gate. It was a clear, sunny June day and as she drove the short distance down Spring Valley Road, she had a sense of well-being.

Turning right into the area that was home to the Marriott, it was immediately apparent that this wasn't just another day for the hotel. The parking lot was a jumble of huge white trucks with broadcast news service insignias painted on their sides. Technicians were busily laying miles of cable from the trucks to the podium and camera positions in the hotel ballroom.

Louise found a spot in the parking lot in the back of the hotel and entered through the rear doors. All she had to do was follow the purposeful men in T-shirts with tool belts hanging low on their hips.

Stepping cautiously into the expansive place, Louise immediately saw Range near the front of the ballroom. Dressed in a striped shirt, open at the neck, and khaki trousers, he stood erect and forceful. Perhaps feeling her eyes upon him, Range turned and spotted her. He strode over immediately, smiling broadly.

He thought she looked terrific. Range knew from pictures that he had seen of Bill and Louise from years gone by that a younger Louise had been pretty in a softer sort of way. As her life evolved, so had her face. It was more defined, more chiseled. Her jaw was strong. Her alert brown eyes glowed warmly, the white parts as white as a child's. Her skin was smooth, but the lines at the corners of her eyes were pronounced. Her honey-colored hair brushed the top of her shoulders. It was shiny and natural-looking, although he knew that women with eighteen-year-old sons generally were not without gray. She moved with grace and assurance. Her body was great!

"Louise, it's great to see you. You look wonderful!" He kissed her on the cheek. She smelled his aftershave. "I wanted to thank you again for the barbecue. I enjoyed myself and I think everybody else did, too."

"I suppose I could act cool and say that your call was no big thing, but I can't tell you how happy I was that you invited me today. I love this kind of thing."

He put his arm firmly around her shoulders. "Come on, then. Let me show you around. The way we do things now is a little different from the last time you were at one of these."

As they walked out to the parking lot, Range explained the latest technology that made coverage of news events ever more immediate. They went into the large white KEY truck that was, in effect, a mini–television transmission station. Pictures and sound from the victory celebration tonight would go through the wires from the ballroom into the truck, which would send the pictures from the satellite dish on its roof to a satellite cruising above the earth. The satellite dish on top of the KEY broadcast center in New York City would be turned in the direction of the sky satellite and transmit the pictures down to the news headquarters. Then the pictures would be sent out to the rest of the country by the KEY television network. If they chose, local stations could downlink the pictures themselves directly from the satellite. All that was needed were the satellite coordinates and a receiving satellite dish turned in the right direction. Everything was transmitted with such speed that the viewer at home would hear Haines Wingard's victory speech with less than a second's delay.

"Amazing, really, how all this is done." Louise shook her head in wonder.

"It is, but we pretty much take it for granted at this point. Anyone with a satellite truck can transmit like this. At one time, the networks were the hot shots when it came to covering events like these, but now individual stations can do their own reporting this way. It's really changing a lot of things in broadcast news. You hungry?"

"Famished."

"Great. Want to have lunch in the hotel?"

"Sure, but if you can leave for a while, I know an excellent little restaurant nearby."

Ten minutes later, they were seated at the Esty Street Cafe. Owner Scott Tremble greeted them at the door and escorted them to a corner table.

"The food here is as good as you'll find just about anywhere around here. You can almost close your eyes and point to anything on the menu and you'll be satisfied," Louise declared.

"In that case . . ." He shut his eyes and read what his finger had chosen. "I'll have the seared scallop and spinach salad with honey dressing."

She smiled. "Make that two."

It felt good to smile. They chatted about the election and the candidates and the mood of the country. Range listened to her observations, responding with points of his own. She hadn't been familiar with his political views but she found them to be quite similar to hers.

"So now we're well into our campaign coverage planning. The conventions in July and August mean I'll be on the road a lot this summer," said Range, a bit wearily.

"I know it's stressful, but you must love your job," Louise observed.

"I used to love it a lot more. It was much more satisfying producing the *Evening Headlines* with Bill than it will ever be with Pete Carlson. I miss Bill. Apparently, America misses him as well. Our ratings are down."

"Any talk of replacing the anchor? I remember Bill saying that a dip in the ratings can mean either a new anchor or a new executive producer."

Range laughed. "Thanks. Well, I certainly hope it's the former before the latter. And if Pete Carlson is replaced, Eliza Blake is next in line. I could live with that. Although she's been having a bit of trouble herself lately. That could hurt her."

"Well, I like her. She's been so gracious about filling in for Bill at a fund-raiser I'm working on. I'd much rather see her in Bill's chair at *KEY News*."

Louise looked up from absentmindedly stirring her coffee. She realized that, until now, for the entire luncheon she had not thought of Bill. She was sure it was the first time since his death that an hour had passed without her ex-husband coming to mind.

"Mmm. I miss Bill, too," Louise continued. "Even though we haven't been married for years, I didn't realize how much I still depended on him, mostly to share in making decisions about William. He was a good one to run things past on just about anything. I miss that most of all." Louise took a last sip of her white wine before adding, "And there's the fact that Bill Kendall was the first man that I ever really loved. Maybe he was the only one. Losing him hurts."

"I know Bill loved you, too. He told me many times how good your good years were."

Louise smiled wryly. "Sad, isn't it? Even with all we had going for us, we didn't keep it together."

"How much do you think William's condition had to do with it?"

"Not much. Sure, that was a big strain. But I think the old saying is true. Stress is threatening to a marriage. But a marriage with the right stuff cannot only survive it, but become stronger for the testing. No, William didn't cause our breakup. It was a cumulative thing. Bill and I were both very strong-willed and as the years went on we saw things in increasingly different ways. Except for our son, we had very little in common anymore. And we were both young enough and honest enough that the thought of staying in what had become a hollow marriage was unbearable. We also had the economic resources to split up, an important consideration when you have kids."

The waiter placed the check on the table, interrupting the conversation. Range looked at his watch.

"I wish I didn't have to leave now, but I do," he said sincerely. "You know, I really enjoyed this. Would you like to have dinner sometime soon?"

"I would. I'd like that very much." As they got up from the table, Louise assured herself that the next time she saw Range she would be sure that she had a pedicure.

✣ Chapter 59

Judge Quinn didn't like Nate Heller calling the Hackensack courthouse, but he took the call in chambers anyway. He deliberately left his office door open so his clerk wouldn't think anything secret was going on.

"Yes, Mr. Heller. How nice of you to call. I know you must be busy with our primary. What can I do for you?"

"It's what I can do for *you*, Judge. Why don't you come down to Houston next month and see how much excitement half a million dollars can buy?"

✣ Chapter 60

By ten o'clock, two hours after the New Jersey polls had closed, the expected happened. Haines Wingard won the delegates necessary to make him his party's candidate. Nate Heller let the word out that Wingard would make his victory statement within the half hour, ensuring that excerpts from the speech would be included in late local newscasts.

At 10:20, Win and Joy entered the Marriott ballroom by a side door and made their smiling and waving way to the podium, basking in the applause and cheers and stopping to shake hands with some of the hundreds of supporters packing the room.

At 10:30, Wingard began his victory speech. He thanked those who had worked so long and so hard for him, pledged to do his best in the months of campaigning to come, and asked for the continued support of his party and the American people. Balloons fell, supporters yelled and whistled and the band played "Happy Days Are Here Again." Win and Joy flashed their white smiles and waved, luxuriating in the sweetness of victory.

By 10:50, the Wingards made their way off the stage and out to a car waiting to take them on the fifty-minute drive to the Waldorf Towers in Manhattan where they would spend the night.

At 11:01, news shows were leading with the Wingard victory speech.

By 11:15, the television technicians at the Marriott were breaking down their equipment and packing up.

Yelena Gregory called to say how pleased she was with the coverage. Knowing that KEY headquarters was satisfied with the editorial and technical quality of the remote, Range popped another antacid tablet and breathed a sigh of relief. As many of these things as he had done, he never sat back and coasted. Anything could, and sometimes did, happen.

But now, able to relax, his thoughts turned to his lunch with Louise. Funny, he had known her for years. While always finding her attractive, he had never acted on his feelings and called her. It was awkward to ask Bill's ex-wife for a date. The dynamic had changed with Bill's death. He didn't think Bill would mind. He might even have been pleased. Bill had often said that he wished Louise a happy life and hoped that she would find love again.

Suddenly he felt the overriding urge to see her. He thought

of getting into his rental car and driving over to Bears Nest. It would be fun to act impulsively for a change. But how would Louise take it if he just showed up on her doorstep at slightly before midnight? Something told him she'd probably take it just fine.

Range decided against spontaneity in favor of what he had planned before he saw Louise. He thanked everyone who had worked for him, stopped for a quick beer in the lounge and then began the drive back to Manhattan.

❧ Chapter 61

The day after the last primaries, Senator Wingard was scheduled to appear on all the morning news shows. After hectic stops at the other network broadcast studios around Manhattan, KEY was the last interview.

The Wingard entourage entered the *KEY to America* studio with energy, excitement and the assurance that comes from winning. His eyes were tired, but the senator was smiling broadly as he shook hands with KEY staffers who had gathered in the rear of the studio to get a look at the man who might be the next president. Joy, stunning in a magenta silk dress, not only accompanied her husband, but got plenty of attention on her own. The first lady factor was at work.

The Wingards were directed to their places in the studio "living room." They sat themselves on the blue couch as a sound technician expertly clipped small microphones to the senator's lapel and the neckline of Joy's dress. Both guests were already wearing their television makeup, but the show's hairdresser quickly did her job, efficiently brushing and smoothing. All this was quietly done while Eliza and Harry were busy on the other side of the studio, in the "kitchen," taking a crash course in making flowers and other decorations from icing, courtesy of a pastry-chef-turned-cookbook-author. The baker was vehement in his conviction that anyone could execute the icing rosettes, thereby saving themselves money and adding a very personal touch to the graduation and wedding cakes so common at this time of year. Harry was having better luck with the flowers than his co-host. Eliza had gotten icing on the front of her yellow suit.

At the commercial break, Eliza and Harry made their way over to the "living room" after washing the sticky icing from their hands. Eliza noticed Nate Heller standing over to the side of the set. What an intense little man he was. An intense little man with an agenda he was very successful pushing.

"Five seconds."

Eliza and Harry sat up straight in the two chairs across from the couch. Eliza started off.

"Last night, Michigan senator Haines Wingard won the final delegates necessary to secure his party's presidential nomination. Senator and Mrs. Wingard are with us this morning. Congratulations and welcome."

"Thank you, Eliza. It's great to be here."

"Well, Senator, you made it. How does it feel this morning?"

"Great! Just great! You know, Eliza, it's been a long primary season and I must tell you that I'm glad it's over. And I must also admit how good it feels to win the nomination. I think I'm just going to let myself enjoy that feeling this morning."

"You know I can't just let you sit back and enjoy the moment," said Eliza, smiling good-naturedly. "I've got to ask about the future. What are you planning to do next?"

Wingard returned the smile. "Well, in the very immediate future, I will be doing some speaking and campaigning here in New York City this morning. This afternoon, I'll be going back to Washington to attend to some Senate business. And tomorrow I'm taking a day off." Wingard gestured offstage. "But I have a campaign manager in the wings who has plans for just about all the days after that. He's a tough taskmaster. Seriously, though, we aren't going to sit back and rest, waiting for the convention this summer. We're going to use all the time we have to get out there and talk with the American people about the issues."

The computer signaled the *KEY to America* theme music to begin playing.

"Senator, I'm sorry but we have to take a break. Can you stay with us? Harry hasn't gotten a chance to ask you anything and we'd like to hear from Mrs. Wingard as well."

"We'd be happy to stay."

"*KEY to America* will continue after this."

During the commercial, Eliza quickly walked the few feet over to the news desk. She could feel a headache coming on and wanted to keep ahead of it. She rifled through her shoulder bag until she found her bottle of Fiorinal. In her rush to open it, the bottle fell from her hands and the green capsules spilled at her feet. A stagehand scurried to clean up the pills and gave the bottle back to Eliza, as one of the broadcast producers handed her the script she would read in the news block after the commercial.

The first three stories were recaps of earlier reported news— President Grayson's physical exam results, the announcement of an economic summit scheduled for late summer, and the end of a labor strike. She didn't have time to read the last spot as the stage manager signaled that they were coming out of commercial.

Eliza started to talk into the camera, routinely reading her copy. Most of the people in the studio watched Eliza on one of several monitors scattered around the room. Joy turned her head and was watching Eliza herself as the anchorwoman began the last story.

"Residents of an exclusive Upper East Side Manhattan neighborhood are stunned this morning by the street murder of a prominent New York physician. Dr. Leo Karas—" Eliza stopped, her eyes squinting unbelievingly at the Teleprompter before her.

There was dead silence in the studio. Everyone was staring at her.

She struggled to begin again. "Dr. Leo Karas, a psychiatrist and author, was the apparent victim of a robber's gun as he was walking home from his East Side office early this morning. Police are investigating. That's it for this half hour. Now back to Harry and Senator and Mrs. Wingard."

Her face flushed and heart pounding, she pulled out her earpiece, unclipped her microphone and walked quickly out of the studio.

℀ Chapter 62

It was easy to hire a locksmith to open the apartment, and make a new set of keys.

I could have dropped it anywhere. The little silver key ring, where could it have gone? It could be anywhere.

Please, God. Let it be anywhere but on East Eightieth Street. That key ring could be easily traced.

℀ Chapter 63

In the desperate, lonely years that he had been living on the streets of New York, he had seen and done a lot of things. He had witnessed men and women eating out of garbage cans and urinating on the sidewalk. He had done both himself. He had watched human beings sleeping on subway grates, huddled to stay warm and making rooms for the night out of cardboard boxes. He had done both himself. He had observed people fistfighting on the sidewalk and having sex in doorways. He had done both himself, though more of the former and less of the latter. He had spent more days than he could count panhandling, scraping together enough to buy a pint of anything, drinking to unconsciousness and waking to find his face lying in his own vomit. He barely noticed anymore the countless drug deals, street robberies and prostitution contracts that crossed his field of vision daily. He had seen more in the years he had been homeless than he had ever dreamed possible.

Almost nothing fazed him anymore.

His rough, cracked hand reached into the pocket of his filthy workpants and felt for the key ring. There it was. He had picked it up from the sidewalk, from beside Dr. Karas's body with the bullets in the back of his brain.

The voices told him to take the key ring lying beside Dr. Karas.

"Tit for tat. Tit for tat. Leave him the elephant, this for that."

He didn't want to give up the golden elephant, it was his favorite. But he had to do what the voices commanded. Eliza Blake's voice had been so calm when she told him to keep an eye on the doctor. The man knew she'd be awfully angry if he disobeyed now.

He carefully placed the precious brass elephant next to the still body. He picked up the shiny ring quickly and scrammed, not wanting the police to catch him.

He hadn't gone back to Eightieth Street since then. He had stayed farther downtown. He had been eyeing three brownstones on the same block in the upper sixties that were being refurbished, waiting for knockers to be installed. Finally, one by one, they appeared.

One night he went by and was disappointed to find an iron oak leaf affixed to a dark green front door.

The next time he went by, there was a brass scallop shell screwed to the neighboring new home.

Nope.

The third time was the charm. A brass wolf's head peered out of the deep red door. Tonight he was going to add the wild specimen to his menagerie. Those people weren't going to like it much. All their hard work, sanding and cleaning and fixing. But a wolf was one he didn't have yet. He ached to get the spray can out of its hiding place.

Just a few more hours until he could do what he had to do.

❧ Chapter 64

Father Alec read about the murder of Dr. Leo Karas in the *Star Ledger*. Karas, the story revealed, had played an integral role in the development of the AIDS clinic at the University of Medicine and Dentistry of New Jersey in Newark and had a pro-bono affiliation there.

Father Alec had the feeling one has when reading or seeing something revealed in an official news capacity that one already knows. He felt like an insider. Father Alec wanted to tell someone. But he couldn't. Instead, he sat quietly in his small office in the rectory behind the cathedral, remembering his first meeting with Bill Kendall.

"Father, I have AIDS."

The priest had heard it a number of times before, but never from someone so well known and powerful. Yet, in the end, Bill Kendall, multimillionaire anchorman, was the same as any other afflicted child of God. He was going to die. It was not likely to be an easy death. It probably would be painful, degrading and ugly. Father Alec knew that the man sitting beside him knew full well what lay ahead.

Bill Kendall's face bespoke his anguish. The priest groped for words, and then remembered that this human being needed someone to listen, not necessarily to talk. He was probably eager to tell his story, to let it out. He needed compassion, not advice.

Bill explained that he had just been at the AIDS clinic. His psychiatrist had arranged for him to see a specialist there. Bill was very concerned that no one recognize him and the specialist had sworn that he would protect his identity at all costs. Kendall supposed that he could trust someone whom his psychiatrist recommended. He trusted his doctor.

Bill also told Father Alec that his psychiatrist had prescribed Prozac for the depression that enveloped him, saying that it would take the edge off the psychic pain. Bill said he wasn't sure if the medication was helping. He still felt miserable. He said he had seen the twin spires of the cathedral when he came out of the hospital and, on impulse, had driven in their direction.

Bill described how he had discovered a lump under his right arm. A diagnosis of lymphoma and AIDS quickly followed. Bill grasped the priest's hand. Father Alec consciously held tightly and looked steadily into the anchorman's eyes.

"Do you think we can talk again? It's helped."

"Anytime you say."

Bill looked around the vast cathedral. The priest read his mind.

"Next time, we could make it in my office."

"But I don't want anyone to recognize me."

"Come with me."

Father Alec led him to the Lady Chapel. It was empty. The priest guided him up behind the marble altar. There was a door hidden from view by the elaborate altarpiece which, like a miniature cathedral itself, spired to the chapel ceiling.

"This leads into one of the rectory dining rooms. No one will see you enter or leave. Just call me first, and we'll meet here."

And so they began to meet and talk. It was during one of those talks that Bill mentioned the psychiatrist's name.

"It just goes to show you, though, that once those nuns and brothers get you in the formative years, they always have a hold.

Talking to a psychiatrist could be enough for most people, but to a Catholic, it's important to cover your bets. That's why I'm talking to you, just to be on the safe side."

The two men had smiled at the truth in the words.

"You know, I really like you and would like to have you for a friend. It's too bad that I'm going to die, just as I'm getting to know you."

Father Alec hadn't known what to say to that.

At their next meeting, Father Alec told Bill that he could anoint him with the holy oil of the sick. Bill had gone for the idea eagerly. Behind the secret door, in the hallway between the Lady Chapel and the rectory, was the oak-carved sacristy where the holy oils were kept.

In silence, Father Alec laid his hands on Bill's head. Then he stuck his thumb into the bottle of blessed oil and made the sign of the cross on Bill's forehead.

"Through this holy anointing, may the Lord in his love and mercy help you with the grace of the Holy Spirit."

Bill hadn't known that he was supposed to answer Amen, so Father Alec said it for him.

"Bill, give me your hands."

They had trembled as the priest anointed them.

"May the Lord who frees you from sin save you and raise you up."

Bill had looked into the priest's eyes and said, "Amen."

Looking back at it, Father Alec wondered if Bill would have committed suicide if he hadn't been anointed. For all intents and purposes, the anointing of the sick was the same as the last rites. On the one hand, the priest felt comforted knowing that Bill had died in the state of grace. He was trying to console, trying to ready Bill for the Lord. He had said and done what he thought to be the right thing at the time. But feelings of self-doubt, of not having said something that would have prevented the suicide, ate at the young priest.

❧ Chapter 65

Thank God, they hadn't found the key ring.

It was hard to think of a way that things could have gone any better than they had. All the reports on the television had virtually the same spin. Karas was the victim of the street violence that was so prevalent in today's society.

Police were leaning heavily toward the robbery theory. Dr. Karas's body was found on East Eightieth Street, between Park and Madison Avenues. A somewhat inebriated gentleman, coming home from an evening at a nearby posh eatery, quickly sobered up when he found the doctor lying on the sidewalk. The man called 911. Police and a paramedic team were there within minutes. It was already too late for Dr. Karas.

No wallet was found on the body, nor was there a watch or any other jewelry. The doctor was primarily identified by the L. KARAS written indelibly into the neck of his shirt in launderers' ink.

A jogger catching an early morning run in the southern part of Central Park found Dr. Karas's discarded wallet, credit cards intact, money gone.

And so, the reports concluded, a prominent member of society, a contributor to the betterment of the human condition, had lost his life in a senseless act of violence.

How eager the police were to close out a case! Didn't anyone suspect some other sort of foul play? An irate patient would be so obvious a possibility, or a disgruntled business partner. Oh well, the New York Police Department's overwork was just pure good luck. Or better yet, God's sign of approval. Clearly, God must be showing that the right thing had been done in getting rid of Dr. Leo Karas.

The doctor certainly had been a hard worker. It had been after one in the morning when anyone who wanted to hear could have overheard the doorman say to the psychiatrist, "Good night, Dr. Karas."

"Good night, Juan. See you tomorrow."

Thank you very much, Juan, for identifying him.

The streets were quiet. As Karas crossed Park Avenue, it seemed as good a time as any. There wasn't anyone to be seen. Seize the moment. Karas was just a few steps ahead. He was an easy target.

He never even heard the shots.

℀ Chapter 66

Detective Colburn read the *Daily News* and *New York Post* accounts of the murder of Dr. Leo Karas. He noted with satisfaction that the police press information officer had done as instructed and withheld the part about the elephant doorknocker found next to the dead man's body.

The last thing they needed was someone coming up with a SERIAL DOORKNOCKER MURDERER theory.

And if the press knew that the knocker was the one stolen from Bill Kendall's townhouse, they'd really go to town with that!

✣ Chapter 67

Louise could tell by the position of the sun that it was time to get inside. She had been lying by the pool for an hour and a half, thinking about dinner with Range.

Just about everything was ready. The townhouse was immaculate, the result of yesterday's thorough going over by the cleaning man. The small round table on the terrace was set with a hot pink cloth and napkins and splashy, glazed Mexican pottery. The refrigerator was stocked with a marinating shrimp appetizer and the club steaks that she planned to grill. Two bottles of Vernaccia di San Gimignano were cooling in a glass ice bucket, and a Chianti Riserva sat on the counter. Louise made a mental note to open it when she got back from the farm.

She pulled her cotton sundress over her head, slipped her feet into matching canvas espadrilles and gathered up her sunbathing paraphernalia. The towel, sunscreen, water bottle and the paperback novel she was unable to concentrate on were shoved into her straw bag. She remembered that her wallet and car keys were in the bag as well and she decided not to bother stopping back at the house. She'd go straight to her car and drive to the farm.

She made her way around the pool smiling and saying hello to other residents lounging in their deck chairs. That was about as far as it ever went. People here liked their privacy and respected the privacy of others residing in the complex. There wasn't much cup-of-sugar borrowing.

Stopping in the ladies' room in the Bears Nest clubhouse, she looked in the lighted mirror. Whoa! You better get going, sweetheart, there's work to do on you. Best to get everything else out of the way first.

Louise drove down Spring Valley Road, windows open, breeze

blowing. Demarest Farm, in neighboring Hillsdale, was less than five minutes away. She pulled into the long, curving driveway to the huge red barn abutting the Garden State Parkway. At one time, not too long ago, Demarest Farm had sold its produce at a tiny roadside stand. Now, like so much in northern New Jersey, the small-time atmosphere was gone, even though the Demarests tried hard to maintain their personal touches.

The help at the farm was courteous and hardworking, the stockboys offering to carry purchases out to the customers' cars. Louise thought back to Mrs. Demarest giving William many polished red apples to chomp over the seasons the Kendalls had patronized the farm. Now daughter-in-law Marsha ran things. Marsha was unfailingly cheerful and eager to answer any questions.

Louise made her way to a bushel basket of fresh green beans, and filled a plastic bag with the best-looking specimens. Next, a head of romaine, some radicchio and a couple of juicy red tomatoes were heaped into the shopping basket hanging from her arm. She decided to cheat a little and go to the salad bar for the rest of the ingredients. She spooned sliced mushrooms, shredded carrots, and some sugarsnap peas into a plastic container.

She hoped that there would still be some good bread left this late in the day. The bakery section did not disappoint her. A long loaf of french bread went into the basket.

Dessert? Better not go for the pie. Some sliced fresh strawberries would do just fine.

At the counter by the cash register was a big metal can full of bunches of snapdragons. The red, yellow, orange and pink blossoms would look great with the Mexican pottery. Marsha wrapped the bunch Louise selected with green tissue paper.

"Having a party tonight?" asked Marsha, eyeing the overflowing shopping basket.

"A small one."

As Louise left the barn, Marsha thought that Mrs. Kendall looked happier than she had seen her in a long, long time.

❧ Chapter 68

Wrapped in a white terrycloth robe, Eliza lay curled on her bed, hair tousled, her eyes swollen from crying.

Again, someone whom she had cared about had been taken.

She listened to the muffled sounds of Mrs. Twomey reading to Janie in the next room. Janie was giggling at the misadventures of P. J. Funnybunny, a mischievous little rabbit who was always getting into trouble and learning his lessons the hard way.

There are no mistakes, only lessons. Where had she heard that? Dr. Karas?

It was a sunny, almost summery day, but Eliza had the drapes closed tightly. Left alone with her thoughts in the quiet of the darkened room, the events of the past few weeks reeled round and round inside her head. Bill's startling death had become a tragic suicide at the same time as her own life was being thrown into another upheaval. Those events had sent her back to Dr. Karas. Dr. Karas. Her doctor. Bill's doctor.

Dr. Karas's last words to her. "Be very careful of Pete Carlson."

And now Leo Karas murdered. A coincidence?

Please, God, let it be a coincidence. Even as she uttered the silent prayer, she knew it was more than mere chance. She didn't care what the police said, Dr. Karas's death wasn't a random act of violence. All her instincts told her Leo Karas had been murdered.

She rose from the bed, pulling the belt of the robe firmly, and walked barefoot to the den. Slowly seating herself at the polished desk, she tiredly switched on the computer. Carefully and purposefully, she opened and closed each of Bill's files, scanning through his notes. The Leo Karas entries were still there. The appointments were next to the psychiatrist's name, dates going back to February.

Why had Bill gone back to see Karas then?

Why right after the New Hampshire primary?

She tried to remember back to the New Hampshire remote. Cold. It had been cold outside the morning after Wingard's victory. She'd worn layer after layer of clothes beneath her down coat. She'd wished the producers had come up with a nice, warm, indoor location for *KEY to America*'s broadcast. But they were adamant about the covered bridge backdrop.

The covered bridge. Eliza tried to concentrate. She had interviewed Wingard in front of the bridge. After the interview, as the show went to commercial, Wingard had gotten up from his chair opposite hers. Think, Eliza, think! Something else. Did something else happen?

She had watched Senator Wingard as he left the set. The candidate approached his wife who was waiting for him off to the side. Suddenly, Eliza recalled!

Joy Wingard was talking to Bill. But Bill's face had looked different. He wasn't wearing his usual confident expression. He looked bewildered. Puzzled. Hurt.

Eliza remembered at the time being a bit surprised to see Bill out so early. There was no good reason for Bill to be out at the *KEY to America* location that morning. He wasn't scheduled to appear.

Had he come to see Joy Wingard?

She typed in Joy's name.

The computer searched.

Chapter 69

Dopey Yelena. She always ended up telling him everything he wanted to know. She did seem somewhat reserved of late, but she still made conversation.

Pete Carlson called his contact at *The Mole*.

"That's right. Eliza Blake and Bill Kendall had the same shrink, Leo Karas. Kendall's dead, and now Karas has been murdered."

He listened impatiently to the response.

"Make of it anything you want. That's *your* job," Carlson snapped.

Chapter 70

It had gotten chilly on the terrace and Louise suggested that they go inside to have an after-dinner drink in the library.

"Come on, let's be lazy and decadent," Louise said, steering Range into the closet-size elevator and pushing 3. "When I was deciding on buying this place, I wasn't sure about the idea of having an elevator. It just wasn't me or something. I hardly ever use it, except to bring up the groceries from the car. It's always easier just to run up or down the stairs. But I suppose it's a nice feature to have in a place with four levels. If I were ever disabled, I'm sure I'd be glad to have it."

Range was listening at the same time as he was making mental note of the buttons in the elevator. G was the lower level with the family room, garage and laundry. The living room, dining room, terrace, kitchen and powder room was 1. And if 3 was the library, that left 2 as the bedroom floor.

The elevator door slid quietly open and Louise led Range into the library. Strategically aimed track lighting from the vaulted ceiling illuminated the room. The walls were painted a deep forest green. The far wall was filled with bookshelves stocked with leatherbound classics and more current fiction and nonfiction. A mahogany partners desk was positioned near the window, a computer terminal perched on top. In the corner was a recessed wet bar, brass sink shining, glass shelves gleaming with crystal cocktail glasses. In another corner, two green leather armchairs faced each other across a game table inlaid with a checkered board and decorated with jade chess pieces. An inviting-looking overstuffed sofa, covered in an oriental print, faced the bookcases. On the well-polished hardwood floor was a hand-cut Chinese rug in shades of green and pink.

Louise gestured to the couch. "Relax."

She went over to the bar, removed two brandy snifters from the shelf and recited the cordial choices. Range begged off anything sweet, so Louise suggested a Remy Martin. "I'll take mine on the rocks," he added. While pouring the brandy, Louise reflected on how well the evening had been going. The chemistry was there, all right. She desired Range Bullock and all the signs were telling her that he desired her, too. Funny how it came back to you, the thrilling feeling of something new and unknown.

Louise made her way toward the couch, extending one of the snifters to Range. She caught the admiring look in his eyes as he appraised her. She wore a sleeveless white silk shell and shortish navy silk skirt that gathered and tied on the side. Heeled sandals with navy patent straps wrapped her pedicured feet, peachy nail polish glimmering on her pampered toes. She was already tanned so she wore no stockings. One thick gold bangle bracelet cuffed her right wrist and large gold hoop earrings dangled from her ears.

Range took the brandy from her and tried to get his mind off imagining what it would be like to untie the skirt.

Louise, for the moment, was more interested in continuing the discussion begun at dinner. They had been talking about *KEY News*, broadcast journalism and the kinds of situations Range found himself in as executive producer of a network news show. She had been getting excited as he related some of his tales. She realized that, for her, the power-as-aphrodisiac factor was at work, but she reassured herself that there was some compassion and sensitivity in his professional reactions to events. She didn't want to overanalyze him. It had been a long time since anyone had even remotely interested her. She knew she was hungry for something and as the minutes passed she was more and more sure that Range Bullock was it.

Louise slipped off one of her sandals and tucked her foot underneath her as she took a seat beside Range.

"I didn't want to bring it up at dinner, but how's it going with Pete Carlson? Is it getting any easier?"

Range groaned. "I can't stand the guy. But I've been doing my best to make him look good. When the *Evening Headlines* ratings go down, it's bad for me, too."

"And . . . ?"

"The ratings are still down."

"Ouch." Louise grimaced. Trying to make him feel better, she said, "You know, I've been making it a point to watch the show. I think those Eliza Blake pieces have been quite good."

Range nodded. "Yeah, Eliza's good, all right. But she's hit a rough patch lately. I'm worried about her. One more thing would be bad for her. Pete may be a blowhard, but at least he's scandal-free. You know, Leo Karas was Eliza's shrink. She's really taking his murder hard."

"Yes, Eliza told me at the barbecue that she'd been to Dr. Karas. In fact, I was thinking of going to talk to him myself. I wanted to see if he knew that Bill was thinking of killing himself."

Louise took a sip of her Remy and recalled, "Bill began to see Karas a short time after William was diagnosed. Bill was really thrown by it. He always said that Leo saved his life."

"So you weren't surprised to see his name in the will?"

"Yes and no. After all, that was thirteen years ago. I suppose Bill never forgot what the man did for him. What relationship they had, since Bill and I divorced, I don't know."

"What about you? How did you deal with the Fragile X diagnosis?"

"At first it was a relief to finally have an answer. For years, we hadn't known why William was having such a hard time. He was slow to sit up, slow to crawl, slow to walk. Talking took years. He was almost six before he was trained. It was good to have an explanation for why he was struggling, why he'd flap his arms and bite his hands. We were one of the first families formally diagnosed. Over the years, much more has been learned than they knew then. Fragile sites on the X chromosome. That doesn't sound so bad, does it? But those little fragile sites can manifest in a wide range of ways, from learning disabilities to mental retardation."

Louise took another sip of brandy and stopped to consider. "I've alternated over the years. At times, I've been a wreck and felt totally overwhelmed. At other times, I've thought I've had the whole thing under control. But most of the time, I've just tried to do the best I could." She laughed vulnerably. "I suppose there are some who would say that I obsessed on it. I tried to learn everything. Many times I knew more than some of the specialists I've had to consult. But what else could I do? He's my child. I didn't choose Fragile X, it chose me. Once dealt, I had to play the cards I had, the best I could. But God, he was such a lovable little boy and he is an incredibly dear young man. Sometimes, I've felt gypped and other times I've felt particularly blessed."

He wanted to take her right then.

"Where's William this weekend?"

"At a friend's." She studied the light brown liquid, watching carefully as it reflected the soft lights of the library. "At a friend's," she repeated. "You know, there was a time when I worried constantly about William and what his life would be like. I wondered what his peer group would be, wondered if he'd even have friends." Looking up from her glass, she smiled. "I needn't have worried so much. He's found his way. In fact, sometimes I think he has a better social life than I do."

Range reached out and took her hand. "I'd like to do something about that."

"I wish you would."

He took the snifter from her hand and placed it beside his own on the end of the table. He stood, gently pulled her up from the couch and guided her to the elevator. His mouth firmly covered hers as his right hand began to untie the knot on her skirt and his left hand pushed 2.

✿ Chapter 71

Eliza and Janie spent Sunday afternoon at the children's zoo. Janie had wanted to see the monkeys for the umpteenth time. Knowing it was good to get out for a few hours, Eliza had forced herself to go. When they got home, the light was flashing on the answering machine. Eliza knew who it would be.

"Eliza, it's Mama. Just wondering how you were. Give me a call if you feel like it." Click.

Eliza listened to her other messages. Mary Cate saying that she had editing time in the morning for a piece they were working on, would Eliza please plan to record her track right after *KEY to America* went off the air? Range suggesting that she come to see him on Monday, he had something he wanted to talk over with her. Harry Granger announcing raspily that she should be prepared for a substitute in the morning, he was losing his voice.

She called Harry first.

"What's with you?" Eliza was concerned.

"Oh, it's just some sort of bug or something. I don't feel rotten enough to be declared really sick, but my voice is not going to cut it on the air."

"I'll say. You sound pitiful!"

"Thanks."

"You know what I mean, Harry. Anyway, what can I do for you? Is there anything you need?" Eliza knew that Harry lived alone. She hated the idea of him sick with no one watching over him.

"Just don't have better chemistry with my substitute than you do with me. I kinda like my job."

Eliza loved working with Harry and really didn't like the idea of doing the show with a stand-in. She felt a pang of annoyance. Just the start of another week in paradise.

You ingrate! Do you know how many women would happily trade places with you?

Feeling duly ashamed, her brain decided to really wallow in guilt. She thought about her mother. She knew from experience that she would bug herself until she eventually returned the call. She might as well do it. Eliza pushed her speed dial and in three seconds was connected to Rhode Island.

"Hi, Mom."

"Hello, dear. Did you get my message? How's Janie?"

"Yes, Mom. That's why I'm calling back. Janie's just fine. How's it going?"

"I wanted to tell you, I didn't like the outfit you wore on Tuesday, the skirt was much too short. And I don't like the way they've been fixing your hair lately. Tell them you want to have it fixed the old way. It looked much better than that crazy way they did it this week."

"Anything you did like, Mom?"

"Well, to tell you the truth, I switched to the *Today Show*, and I like Katie's clothes and hairstyle much better than yours."

"Great, Mom."

"Now, Eliza, don't be mad at me. I'm only telling you these things because I want what's best for you. Don't you know that?"

Eliza had found that stopping and counting to ten really did help.

"Eliza?"

"Yes, Mother?"

"Do you have to interview those authors with the horrible ideas? They are nothing but Communists and you shouldn't give them any attention."

"Mom, the Cold War is over."

"That's what they want us to believe."

"How's Daddy?"

"He's fine. He's down at the gas station."

"Well, tell him I said hello. I'll talk to you next week."

"Fine, dear. Goodbye."

She knew where they were hidden. The emergency supply. Appearing on national television every day, having trash printed about her in the tabloids, knowing the secret that a network anchorman had an affair with the next president's wife, and suspecting that her psychiatrist had been murdered because he knew too much—what these pressures had not succeeded in doing, talking to her mother did. She found them, fought for thirty seconds and gave in. She parked Janie in front of the television and rolled the Barney tape. She went down the hall to the bathroom, locked the door, sat on the edge of the tub and lit up a Marlboro Light.

❧ Chapter 72

Range peered at Eliza over his bifocals, a scowl on his face. His desk was cluttered with papers and she noticed that the ever-present Tums bottle was almost empty.

"Eliza, I'm concerned about you. The ratings are down. That could ultimately be good for you. Now, of all times, you have to be strong. This is not the time for you to cave in. Your career depends on it."

"Range, it's a little hard for me to focus on my career right now."

"Well, you better."

That happy salutation completed, Range told her that Joy Wingard would be coming to KEY later in the week to tape public service announcements for the AIDS Parade for Dollars. Range wanted Eliza to do a story focused on the candidate's wife as fund-raiser.

She felt she had to tell him. Maybe as Bill's best friend, he knew already.

"I happen to know that Bill and Joy Wingard were having an affair," she said.

"And how do you know that?" he asked calmly.

"A confidential source. A confidential, reliable source."

His face remained expressionless. Eliza could not tell if her statement had surprised him or not. He stared at her for a few long moments. When he finally spoke, Eliza knew in no uncertain terms what his position was.

"I am not going to ask you again how you know because, frankly, I don't care. If Bill Kendall and Joy Wingard were involved, that was their business. As far as I'm concerned, it doesn't have anything to do with Haines Wingard's ability, or lack thereof, to govern this country. As you know, Bill Kendall was my best friend. If information less than flattering about Bill, but crucial to the national interest, were at stake here, I like to think I would report it regardless of Bill's memory. But this is a private matter. Each of us is entitled to some privacy and I'm going to respect that. We will not be reporting on the *Evening Headlines* that our deceased anchorman and our probable next first lady slept together."

Range stared at her as Eliza took in the power of his words. His next words made her feel he could read her mind.

"Of course, you can go to Yelena with this. That's up to you. She may or may not override my decision."

ℛ Chapter 73

Daily Campaign Schedule for Joy Wingard

NEW YORK CITY	7:15a	*Today Show*, NBC, Live Interview
	7:45a	*Good Morning America*, ABC, Live Interview
	8:15a	*CBS This Morning*, Live Interview
	8:45a	*KEY to America*, Live Interview
	10:00a	AIDS Public Service Announcements Taping
	Noon	Lunch, Private Time
NEWARK, NJ	2:00p	Tour, AIDS Program, Children's Hospital

3:15p   Tour, Boarder Babies Program,
        UMDNJ
4:30p   Tour, AIDS Clinic, St. Michael's
        Medical Center
6:30p   Wheels up, Newark Airport, for
        Washington

At 6:00 A.M., Eliza sat in the red leatherlike barber's chair in the makeup room off the *KEY to America* studio. While Lucille was brushing her out, Eliza read Joy Wingard's itinerary for the day. Joy sure was moving fast. She was relieved that Harry was back and scheduled to conduct the Wingard interview on the broadcast this morning. Eliza just wanted to concentrate on observing Mrs. Wingard today.

Since her conversation with Range Bullock, Eliza had been debating with herself. Never in her career had she felt so torn. She agreed with Range that the individual's right to privacy was essential. Yet news was news. If you defined news as information that people had an interest in, the Kendall-Wingard story would certainly qualify. But if news was knowledge that people needed because it was important to their lives, Eliza wasn't sure that the affair would fit the bill. On the one hand, she felt that Range might be letting his friendship with Bill Kendall color his decision and, on the other hand, she herself knew what it was like to have one's private life splashed across the headlines.

She wondered if watching Joy over the next twelve hours would help her decide how to proceed. But afraid to leave a decision of this importance to herself alone, she had scheduled a ten o'clock appointment with Yelena Gregory.

Eliza planned to devote the day to Joy and the piece that Range wanted on the candidate's wife as the AIDS fund-raiser. After her meeting with Yelena, Eliza would look on as the end of the public service announcements was taped and then travel with the pool press assigned to the candidate's wife's trip to Newark.

Taking a last gulp of coffee, she tilted her face upward for

Lucille's makeup application and listened to the makeup artist nag her about drinking more water. Eliza silently cursed the financial cutbacks at KEY. She wanted her own *KEY News* crew to accompany her as she followed Joy but, to save money, the networks increasingly depended on designated pool camera crews to cover campaign events. One cameraman's tape would be dubbed or fed to the other networks. Consequently, in a situation like today's, the available pictures of Joy Wingard would be the same for CBS, NBC, ABC and KEY. The reporter's script and the soundbites selected became the unique elements of the news piece.

Eliza preferred to have her own crew. Inevitably, there would be some opportunity to get that extra video impression that would distinguish a story visually. A good crew would recognize and seize those special images. A mediocre crew could at least be directed to record a moment that she wanted captured. If you didn't have a crew of your own, you had to depend on the pool crew's getting it. Their job was to get the basics for everybody. They weren't interested in special instructions from individual correspondents or producers.

A nattily dressed Harry Granger loped toward her, coffee cup in hand, *New York Times* tucked under his arm. He carefully lowered himself into the chair next to Eliza's. His skin was unusually pale and he looked tired.

"Your tie looks great, but you sure don't."

"Thanks, I like you, too."

Eliza laughed. "I'm sorry, Harry, but you don't look too good. Aren't you feeling any better?"

"My voice is back, but I must admit I've felt peppier in my day."

"Don't say that too loud, my friend. TV is a young man's game, you know. They'll start looking for your replacement." Eliza's eyes twinkled.

Harry smiled wryly. "Good, I was feeling guilty about the favor I was about to ask, but now I don't."

"Why do I have a hunch I won't like what's coming?"

"Actually this makes some sense, seeing as you are doing a

story on her. Would you do me a big favor and do the Joy Wingard interview this morning? I'll owe you one."

Eliza looked hard into Harry's face. "You must really feel lousy. You never give up your air time. Sure, I'll do it."

Harry brightened and looked relieved. "Hoping you'd say that, I took the liberty of bringing the research packet with me." He unfolded his newspaper revealing a manila folder resting inside. He handed the folder to Eliza.

She opened it and began to peruse the newspaper and magazine articles inside, recognizing most of them as ones she had already read. She preferred not to do this interview, but she said yes because she wanted to come through for Harry. Now that she was committed to asking Joy Wingard questions, she might as well make her questions count.

❧ Chapter 74

"Wake up, Janie. Time to get up, my little faerie."

The big blue eyes opened slowly and sleepily. Mrs. Twomey leaned over and kissed the top of Janie's head, gently patting the back of the quilt-covered child.

"Come now, love. I've made your favorite french toast this morning. Come now, while it's still hot."

Janie sat up quickly and Mrs. Twomey guided her feet into fluffy bunny slippers. The pair made a quick stop in the bathroom and were just arriving in the kitchen when the phone rang.

"Hi, Mrs. Twomey. It's me. Everything okay?"

"Sure it is, Mrs. Blake. Janie's just after getting up and she's about to eat her breakfast. Do you want to talk to her?"

"No, don't interrupt her. It's you I really wanted to talk to,

Mrs. Twomey. I've left my notebook home and I need it today. I'm sending a courier over to pick it up."

"Where is it?"

"In my bedroom, on the night table. Please get a yellow legal envelope from my desk in the den and put the notebook in it, seal it and mark my name on the outside of the envelope. You can leave it with the doorman, or if it's easier for you, just have the doorman instruct the courier to come up."

"Fine, Mrs. Blake. I'll see to it right away."

"Thanks, Mrs. Twomey. Don't forget, I'm going to Newark this afternoon and I'll be getting home later than usual. Take good care of my sweetheart."

While Janie concentrated on her syrupy french toast, Mrs. Twomey went to Eliza's room, finding the notebook just where it was supposed to be. Idly flipping through it, she recognized many of the names that were so much in the news these days. Mrs. Blake had such an important job and Mrs. Twomey was proud to work for her. Imagine talking with movie stars and presidential candidates just like they were regular people!

As the housekeeper went to the den to get an envelope, she came to a page headed *Bill Kendall*. Listed underneath was the name Joy Wingard and, in parentheses, the word "affair." Beneath that was the name Leo Karas next to which there were more parentheses around the word "psychiatrist." There was another notation, "DQ," with a question mark.

The intercom buzzed. Mrs. Twomey guiltily snapped the notebook shut and went to the box next to the front door.

"Send the courier up, please."

Quickly sliding the notebook into the envelope and marking the front *Eliza Blake, KEY News*, she wondered at the thought of Bill Kendall being mixed up with the presidential candidate's wife. How the ladies at the Irish-American Club would love that piece of gossip! But she wouldn't say anything. Having the momentary importance of being able to tell that news wasn't worth risking the long-term prestige of working for Eliza Blake.

Handing the envelope to the courier, she locked the front door and made her way back to Janie. She sat down on a kitchen chair and rubbed her swollen ankles.

"Good, my little faerie! You've eaten your breakfast all up!"

✣ Chapter 75

It was front page news in the *Star Ledger* that Joy Wingard was going to be in town that day. Father Alec noted with interest that she was touring AIDS facilities. How ironic, but how opportune.

He had the day to himself, the first time off in over three weeks. Every day and night were filled with cathedral duties and archdiocesan meetings. He knew that business was important, but he worried that he was spending more time on the mechanics of the Church than on its mission. He wanted more direct connection with people who needed help.

He never forgot that he had taken a vow of obedience. He intended to honor that sacred promise. He carried out the assignments he was given capably and diligently. His superiors were pleased. Maybe too pleased. He kept getting more and more administrative jobs.

Studying the picture of the beautiful woman on the front page, Father Alec turned his attention from thoughts about his ecclesiastical career to something else that had been bothering him. Joy Wingard. Did she know that Bill Kendall had had AIDS?

Father Alec hadn't been sleeping well at all over the last several weeks, tossing and turning and having strange, disturbing dreams. He knew what he was grappling with. His conscience was bothering him. He felt that he was bound to stay out of it, with Bill's confidentiality at stake. Yet if Joy was HIV-positive, she should know it. Early medical treatment might make a difference. Not to mention the possibility of spreading the infection. Experts said it was seven times less likely for a woman to transmit the virus to a man than vice versa, but it did happen. Haines Wingard could be the next president of the United States. The priest closed his eyes, not wanting to contemplate the consequences.

He had briefly toyed with the idea of writing to her anonymously and suggesting that she get tested. But he decided that was the coward's way out. It also occurred to him that even letters marked Personal and Confidential might first be opened by the Secret Service. She might never get to see the letter.

Was God providing this opportunity? It would be easy for Father Alec to show up at St. Michael's this afternoon. A priest at a Catholic hospital would go virtually unnoticed. Perhaps he could pull her aside and talk to her. He was increasingly sure that he had no other choice. She had to know that she was at risk. It would be wrong not to tell her. He hoped that God and Bill Kendall understood. After all, he rationalized, Bill hadn't talked about Joy under the seal of confession. Even though the anointing he gave Bill carried with it a forgiveness of sins, Bill had never actually gone to confession to him.

His mind made up, Father Alec didn't quite know how he was going to talk to Joy Wingard, but something inside him made him confident that he would be able to complete his mission.

❧ Chapter 76

Joy handled herself impressively. She had studied hard about AIDS and it paid off. She fielded questions of the anchorpeople on the morning shows with ease, grace and earnestness. She had been somewhat surprised that no one had raised the Bill Kendall bequest at the first three shows. Then she got to KEY.

The interview started out routinely enough. Eliza Blake asked her about the status of the fund-raising effort. Joy was proud to report that the American people were being enormously generous. The contributions were flowing in to the AIDS Parade for Dollars Washington post office box.

"Still, Eliza, until there is a cure or a vaccine, there is so much more to be done. So much to be done for those living with AIDS. It's a disease that doesn't care if you're male or female, rich or poor, black or white, old or young. Pediatric AIDS is particularly heartbreaking. This afternoon, I'll have the opportunity to tour AIDS facilities in Newark that have implemented programs to help."

"Why Newark?"

"New Jersey ranks third in the nation, behind New York and Florida, in the number of pediatric AIDS cases. New Jersey also has the highest percentage of females with AIDS. The state has been forced to deal with AIDS and to be innovative in its programs. And the Catholic Church has provided more hospital beds for AIDS patients than any other institution in the country. There's a lot to learn there."

"Mrs. Wingard, following this interview, you are scheduled to tape some public service announcements on AIDS and your fund-raising effort. Here at KEY, we've noted with interest that our own Bill Kendall left $100,000 to the AIDS Parade for Dollars in his will."

"Yes, that's right."

Eliza detected a tensing of Joy's jaw. She decided to remain silent for a few moments and see if Joy would continue on her own, but the candidate's wife just stared back. Eliza had the feeling that Joy was daring her to insinuate anything else. In that moment, Eliza decided not to push any further. There would always be another time.

"Did Bill Kendall have a particular interest in AIDS?"

Joy Wingard went with what she and Nate Heller had planned.

She hoped it didn't sound rehearsed. "Bill Kendall was a fine human being. He was interested in just about anything that affected his fellow man. We had talked about various charities. As you probably know, he did a lot of work as a supporter of the developmentally disabled. But he was one of those who realized, early on, the scope and seriousness of the AIDS threat."

The theme music began to play. Eliza thanked her guest and teased to the movie review coming up after the commercial. Joy Wingard unclipped the microphone from her shrimp-colored linen suit and rose from the couch, taking time to shake Eliza's hand and smile graciously. Eliza mentioned that she was working on a story on the Wingard fund-raising effort and would be following her to Newark later in the day.

"If I can help with your story in any way, Eliza, please don't hesitate to call on me." Beneath the gracious words, Eliza thought she detected a tightness in the candidate's wife's voice.

✣ Chapter 77

Hearing himself paged, the orderly stashed another ravaged patient against the wall of the busy hospital hallway and went to the house phone.

"It's me."

"I'm not supposed to receive personal calls at work!"

"Sorry, couldn't reach you before this. I'll be brief. Joy Wingard is going to be there today. Just keep your eyes open."

"Don't I always?"

"True."

"Hey, Peter, while I've got you on the phone, I've been thinking. You didn't pay me enough for that bit of info on Bill Kendall. If I spread that news around, I could make *a lot more*."

"Okay, okay," came the resigned response. "How much more do you want?"

❧ Chapter 78

"You were wonderful this morning, darling. I got to the office early and watched you on all four shows. There wasn't a question that you didn't answer well. I was very proud of you."

Joy was sitting in a small KEY studio, practicing reading from the Teleprompter her public service announcement scripts when the call from Win was put through. Before she could answer, he continued.

"Today is all yours. Since I have to be here in Washington for Senate business, you'll be our representative out there again today. Your performance this morning was a terrific start. Go get 'em, sweetheart."

Win dealt best with the concrete. He didn't do well with suggestions and nuances. Joy concluded that the Bill Kendall questions hadn't bothered Win at all.

Nate Heller, on the other hand, had not missed any of the subtleties of Eliza Blake's questioning. Wanting to be there when the PSAs were taped, he met Joy as she was entering the studio. Having watched the interviews from his hotel room, he too had been delighted with the way Joy conducted herself. But he had not been thrilled with Eliza's probing.

"Damn her," he hissed, corralling Joy to the corner of the studio. "Damn her and her nosy questions."

"Come on, Nate. She was just doing her job."

"Oh, wonderful. 'She was just doing her job,' " he parroted. "Aren't you the benevolent, understanding one?"

"I think we should be thankful that no one else asked the same question. It's really a fairly obvious one."

Nate considered her words. "You're right. I guess we were lucky. Besides, there isn't anything we can do about it now. Maybe that'll be the end of the Bill Kendall factor."

"Wishful thinking, Nate?"

Nate's eyes followed her as she broke away from him, crossed the small room, mounted the platform and arranged herself carefully in the speaker's chair behind a curved gray Formica-topped desk. "No, thank you," was her response to the KEY makeup woman. She preferred to do her own. The voice of the director came from a speaker in the ceiling. He was watching her on his screen in the control room. He told her that she looked sensational, and asked the cameraman to tighten up on her just a bit.

Unexpectedly, Joy realized that she was not nervous. In fact, she was getting a charge out of the tension in the studio as everyone concerned prepared to tape. She liked this better than a live interview. If she made a mistake, they could just tape again and she could fix it. She had nothing to lose.

℀ Chapter 79

In a large office three hundred yards away, Eliza sat with her boss. She explained to Yelena Gregory what she had found in Bill Kendall's computer notes.

"So I'm here today, uncertain about *what* to do. This thing and its implications are big, and I want to talk about how I— we—should proceed."

Yelena nodded, her broad face somber. "You're right. If I don't seem surprised at what you've told me, it's because Range already talked to me."

Eliza felt a pang of something. Annoyance? Betrayal? What was Range trying to pull, anyway? Telling Eliza in no uncertain terms that Bill's affair was Bill's business and then rushing to talk it over with Yelena.

Yelena was quick to respond to Eliza's unspoken doubts. "Please don't get the wrong impression, Eliza. Range wasn't coming to me behind your back. On the contrary, he was concerned that he had come down too heavily. He was second-guessing himself and he wanted another opinion on how to deal with this."

Somewhat appeased, Eliza decided to let the Range Bullock issue rest, at least for the time being. "Well, what did you and Range decide?"

Yelena rose from her seat, walked around the big desk and rested her imposing figure on the edge of it. She ran her large hands through her closely cropped hair, pulling it back from her face in an expression of beleaguered contemplation.

"I considered this all last night. Didn't sleep much, thinking about it. What is our responsibility here? Someone's got to draw the line somewhere as to what is personal in a public figure's life. It's a tough, tough call." Yelena paused, rising to look out the window onto the city street. She turned back to face Eliza. "But my inclination, at this point at least, is to agree with Range. Bill Kendall and Joy Wingard's affair—if, indeed they had one—isn't something that the country needs to know about to make a decision on Haines Wingard's ability to govern."

Eliza didn't like the intimation that the affair was something less than real. But she also felt somewhat relieved. The buck had been passed, and Yelena had made her decision. Eliza was grateful that the older woman was there to turn to; her wisdom and years of experience were reassuring. Eliza really didn't want to invade Bill's privacy either.

But what about Leo Karas's murder?

"Yelena, something else is bothering me."

"What?"

"The murder of Dr. Leo Karas."

Yelena looked puzzled but interested. "From the account I read, it was my understanding that the police think it's a simple robbery-shooting. Not, of course, that any murder is simple." .

Eliza paused, wondering if she should say more. If she couldn't go to the head of the news division with her suspicions, who could she go to?

The intercom buzzed. "Yelena, Pete Carlson is here."

"Ask him to have a seat. I'll be with him in a few minutes."

A sign. Be quiet. Don't go any further. For now.

Yelena was waiting, looking at Eliza expectantly.

"I guess I'm just a little paranoid these days. The police must know what they're doing." Eliza rose from her seat. "Okay, Yelena. And thanks. I'm glad we talked."

"That's what I'm here for, kiddo. It's an interesting time, and an interesting campaign. We'll see how it all works out. I see on the 'Insights' that you're working on a Joy piece today. I'll bet she's really in love with you after the Kendall question this morning."

Eliza answered, slightly embarrassed. "Oh, you caught the show this morning? I. . . ."

"No need to explain," Yelena reassured. "Regardless of the conversation we just had, that question about Bill had to be asked."

Eliza glanced at her watch. "I better run. I want to catch the end of Joy's taping. Thanks again, Yelena."

The two women smiled and shook hands firmly. As Eliza was leaving, the news president asked, "You've still got Bill's computer notes?"

"Yes, they're safe with me. They're just copies, though. I'm sure Jean's still got the originals."

"Oh," laughed Yelena, "that's fine. They'll be safe with Jean. She'll guard them ferociously. Probably build a shrine around them."

Yelena crossed to the door and, ushering Eliza out, motioned to Pete Carlson. Eliza forced herself to say "Good morning" as she brushed past him.

Pete closed the door behind him as he entered Yelena's office. He didn't know why Eliza had been there, but he was sure of one thing. Yelena didn't seem as happy as she used to whenever she saw him.

"What's the matter, Yelena? You're not yourself lately. Is it something I've done?"

Yelena shook her head, but her brusque manner said it all. She was definitely angry about something.

There had been only one long-distance call that night on last month's phone bill. The night she'd heard of Pete's disgust in sleeping with her.

Yelena's heart had pounded as she dialed this number and listened to the gruff answer.

"Nate Heller."

✣ Chapter 80

Back in his office after the meeting with Yelena, Pete Carlson immediately went for the phone. He jabbed the buttons angrily.

"Why didn't you tell me Joy was having an affair with Bill Kendall?" demanded Carlson.

"If I had, what would you have done with the information?" came Nate Heller's response.

"I would have scooped the world, that's what!"

"Think about it, Pete. That's why I *didn't* tell you. That would not have helped Haines Wingard become the next president of the United States. Are you forgetting your bigger goal?"

Carlson didn't answer. He didn't like being kept in the dark about anything, especially something as potentially explosive as this. Heller was right. Pete wouldn't have reported the affair— that would have severely hurt the Wingard candidacy. But he wanted to be in on all the dirt just the same. Knowledge was power.

"And where did you hear it, anyway?"

"Yelena."

"Christ!" Nate tried to contain his anger. "Now the whole world will know."

"Uh-uh. Don't worry. Yelena's not going to say anything. She cares too much about the reputation of *KEY News* and she doesn't want Kendall's memory besmirched. Apparently, Range Bullock knows, too. But according to Yelena, he's not going to say anything either. Bill was his best friend."

"But there is one problem."

"What's that?"

"Eliza Blake knows, too."

"Will she tell?"

"I don't know. But it's something else we have to worry about."

℀ Chapter 81

The Boarder Babies program at University Hospital was established to provide emotional nourishment for babies born too soon, too small or too sick. Volunteers came to the hospital to hold, rock and provide some human warmth to the tiny human beings who were fighting for their lives. AIDS had increased the already booming business the Boarder Babies program was doing.

Some of the troubled, diseased, overwhelmed mothers who

passed through the delivery room had abandoned their babies. The newborns remained in the hospital for months while efforts were made to place them in foster homes. While the babies waited, they had the benefit of the volunteers, who sat in rocking chairs near the incubators, talking and singing to them. The luckier, stronger infants could be lifted and cuddled and played with.

The volunteers, as well as the staff nurses, became attached to the babies. Some ended up taking the babies home and adopting them. Others, when homes were found for the infants they had grown to love, experienced the pain of deep loss. The volunteers and the nurses said they often got as much emotional satisfaction and nourishment as they gave.

"The warmth of another body, skin-to-skin contact, is central to the human experience," the nursery supervisor explained to Joy. "The babies, like all little ones, need the personal interaction of a mother or at least a mother figure. Would you like to hold one?"

Joy hesitated for a moment, looking uncertainly at the fragile creature lying in the Lucite crib. The head nurse smiled encouragingly, nodded for Joy to take her seat in the nearby rocking chair and carefully lifted the tiny bundle. The baby was placed in the crook of Joy's arm. With her free hand, Joy gingerly searched beneath the cotton receiving blanket until she found the miniature version of her own. The tiny fingers wrapped themselves tightly around her pinky. A tear fell from the corner of Joy's eye.

Yes, thought Nate Heller. Great picture!

❧ Chapter 82

Father Alec waited quietly and alone in the hospital chapel of St. Michael's Medical Center. A Secret Service agent, shoes shined and radio earpiece visible, came in and looked around. Appraising Father Alec sitting in a rear pew in his black suit and Roman collar, the agent apparently saw nothing amiss.

Father Alec was disappointed and distressed. What if his mission today had been to hurt Mrs. Wingard? He speculated on how easy it would be for anyone to dress like a cleric. The agent's cursory glance shouldn't be called security. Of course, they couldn't investigate every single person who came across Mrs. Wingard's path, but he wanted to believe that the Secret Service wasn't missing suspicious and nervous-looking characters. He was sure he must look nervous. In truth, he *was* going to hurt Joy Wingard today.

He rose from the pew, genuflected, turned and walked to the door at the rear of the chapel. Poking his head out, he looked down the corridor. Nothing yet.

The *Star Ledger* had said she was focusing on AIDS in her Newark tour. The archdiocese was proud. St. Michael's with its clinic, support groups and private counseling served about 40 percent of the AIDS patients living in Essex County. Mrs. Wingard must be getting her eyes and ears full. How horrible it would be for her, after observing AIDS cases close up, to hear that she, too, had been exposed to the disease!

Movement down the hall caught his eye. A woman dressed in pink was moving slowly in his direction, her head turned toward a nun who walked beside her. She was listening attentively to what Sister had to say. Cameramen were walking backward in front of her. Several other men and women surrounded her. He assumed they were Secret Service, campaign aides and media types.

What if this doesn't work? What if she won't stop?

Suddenly, she was right in front of him. Joy stopped and her entourage stopped with her. She smiled openly and extended her hand to the young priest standing in the chapel doorway.

"Hello, I'm Joy Wingard." He thought he detected a look of semirecognition in her eyes.

"Mrs. Wingard, I'm Father Alec Fisco from Sacred Heart Cathedral. I was wondering if I could have a few moments of your time?"

She turned to a short, intense-looking man standing beside her. He glanced at his watch and brusquely told her that they were running behind. She turned to Father Alec with an apologetic look and was about to make her excuses when she suddenly placed him.

"Sacred Heart Cathedral? Yes, what can I do for you?"

"I was hoping we could talk in private."

She smiled and gestured to the group around her and shrugged helplessly.

"Perhaps we could talk in the chapel for a minute? Please." The priest's eyes implored.

"Nate, I want to talk to Father in the chapel. Will you please arrange that?"

The short, intense one looked annoyed. But he muttered the necessary instructions. The camera people turned and broke away from the group, eager to get outside and grab an exterior shot of the hospital before it was time to get back in the press cars again. They had enough video of the priest and Mrs. Wingard.

In an instant, Father Alec found himself sitting in a pew in an empty chapel beside the very possible next first lady. She tried to put him at ease.

"Father, that was a beautiful homily you gave for Bill Kendall. I'm sure it must have comforted his family."

"Thank you. I hope so. I'm flattered you remember me."

"Did you know Bill very well?"

"I only knew Bill Kendall for a very brief time, but I think it's fair to say I knew him well."

There was a pause, neither one sure of where to go next with the conversation. The priest looked pained and extraordinarily uncomfortable.

"What is it, Father?"

"Mrs. Wingard, I'm so very sorry to tell you this, but I feel that I must." He stopped and looked like he might actually be sick. She prodded.

"What? What is it?"

"Mrs. Wingard, Bill Kendall had AIDS."

He saw her intake of breath, watched her bite her bottom lip. Otherwise, her face remained expressionless. She rose, smoothed the skirt of her suit, and adjusted a stray strand of hair. If she had just been hit with the psychic equivalent of a body blow, she gave little sign. Instead, she took the priest's hand.

"Thank you, Father. I appreciate that you told me."

His mouth hung slightly open as he watched her walk erect to the chapel door, open it, and face the throng waiting for her on the other side.

❧ Chapter 83

Senator Wingard returned to his office after casting his vote on the Senate floor. The bill that he co-sponsored had passed by a wide margin. He did not feel triumphant.

They think I buy it.

The thought sickened him. He hadn't realized Joy was such a smooth liar.

Nate was another story. He didn't look him in the eye when

the subject of the Kendall bequest came up. It was so out of character for his suspicious campaign manager not to comment on a charitable bequest's being made before the charity had been announced. Nate must know that Joy had been seeing Kendall.

Win was playing along. He didn't want to confront Joy about it now. The campaign was much more important than his marriage. He wanted to put all his energies into becoming president.

But now he knew that neither Joy nor Nate could be trusted. They didn't speak the truth. What else could they be hiding?

He couldn't say he was heartbroken. "Resigned" would be a better description of how he felt. He'd known for a long time that he and Joy didn't have much going on between them. They were thoughtful and polite with one another, but there was none of the easy bantering they'd shared in their early years together. No spark, no excitement. Their lovemaking was perfunctory. They both just went through the motions.

The pursuit of the White House was not bringing them closer. Their marriage was a political business deal.

In a strange way, Wingard was more upset over Nate's betrayal. He'd trusted his campaign manager utterly and completely. But now he knew he'd been naive. He should have known better. Just because they'd cheated on the law boards together all those years ago, and had been friends and allies all of their adult lives, didn't mean that things couldn't change. Brothers betrayed brothers. He just hadn't expected it from Nate.

In the end, how much did it all matter? As long as the presidency was Wingard's.

There was nothing to do now but to go along with the lie. Maybe they would all get away with it in the end. He had watched Joy's morning news interviews with a lump in his throat, but she hadn't betrayed a thing. Even in response to Eliza Blake's questions, Joy had remained calm and collected. If Win hadn't read her journal, he would have believed Joy's explanations himself.

But he had read it. The journal and the letter tucked inside had explained it all.

� Chapter 84

"What did the priest want?" asked Nate the minute they got into the car for the drive to Newark Airport.

"Oh, he wanted to make a point about the evil of abortion," Joy lied carefully. "He was just a very sincere young man. He said that in my position I could do a lot of good by influencing public opinion."

Nate rolled his eyes. "What did you say?"

"I said I understood and respected his feelings and I thanked him."

"Good. Stay off abortion whenever you possibly can."

Joy was relieved that she had an interview with an AP reporter on the flight back to Washington. She didn't have to sit next to Nate. She resented that they had been forced to become allies of a sort, united in their common knowledge of her affair with Bill. As far as she was concerned, the less she saw of Nate Heller, the better she liked it. She especially didn't want to talk to Nate now, after her conversation with Father Alec.

Once settled in her coach seat on the commercial shuttle flight to National Airport, Joy amazed herself at her ability to field the reporter's questions. Sipping an icy ginger ale, she responded appropriately and carefully. Attentive and poised, she made it a point to inject some self-deprecating humor. She was getting quite adept at winning over the reporters. Lately, she had been playing a little game with herself. Before an interview, she'd think of two or three clever statements that she'd find a way to squeeze into the conversation. When she checked the reporter's subsequent story, sure enough, her preplanned quotes would be included with amazing frequency. It worked in print and she had begun to be more aware of doing it with the broadcasters, too. She liked to see if she could pick her own soundbites.

The airliner began its descent to the runway. She noticed that though the early summer evening wasn't dark yet, the landing lights were already lit, rimming the macadam plane path. Joy wondered at the fact that she had been able to do the interview so smoothly, pouring on some charm as well, right after Father Alec's biting pronouncement.

❧ Chapter 85

With less than two minutes until air, Yelena joined Range, Louise and Jean as they settled themselves in the Fishbowl to watch the show on the monitor mounted against the wall of the office. There were several television sets lined up alongside the one turned to KEY, their audio turned down, affording a chance to see what the other networks were doing at the time.

Yelena turned to Jean. "It's good to have you back."

"I second that," added Range.

Jean smiled appreciatively. "I'm surprised at how good it is to be back." Jean had ample reason to smile. She had come back to work on her own terms, having decided that she couldn't face being some other KEY hotshot's "girl." She had always secretly wanted to work in production and, somehow, Bill's death and the time off she had taken to sort things out had emboldened her to ask for what she really wanted. After just two weeks away, she called Range and told him of her desire. She was very pleasantly surprised when he immediately offered her an assistant producer's job on the *Evening Headlines*. What was it they said about adversity being an opportunity for growth?

Louise sat on the office couch, legs crossed, long slit skirt revealing a nice section of thigh. She was looking forward to dinner with Range after the show. In fact, she'd been thinking about it all day. The delicious early summer warmth outside translated into a hunger for Range's male companionship. She knew Range had dinner reservations at Lespinasse. What he didn't know was that she had taken a room for the night at the St. Regis.

Louise glanced out through the glass wall of the Fishbowl. Pete Carlson was in his anchor chair, poised to begin.

Tonight, all the networks led with campaign stories. Coming out of the opening story, Carlson voiced over some pictures of Joy Wingard in Newark visiting the AIDS care facilities. Louise noticed it first.

"Hey, isn't that the priest from Bill's funeral talking to Joy Wingard?"

The camera closed in on the young man's face as Yelena, Range and Jean peered.

Yelena nodded, impressed. "Yes, I think you're right. Nice catch, lady. Sure you don't want a job in news?"

❧ Chapter 86

Returning from Newark, a very tired Eliza inserted the key and opened her apartment door. As she dropped her canvas carry bag in the foyer, she kicked off her black and white spectators and unbuckled the wide patent leather belt cinching her waist. A squealing Janie, fresh from her bath and dragging her stuffed monkey, greeted her.

"Mommy, Mommy!"

"My sweetheart! I missed you!"

She gathered the little girl in her arms and inhaled the deliciousness of her. Mr. Bubble on four-year-old skin.

"Did you have a good day?"

"Uh-huh. Zippy and I had friends over."

"You did? Who?"

"Billy and Chris."

Eliza spotted Mrs. Twomey coming from the bathroom, Janie's clothes gathered in her arms. Mrs. Twomey looked beat.

"Hi, Mrs. Twomey. How did it go today?"

"Fine, fine," Mrs. Twomey responded in her light brogue. "The little Haffler twins came over to play this afternoon and the three of them had a grand time." Eliza envisioned what her day had been. If she was tired, she didn't complain about it. It was a given in Mrs. Twomey's world that people worked hard. That's all there was to it.

"We made cookies, Mommy!"

"You did? What big kids! I hope you saved some for me."

"We did. And Mrs. Twomey made applesauce. We saved some of that for you, too." Janie was enthusiastic. She loved Mrs. Twomey's applesauce.

It was at moments like these that Eliza felt she was missing something. She should be home, supervising the play dates, baking the chocolate chips with her child. It was a recurrent theme.

Janie prodded her toward the kitchen, eager to show off her cookies. The two sat at the glass table, Janie drinking milk, Eliza sipping a Diet Coke. Janie nibbled on her cookie, making only small progress. Eliza popped down three in short order and knew she could easily devour the rest of them. She pushed the plate aside.

Mrs. Twomey, having straightened up after the bath and turned down Janie's bed, came in to say good night.

"Night-night, Mrs. Twomey. See you tomorrow." Janie rose and gave her a big hug. Mrs. Twomey hugged back, genuinely and affectionately.

"Good night, Mrs. Twomey, and thank you."

The housekeeper looked like she wanted to say something. "What is it, Mrs. Twomey? Is something wrong?"

"Mrs. Blake, I've been wanting to tell you for quite a while and I'm just going to come out with it. I've been watching that Pete Carlson on the news and I think you are so much better than he is. I think you should have gotten Bill Kendall's job." She exhaled with a deliberate nod of the head. "There. I've said it."

Eliza smiled. "I think you're a bit prejudiced, Mrs. Twomey. But thanks all the same. I appreciate it."

Hearing Mrs. Twomey lock the front door behind her, Eliza glanced at the microwave's digital clock—8:15. Already. Janie went to bed at 8:30. A big half hour at the end of the day to spend with her little girl. Quality time, schmality time. It wasn't enough, and she knew it.

Mother and daughter walked down the hall to the little girl's room and started their routine. *Goodnight, Moon*, Walt Disney's version of *Button Soup*, *Clifford the Big Red Dog*, and *Curious George*. Most kids, Eliza speculated, would want *Goodnight, Moon* read last, just prior to lights out. Not Janie. Janie liked to be prepared. *Goodnight, Moon* was the stage-setter and got her mind thinking in the direction of going to sleep. The other stories were the ones she really enjoyed, always saving *Curious George* for last.

"I love monkeys. Can we get a monkey, Mommy? Please?"

"You have Zippy, sweetheart."

Janie wasn't buying it. "I mean a real monkey."

"No."

"Why?"

"We can't keep a monkey in an apartment."

"Please?"

"Sorry, Janie. The answer is no."

The afternoon spent with Billy and Christopher Haffler had left Janie tired enough to give up fairly easily. A half-dozen hugs, kisses, "night-nights" and "I love yous" later, and the little girl was settled in for the night.

Eliza padded back down to the kitchen, peeling off her pantyhose as she walked. Instinctively, she went over and turned on the television that rested on the counter. She hit the rewind button of the VCR, rolling back the tape of the *Evening Headlines*. She had the VCR programmed to tape the show every night.

A fifteen-hour day, and in less than seven hours she'd be up to do it again. Eliza groaned and mentally checked off what she wanted to do before she could crawl gratefully into bed. A good, hot bath was high on the list.

She hit the Play button. The tail end of the local news sports report popped on the screen. The Mets lost again. So did the Yankees. The sports announcer was disgusted.

Mrs. Twomey had left some roast chicken, green beans and a baked potato on a covered plate in the microwave. Not really tasting what she was eating, Eliza listened as the *Evening Headlines* began. She watched entranced as Pete Carlson delivered the day's news.

Pete might not be impressive in person, but Eliza had to admit that on television he came across powerfully. Funny, how TV could do that. She had seen people who had great personal magnetism not make the grade as TV personalities. Carlson was the reverse. In the flesh, he had the charisma of day-old bread, but on the screen, he shone. It was surprising that the ratings were down. Maybe the public somehow sensed what a rat he was and tuned out.

"Meow!" Eliza purred out loud, disgusted with herself for dwelling on Carlson. She was jealous and she knew it. Increasingly, she realized she wanted the anchor job. Just run your own race, she told herself. Focus on your job and do it in the best way possible.

Carlson was talking over the pictures of Joy Wingard. Predictably, the screen showed Mrs. Wingard's eyes filling up as she held the AIDS baby. Eliza knew the moment she had seen the tear in Joy's eye that afternoon that the picture would make the evening news. It was a natural.

The last tel-op was Joy talking to the young priest. Standing near Joy, Eliza had heard him introduce himself as Father Fisco from Sacred Heart Cathedral. She had immediately placed him as the priest who gave the memorable sermon at Bill's funeral. What had he said to Joy behind closed chapel doors? What had he wanted from her?

Eliza poured scalding water over a decaffeinated tea bag in a yellow ceramic KEY mug. She was too tired to speculate further about Joy Wingard and Father Fisco. Her mind was already looking ahead to tomorrow. She had to be up at her usual painful hour, anchor the show, go out and do a couple of interviews with outside observers of Mrs. Wingard's AIDS fund-raising efforts and, then, hopefully, sit down to write the script for the piece. The video shot today would definitely be worth using again in the takeout piece, even though some of it had already aired on the show tonight as hard news. In addition, the Washington bureau was shooting pictures of the office where volunteers were busy counting the money that was flowing into the D.C. post office box. Other KEY bureaus around the country were getting reaction from people in the street on what they thought of Joy Wingard's efforts for the AIDS Parade for Dollars.

Yes, Eliza decided, the elements were well covered. The piece had all the makings of a winner and Eliza was determined to have her best effort air on the *Evening Headlines*.

But right now, the bathtub beckoned.

℀ Chapter 87

Jean opened a pouch of dried cat food and emptied it into Sylvester's bowl. The black and white cat stared indifferently from beneath the kitchen table. Jean scooped the contents of a can of corned beef hash into a microwavable bowl, covered it and zapped it for six minutes. As she ate in silence, she reflected that her dinner was not that much different from her pet's.

Jean's mood was not improved by thoughts of what she had witnessed in Range's office. Louise and Range had become quite an item in her absence and she didn't approve, not one bit. Seeing Louise in the Fishbowl tonight was a reminder of Bill. How any woman could ever be interested in another man after she'd had Bill was beyond Jean. He was the best and anyone else fell short in comparison.

Sylvester finally arose, stretched and glided over to his bowl. He halfheartedly took a few bits of the ersatz chicken concoction and then walked away in disdain.

"Aren't you the high and mighty one? You should be glad that you are fed at all, for all the feedback I get from you!"

High and mighty. Louise Kendall thought she was so high and mighty. Sashaying in there this evening dressed like a common floozy. She was so sure of herself, sidling up to Range and flirting unabashedly. She should be ashamed!

And Range. What came over him as soon as that woman walked into the room? He acted like a fool. Didn't he have any loyalty to Bill? It was disgusting!

A job in news, indeed. Sure, Yelena, that's just what they all needed. Louise Kendall in the newsroom, another office affair. Jean grimaced at the thought. She had witnessed dozens of personal relationships develop in the news department over the years. Some lasted, most didn't. But all of them had turned her off. Work and love, not to mention sex, just didn't go together. She would never allow herself to get involved with anyone at work.

Not that anyone had ever asked.

In all her years at KEY the only one who had ever interested her, the only one she had guiltily fantasized about, was Bill. He was the only one she had ever loved. And she was very sure there would be no other. Louise Kendall should get down on her knees and thank God that she'd been married to Bill and be forever grateful that he'd fathered her child. The fact that Louise

Kendall was showing interest in another man was revolting. Being Bill Kendall's widow, even if they had been divorced, should be enough for any woman.

Bill Kendall's widow. What a grand role that would be! To have been able to mourn for Bill for all the world to see. Jean would have given that role the respect it deserved, beginning from the day of the funeral. It would been her privilege to walk behind Bill's casket, to have the priest address her in his sermon.

The priest. That's what had her thinking so much about Bill. Jean looked down and began fingering the ivory bracelet on her left wrist. A Christmas gift from her precious Bill.

She wondered what the priest had been talking to Mrs. Wingard about.

She brought her plate over to the kitchen sink, bent down to the cabinet beneath and began to rummage through it. Finding the can of paint thinner, she grabbed a clean rag and made her way to the bathroom. Those painters had been slobs. There were paint splatterings all over the place. She breathed in the turpentine vapors as she methodically began rubbing and loosening the tiny specks of stray paint that had affixed themselves to the tiles. She liked things to be spotless.

As she worked diligently, her thoughts turned to her new job. She wanted so to make a success of it. Range had told her today that she would be traveling with the news staff to the conventions this summer. She was thrilled. She wanted to do a good job, wanted everyone to see her value. She planned to study up before the trips.

Pete Carlson would be anchoring at the conventions this year. She hoped he flopped. Failed miserably. Carlson had nerve, thinking he could replace Bill.

It still bothered her having to leave Bill's personal files on the computer in what was now Pete Carlson's office. What if that slug ever accessed them?

That's impossible, Jean consoled herself. If she couldn't figure out Bill's password, then Carlson couldn't either.

As she scrubbed away, Bill's bracelet smashed against the tile wall, breaking apart. She knelt down to pick up the pieces, tears welling up in her eyes.

Bill's gift. Ivory.

" 'An elephant never forgets.'

"Elephant!"

❧ Chapter 88

Mack was waiting for Eliza when she arrived at the *KEY to America* studio at 5:00 A.M. As she approached him, her face lit up in a smile and she felt her heart beat faster.

"What in the world are you doing here so early? Never mind. I've missed you." She wanted to kiss him but, mindful of where they were, she held back. Her initial reaction of happy anticipation was quickly replaced by a sense of foreboding when she saw the strange expression on Mack's face.

"Let's go up to your office."

"What? What is it? Just tell me now."

"Trust me."

He took her arm and guided her out of the newsroom and down the hall to the elevator. Once inside her office, he closed the door and indicated she should take a seat.

"Okay, now. What is it?" she demanded.

"Here."

He pulled a rolled-up copy of the newest issue of *The Mole* from his jacket pocket. Eliza felt her pulse race as she read the headline:

ELIZA BLAKE: THE TIE THAT BINDS DEAD ANCHOR AND MURDERED DOCTOR!

As Eliza scanned the innuendo-filled story, Mack said, "You've got to confront this head on."

❧ Chapter 89

The last few minutes of every *KEY to America* were usually devoted to off-the-cuff banter between Eliza and Harry. But today, everyone was talking about Eliza's soliloquy on this morning's broadcast.

Yelena re-cued the videotape to watch it again. Eliza, in a honey-colored jacket, looked resolutely into the camera, her blue eyes clear.

"In closing this morning, I want to talk to you about something very personal. It's about a time of my life, a very painful time, a time that I'd always thought I could keep to myself.

"Unfortunately, now, due to recent published reports, erroneous reports, I feel I must set the record straight."

The camera pulled tighter on Eliza's solemn face.

"Four years ago, after the death of my husband and the birth of my daughter, I went through a very difficult time. Simply put, I collapsed emotionally. At that time, Bill Kendall, our former anchorman and my dear friend, was very supportive, going as far as recommending a good therapist, Dr. Leo Karas.

"It's been reported that I was hospitalized. And that is true. I spent almost a month at a hospital in New Jersey recuperating and I continued therapy with Dr. Karas after my clinic stay. Fortunately for me and my child, I was able, with wonderful care, to get through that hard time. I am very grateful for that."

Yelena watched as Eliza stared determinedly from the screen.

"It's also been reported, however, that I had a drug problem. *That is not true.* I have never used cocaine or any other illegal drug in my life. I hasten to add, though, that people who *are* addicted to drugs need to be helped, not attacked.

"Within the past two months, we've lost Bill Kendall to suicide and Dr. Karas has been murdered. I, as much as and perhaps more than anyone else would like to know what, if any, connection there is between these two tragic deaths."

Here, Eliza was adamant.

"But to suggest, as has been done in print, that I may have had something to do with these events, is libelous, malicious and outrageous. Both of these men were very dear to me, and important in my life."

Yelena stopped the videotape. The *KEY News* switchboard had been inundated with calls, and faxes had been coming in all day. The overwhelming majority of viewers were supporting Eliza.

The news president was relieved, but not just because it was good for *KEY News*.

℀ Chapter 90

Jean sat in the back of a yellow cab riding up Tenth Avenue, eager to get to Eliza's Upper West Side apartment.

It hadn't been too difficult to get to the computer. She still had her key to Pete's office—no, she corrected herself—*Bill's* office. She waited until everyone had cleared out after Friday's show. She'd simply let herself into the office, sat behind the desk and typed in the eight letters.

E-L-E-P-H-A-N-T. Magic.

Bill's Remember directory opened. The first file in the alphabetical list was 'ETHICS.PC.' Jean had almost bypassed this file, thinking PC stood for "politically correct." When she double-clicked on it, the file opened and she discovered that the letters stood, instead, for Pete Carlson.

The cab pulled up in front of Eliza's building. The doorman

announced her and Jean was let into the apartment by Mrs. Twomey. Janie was at the housekeeper's side.

"Mommy is getting ready for a big party," she announced proudly.

Eliza came down the hall, wearing a bathrobe, her hair wrapped in a towel, looking worried.

"Jean, is everything okay?" Jean had never come to the apartment before.

"Eliza, you have to help. I have to tell you what I found on Bill's computer. Pete Carlson!" Jean was out of breath.

Eliza took her arm. "Here, Jean, sit down. Calm yourself. Now, what's the matter?"

"It's Pete Carlson."

"Mrs. Twomey, would you please take Janie into the kitchen and get her some ice cream for dessert?" Eliza didn't want Janie in on this.

"Now, start again, Jean."

Bill's secretary tried to collect herself. "Okay. You know how Bill was planning on writing a book?"

"Yes."

"Well, he kept notes on his computer for it. Notes that were password-protected. I couldn't access them after he died, couldn't erase them from the computer, the computer that is now in Carlson's office."

"Go on."

"Well, I figured out the password."

Down the hall, Eliza could see Mrs. Twomey in the kitchen. Beyond the housekeeper, she saw Janie globbing Hershey's syrup on her vanilla ice cream. So normal a scene in what had become such a complicated life.

She forced herself to ask, "What did you find?"

"Something about Pete Carlson and the Wingard campaign. Oh, God, it's all in the computer. I didn't want to make a hard copy of the files. But you can come and see the notes yourself."

Eliza glanced at her watch. In twenty minutes, Mack would be picking her up to drive out to the New Visions dinner. She had to give the speech tonight. She'd promised. First, the lies in *The Mole* yesterday, then her defense before a national audience, now this.

"Look, let's take this one step at a time. Tomorrow, I have a shoot all day. Why don't you make a copy of the notes and bring them over here on Sunday. We'll go over them and decide what to do next."

Calmer now, Jean nodded. "I'll make copies of everything. There's more in there I didn't even get to read . . . something about a judge, and a file named JOY.ALL. Maybe I should call Yelena."

Eliza wanted to go to Bill's old office right then. But another day wouldn't matter.

❧ Chapter 91

Many heads turned to stare as Eliza Blake entered the crowded Marriott ballroom. She stood in the doorway, erect and elegant in a form-fitting white strapless gown. Her hair was swept up in a French twist which showed to advantage her long, graceful neck and the twinkling diamond studs decorating her earlobes. She wore no other jewelry.

"So this is how it feels to make an entrance with a star," Mack whispered in her ear.

Eliza smiled up at him in reply.

"You're beaming," he said.

"Mack, I actually feel glamorous tonight. I haven't felt glamorous in a very long time."

"I'm glad I'm here to see it."

She took his hand. "You've certainly made your contribution to making me feel this way."

He wanted to kiss her, long and hard. But that would have to wait. Later, after an evening of anticipation.

"Eliza. Mack." Louise Kendall, smashing in a tuxedo-style suit with a very high slit in its long, black skirt, came to their side. "Eliza! You look wonderful. Thank you again, so much, for coming tonight. We're sold out! Everyone wants to see and hear you!"

Louise steered them to one of the fifty round tables that dotted the festive room. Five hundred well-turned-out people had paid five hundred dollars a ticket to support New Visions for Living and its goal to open yet another group home for the developmentally disabled. The theme this year was "Black and White" and the ballroom was decked out accordingly. Black and white helium-filled balloons covered the ceiling, white dinner plates lay on top of black porcelain chargers, and flower arrangements of white blooms dominated each table. In a corner of the room, a white BMW coupe with a black convertible top preened seductively. Some lucky raffle winner was going to drive home in style tonight.

"I hope you won't mind, but I've seated you next to William."

"Fine. I'd especially like to get to know William a little better."

Louise smiled gratefully. "Well, don't let him chew your ear off."

What a gentle soul the young man was! He cast his eyes down bashfully as Eliza extended her hand to him, but he managed to shake it firmly. Eliza complimented him on how handsome he looked dressed in his dinner jacket.

"You look pretty, too," William said, blushing.

Eliza gently tried to draw him out and they talked for a while about his group home and his computer. "My dad and I worked on the computer," he said quietly. "I miss my dad."

"I miss your dad, too, William. Many people do."

"They do? I thought I was the only one."

Eliza felt the sting of tears. The poor kid. Bill was central to William's life, as John had been central to hers. Just a few weeks after his father's death, William must be hurting terribly.

She felt the faint stirrings of a headache.

Now, Louise was standing next to her chair.

"Eliza, have you met Father Alexander Fisco?"

"I remember you, Father. From Bill's funeral. It was a beautiful Mass."

The priest smiled, almost shyly, Eliza thought. "Thank you."

Louise was going on. "We're blessed to have Father Alec here tonight to give the invocation before dinner."

Eliza made a mental note to talk to the priest before the evening was over. Father Alec took the seat on the other side of William.

People kept coming over to the table, wanting to be introduced to the anchorwoman. Louise did so enthusiastically. Satisfied diners this year would mean guaranteed ticket sales next year. Louise stood again, now accompanied by a slick-looking man in a tuxedo. Eliza finished swallowing her Fiorinal.

"Eliza, I'd like you to meet Judge Dennis Quinn. Dennis and Bill worked on fund-raising for New Visions years ago. After a hiatus, Dennis is back working with us again, and we couldn't be more pleased."

Eliza rose to shake the man's hand, but she was interrupted by her young dinner partner.

"The man with the funny red hair." William was staring at the judge with a dark scowl on his face.

Eliza looked back at the judge. His hair was jet black, streaked with a few grays.

William looked down at his plate and began speaking to himself. "Well, you're gonna give it back every bit, how can I do that, we'll figure out a way, well you're gonna give it back every bit, how can I do that, we'll figure out . . ."

No one moved. Louise tried to quiet the young man, placing his spoon in his hand, telling him, "It's okay, William."

Louise looked up apologetically.

Judge Quinn shrugged and smiled uneasily. "Poor kid," he said.

William went back to eating his fruit cup. Father Alec stared at the judge.

℀ Chapter 92

How could late June be so hot? It must be that global warming thing.

A blast of scorching air shot through the window at the toll plaza. The black Lincoln Continental pulled off the New Jersey Turnpike at 15W and headed for Route 280, the highway that led to Newark and points west.

The advance call this morning had been a good idea. The priest had not asked for identification. When asked about the possibility of confession, Father Alec had answered that the sacrament of reconciliation was celebrated in the cathedral every Saturday at 11:30. After learning that anonymity was essential, the priest had been very reassuring: it was unlikely that many people would be coming to confession on a sweltering Saturday morning.

"Father, I'd rather even you didn't see me."

"Fine." The priest had not missed a beat. "I could wait for you in the confessional at the fourth station of the cross, at the right rear of the cathedral at 11:30. I won't be able to see you from inside the box. And once you get inside, you'll be able to see my outline through the screen, but I won't be able to see you."

"You're sure?"

"Absolutely."

Maybe he was telling the truth, maybe he wasn't. But the chance had to be taken. It was important to know if Father Alec was going to present a problem. A problem that would have to be dealt with.

Route 280 was a real garden path. Industrialized Newark was the garden. Driving this way every day would be really depressing. Fortunately, there was no need for that. Today would be a one-shot deal. Unless, of course, it was necessary to take care of the priest.

Getting off at Exit 14, the Lincoln turned right onto Clifton Avenue. Immediately after Branch Brook Park, the granite cathedral loomed. Heat waves rippled over the brick courtyard of Pope John Paul II Plaza, as the car passed slowly in front of the cathedral and then took a turn to the right onto the street that separated the church from the public high school. The rectory was attached to the rear of the cathedral.

Father Alec had explained that it would be necessary to enter the cathedral through the side door of the rectory. The beautiful, massive front doors of the cathedral were only open on Sunday and for major services. At all other times, anyone entering had to pass through the rectory lobby. A chance to be seen, but a chance that had to be taken.

The car clock read 10:45. Okay, find a place to park. The Lincoln continued down the street and pulled into a spot at the corner. It would be easy to pull out from here.

There was no one to pass on the short, hot walk back down the street to the rectory entrance. Inside the welcoming coolness, the teenager at the office window barely looked up. The youngster's demeanor suggested that his policy was to answer, not ask, questions. Lucky.

A black and white sign indicated that the cathedral was to the right, down a long hallway flanked with stained glass depictions of rather dour-looking saints. Entering at the side of the main altar and looking around carefully, Dennis saw that the priest had been right. The cathedral appeared to be empty. There were no

Catholics hanging out in church on this unusually hot Saturday in June.

The best thing to do would be to act like a tourist and slowly make the path around the interior walls of the building until the fourth station was located. A pious pilgrim would have walked across the width of the nave to begin the Way of the Cross on the eastern wall. Here, at the western end of the transept, was where the Savior's sorrows ended.

Walking down the west aisle, the impious could begin at the fourteenth station, which was a multicolored mosaic of the lifeless body of the Christ being lowered into the tomb.

Ah, the last shall be first.

The next station was Jesus coming down from the cross, followed by Jesus expiring on the cross, Jesus being nailed to the cross, Jesus being stripped of his garments, Jesus falling a third time and, then, Jesus consoling the holy women of Jerusalem.

The vestibule was a welcome break from Jesus' travails. It might also be a good place to hide and wait. Up the east aisle of the nave, to the fourth station, "Jesus Meets His Afflicted Mother." The oaken confessional box was right beside it. No need to go farther. Find a place to hide where the confessional was visible.

11:00 A.M.

The vestibule provided as good a spot as any. No one would look askance at someone admiring the carvings there or reading a pamphlet on the cathedral basilica. A quick look down a short hallway off the vestibule provided a bonus. A small area with double doors. The slit between the doors provided a perfect view of the fourth station. It was very unlikely that anyone would come upon this spot. It was a good place to sit and watch.

Time passed. A small pleasant-looking, white-haired man with a large key ring attached to the belt loop of his workpants entered the nave and began making his way along the eastern wall of the church, methodically shining the marble floor with his large, electric floor polisher. At the same time, Father Alec, dressed in a black clergy shirt, crossed the church and stopped to genuflect in front of the main altar. He quickly caught up to the older man.

"*Buon giorno,* Vittorio."

"*Buon giorno,* Padre. How are you today?" Vittorio asked with a thick accent.

"Fine, Vittorio. *Un po' caldo, no?*"

"*Si,* Padre."

The priest traveled on, opened the confessional door and entered, closing the door behind him and settling himself on the hard seat. He placed a small purple stole around his neck. In the silence of the cathedral, he strained to hear footsteps over the noise of the floor polisher. The design of the confessional called for the small light in his box to change from green to red when someone knelt in the adjoining box. That was the design.

The reality was that the light had long ago burned out and no one had bothered to replace it, especially since so many confessions were now done face to face in "reconciliation rooms" on the other side of the cathedral.

The shoes clicked on the marble floor.

Parting the heavy red velvet drape and going into the box, Dennis knelt on the small wooden kneeler in the darkness. The walls were lined with soundproofing tiles, a touch of modernity seemingly out of place in a Gothic cathedral. Through the pindots in the screen, the outline of Father Alec's profile could be seen. There was an awkward silence.

"Father, I'm the man with the funny red hair. I wanted to talk to you last night at the dinner, but you left right after the invocation."

"Go on."

"Well, I'm afraid you know that Bill Kendall and I had a financial arrangement. I borrowed a good deal of money and Bill Kendall was making sure that I paid it back. But I think you know this already."

"I can't say whether I know anything or not," said the priest.

"Okay, Father. I understand. But you can imagine that I

wasn't unhappy when Bill Kendall took his own life. I thought I was home free."

Silence.

"But then, Bill's psychiatrist decided to turn the screws. Now he's dead, too."

Father Alec felt he needed to ask the question. "Did you have anything to do with his murder?"

"No."

Did the answer come too quickly? Father Alec couldn't tell. But if his penitent was not here to confess the sin of murder, then what was it? "Why are you here?" the priest asked pointedly.

A pause.

"As far as I know, there were only three men who could ever expose me. Two of them are dead. There's only one left."

"Is this a threat? Are you threatening a priest in his own confessional?"

The wooden kneeler was uncomfortable. Dennis shifted his weight.

"I just want to feel safe. I haven't felt safe for a long time."

"You can trust the seal of confession. I am bound to go to my grave with anything you tell me here."

Dennis realized that the priest was offering him the chance to unburden his heart. That wasn't why he'd driven down the turnpike this morning. But maybe he shouldn't miss the opportunity to bind the priest to the sacramental seal. After a few moments, the fallen-away Catholic found that the words came back so easily. "Bless me, Father, for I have sinned. It's been twenty years since my last confession. These are my sins."

The priest listened.

"What do you plan to do now?"

"I'll take care of things in my own way, Father."

❧ Chapter 93

Nate Heller was giving himself a birthday dinner. Admittedly, it was a Saturday, but it was his forty-sixth birthday and no one had called all day. He was surprised Win hadn't said anything. His friend had always remembered.

Win concentrated on the campaign. It seemed as though there was nothing else in the world.

The waiter brought the covered dishes to the table. Beneath the lids rested Nate's favorite orange-pressed duck, shrimp and lobster sauce, and fried rice. Nate took a sip of cold Chinese beer and licked his lips. Happy birthday to me.

Today had been spent like the others before it, working toward the goal. Nate, Win and Joy met to discuss the last of the pre-convention traveling schedule. Joy had been preoccupied and didn't really seem to be focusing on the business at hand. It worried him. She had to be on top of things. None of them needed her slipping up.

He had let her think that he'd bought her explanation of the meeting with the priest in that Newark hospital.

Damn it! Another complication. The priest from Bill Kendall's funeral. The priest in the will. For sure, Father Fisco had not wanted to talk about abortion.

Just what he didn't need. Things were going so well. The AIDS Parade for Dollars was succeeding beyond his best expectations. The publicity for the campaign had been wonderful and public approval ratings for the project were high. All from his idea.

Nate felt his throat constrict and the crispy duck was hard to swallow. Joy's damned affair wasn't going to muck things up.

No way. Did that damn priest know something? God, he hoped not.

Nate stifled a burp as the waiter cleared away the empty dishes and brought a steamy hand towel along with a plate of sliced oranges and a fortune cookie. He tore the orange away from its rind with his teeth, intent on getting every last bit of the juicy goodness. Cracking open his cookie, he read the Confucian version of God helps them who help themselves. That was true in any society, in any language. Nate had spent most of his life helping himself, realizing that no one was going to do it for him. He reached for his wallet and checked his watch.

He had to catch the late shuttle to Newark. He wanted to schmooze the judge, take him out to dinner tomorrow night maybe, let him get the idea that he's a sure bet for a federal position. Pete needed a little stroking, too. Keeping it up for Yelena was getting more and more difficult for him, but she was too valuable a resource for the cause.

Nate felt a burning feeling in his chest. He must have eaten too quickly. Or it was simply that his stomach always churned these days. Worrying about the loose cannon didn't help.

The loose cannon. Eliza Blake. As far as he was concerned, Eliza Blake couldn't be trusted.

"Happy birthday, dear Natey, Happy birthday to you."

❧ Chapter 94

New York's Fifth Avenue was almost deserted on Sunday morning. Early as it was, it would be good to get inside the cool cathedral. The sun, barely poking through the skyscrapers, was already heating up the city's macadam and concrete.

Arriving half an hour early for the 8:00 A.M. Mass ensured that Jean's entrance wouldn't be missed.

Sad that it should have to be this way. But there was really no choice. Jean knew, or would soon know, everything in Bill Kendall's personal files. Everything.

There she was! Clutching her little white summer pocketbook in front of her, her face looking pinched and strained. Genuflecting at an empty pew, Jean stepped in and knelt to pray. Throughout the Mass, her bony fingers rubbed the glass beads of her rosary, her lips moving silently.

At Communion time, Jean rose to take her place on line. Her head was bowed so reverently as she approached the priest. What a sanctimonious prig! Why couldn't she have just kept her nose out of it?

There was a special term for it, wasn't there? Viaticum. The *last* Communion.

As the priest placed the thin wafer on her tongue, Jean was unaware that she was receiving her viaticum, the spiritual food for her final journey.

The cathedral pews were far from full at such an early Mass, so there was no problem keeping Jean in sight as she moved to her seat. Jean in her prim cotton dress and cardigan, God forbid she should have bare arms in church.

Soon that pious busybody would be silenced forever.

Funny, if you've killed once, it was easy to kill again.

"The Mass is ended. Go in peace."

"Thanks be to God," Jean replied.

Chapter 95

As she descended the steps of St. Patrick's, Jean didn't notice that she was being followed. Walking toward the subway station, her mind was on getting to KEY, making a copy of the files in Bill's office and going to meet Eliza.

Jean was thinking of her beloved Bill as the train roared into the station and she felt the violent push from behind.

July

❧ Chapter 96

"It's freezing in here."

Eliza rose from her desk, rubbing her arms. She was sure that it was a good ten degrees cooler in her den than the wall thermostat indicated. She hesitated to complain too loudly. Only early July, it was blistering outside. The weather forecasters were predicting a scorching summer.

Janie and Mrs. Twomey were in the living room working on some Sesame Street puzzles. Eliza and Mack were going over convention research, or were trying to. Jean's death had shaken everyone.

The police thought it was an accident, or perhaps another suicide. There had been no witnesses on the subway platform so early on a Sunday morning.

With the *Evening Headlines* story on Joy Wingard behind her, Eliza was trying to immerse herself in convention research material. Houston's Astrodome had been selected as the Convention Hall. Almost 5,000 delegates and alternates, as well as 15,000 members of the media, and another 40,000 guests and convention participants were expected to converge on the largest city in Texas. The greater Houston metropolitan area roughly measured that of the state of Rhode Island and Houstonian hospitality would earn a huge economic boost for the town.

In addition to anchoring *KEY to America* from the KEY skybox atop the Astrodome, Eliza would report from the floor during the evening convention sessions. She had a preliminary copy of the *KEY Convention Handbook*, a guide that contained just about every imaginable piece of knowledge helpful in covering this major political event. Delegate seating charts, procedural rules, delegate counts broken down by state, convention staff and officials and their phone numbers, biographies and background information on the players, as well as a history of the campaign thus far—all of it was efficiently included in the handbook. Reading it carefully, Eliza couldn't think of much the research staff had missed. Yet she knew there would be additions and corrections to the three-ring binder right up until the convention began.

The convention planners wanted a "newsless" convention, one where there was little controversy and the focus would be on Haines Wingard, the shining candidate and leader of his country. With America watching at home, a national show of party unity was the goal. This convention promised to be a lovefest. Eliza knew it was especially important to have a mental cache of anecdotes and background material to use when there was air to fill while the delirious delegates demonstrated and minor speakers droned.

She'd done some research of her own, reading books and articles on past presidential candidates and their wives. She wasn't surprised to learn how many of the powerful men had been involved in extramarital activities. She wondered if anyone had ever thought of doing a book on the "activities" of the wives. Perhaps there weren't enough first ladies who had dallied outside their marriages to do a book about it. Maybe down the line, when Eliza's broadcasting days were over, she could do the research and see if there was a book there. She knew that the Joy Wingard story would make a great chapter. Eliza also knew that the knowledge she possessed could make this convention anything but newsless.

Eliza absentmindedly rubbed the tiny gold charm that hung from her wrist.

"Mack, I keep going over it in my mind. Jean coming over here with her allegations about Pete Carlson and mentioning something about other computer files." Eliza tried to remember just what Jean had said. "There was a file about a judge, she mentioned, and a file about Joy. I was in such a rush, Mack, and she was going on and on, and asking for help. You were on your way over, and I'm afraid I didn't realize how serious it all might have been to her.

"And then we get to the New Visions dinner, I'm trying to keep my speech in my head and look after Bill's son, and Louise introduces me to this Judge Quinn. You remember him. Just as he says hello, young William calls him 'the man with the funny red hair.'

"And now Jean is crushed by a subway train. I know it sounds crazy, but I feel that it's all connected somehow. I just know it is."

Mack considered. "Look, we can't get into Bill's notes. We don't know the password. Let's sleuth around in Houston. Maybe we'll find out more there."

Eliza crossed the room and perched herself on the arm of Mack's chair. She circled her arms around his neck.

"Mack?"

"Hmm?"

"I'm excited about the Houston trip."

"I know. I know there's nothing you like better than politics and intrigue."

"That's not what I was thinking about. Do you realize this is the first time we'll be away together?"

"If you can call it that. There will be thousands of people there. And we'll both be working excruciatingly long hours. We won't have much time together at all."

"Remember the old expression, 'Where there's a will . . .' "

❧ Chapter 97

Louise kissed the brown wavy hair and gave the fluffy comforter covering her son one last tuck. Then she tiptoed out of the room. William was home for a few days while some repair work was being done on his group home.

She listened outside the door a minute, as she had hundreds of times before. She could hear the muffled sounds of her son talking to himself as he so often did before he fell asleep. Memories of the two-sided conversations he had replayed as a little boy usually made her smile, as it was his special way of working out in his mind at night what had happened in his school classes each day. Louise had learned what was being taught, what his teachers had corrected him on, even whom William had fought with, just by listening as he talked himself to sleep.

Tonight, she was reminded of the New Visions dinner and his replay at the table. Louise thought that getting embarrassed over William was a thing of the past, but everyone had felt so uncomfortable.

Louise slowly climbed up the flight to the third-floor library and made her way to the mahogany partners desk. The glass bowl resting on the corner of the desk was filled with unopened bills and unanswered correspondence she wanted to go through before she hit the hay herself.

She knew she had been neglecting things. Burning the candle at both ends, hey, old girl? In the days before Range, Louise's weeks had been fairly routine, filled with work and reasonable bedtimes. When William came home for weekend visits, she had plenty of energy for him.

Now, with Range a very important part of her life, she gladly traveled into Manhattan two or three nights a week. Range came out to New Jersey on weekends. Louise smiled, thinking of Range's pronouncement that he would not want to spend the night anytime William was home. Louise was glad that Range had said it before she had.

She'd also spent a good deal of time on the New Visions fundraiser. It had been worth it, though. The dinner had been their most successful moneymaker yet. Eliza Blake had been a big hit as the dinner speaker. And, happily, when Louise asked her if she'd do it again next year, Eliza had agreed.

Indeed, everything was better than it had been in a very long time, and Louise was grateful. Still, the pace of her very full life was tiring, and now she was looking forward to accompanying Range to Houston. Tonight, she was just glad to have a chance to get caught up on her paperwork, write some checks, and go through the printouts of the newest multiple listings. She had three clients who were aching to buy and she didn't want to miss an opportunity to close them.

For the next forty-five minutes she systematically wrote checks to pay the condominium maintenance fee, the Public Service Electric and Gas bill, the American Express and Visa bills, her monthly health insurance, and the car and life insurance premiums that always came due at this time of year. Then there were the envelopes asking for donations for charitable causes. She worked her way through the bowl until there were no more checks to be written for the month.

Louise decided to plow away and try to make a dent in responding to the condolence letters that were still coming in about Bill. She had been answering the letters with a personal note of her own, rather than sending the standard engraved cards. The first order of business tonight was a letter from the vice president himself, who recalled his dealings with Bill in interview situations over the years. Bill was, the vice president wrote, always straight-shooting in his questioning. The VP also went on to remark how impressed he had been with Bill's funeral service and thought that it had been a fitting sendoff for such a fine man.

Louise's mind traveled back to the funeral. It had been impressive and she had Father Alec to thank for it. He had handled everything.

Father Alec. Joy Wingard. Leo Karas. Bill's will. There was some sort of connection there. It was bothering her. Seeing the priest talk to Joy in the videotape the other night was just too much of a coincidence. What was going on? She would ask Range what he thought.

She answered the vice president and three other messages of sympathy and decided to call it a night. As she capped her pen and went to switch off the lamp, she noticed a small stack of diskettes piled carefully next to the computer. William must have been busy up here. She smiled with satisfaction, still thinking that it was quite remarkable that her son was so good with the machine. She knew so many "normal" people who were mystified by anything having to do with computers.

Louise didn't bother looking through the diskettes, didn't notice the one at the bottom marked DAD in large, amateurish letters.

❧ Chapter 98

"Never, ever take more than one of these. Too much of this medication can cause potentially fatal arrhythmias."

That's what the doctor had said.

Four of the pale green, half-milligram pills. All together, two milligrams. That should do it. The pills were pulverized and carefully placed into the Fiorinal casing. The green Fiorinal capsule covered the new green powder very well. The untampered capsules were discarded.

Once the pills were in Eliza's bag, it would only be a matter of time, given the frequency of her headaches.

The sooner the better.

❧ Chapter 99

If this plane goes down it will change the face of television news as America knows it, Eliza thought as she made her way to her seat. The commercial flight from New York to Houston was packed with newspeople and delegates from the tristate area on their way to the national convention. They were easily distinguished. The delegates wore WINGARD FOR PRESIDENT buttons and had the air of people who were on their way to a party. The journalists looked as though they were going to work.

Heading down the aisle of the 737, Eliza recognized Dan Rather sitting in first class. So, CBS was still springing for the expensive seats for their anchor. KEY was not. Eliza felt a little better when she saw that the public television anchor was sitting in coach, too. There were many other familiar faces in the cabin. Several print journalists were sprinkled about the broadcast passengers. Eliza noted ironically that the reason she recognized the newspaper reporters and columnists was that they often appeared as panelists on the television talk shows.

KEY News was heavily represented on the flight from LaGuardia. Range was already in his seat, with a very attentive Louise Kendall sitting beside him. Those two must really have something going for Range to have asked her to accompany him to the convention. The executive producer was known for being all work and no play on a big remote.

Eliza wished Mack was taking this flight but he would be coming down later.

Finding her place, she stowed her canvas shoulder bag underneath the seat in front of her and sat down at the window. She was adjusting her lap belt when Yelena Gregory sat down beside her. The older woman seemed pleased to see Eliza.

"What a nice surprise! You never know who you're going to get stuck with for three hours."

Eliza grinned. "I must say, I'm impressed. The president herself sitting in the back with the rest of us. I thought for sure you'd be sitting up front with the big boys."

"That's the whole idea, my friend. I'm setting a good example for the troops. We're all in this together, and all that. They'll love me for it."

Eliza recognized the truth in Yelena's words. The news staff liked the brass and the stars mingling among them. It made the off-camera team feel they were all part of a powerful team. A plane ride like this was a good chance to strengthen morale.

As the jet gathered runway speed and pressure built in the cabin at takeoff, Eliza noted that Yelena held onto the armrests so hard that her knuckles turned white. Funny, she had never envisioned Yelena as the type who would be afraid of flying. Then Eliza recalled a story on a fear-of-flying class that she had worked on. The students were a real cross-section of life. A business executive, a housewife, a doctor, a waiter, two grandmothers and a dress designer were enrolled in the class, united in their terror of flying and in their determination to deal with it. Add the first woman president of a television news division to the list of phobics. It wasn't until the plane had ascended and the seat belt sign flicked off that Yelena let go of the armrests.

Yelena turned to Eliza, a weak, embarrassed smile on her face. "Not very macho, I'm afraid. It's not something I'm very proud of, but I'm scared to death of flying. Yelena changed the subject. "How's your little girl?"

"Janie's fine. There were fewer tears this time. I think she's

getting used to my traveling. I'm not sure if that's good or bad."
Eliza's smile was bittersweet.

Yelena reached out and patted Eliza's arm. "I can only imagine
how hard it is. I have no children. It's the major regret of my
life. I had a hysterectomy back in the early eighties. I envy you
your little girl."

Eliza wasn't sure how to respond. She nodded. "I know I'm
lucky, blessed really, to have Janie."

The flight attendant brought lunch and the conversation ended.
By the time the plastic plates of creamed chicken, rice, and cu-
cumber and tomato salad were cleared away and the tiny tray
tables were refastened to the seat backs in front of them, Eliza
had decided to bring it up.

"Did Jean White call you the weekend before she died?"

"No," Yelena lied.

Eliza put her head back against the seat and closed her eyes.

"God, I wish I'd paid more attention. Something about Bill's
computer notes."

Yelena didn't seem very interested.

"Look, we'll try to figure it all out when we get back to New
York. Now, Eliza, you've just got to concentrate on your convention assignments. Give those all your attention."

Yelena excused herself. Taking the opportunity to schmooze
along the way, she made her way toward the lavatory at the back
of the plane, stopping to chat with every KEY face she recognized. Pete Carlson sat with Mary Cate Ryan, poor Mary Cate
looking none too enthusiastic. Range and Louise sat holding
hands.

Eliza turned back around in her coach seat and pulled a copy
of the current *Newsweek* from her carry bag. The cover story was
Haines Wingard and the convention that was to begin Monday.
The latest polls indicated that if the election were held tomorrow,
Wingard would probably beat the incumbent President Grayson.
Eliza had finished the seven-page article when Yelena returned to
her seat.

"Eliza, will you do me a favor and not mention my fear of

flying to anyone. It's not that I think it's anything to be ashamed of, really, but it doesn't quite fit the strong image that I would like to project. Let's face it, we're still operating in a man's world and vulnerability is viewed as weakness."

Eliza felt camaraderie with the large, plain woman. Yelena always appeared completely in control, so strong, so invulnerable. That her boss had another, struggling side made Eliza like her even more.

"Absolutely, Yelena. I understand. Maybe when we get back home from Houston, you'd like to come over for dinner some night with Janie and me."

"That's the best invitation I've had in quite a while."

Yelena was feeling increasingly guilty about Eliza Blake.

ℋ Chapter 100

The hundred aides, Secret Service agents, and journalists aboard the chartered Wingard jet traveling to Houston watched stunned as their usually reserved candidate aisle-surfed down the middle of the plane. Haines Wingard stood in a little rubber tub, the kind usually reserved for bathing babies, and swooshed down the aisle in a clearly exuberant mood.

Going into the convention, the major polls predicted a very bright future. President Grayson was making one mistake after another. Wingard, on the other hand, could almost do no wrong. His ideas on taxes, health care, crime and gun control, and education were finding a receptive audience in the American electorate. The AIDS Parade had appealed to the national imagination. Americans were rallying around the man who had made the eradication of AIDS a real cause. Haines Wingard had taken on the aura of a hero.

Even the intense Nate Heller had allowed himself to feel the excitement of the day. But he kept it in check, knowing that good generals never let up. He would always be on guard. He did think it was okay, though, for Win to at least appear to lighten up before the troops. The planned aisle-surfing was part of the new exuberance.

Joy also made her way around the plane, radiant with the flush of adrenaline. She continued to be surprised by how much she now enjoyed the campaign. And though she tried not to, more and more she thought about what getting to the White House would actually mean in her life. Not long ago, she had been deeply depressed by her childlessness, the condition of her marriage, the definition of her life as "the wife of Senator Haines Wingard." Today, it looked most likely that she would be the next first lady of the land.

If nothing went wrong.

℁ Chapter 101

Eliza's rental car pulled across the acres of white hot parking lots that surrounded the fifteen-story Astrodome. The structure resembled a gigantic gray alien spaceship plopped down in a sea of asphalt. Eliza could picture little figures with antennae and silver space suits disembarking through the dome's wide metal doors. Huge red, white and blue banners hung in front of the spaceship and state flags lined the walkway to the main entrance.

The Houston Astros, the Dome's usual summer occupants, had been banished for nearly a month while it was readied. Bats and balls were replaced with the nuts and bolts required for converting the structure into a convention hall.

Literally nuts and bolts—120,000 of them. Huge grids holding thousands of lights hung from the ceiling and nets constraining 225,000 red, white and blue balloons were fastened to the top of the dome. Any evidence that baseball had been played in the space was banished. The scoreboards, billboards and advertisements that plastered the inside of the stadium were covered. An 88-foot podium had been constructed, with Haines Wingard's lectern positioned where second base usually rested. Behind the podium, a 570-foot-long blue curtain sealed off about one third of the stadium's 55,000 seats in an effort to make the massive dome seem more intimate.

The Astrodome transformers had worked their magic well. The backdrop for Senator Wingard's official nomination and formal acceptance of his party's candidacy for the nation's highest post was powerful, patriotic and presidential. Eliza took a deep breath as she entered. It was spectacular! Even the most jaded journalist would have to admit that the convention hall was very impressive indeed.

Most of the 15,000 journalists who were covering the convention were stationed in a workspace set up in the adjacent Astrohall. Five hundred thousand square feet, about fourteen football fields, had been set aside for the broadcast and print reporters, producers, editors, researchers, columnists and managers who poured in from across the country and from around the globe to observe and report on the political spectacle. *Time, Newsweek*, the Associated Press, Reuters and Knight-Ridder hung out their identifying flags in front of their flimsily partitioned encampments. The *Wall Street Journal* worked across the way from the *Chicago Tribune* which abutted the *New York Times*. The *L.A. Times*, the *Boston Globe* and the *Baltimore Sun* were neighbors. A large area was reserved for foreign broadcasters. KEY shared a hallway and bathrooms with CBS, ABC and CNN. C-Span and NBC occupied their own sizeable portions of the Astrohall maze. The networks, though visible, were far from the only television representation.

Local stations from throughout the United States had sent their own reporters and crews to give the convention a hometown perspective.

Wearing her mandatory-for-survival running shoes, the sneakers that would be on her feet all week, Eliza made her way from the Astrodome to the Astrohall and the KEY work area. She couldn't help but appreciate the logistics and planning that went into the operation of this gargantuan machine called a convention. Once the banners were down and the cables ripped up at the end of the week, the planning would begin for the next convention four years ahead.

Eliza showed her press pass to the security guard at the entrance to the KEY area, realizing that he did not recognize her. Perhaps it was because her face was makeup-less or because she wore khaki walking shorts and a T-shirt. She was not particularly offended. The guard did not look like the type who rose early to watch morning news.

The KEY workspace had been designed as a small-scale broadcast center with areas for special events, finance and senior management. A closed section was marked off as a private office for Yelena. There was a correspondents and producers room, a crew room, and offices for the *Evening Headlines* and *KEY to America*. A central news desk had easy access to computers, copiers and fax machines. In the rear of the workspace, six editing rooms had been set up with equipment shipped from KEY in New York. A videotape library, a conference room and food service area completed the self-contained headquarters.

Pete Carlson was the first person Eliza saw. Ugh. She hoped this wasn't an omen for what the rest of the convention would be like.

"Nice setup, hey, Eliza?"

God, he was so obvious in the way he stared her up and down. Creep.

"It looks that way, Pete," she answered unsmilingly. "Have you been over to the Dome yet?"

"Sure have. Looks good. I'm on my way over there for a rehearsal right now." Not wanting to sound tense, he added, "I sure hope they get the air conditioner to work inside the anchor booth."

"I'm sure they will, Pete." She couldn't bring herself to wish him good luck and she was mad at herself for feeling the least bit sympathetic toward the snake. He was prime-time anchoring a national political convention for the first time. Though his ratings had edged up a bit in the last weeks, it was crucial that he deliver this week. The heat was on.

Sap! Don't feel sorry for Pete Carlson. He's been happy to screw you any way he could. Eliza considered what made a guy so sneaky and mean. Ambition? Insecurity? Probably both. But Pete had shown his true colors to Eliza when he sabotaged her in the live studio Q and A. Fool me once, shame on you. Fool me twice, shame on me.

If Pete Carlson knew about Bill and Joy, he could break a very sensational story and his ratings would be assured. Then it occurred to Eliza that, as anchor and managing editor of the network's flagship broadcast, Carlson might well have been told by Range or Yelena. And if that was the case, she couldn't imagine Carlson keeping it to himself. He could make a big splash with the news of the Bill Kendall–Joy Wingard love affair. No, he wouldn't keep that to himself. Not unless he had something to gain by not reporting it.

❧ Chapter 102

It was getting harder and harder to do what he needed to do. The doorknockers, at least the kind he needed, were becoming increasingly more difficult to find. Were people catching on? Was there a plot to stop attaching his beloved animals to the formidable front doors of Manhattan townhouses? That thought depressed him further.

He didn't ask for much. He loved his animals, and adding to his menagerie was the only pleasure he got. Besides, he only did what he was told. It had been almost two weeks since he'd found a new pet. Several new knockers had sprung up in the blocks he covered. Rosettes and dogwood blossoms, iron rings and brass ropes, even two sweethearts, their kiss captured forever in metal. But no new animals guarded their masters' homes.

The man shuffled along slowly, discouraged, pushing his overstuffed cart. It was a hot night. He knew he had too much clothing on for July, but he was always cold. A trash can was up ahead, a chance for something to eat, or some cans and bottles he could trade for some money. He rummaged through. Someone had already been here. These days, there was even competition for garbage.

He glanced at a discarded newspaper. There was a picture of a man and a woman, smiling and waving from the top of a stair leading to an airplane. Underneath the picture, it was proclaimed that Haines and Joy Wingard had arrived in Houston, Texas, for the national political convention. Big deal. It didn't and wouldn't affect his life. No matter who became president, he'd still be homeless, wandering the streets.

He continued on his urban safari.

Two blocks later, his heart leapt. A shiny brass longhorn stared defiantly from a green lacquered door! He'd never done a longhorn bull before. The thought of those horns ignited the first pleasure he had felt in a long time. He closed his eyes and took a deep breath. When they opened, his eyes traveled to the small space next to the front stoop.

There was a spanking white wall. A WET PAINT sign was taped to the railing above, with an arrow pointing down.

"Tit for tat. Tit for tat. Spray them a longhorn, this for that."

The homeless man found his spray-paint can buried deep within his plastic bag, and the video camera hidden in the parked car at the curb recorded as the rodeo art began.

✿ Chapter 103

Only the last four days of the convention got full-scale network coverage. The platform and rules committees had met the preceding week to hash out party specifics. Those dry and grueling sessions were not the stuff of which television news was made. The first session on Monday night at the Astrodome was when America would tune in to watch. From the opening gavel to the delirious demonstration planned to erupt after Haines Wingard's acceptance speech on Thursday night, the convention was very carefully scripted by party planners. Scripted with television in mind.

KEY to America, with Eliza Blake anchoring, was broadcasting every morning from the KEY skybox in the Astrodome. Harry Granger had remained in the New York studio. Monday morning's show featured pieces on Houston's preparations for the convention, how the Wingard presidential campaign was coming across in middle America, and how delegates viewed the Wingard ticket.

The last segment from Houston was a live interview Eliza conducted with Joy Wingard. The campaign staff made it clear beforehand that Mrs. Wingard wanted to promote the AIDS Parade for Dollars. One of the planned convention highlights was to be Joy's speech on the AIDS battle. Eliza noticed that Nate Heller accompanied Joy to the skybox for the interview.

The stage manager, crouched next to the anchor desk in the cramped skybox, signaled for Eliza to begin.

"Mrs. Wingard, how do you think the publicity over Bill Kendall's donation has helped the AIDS Parade?"

Joy answered the question predictably and smoothly. "The Kendall donation helped our fund-raising effort a great deal because Bill Kendall was a respected and well-liked public figure. People responded to him and trusted him. His support gave the AIDS Parade not only publicity, but credibility as well."

"Last month, Mrs. Wingard, you toured AIDS facilities in Newark, New Jersey. Did you learn anything that you hadn't known before?"

Joy looked sharply at Eliza. "I observed, Eliza, that while there are too many people who are HIV-positive or suffering from full-blown AIDS, there are, thank God, many people who are trying to help. They are trying to find cures, they are caring for the afflicted, they are trying to bring comfort to their fellow human beings. My husband has promised that he will do all he can as president to find an answer to this plague." Joy stared at Eliza. Was there defiance in her look?

Eliza shuffled through her index cards. "To change the subject for the moment, Mrs. Wingard, figures released this morning show that violent street crime in America is on the rise. Realistically, what do you think your husband can do about a society where a man can be shot down in the street just for the few dollars in his pocket?"

This time, Eliza thought she might have hit a nerve. The color rose on Joy's neck as the master of the smooth answer stammered a reply.

"Ah, I haven't seen the statistics you, ah, speak of, Eliza. Ah. . . . off the top of my head, I'd have to say that our society is basically a good one, but . . . but we have problems that must be addressed. Street crime does not exist in a vacuum. It's often rooted in hopelessness and, um, powerlessness. If we could work toward building a society where people felt better about themselves and their abilities to make decent lives, perhaps they wouldn't turn to drugs and crime."

Nice recovery, thought Eliza.

As both unclipped their microphones after the interview, Joy thanked Eliza, without looking her in the eye. Nate Heller stepped up in an attempt to break the awkward tension.

"Where are you staying?" he asked Eliza politely. It was the first question that everyone working at the convention asked each other.

"The Oaks."

"Oh. We're all staying at the Galleria."

"I know."

It was, of course, common knowledge where the presidential candidate and his entourage were headquartered. The two Westin hotels were linked by Houston's famed Galleria, the glamorous, glass-covered shopping mall that featured Tiffany's and Neiman Marcus, along with video arcades and an ice-skating rink.

"Are you planning to come to the party after the session tonight?"

"If I can keep my eyes open," Eliza smiled.

"Good. Hope to see you there," Joy responded perfunctorily.

The Houston Chamber of Commerce was throwing a party in the Westin Galleria ballroom. Members of the media were invited. The Wingards were scheduled to make an appearance.

As soon as Joy and Nate left, Eliza gathered up her convention handbook and her shoulder bag from the long control desk at the rear of the skybox. She picked up the nearest of the two dozen phones on the table and dialed the 212 area code. She felt a catch in her throat when the small determined voice answered.

"Hello?"

"Janie? Janie, honey, it's Mommy."

"Mommy! I miss you, Mommy."

"I miss you, too, my sweetheart. Are you having a good time with Mrs. Twomey?"

"Yes. Mrs. Twomey made me pancakes in the shapes of an'mals for breakfast."

"She did? Aren't you lucky!"

"Here's Mrs. Twomey."

That was Janie. She might miss her mother, but she had no problem in getting off the phone if there was a more attractive offer on the television set. It was 9:15 in New York. *I Love Lucy* was on. Little though she was, *I Love Lucy* fascinated Janie.

Mrs. Twomey came to the phone and assured Eliza that everything was all right.

"Would you tell me even if everything wasn't okay?" Eliza asked.

"Of course I would. Of course I would. But everything *is* just fine. Janie watched you for a little while on the TV this morning, just like she always does. Then she switched to *Sesame Street*."

That was a good sign. If she was obsessing over missing her mother, Janie probably would have glued herself to the screen.

"What are you two doing today?"

"We'll be going to the park this morning while it's cool."

Eliza made a mental note for the thousandth time that she wanted to buy a house in the suburbs. A house with a swimming pool or a nearby outdoor swim club. A child should be playing outside in the summertime, not cooped up in an air-conditioned apartment. Maybe by next summer, Janie could be doing the jellyfish float in a nice, clear, clean pool.

"Thanks so much, Mrs. Twomey. I don't know what I would do without you. Hopefully, the week will fly by, and I'll be home before we all know it. I miss Janie so much when I'm away like this. I keep consoling myself with the idea that we're going on vacation when I get home."

"Don't worry, Mrs. Blake. Janie is just fine. And the little faerie is excited about going to the beach next week, too."

Putting the receiver back in the cradle, Eliza swallowed hard to keep back the tears she felt coming. The little faerie.

Being a mother with a career outside the home was conflicting enough. Being a single mother added another painful dimension. There was no Daddy for Janie, no other parent to be there for the little girl. And Eliza knew she was one of the rare, lucky ones. She was a single mother who made a lot of money. A single mother who could afford excellent child care. A single mother who could afford a beautiful, basically safe place to live. A single mother who didn't have to worry about paying bills. Unless, of course, she were to lose her job.

She knew that was what kept her driven to do so well. Not just an inner need for success for its own sake, but the knowledge that the buck stopped with her. If she didn't make her own money, it would all come tumbling down. Mrs. Twomey and the private nursery school and the expensive sneakers that Janie outgrew every three months. The doormanned building and the circus tickets and the Zabar's treats. She liked her life, the life she was able to offer Janie. Without that paycheck, their world would be a very different, very scary place, one that Eliza did not like to think about. That's why she rarely said no to an assignment. She wanted KEY to value her.

But at moments like these, a thousand miles away from the little girl watching *I Love Lucy* reruns, the little girl being cared for by someone else, Eliza would have gladly traded some of the glamour, money and excitement for the security and simple pleasure of watching Janie run under a sprinkler.

✣ Chapter 104

Detective Colburn had set his trap for the bold, persistent artist.

It was easy enough to get an owner to volunteer his townhouse. Civic duty and all that. Also, the detective theorized, the owner's foray into police work would provide good cocktail party conversation for quite some time.

Colburn himself picked out the doorknocker. It was the largest, shiniest, showiest one he could find. A brass Texas longhorn whose horns spread a good ten inches across. If doorknockers were his thing, Colburn knew he would be turned on by this one. He was counting on it.

The wall was painted spanking white. The small video camera, timed to click on at 9:00 P.M., was positioned inside a nondescript police surveillance car parked curbside. The wide-angle lens was aimed at the fresh, white wall.

Detective Colburn knew that the trap had succeeded when he cabbed to the site early in the morning. The brass doorknocker was gone and a rather good spray-painted rendition of the longhorn bull stared out defiantly from the white canvas. Colburn took a picture for evidence later on. Then he unlocked the police car, climbed inside and drove it back to the precinct. At a red light, he unloaded the tape from the recorder.

Inside the station house, he rewound the time-coded tape and then forwarded it at a speed just slow enough to be able to view the action. Just after midnight, the culprit appeared.

A homeless man! Colburn had been expecting a kid.

The detective isolated two images of the man with the shopping cart. The first was a long, full shot showing a thin man of medium height, wearing baggy pants, a winter jacket and a Yankees cap. The other picture offered a better view of his weather-worn face as he turned after completing his masterpiece. Colburn could make out deep creases at the corner of the man's eyes and mouth. He was unshaven. Dark hair peeked out shaggily from beneath the cap.

Colburn would have some copies made and then start flashing the fuzzy shots around. Hopefully, somebody on the beat would recognize the guy. Maybe they could pick him up tonight.

✣ Chapter 105

The door clicked shut and Louise rolled over in the king-size bed. Range was on his way to the Astrohall. Louise felt uneasy about what they had just viewed and their conversation that followed.

They had lain in bed and watched Eliza Blake interview Joy Wingard. Alone now, Louise felt she now had to acknowledge what she had known all along but hadn't wanted to face. She knew there must have been something going on between Joy and Bill. Louise had her suspicions aroused when she'd watched Eliza Blake's first interview with Joy Wingard. Until then she hadn't realized that Bill must have known about the Parade for Dollars before its official announcement. She had dismissed the thought, not particularly wanting to think about Bill with anyone else.

She and Range had never discussed the connection. It was the great unspoken between them.

After this morning's interview, she asked Range what he thought of Eliza's questions.

"I think she'd better watch herself," Range snapped angrily.

Seeing Louise wince, Range softened. "I don't know why she continues to pursue the Bill thing. That's old news."

"Why are you reacting so?"

Range ran his hands through his red hair.

"Listen, Lou, I loved the guy. You want me to come out and say it? Fine. He was my best friend. I don't want him to be remembered as the man who slept with the president's wife. I want him to be remembered as the pro and terrific human being that he was."

There was a silence between them.

"Surely you suspected it," Range said softly.

"Mmm. I don't want to think about it. It depresses me. It was over between us, but somehow the thought of him with another woman doesn't sit well with me. Not to mention the media frenzy that would ensue if it got out. I just can't deal with that." Louise's face expressed her distaste.

She considered the interview for a minute. "Well, what did you think about Eliza's question about Newark? Could that question have had a double meaning? I keep thinking of Father Alec showing up in those pictures with Joy. And the crime question, the description fit Dr. Karas's murder."

Before he could respond, Range's beeper went off. "We'll have to talk about all this later. I've got to get going." Range Bullock was eager to avoid that conversation.

❧ Chapter 106

The good news was that it was only 10:30 P.M. local time when the gavel fell marking the close of the first convention session. The bad news was that it was 11:30 in New York. That meant that Eliza had to be in at 4:00 A.M. local time to prepare for her six o'clock interview in Houston that would lead off *KEY to America* at seven in New York. Forget it. Eliza was dog-tired, there was humming behind her eyes, and her feet were killing her. She and the other correspondents, producers and camera crews wore running shoes on the convention floor as they searched out interviews and hustled from delegation to delegation looking for stories to report. The sneakers could only do so much. Her feet were still sore from hours of pounding the hard cement floor. She ached to go back to the hotel, soak in a hot tub and slip between the crisp white sheets.

Eliza met up with Mack as she walked from the Astrodome back to the Astrohall to pick up her bag.

"How'd you do tonight?" he asked.

"I got everyone I needed to get, including the governors of Texas, California and New York, the right-to-life and pro-choice honchos, the women's caucus spokesperson and Mr. Personality himself, campaign manager Nate Heller." Eliza stopped, out of breath.

Mack smiled. "Yeah, Heller's a real charm boy, isn't he? But he must be in his glory this week and after all the exposure for Wingard in this enthusiastic setting. I didn't find anyone saying a negative thing about Wingard or his campaign tonight. How about you?"

"Nope. These people are head over heels for him."

"They know that they have a winner and that's real seductive stuff."

Eliza and Mack walked along with the throngs of delegates and media people who poured out of the Astrodome. The delegates looked revved up and ready to party. The media people were dragging. Eliza was thinking of Joy Wingard and Bill Kendall. The convention would take on a whole new tone if their story got out. She wondered about her gut decision to trawl with Joy in the interview this morning. Had it been a mistake? Eliza was pushing with the questions she put to Joy. The candidate's wife knew that Eliza was on to something. Eliza could sense it. Joy smelled it and it scared her. Or did it excite her? And what about Yelena and Range? Did they think she was going against the decision not to push disclosure of the affair? They must have picked up on her leading questions, yet neither had said a word about the interview.

Mack interrupted her thoughts. "Are we going to the party at the Galleria?"

"No way. I can't, Mack, I'm exhausted."

"Sure you don't want to make a quick stop? It's literally right next door to our hotel and I hear they're putting out quite a spread. Plus, The Man and his wife will be there."

Eliza considered Mack's scenario. An extra twenty minutes tacked on to this endless day wouldn't matter that much. "Okay. Quick stop."

Once inside the ballroom, Eliza was glad she had rallied. In true Texas fashion, the party planners had gone for the big bang. The walls were solid seas of shimmering silver balloons. A long, well-stocked open bar was set up in each corner of the room. Black-jacketed waiters offered flutes of champagne. Others passed silver trays of hors d'oeuvres, each with a tempting array of Cajun, Mexican and southwestern morsels. The place was mobbed.

As Eliza sampled some delicious blackened redfish with Cajun sauce, she spotted the KEY group. She and Mack made their way toward Pete Carlson, Yelena, Range and Louise Kendall, and Mary Cate. Over the din of musicians and revelers, Eliza tried to make small talk with Louise, asking about young William.

"To tell you the truth, Eliza, it's hard to gauge *how* he's doing. Sometimes he just goes along like everything is fine and other times, he seems so sad. I guess that's about what you'd expect from any kid who has just lost his dad." Louise shook her head and smiled. "But I'll tell you something. If he says 'An elephant never forgets' one more time, I think I'll lose my mind."

Eliza didn't get a chance to respond. The country band struck up a boisterous rendition of "Deep in the Heart of Texas" as Win and Joy entered the ballroom. Eliza watched as the shining couple worked the room, making their way slowly up to the podium in front. Nate Heller and the Secret Service cleared the path for them. They're enjoying this, she thought. The adulation and attention that filled the room was intoxicating.

Once at the microphone, it took a lot to quiet the room down. At last, the candidate was able to say a few words about how happy he was to be with them and joked that it was good to be allowed out of his room after working there for most of the day on his acceptance speech. The audience laughed and cheered. Win thanked Houston and Texas and his supporters from across the nation. He even thanked the media for doing their jobs conscientiously and fairly.

"Oh, brother," Mack muttered in Eliza's ear.

"Don't be cynical," she hissed back.

And then, quickly, it was time to go. The Wingards smiled and waved their goodbyes to a cheering audience. The couple descended from the stage, and Eliza saw Nate Heller leading a man toward the candidate. Wingard was smiling and shaking the man's hand.

It was Judge Dennis Quinn!

She nudged Mack and yelled in his ear to be heard over the din in the room.

"What more do we need? Something funky is going on over there, I'm sure of it. Now more than ever, I've got to figure out a way to get into Bill's computer."

Eliza turned to the KEY group. "Unlike the rest of you lucky dogs, I have to be up and at 'em very, very early tomorrow morning. I'm gonna to pack it in."

"How 'bout an escort back to your room?" Mack asked.

Eliza smiled. "Don't tempt me. I've got to get up bright-eyed and bushy-tailed. It's just a short walk through the Galleria. I'm sure I'll be safe."

"Okay, if you're sure. There are a few people I need to talk to before calling it a night."

Eliza strolled along the deserted second floor of the mall, browsing at the shop windows, her mind going over the events of the day. It had been a successful, tough and achingly long one. She was satisfied with the job done.

But Dennis Quinn shaking hands with Wingard. . . . What was that connection all about?

She paused at a toy store. Little pigtailed dolls wearing jean skirts, red bandanna neckerchiefs, cowboy hats and boots were sitting on a split-rail fence display. She'd make a point of coming back when the store was open to buy one of the brown-haired dolls for Janie. Eliza made a mental note of the store's name and moved on.

She was exhausted and foot-sore. And her head was beginning to throb.

❧ Chapter 107

Haines Wingard looked over at his wife. Was she really sleeping, or was she faking it? He found himself questioning everything Joy said and did now.

They hadn't had sex in months, not since the night of Bill Kendall's funeral. He wondered how he would explain the condoms he planned to wear from now on when he had sex with her. *If* he had sex with her. She disgusted him.

Maybe he should say he was only thinking of protecting her. Maybe he should let her think that *he* was out cheating. At this point, he really didn't give a damn what Joy thought. He did know one thing. He sure as hell didn't want to get AIDS, and Joy's catting around had already exposed him.

He did not want to think about it. The AIDS virus couldn't be detected for up to six months after infection. He would be president by then. He was sure she hadn't seen Kendall since New Hampshire.

He'd get tested later this month. By then, the test would make no mistake.

❦ Chapter 108

Eliza awoke in the darkened hotel room. The digital clock told her she had been asleep only two hours. She felt sick to her stomach.

She flipped on the light, made her way to the white bathroom and knelt on the cold floor beside the toilet. She remembered briefly the feeling she'd had once on a small sailboat on Long Island Sound. The nausea that wouldn't go away until the body relieved itself. Being seasick was worse than having a virus or a flu. Or so she had thought until now.

She retched violently. Then again. And again. She vomited until there was nothing left to throw up. Then she vomited green. She knew it to be bile.

She was scared. Alone in her hotel room, hundreds of miles from home. The nausea was not going away. She lifted her heavy head from the bowl. The room spun. She was afraid she was going to pass out. She had to get to the phone. Call Mack. Crawling across the tile floor she knew there was something wrong. Something terribly wrong.

The entire room had turned yellow.

❧ Chapter 109

"Mrs. Twomey, Mrs. Twomey," shouted Janie from the living room. Mommy isn't on the TV this morning."

Mrs. Twomey walked from the kitchen to the living room, wiping her floured hands on a dish towel. She looked at the television. Janie was pointing at the screen.

"See? Mommy's not on."

Janie was right. Mrs. Blake's friend Mack was sitting in the skybox where Eliza was yesterday.

"Okay, Janie. Let's turn on *Sesame Street* instead."

"But where's Mommy? I want to see my mommy!"

❧ Chapter 110

She wasn't on! It worked! Eliza had taken the pills.

The murderer smiled. Now everything was taken care of.

Chapter 111

Dr. Randi Hagerman didn't usually find herself at work so early in the morning.

Though the emergency room doctor at Twelve Oaks Hospital suspected flu or food poisoning, he had thought it wise to call the sharpest internist on staff. Considering who the patient was, he didn't want to be held responsible for any misdiagnosis.

Dr. Hagerman had listened as the duty doctor described over the phone Eliza Blake's violent vomiting and yellow vision. She immediately ordered an electrocardiogram. By the time Dr. Hagerman got to the hospital, the answers were back.

She had expected to see the "hockey stick" pattern on the EKG tape. The surprising thing was the patient. Young, healthy-looking Eliza Blake was the owner of very disturbing, inexplicable test results.

Chapter 112

"I want to see my mommy." Janie's lower lip was protruding dangerously.

"Honey, I'm sure Mommy must be busy doing something else. She'll probably be calling us soon." Mrs. Twomey tried to sound nonchalant.

Janie looked uncertain. Mrs. Twomey changed channels and

Big Bird appeared. Janie's curiosity over what the big yellow fellow was going to do today distracted her for the moment.

Mrs. Twomey returned to the kitchen and her blueberry muffin batter. She switched on the small kitchen set, already tuned to KEY and adjusted the volume lower, insuring that Janie would not hear anything. Mack was on the screen talking to Harry Granger in New York.

"Middle of the night, major league stomach upset, Harry. She's resting well enough, though. In fact, she had to be forced to stay in bed and take it easy this morning. But the last I heard, she is determined to be working the convention floor tonight."

As she slid the muffin tins into the oven, a worried Mrs. Twomey wondered if what she had just heard was the whole story. When she heard from Eliza herself, she'd know for sure.

℘ Chapter 113

Detective Colburn got to the precinct a little later than usual. Bunny and the kids were leaving for the Cape and he had wanted to see them off. He was going to join them up there in a couple of days. Unless, of course, something big came up between now and the weekend.

Colburn had just taken a seat at his desk and was pulling the plastic lid off his coffee when his chief walked over and informed him that the patrol guys had picked up the graffiti artist the night before. He was being held downstairs.

"Let me go get a look at him," sighed the detective, putting the lid back on the Styrofoam cup.

"Don't get your hopes up about getting any answers that make sense. He's a schizo."

The man in the holding cell was lying on his side in the corner. His eyes were closed and his mouth was hanging open. Watching closely, Colburn could see the man's shoulders and chest moving slowly up and down. He was sleeping. Probably the best sleep the poor bastard has had in quite a while, thought the detective. Colburn decided to let him sleep. Whether he was questioned now or after lunch wouldn't make a whole lot of difference. Let the guy rest and get something to eat. This sad soul wouldn't complain about the jail food. He'd be grateful to get it.

On his way back upstairs, Detective Colburn stopped to check the homeless man's personal effects.

"Pathetic," said the property sergeant. "The poor guy's whole life wrapped up in a couple of lousy garbage bags." He gestured to the black plastic lawn bags piled next to the wall.

"Anything in them?"

"Take a look for yourself."

Colburn let out a low whistle as he surveyed the booty. A zoo's worth of brass animal doorknockers, plus four cans of spray paint. . . .

"Four cans of spray paint, old clothes, a blanket, a ratty old pillow, a pot and a frying pan, a couple books, a cardboard container of half-eaten Chinese food and a package of noodles. God knows what garbage can he picked those out of. And a few old programs from the Guggenheim."

Colburn pictured the bedraggled homeless man stooping down to pick up the discarded programs in front of the beautiful, smooth white building.

There was also a small silver key ring.

The detective turned the key ring over in his hands. It was a loop with a small ball attached to the end that could be screwed on and off to accommodate added or subtracted keys. Two keys and a tag, slightly larger than a quarter, hung from the loop. "Sterling" was stamped in tiny letters at the bottom of the tag. On the other side, Colburn read the inscription "Please return to Tiffany & Co., New York." Beneath that was a registration number. Colburn wrote it down.

He returned to his desk and his now lukewarm coffee. He was about to call Tiffany's when he got a call to go to a robbery scene at a luxury high-rise on East Seventy-ninth Street.

Tiffany's would have to wait.

✣ Chapter 114

"Do you have a heart condition?"

In an examining room at Twelve Oaks Hospital, Eliza stared back quizzically at Randi Hagerman. "A heart condition? What do you mean, a heart condition?"

"Are you taking any heart medication, like digitalis or digoxin?"

"No, of course not. My heart is fine. I'm fine. What are you talking about?"

Dr. Hagerman held the electrocardiogram record for Eliza to examine. "See this pattern here?" She pointed. "The one that looks like a hockey stick repeated over and over?"

Eliza nodded.

"Well, that and the facts of the vomiting and the yellow vision, taken together, indicate that you may have had too much digitalis. Digitalis is a common medication for congestive heart failure."

"Digitalis?" Eliza was incredulous. "I've never taken digitalis in my life! And I'm as healthy as a horse . . . or I was until a few hours ago."

Eliza thought back to last night. She'd eaten that blackened redfish at the reception.

"Are you sure this isn't food poisoning?"

Dr. Hagerman shook her head. "Food poisoning would cause the vomiting. It wouldn't make you see yellow or make your heart beat the way it did when you took this test. Are you sure you didn't take any medication? Maybe someone else's medication by mistake?"

"The only thing I took last night was Fiorinal before I went to bed."

"Do you have the rest of the bottle?"

"It's in the wastebasket at the hotel. That was the last of it. I cursed myself for not bringing more with me." Eliza paused, recalling the night before. "In fact, I remember being surprised that it was the end of the bottle. I thought I had more left than that."

✣ Chapter 115

Someone wanted to kill her!

Who? Even Mack, usually so calm and steady, was crazed.

Eliza felt panicked. Why would someone want me out of the way? She remembered the scene at the party last night. Wingard, Heller and Judge Quinn.

Get right back into the saddle again, Eliza told herself as she dressed slowly. As she maneuvered her aching legs into her hose, she cursed the fact that her legs weren't tanned enough to go bare. Carefully sliding into a red linen skirt, she wondered how she was going to make it through all the hours to come on the convention floor.

From the hospital, she had called home to check on Janie and to suggest to Mrs. Twomey that she permit the little girl to stay up for the start of the convention coverage tonight. She wanted Janie to see her and know that her mommy was all right and at work as usual.

Dr. Hagerman's words echoed through her mind. Any more of the digitalis in her bloodstream could have killed her. She could not allow herself to think of the near miss in terms of her daughter. The idea of a motherless, parentless Janie shut her down and she had to do her job. There would be enough time next week, at the beach, to let go. Now, Eliza had to concentrate on surviving the convention.

The phone rang loudly in the quiet hotel room. It was Yelena Gregory.

"How are you holding up?"

"About the same as I was an hour ago when you called. I'm fine, Yelena, just fine. A little spent maybe, but I should be okay."

"Thank God for that." There was a short pause. "Eliza, I want to have some security men assigned to you tonight."

"That's not necessary."

"I think it is. I wouldn't forgive myself if something else happened. If someone deliberately tried to poison you, you must have protection. I'm not taking any chances."

"Yelena, if something else happens, I doubt it would be on the convention floor. You know the security, the metal detectors that have to be gotten through to get into the Astrodome, the Secret Service, the police. Unless whoever wants to get me wants to be caught, he isn't going to do anything at the convention."

Yelena relented slightly. "All right, but I sure as hell want you to have a bodyguard outside, the rest of the time we are in Houston."

Eliza considered Yelena's words. She felt safe inside the Astro complex with thousands of delegates and journalists milling around. She'd be distracted and feel ridiculous with bodyguards hovering around while she worked. But maybe an escort going back and forth from the hotel to the convention would be a smart idea.

"Okay, Yelena."

"Good. Have you been out of your room yet?"

"No."

"Well, there's a guard outside your door right now. He'll drive you to the Astrodome."

ℋ Chapter 116

The highlight of the evening was the speech Joy Wingard gave on the AIDS Parade for Dollars. Joy asked the American people to continue their grass roots efforts to eradicate the deadly disease. She paraphrased a JFK statement—or was it FDR?—saying that much could be told about a country by how it treated the weakest of its citizens. She called for patriotism and determination in conquering the scourge that was sapping the whole country. It was a compassionate and moving address. Thousands on the convention floor gave her a standing ovation.

When the gavel came down for the night, Eliza met her bodyguard. He drove her directly back to the hotel, positioning himself outside her door.

Mack called, offering to come over.

"Thanks, Mack, but I really am exhausted and I have to be up in just a couple of hours. I just want to crash. I feel secure with the guard outside."

"Okay, but remember, I'm just a phone call away."

"How could I forget, sweetheart?"

Eliza undressed and got into bed quickly but she did not sleep soundly.

Five hours later, another bodyguard drove Eliza back along dark Highway 610, the city loop, to the Astrodome for her *KEY to America* duties.

Her dream last night was nagging at her. It started out the

same way as the dream she'd had the night Bill died. Pete Carlson was pursuing Bill down a long hallway and Eliza was trying to warn Bill of something. But this time, Pete Carlson changed into a big, greasy black rodent with tiny eyes and fierce front teeth. Yelena Gregory then appeared. She was petting the slick fur of the ratty animal. The rodent began sniffing around at Yelena's feet. Suddenly, Eliza heard Janie calling out to her, "Mommy, Mommy," but Eliza had not been able to move. She could not get to her daughter. She was paralyzed, transfixed by a large, black mole on Janie's face.

℀ Chapter 117

Detective Colburn scanned the *Daily News* headline. WINGARD NOMINATED TONIGHT, JOY WOWS 'EM WITH AIDS SPEECH. Colburn wasn't sure yet whom he would vote for in November. As far as he was concerned, President Grayson seemed like a nice enough guy, but he hadn't gotten all that much accomplished in the past four years. Wingard didn't really excite him either.

He had been tied up most of yesterday with the high-rise robbery and he knew that he had more work to do on it today. First, he wanted to tie up loose ends on the graffiti case. The homeless man was still in the cell downstairs. Had he been the one who had taken the knocker from Bill Kendall's door the night after his suicide and left it next to the body of Dr. Leo Karas? Colburn hoped to God it didn't turn out that the mentally ill man had murdered the psychiatrist.

He called Tiffany's, identified himself and made his request, reciting the identification number on the silver key ring tag. The woman at Tiffany's was exceedingly polite but said that it was contrary to company policy to give out such information over the telephone. If the detective would like to come in person, with the proper identification, Tiffany's would be delighted to cooperate.

Colburn sighed. It had been worth a shot, but he hadn't really expected Tiffany's to give him the information over the phone. He'd have to find time to drive down to Fifty-seventh Street.

❧ Chapter 118

Father Alec Fisco sat in his living room on the quiet third floor of the cathedral rectory and watched as the huge red, white and blue balloons fell from the top of the Astrodome. Fireworks exploded in an ambitious pyrotechnic display. The delegates danced, sang and cheered, delirious with their promising choice. It was the grand finale of Haines Wingard's convention.

Watching Haines and Joy Wingard smiling ecstatically from the Astrodome stage, Father Alec thought of Wingard's acceptance speech. It had been a masterful piece. The camera had cut to the intense little man who had been with Joy that day at St. Michael's. NATE HELLER, CAMPAIGN MANAGER was the identification at the bottom of the screen. Nate had a reverential, almost trancelike expression on his face.

Would the presidential candidate develop AIDS?

Father Alec rose, switched off the television set and walked over to the window. From Cathedral Hill in Newark, the whole New York skyline, from the Twin Towers to the George Washington Bridge, sparkled in a summer night's haze.

The president of the United States and AIDS. Maybe it was God's plan. Maybe that's what it would take.

✕ Chapter 119

Breakfast had been good and the homeless man wondered what they would be serving for dinner. The beef stew had been delicious last night. He hoped for meatloaf and mashed potatoes. He hadn't had meatloaf in a long, long time.

He wished he could stay in this place. He ate well and slept well. No one bothered him or poked him along, urging him to keep moving. In fact, that cop had actually been nice to him.

What did he say his name was? Cochran? Kelberg? Something like that. Oh no, Colburn—that was it.

He wasn't bad to talk to. He had listened to the treasured safari stories, the stories that represented the only pleasure and satisfaction the homeless man derived from his life. Detective Colburn seemed really interested. He had a list all drawn up of the animals in the menagerie. He knew all about the fox, the wolf, the cat, the lion, the horses and even the unicorn. The policeman knew about some that he himself had forgotten all about.

Then the cop asked about the elephant. Ah, his favorite. He explained that the pretty woman on television told him to take that one. Like she told him to follow the doctor.

Then Colburn asked him about the key ring. The friendly policeman left the cell when the graffiti artist told him where that had come from.

Tit for tat. Tit for tat.

✣ Chapter 120

Yelena insisted on sitting with Eliza on the flight back from New York.

"You were almost killed," Yelena cried as she took a long drink of her Scotch. "And I'm so afraid."

"I'm afraid, too."

"But you don't understand. I told Pete things about you, about your hospitalization, about your seeing Dr. Karas. I didn't want to face it, but he was using me. I knew it, but I so wanted someone in my life."

She was now openly weeping. Eliza found herself feeling sorry for her. Like all human beings, Yelena needed love. But she had lost her self-respect in trying to get it.

"Pete's afraid that I want his job," Eliza stated.

"Not anymore. Not now that Wingard's going to the White House. He was only after you in case Wingard didn't make it."

"So he planted the *Mole* stories and he tried to kill me?"

Yelena took another drink.

"*The Mole*, yes. But he has no reason to kill you. He's going to get what he wants. I know—I think I've always known. But he's not a murderer."

Eliza was scared, for herself, for her child.

"Well, somebody wants me dead. Somebody thinks I know something. My psychiatrist is dead. And Jean, poor Jean. I didn't listen. She wanted me to know something about Bill. Something in his computer. She was concerned about Pete. But there was more. I have to get into Bill's files."

"Well, I have a key to Pete's office," Yelena said.

ℜ Chapter 121

He didn't want to lose her.

He wanted to stay by her side as much as possible but no matter how many strings he tried to pull, Mack couldn't get a seat on the plane back to New York with Eliza. He was booked instead on a flight forty-five minutes behind her.

The *Mole* smears, the murder of Leo Karas, the death of Jean White, Dennis Quinn with Wingard, the digitalis poisoning. It had all gone too far.

Mack checked his watch. He still had a few minutes until boarding. He pulled out his cell phone, called information and dialed the number for *The Record* in Hackensack, New Jersey.

ℜ Chapter 122

He repeatedly reminded himself that nothing should surprise him, but this did.

Detective Colburn stood in Tiffany's business office. The name and the return address registered to the key ring were well known. Extremely well known.

Eliza Blake, *KEY News*, New York.

❧ Chapter 123

When the plane landed at LaGuardia, Eliza and Yelena went directly to *KEY News*. Yelena opened Pete's empty office.

Eliza sat at the computer, Yelena kept guard at the door. Eliza clicked and double-clicked her way through the directories and subdirectories on Bill's hard drive. She made her way to the REMEMBER directory, with an alphabetical list of files staring back at her from the screen.

Now came the hard part.

Password.

It could be anything. What would Bill choose? Something he wouldn't forget. Eliza thought of Bill, the man, the professional, the friend, the father.

When she double-clicked on ETHICS.PC, the first file in the list, a Password Dialog box appeared. She typed in K-E-N-D-A-L-L.

No.

K-E-Y-N-E-W-S.

No.

N-E-B-R-A-S-K-A. Nothing.

"How about 'William'?" volunteered Yelena.

No go.

Eliza tried F-R-A-G-I-L-E-X.

Zip.

Eliza thought of Bill's son. Louise said he was still struggling with his father's death. He was repeating over and over, "An elephant never forgets. An elephant never forgets."

Elephant!

Eliza typed in the eight letters.

Chapter 124

"Somebody thinks I know something. I hope these notes tell me who." Eliza opened the door of the cab that pulled up in front of the broadcast center. "I'll call you."

"I have some work to do. I'll be here in my office." Yelena closed the car door.

On the ride home, Eliza began to read the hard copy. The ETHICS.PC file confirmed everything Yelena had said and more. Pete had threatened Bill with going public about his—*AIDS?*

Bill? AIDS? God help him. Her mind raced, but that meant Joy Wingard could be at risk.

And the future president!

The cab reached its destination. Eliza stashed the rest of the papers in her bag.

Eliza could hear Janie laughing through the apartment door. What a joyous sound her giggles were! She eagerly put her key into the lock.

"Mommeeeee. You're home!" Janie, dressed in violet sunsuit and pink sneakers, ran to her mother. Eliza gathered the child into her arms, hugging and kissing her and holding her tight. Oh, it felt good!

"Thanks, Mrs. Twomey. It's good to be back. I missed my little sweetheart so!" Eliza gave Janie another squeeze.

The housekeeper stared at Eliza. "You look pale, Mrs. Blake."

"Our vacation next week will be a good remedy for that, won't it, Janie?" Eliza forced herself to take her eyes off the child, turning to Mrs. Twomey. "Thank you for taking such good care of my baby. Talk about me, *you* look tired! You must be eager to get home."

"Oh, that can wait a bit. Janie's already had her supper, but I thought I'd stay and get supper ready for you."

"You are so good, Mrs. Twomey. Okay, if you don't mind, while you get dinner ready, I'll give Janie her bath."

ℐ Chapter 125

Mack hailed a cab on the arrivals platform at LaGuardia Airport.

Once settled in the back of the car, he took out his cell phone and called his office.

"Any messages?"

He listened as a fax from *The Record* was read to him. The newspaper article was an in-depth interview with Dennis Quinn after his appointment to the Superior Court bench. Mack was bored until Quinn spoke of his background. The man who would be a Bergen County Superior Court judge had suffered the loss of his father when he was very young. His mother had remarried. Quinn's stepfather died of congestive heart failure.

"What was Quinn's stepfather's name again?" he asked incredulously.

❧ Chapter 126

Two New York City detectives stood in the offices of the president of *KEY News*.

"You missed her. She was just here," Yelena answered Detective Colburn.

"We've already tried her apartment. She wasn't there."

"Well, you must have passed each other on the way here. What's this all about?"

"We want to question her. A key ring registered to Ms. Blake was found next to the body of Dr. Leo Karas." Colburn looked uncomfortable.

Yelena jumped from her seat. "What! I don't know what you're thinking, but if you think Eliza Blake had anything at all to do with the death of Dr. Karas, you're completely wrong. Ms. Blake and I have just returned from Houston. She's scared out of her wits herself."

She took a breath and stared into Colburn's eyes. "She's not a murderer. She's a *victim*!"

"Please understand, Ms. Gregory, we're certain that Ms. Blake only lost or misplaced the key ring. We just need to speak with her to clear this matter up."

Chapter 127

"Make sure there are lots of bubbles, Mommy."

Janie grinned as Eliza poured more Mr. Bubble into the tub.

"I love Mrs. Twomey, but I missed *you*, Mommy."

Janie, her precious Janie. How close they had come to losing one another!

Eliza longed to sit here and just watch her child splash away, but she knew that they would never be safe unless she figured out who had tried to kill her.

"Why did you bring your work bag in here with us, Mommy?"

"I have something I have to read now, sweetheart. It won't take me long. I promise."

"Promise?"

"Cross my heart."

Janie began playing with her plastic tub toys and Eliza picked up Bill's personal notes. On top of the sheaf of papers they'd printed out in Bill's office was the file on Joy Wingard.

With tears in her eyes, Eliza read of Bill's love for the woman and his heartbreak over the end of their love affair. The text rambled on a bit, especially when he began to describe his fear that he might have exposed Joy to the horrible disease.

At the end was a direction: "See ROMANIA.AID."

Eliza remembered that this file had been toward the end. She quickly rifled through the pages until she found Bill's recounting of his trip to Romania to do the special on the hellholes there called orphanages. He described the sickening, outraged feelings he'd experienced as he witnessed the retarded and physically deformed children stockpiled, mistreated and forgotten in the filthy, dangerous warehouses. He included snatches of dialogue between himself and some of the civil authorities there, venting his feelings of frustration with the Romanian government that valued its own citizens so little.

"When are you going to be done, Mommy?"

"Soon, sweetheart. Thank you for being so patient."

Eliza caught her breath as she read Bill's next words.

> In the end, I, too, was a victim of their callous disregard for human life. When Range and I drove back from shooting at an orphanage outside Bucharest, we had a serious car accident. Range and I were both pretty badly injured, but only I required a blood transfusion.
>
> Imagine how I felt upon later discovering that a full 10 percent of the blood collected and tested in Bucharest was found to be tainted with HIV.

"Oh my God."

"Mommy, what's wrong, what's wrong?" Janie looked at her worriedly.

"Oh my angel, I'm sorry. I didn't mean to scare you."

"Mommy, please stop reading and play with me."

❧ Chapter 128

The phone rang and Mrs. Twomey answered.

"Mrs. Blake is giving Janie her bath, Ms. Gregory."

"Well, tell Mrs. Blake, please, that the police were just here and they want to talk to her about a lost key ring."

❧ Chapter 129

Eliza was eager to read the notes from the filed labeled JUDGE.$. She knew it would have something to do with Dennis Quinn.

"Janie, if you just bear with Mommy a few more minutes, I'll read you two extra stories tonight."

"That would make six all together?" Janie asked guardedly.

"Six."

"Okay."

Eliza read that municipal judge Dennis Quinn had once been the treasurer for New Visions for Living. He'd seemed, in Bill's estimation, to be a good man, Quinn even dressing up as a clown at New Visions parties.

Two years ago, the notes continued, Bill had discovered that Quinn had embezzled $500,000 from New Visions. When confronted by Bill, Quinn, who'd just been nominated for a seat on the Bergen County Superior Court, had begged Bill not to turn him in. The encounter was a bizarre one, as Bill had pulled the man aside during a party at one of the group homes. The judge was in his clown makeup when Bill confronted him.

"William's 'man with the funny red hair'!" Eliza blurted out loud. "He played a clown!"

"Ronald McDonald?"

"No, sweetie, someone else."

Eliza continued reading.

"Please, not for me. This would kill my mother. She's already buried two husbands. She's worked hard all her life. It would kill her if she knew about this."

Bill doubted that Quinn was getting the Superior Court slot based on his legal expertise and merits. His suspicions had been confirmed when he demanded that Quinn replace the funds. The judge admitted he had financed his new position on the bench with the retarded people's money.

Bill had written down the dialogue.

"You mean all the money is gone?"

"Almost."

"Well, you are going to give it back. Every last bit of it."

"How can I do that?"

"We'll figure out a way. And you're damned lucky I don't expose you and that crooked little bunch you hang out with on the other side of the Hudson. But I'm a sucker and I do feel sorry for your mother. Tell me her name, I want to see if she really exists."

Then Janie said, "Mommy, I forgot to tell you. A real policeman was here today.'

ℋ Chapter 130

Eliza's phone was busy.

Mack's cab was stalled in traffic on the Fifty-ninth Street Bridge.

He had to tell Eliza—she and Janie were in danger.

Urgently, he punched the numbers again.

Busy.

Chapter 131

Again, the phone rang. It was her Dennis, full of news about his trip to Houston and the convention. "It was grand. The best time I've had in years. It's so wonderful to have the load of those payments off my back. Things are really turning around for me. Isn't it strange, Ma, how things take care of themselves sometimes? First, Bill Kendall killing himself. Then Leo Karas being murdered." A lighthearted Dennis chuckled.

Their conversation over, she left the phone off the hook.

Ah, Denny. You've no idea what I've done for you. What I'm *doing* for you. For you, my son.

I didn't tell you how close Eliza Blake was getting to you. Much too close.

Frances Twomey thought of the woman down the hall bathing her daughter.

Things *don't* take care of themselves, Denny. They have to be helped along.

Chapter 132

Oh my God! My baby's in here and the killer is in the kitchen.

When Eliza saw the name of Dennis Quinn's mother in Bill's notes, she dropped the papers on the bathroom floor. She lifted the child from the tub and wrapped a towel around her.

"Janie, just stay here. Promise me you'll stay here."

The child looked scared.

"It's okay, sweetheart, but you have to stay right here for Mommy. Don't move. Promise me."

Janie nodded.

Eliza opened the bathroom door. The hallway was empty. She darted to her room and went straight to her closet. She stood on tiptoe, reaching to the back of the high shelf. She felt the wooden container and pulled it down. With trembling fingers, she opened the mahogany box.

It was empty!

Eliza turned to run back to Janie.

Mrs. Twomey stood in the doorway. Eliza's gun was in the housekeeper's hand.

ℋ **Chapter 133**

The unmarked police car pulled up again in front of Eliza Blake's building.

As they waited for the elevator, Detective Colburn turned to his partner.

"Eliza Blake may not have killed her psychiatrist, but she knows who did."

Mrs. Twomey pointed the gun steadily at Eliza. She was amazingly calm as she spoke.

"Ms. Gregory called. The police are on their way. I can't have you telling them that I dropped your key ring at Dr. Karas's body—my son's career will be over. I can't let that happen."

"You killed Dr. Karas?" whispered Eliza incredulously. "But why?"

"He was blackmailing my son, Dennis."

"And now you're going to kill me? No, Mrs. Twomey, you can't."

The housekeeper's eyes narrowed.

"I killed Bill Kendall's nosy secretary when I thought she was on to Denny's secret. I can kill you, too. I have to."

"You pushed Jean in front of that train?"

"I don't want to kill you, Mrs. Blake, but I have no choice."

"You'd leave Janie motherless?"

The housekeeper seemed to hesitate.

And suddenly, Janie was behind Mrs. Twomey at the bedroom door.

"Mommy . . ." Mrs. Twomey started to turn and Eliza lunged for her gun.

❧ Chapter 135

As Detective Colburn and his partner exited the elevator, they heard a shot.

Rushing shoulders first through Eliza Blake's apartment door, both men burst in with guns drawn.

A little girl wrapped in a pink towel stood crying at the end of the hallway. The detectives raced down the corridor, one pushing the child aside, the other taking down the woman standing in the doorway.

Eliza Blake lay on the bloody bedroom floor.

❧ Chapter 136

The cab screeched to a halt and Mack sprang out, throwing money at the driver. The angry flashing lights of an ambulance parked in front of Eliza's apartment building warned that it might be too late.

It can't be too late.

Mack ran past the doorman and sprinted to the elevator, pounding the Up button.

Hurry. Hurry.

The elevator door slid open. Two EMS paramedics flanked a chrome stretcher.

Eliza lay white and unmoving.

"Buddy, get out of the way. She's losing a lot of blood."

Chapter 137

Judge Dennis Quinn was leaving for the PNC Bank branch office to draw out a $500,000 cashier's check when his phone rang.

"Judge Quinn, we're sorry to inform you, sir, but we've arrested your mother for murder. She refuses to speak until she has legal representation and she's asking for you."

Dennis hung up, realizing that when Haines Wingard made it to the White House, he could never appoint the son of a murderer to a federal judgeship.

Chapter 138

Mack's kiss was warm and sweet.

"You look much better today, darling."

Mack had broken away from work at lunchtime to visit Eliza at Roosevelt Hospital. The bullet wound to the torso had caused a lot of bleeding, but miraculously no vital organ had been hit. As he gazed at Eliza smiling from her hospital bed, Mack was relieved to see that color was returning to her cheeks.

"You just missed my mother and Janie. I can't wait to get out of here. Tell me what's going on," she said eagerly.

Mack grinned. "Now I know you're feeling better." He pulled up a chair next to her bed. "The Wingard campaign is disavowing any connection to Dennis Quinn."

"Of course." Eliza nodded.

Mack continued. "And since Quinn didn't break any laws himself, save the embezzlement, which can't be proved, he'll likely be keeping his Superior Court seat."

"Well, the embezzlement could probably be proved if we handed over Bill's notes."

For a few moments, they considered the implications.

"Let's let Bill Kendall rest in peace," Eliza said.

Mack nodded. "My sentiments exactly."

"It's a good example, though, isn't it?" Eliza asked and then answered her own question. "We have a legal system—not necessarily a justice system." Shaking her head wearily, she asked, "And what about Pete Carlson?"

Mack spoke solemnly.

"He has no career left at *KEY News.*"

✄ Chapter 139

Nate Heller snapped off the set with a sigh of relief. The story about the apprehension of the murderer of Dr. Leo Karas and Bill Kendall's secretary, and the murder attempt on Eliza Blake, did mention that Frances Twomey was the mother of a New Jersey Superior Court judge, but there had been no hint of any sort of connection with the Wingard campaign.

Thank God Quinn had delayed coming up with the money.

As all good generals do, he looked at the bigger picture.

I may not have gotten half a million bucks, but I *will* be going to the White House.

❧ Chapter 140

The results were back.

Negative.

Haines Wingard was grateful. He was also bitter. He could never trust his wife, or his campaign manager, again. He'd like to ax Nate, but he couldn't. Nate knew that the future president had cheated on the bar exam.

❧ Chapter 141

Eliza sat on a gaily colored beach towel fiddling absentmindedly with her grandmother's charm and watching Janie dig in the powdery sand of Gooseberry Beach. The baking, late July heat was eased by the ocean breeze blowing gently off the Atlantic. Eliza looked out at the open sea, entranced. It was so beautiful and soothing here. Therapeutic.

Janie's shoulders were looking too pink. Rummaging through the canvas beachbag for the sunblock, Eliza didn't want the week to end. It had been so good for the two of them to have this time away together.

She brushed away the sand that was sticking to Janie's arms and rubbed the lotion smoothly over the soft skin. Silently, she prayed. Thank you, God. Dear God, thank you. The thought of how close she had come to losing her precious Janie still took her breath away.

"Want to make a castle with me, Mommy?"

"You bet, sweetpie!"

Together, mother and child scooped the sand.

Eliza still hadn't taken it in fully. Her beloved and trusted Mrs. Twomey, capable of cold-blooded murder. How could she have so misjudged that woman? It frightened her to think her antennae could be so faulty.

But Mrs. Twomey had never, ever given Eliza any reason to mistrust her. She'd been a wonderful caretaker for Janie. Until the end. . . . Mrs. Twomey had wanted to protect her son. She shivered in the summer heat.

And now the press release that Yelena read in New York this morning made it official. Pete Carlson, anchorman of the *Evening Headlines*, had resigned. Eliza Blake had been named the new anchor.

Eliza knew her life was about to change. Whatever little anonymity she had would soon be gone completely. She wondered if she'd be able to handle that. And still, it was the top of the heap. In her profession, it didn't get any bigger than the anchor chair!

Mack ducked under the beach umbrella, balancing two iced teas and a grape juice. He carefully placed the cardboard tray on the blanket.

"Thanks, honey." As she looked up at Mack, Eliza thought just a moment about John. She wished she could share with him this incredible accomplishment and the concerns that went with it.

But John was now part of her precious past. Mack was the wonderful future.

Mack. How he had been there for her when she lay in the hospital. She'd read the concern in his eyes that he tried to mask with his wry humor. Afterward, he'd admitted how scared he'd been, scared of losing her. As she recuperated, Eliza had plenty of time to think. She'd realized that she, too, was afraid of losing someone that she loved. Again. But she knew she couldn't let the fear paralyze her, keep her from living and loving fully. She knew now that she was ready. Ready to take a chance again, with Mack. She thought of Dr. Karas and how happy he'd be to know that she was moving on.

Sadly, Eliza thought of Bill Kendall. His life had touched hers in so many ways. She was sure he would be happy for her now.

Janie, oblivious to the wisps of fine brown hair which blew across her face, diligently decorated their lopsided sandcastle with some tiny seashells she had collected from the water's edge. She considered her handiwork.

"Isn't this a pretty house, Mommy?"

"Beautiful, Janie."

"I wish we had a house, Mommy."

"I do, too, sweetheart. When we all go home, I think we should look for one."

"You do?" the child asked gleefully.

"Yep, I do."

Janie sat thoughtfully for a moment, considering her mother's answer.

"Will Mack live there with us?"

Eliza and Mack's eyes locked. Neither one was uncomfortable with the child's question.